The Lochnetters

Ella Henderson

Dedication

For Derek. David and Catherine
and all our "Jellies"

Foreword

Crudely speaking *Lochnetting* could be defined as inverted Munro-bagging, the aim being to collect lochs instead of mountains. The inventor of the sport, John Maitland, typical Edinburgh schoolmaster, average family man, does love lochs but is also remarkably unfit. It is his very unfitness and the unsuitability of the team that he builds to accompany him, that make the whole venture a "cuckoo" idea. Those who do not love lochs might be tempted to dismiss lochnetting merely as suitable exercise for those who are not fit enough to tackle heights. This is an account not only of the physical activity involved but of the way the very different characters rub off against each other during their pursuit and how they learn not only more about lochs but even more about themselves, seeing themselves in the eyes of others. This knowledge is helpful and hurtful. Let those who wish to follow in their footsteps be wary.

All characters are purely fictitious and all hotels, B&Bs, other accommodation and sporting facilities are also fictitious.

Most grateful thanks to David, Derek, Bethinn J.J. Parry, Iain, Ali and Isaac Clarke and to all the other friends who helped.

Ella Henderson
June 2018

Contents

A Cuckoo Idea

The Team

The First Expedition

The Second Expedition

Going Public

The Third Expedition

The End of the Beginning

Chapter One

A Cuckoo Idea

The Hosts – Cuckoo HQ

Lochnetting was conceived on a day so like any other day that it was difficult – afterwards – when it mattered – to pinpoint the exact date and the exact date became just another source of family argument. It had been laid in the nest of 10 Damhope Road like a cuckoo's egg; a strange idea, very different from the sibling ideas which it rapidly displaced as it grew over the months, demanding more and more time, monopolising more and more attention.

To put the record straight: early on the day on which it was laid, an unmaternal, irresponsible ideas-cuckoo perched for a cursory inspection on the ridge-pole of 10 Damhope Road, for a brief check on the potential host family, watched them squabbling, frowsy and bad-tempered, in the pre-school kitchen and classified them as normal. Then she popped out the egg with a dismissive twitch of her tail and left them with a valedictory squawk which could not be detected amongst:

"Mum, does he have to slurp like that? I can see all his corn flakes in his disgusting gob!"

"You said we could have a dog. You always ..."

"You two are making me late again. Jane, do your children ..."

"Why do they always become mine, instead of ours when ... Jenny, you do not have to do your hair again ..."

"Get in the car now! Bye, love ..."

"Have a good ..."

Gravel crunch. Brake squeal at the gate. Lingering exhaust fumes.

Just Jane left alone with an invisible cuckoo's egg and a mug of coffee. At peace. At cuckoo H.Q., No. 10 Damhope Road.

No 10 Damhope Road. After five years of ownership John still warmed to the sound of his address and although in the right company he occasionally flippantly abbreviated it to "Number 10", he seldom, if ever, referred to it simply as "home". *No. 10 Damhope Road* had a solidity about it, a common-sense security, that matched the square, stone Victorian house fortified by its five foot stone Victorian wall. On their bills their gas company insisted on prefixing *The Rookery* to the address. *The Rookery* was the name given by some previous owner and apparently so indelibly inscribed on the company's computer that to delete it would mean crashing their entire accounts system. John had unscrewed the name-plate soon after moving in, prising it off brutally and leaving two holes and a reddish-brown rectangular scar on the grey stone of the front wall.

"No need for that sort of sentimentality," he had replied to Jane's quizzically raised eyebrows when he had gone into the kitchen for a plaster, name plate in one hand, bleeding finger on the other. "Do you think I need an anti-tetanus jag?"

"Among other things," she had replied obliquely. During their sixteen or so years of marriage she had become increasingly oblique. "And I rather liked it. The name, I mean, *The Rookery.*"

"Where are the rooks then?" he had smirked conclusively.

Damhope Road was a 'no-through' road. It had originally led to the Hope Dam, a reed-fringed, shallow stretch of water providing a year-long home for ducks and a summer breeding-ground for midges. The dam had been named in honour of one, Sir John Hope, who had donated funds to set up a charitable trust for the conservation of wild-life within the city of Edinburgh. Eighty years after his death the funds and the dam had largely dried up. Its muddy socket had recently been filled in to form part of the extension to the Buchanan Golf Course, now given the conciliatory title of the *Hope Buchanan Golf Club* – although of course the gas company continued to bill the clubhouse as merely the *Buchanan Golf Club*. The previous owner of No. 10, presumably the one who had conjured up *The Rookery* as the name of the house, had been something of a duck fancier and had been so incensed by the filling in of the dam that he had put his house on the market for a fixed sum which John, having recently inherited from his mother, had been in a position to match. The previous owner had been frank, even voluble, about the desecration of the land use at the end of the road and would actually have been prepared to lower the price if John had shared his outrage over the filling in of the dam. John, however, had been quite unconcerned about the golf course extension: he knew the subscriptions to *Hope Buchanan* to be beyond the means of the hoi polloi and as Damhope Road did not lead directly to the club-house, golfers seldom used it and those who did purred past with expensively understated engine noise.

To Jane No. 10 Damhope was simply *home*, the address holding no particular magic for her. At the start of their house-hunting she had fancied a bungalow, not one that squatted compactly, but rather sprawled, with verandahs spilling out into a large, colourful garden. It was John who had double ringed the advertisement for No. 10 and made the appointment to view it and at first sight of the property Jane had actually shuddered.

"You're cold?" John had frowned hopefully.

It had certainly been bitterly cold standing on the path inside the gate on the sodden mat of frosted dead leaves. The house was north facing and its solid, monochrome bulk blocked out what there was of February sun. While John had cast his newly acquired expert eye over the roof and paintwork, she had stamped her feet against the cold that was coiling itself restrictively round her ankles and thrust her hands deep into her pockets.

"Bungalows are colder by and large," he had hissed authoritatively against the deep barking of a dog. "Nearer the ground." And he had strode towards the front door out of earshot of her reply.

The owner, whose features receded behind his dark-rimmed, thick-lensed spectacles so that she had difficulty in later recalling his face, had made no attempt to show them around, had shaken their hands limply and then shrugged them off with a "Have a look! Go wherever you like!" and retreated. Jane had left John to tap woodwork and sniff for wet/dry-rot and followed the large black labrador through to a kitchen where it curled up in front of the Aga, ignoring her, showing the same casual indifference to her presence which its master had displayed. She stood and thawed in unexpected warmth and brightness. The sun slanted through the kitchen window and, outside in the garden, glinted on the metal mesh of the bird feeders swinging from the bare branches of trees. A blackbird squawked protestingly as she pushed open the back door and went out.

Any colour there was seemed to have shrunk back against the wall of the house into a narrow border of crocuses. The two apple trees bearing the bird feeders stood on a yellowed lawn, soured by frost. A rusty wire clothes line was strung between them with faded plastic clothes pegs at almost regular intervals, presumably to prevent the absent-minded from garotting themselves. Beyond the lawn the garden, which sloped down towards a stream that used to feed the Hope Dam and now haunted the golf course with recriminatory drainage problems, had been terraced into two levels to prevent excessive erosion. On the lower section the earth was neatly raked and on one side currant bushes were beginning to form buds; on the upper level the soil was rumpled like an unmade bed with clumps of the brown twigs of perennials showing where blooms might be expected.

"Not dead, just dormant," she said to herself contentedly.

Returning to the house she startled the owner emerging from the shabby little greenhouse on one side of the house. He grunted when he recollected who she was.

"Not much of course at this time of year." It was a statement not an apology.

"All that!" she had replied indicating the purple and gold crocuses and noticing the mitred green heads of daffodils as she did so.

"You a gardener?" The sun glinted on his glasses so that she couldn't see his eyes.

"Not really!" The garden behind their upper villa flat had merely been a patio with containers.

"Well you'll have to learn. Can't have this neglected!"

It was not to be neglected. The garden had been what made No 10 feel like home to her and her love for it had extended, gradually transfusing its warmth and colour through the house as well, until after five years of living there she felt a glow of satisfaction when she opened the front gate even on the coldest of February days.

At the time of the move Jennifer, aged nine, had been a child with few problems. Her younger brother, Hamish, was considerably smaller than she was with limited powers of retaliation and although, for reasons of family pride and economy, she had to attend the same fee-paying school in which her father taught, their paths had yet to cross, because the junior and senior sections of the school were separately housed. Schoolwork presented no problems; more importantly she was very popular among her classmates and finally such a good swimmer that she had actually overheard her father referring to her as "the swimming hope of the nation", a phrase which she stored up and repeated frequently. Possible separation from friends in the neighbourhood had raised a certain level of anxiety which her mother alleviated by promising frequent week-end sleepovers. Her father had gone as far as to promise riding-lessons if she moved without fuss. This was more than she had expected to make out of the bargain but, being an acquisitive child, she had the instinct not to overdo the gratitude and thus managed to persuade him to throw first choice of bedroom into the bargain. She chose the largest of the bedrooms, the one which was probably the master bedroom, but as it was at the front of the house and her mother wanted to overlook the garden, there was no clash of interest - so much so that Jennifer almost wished she had hung out for a Disneyland holiday.

Hamish at six had not put down as many roots at the time of the move. He was supposed to have been called James, both parents having agreed that a common family initial was desirable. He would have been James too if his paternal grandmother hadn't forbidden it outright on the grounds that James was the name she had bestowed on her favourite cat. She always did prefer cats to children and John always did obey his mother implicitly so, somewhat to Jane's chagrin, James had become Hamish, modified just before his baptism to Hamish Jeremy as a concession to the J's. His sister and ultimately everybody else called him Ham.

Ham had been quite simply delighted at the prospect of the move. He had liked both the house and the garden but the cellar had been the main attraction: who could know what or who could be lurking in its darkness? Possessing neither the sense nor the guile to match his sister's demands, all he had asked had been a torch together with a reasonable supply of batteries. He did, however, react quite violently to his sister's suggestions that he live, eat and sleep down there but, as usual, his violent reaction was ineffective because Jennifer was able to inflict more pain and had a louder voice with which to demand his punishment.

Now, after five years of living at No. 10, both children felt almost as though they had never lived anywhere else. The "swimming hope of the nation" had given up training for fear of overdeveloping her shoulders, replaced her black racing lycra with something far more suitably skimpy in which she was given to holding sunbathing sessions with friends in the suntrap of a garden, primly informing her father and her brother that they would be unwelcome in the garden at these times. She objected only mildly when Ham ignored the prohibition because she had her eye on 'his' cellar and was, unbeknown to him and her parents, planning a dimly lit, subterranean fifteenth birthday party in it for her entire class and a few boys from the class above. Ham's interests had also expanded over the five years and some of the expansions had left their marks on the property: the white pebble-dash wall of the garage bore round football-shaped mud stains as he used it increasingly for goal-practice; the wooden ceiling of the cellar was scorched black over the place where he had decided that a cheerful, roaring fire would warm the place up and there was still a bit of a muddy mess at the bottom of the garden after he and a couple of mates had decided to dam the stream, flooding the strawberry beds and washing away soil and some of the plants with it. For the latter offence he had been sentenced to mowing the lawn for the duration of the summer, a wearisome task but at least it gave him the pleasure of dislodging his sister and friends from the lawn at peak sunbathing times.

The lawn-mowing, Jane felt, was a punishment imposed by John too swiftly and with too much self-interest. Ham would have been equally disgruntled if he had been asked to help out on a regular basis with forking, weeding and other necessary garden maintenance. John's satisfaction with his life at No. 10 had expressed itself most tellingly in the gradual increase of his girth, with particular expansion around his waist, and lawn-mowing had become about the limit of his exercise. Jane had tried to draw his attention to the problem, first with gentle tact and then going as far as to remark, "Your mother would have been horrified ..." Jennifer had been significantly more blunt. John, however, turned a deaf ear, refusing to admit any problem.

He continued to admit any problem right up until the annual staff medical, required by the school and carried out on the very day on which the cuckoo-egg was laid, exposed his blood pressure, his cholesterol level and his BMI in bleakly uncompromising statistics. At the time of the test, the school doctor, a terse, monosyllabic individual with thin lips overlined by a pencil thin moustache confined himself to an impassive "Not too good," after taking John's blood pressure, showing as much concern as if he had been commenting on the weather, an assessment which was later translated to Jane as "O.K." The full medical reports arrived on a Friday about a week later, presumably after the results of the blood tests had come through. The sealed envelopes slotted into the pigeon-holes in the staffroom were marked private, but that didn't prevent John's break-time clique from indiscreetly comparing notes over their coffee. They tended to be a competitive clique, all men except for the occasional addition of Sheena Antrobus, the librarian, who believed in circulating. They occupied the circle of worn, brown leather armchairs furthest away from the coffee table and injected new cars, new houses, exotic holidays, etc. casually but challengingly into the general conversation. The subject of the medical records was eagerly seized on by the fitter among them as yet another chance for one-upmanship. Feeling curious eyes upon him, John opened his envelope, digested its contents and immediately stuffed it into the inner breast pocket of his sports jacket.

"O.K. old chap?" enquired the fittest who was also the loudest.

"Fine!" replied John and repeated it. "Absolutely fine! Must go and do some photo-copying."

For the remainder of that school day he gave his break-time clique a wide berth, avoided the staffroom after the last lesson of the day by volunteering for detention duty and left for home as soon as the slowest miscreant had completed his punishment work.

"Hello there! I'm home!"

His voice sounded brittle even to his own ears as he called out the customary greeting with uncustomary cheerfulness. He aroused Jane's worst suspicions. She immediately abandoned a self-assembly rocking-chair kit and followed him through to the study, leaving Jennifer to hold bits together and moan.

"What on earth …?"

"Sh! Shut the door!" Whereas it could be a relief to unburden himself to Jane, he didn't fancy input from his children who had yet to develop sympathy, or rather sympathy for him. "It's the result of the medical. I'll let you see it for yourself."

She drew close to him, holding her breath as he groped in the depths of his brief-case, underneath two copies of *Macbeth,* one of *To Kill a Mockingbird,* a recently confiscated girlie magazine and a pile of jotters.

"I don't want anyone else to know! Not anyone!"

He held the envelope which he had resealed with sellotape away from her, out of her reach, waiting for her assurance before divulging its contents.

"All right, darling."

Slowly he brought his arm down and surrendered it, watching her face while she opened and studied it until, seeing her expression change from anxiety to annoyance, he busied himself replacing the contents of his brief-case with unnecessary precision.

"Just how long have I been trying to get through to you …?" she hissed triumphantly and then read further. "And I've *told* you that you eat all the wrong things." She put it down on the edge of the desk. "It's up to you. You'll have to change your lifestyle; take up some activity; get rid of that paunch." Her hand was on the door-handle. "I'm busy making up the rocking-chair. If you want a cup of tea, you'll have to get it yourself and stay OFF the chocolate biscuits!"

"Something wrong?" Jennifer was only semi-curious but she felt that it was polite to ask.

"Absolutely nothing that can't be fixed except …" and she remembered her promise, "except this chair is taking forever and we've got the Patersons coming round this evening to show off the evidence of their latest holidaying triumph."

"Count me out!" said Jennifer. "I've a Geography test to revise for and I've wasted enough time already helping you with this chair."

Jane bit back the easy retort that Jennifer had been lolling in front of the television without a Geography book or any other book in sight when she was asked to help because she was in no mood for a slanging match which she would inevitably lose. Initially, after John's insistence on secrecy, she had held her breath in expectation of some irreversible, terminal ailment and she had felt anger as well as relief at his disclosure. Now, the anger had evaporated and she was left with a wearying complication of sympathy and pity. The sympathy was for him; the pity for herself. "It's up to you!" she had snapped at him, knowing that the burden of his rehabilitation to fitness would fall just as heavily on her because that precious outer shell of his smug self-assurance, was nothing but the excrescence of an inherent self-mistrust. He had been an only child whose mother had encouraged and rewarded his dependency so that he had grown up motivated by a need for approval. Jane had known when she married him that he would pronounce with authority and look sideways, covertly, to her for support and she had found it endearing then. Now, depending on the circumstance and her mood, she could find it endearing, boring, or even irritating. She still gave him unfailing support in public but within the solid walls of No. 10 she would sometimes play games with him: she would tease and tantalise him by remaining silent when he looked to her, withholding the support temporarily, suspended like a large, juicy bone held just out of reach of a hungry, slavering dog, to be relinquished just before the leaping and floundering could turn to the humiliation of grovelling and whining. Afterwards she felt guilt for his weakness and for her own exploitation of it.

He stood now, only just inside the door, his hands wrapped round a mug of tea.

"I'm taking it without sugar," he said, hoping for approval.

She smiled and responded, "Come and show me how to finish this chair, will you? Jennifer has homework."

The Patersons lived at No. 9 Damhope Road, the houses being numbered on one side of the road only, and had been quick to draw the Maitlands into their ever-revolving circle of acquaintances. They were one step ahead, chronologically speaking, about a decade older and therefore in a position to offer advice to the Maitlands on a wide gamut of topics, ranging from child-raising through property maintenance to which neighbours it was advisable to cultivate. All three of their children, none of whom had ever slammed doors or engaged in slanging matches, had been very successful academically, were enjoying meteoric careers and only touched down occasionally to off-load their latest trophies. Patrick Paterson had taken early retirement in order to spend the best years of his life at the golf club where he was currently president. Moira Paterson led a somewhat cyclical existence, shopping energetically and then decluttering into charity shops. The Patersons' house would have been a rather attractive, stone built, gabled structure were it not for a neo-Gothic arch over the front door which was somehow at odds with its stone plainness. The fact that it was basically slightly smaller than the Maitlands had been compensated for by an extensive conservatory which stretched the length of the back of the house, concealing the bathroom waste pipes which Moira had never liked. The garden was terraced similarly to the Maitlands' but the layout of the land was the only similarity. The top level was paved beyond the conservatory with a large oblong pond sunk into it. A metre high 'safety-wall' from which any self-respecting toddler could launch itself with ease surrounded it and a fountain in the form of a large S-shaped fish played in the middle of it whenever the Patersons entertained. The two lower levels were lushly and uniformly green. The upper level had been converted into a putting green cum croquet lawn. The lower was purely ornamental. In the middle of it a stone mermaid whose hair hung discreetly over her nipples, gazed up at the large shell-shaped bird bath which she held above her head. The bird-bath was never filled because Moira disliked having to scrub bird-droppings off the mermaid. At each of the four corners of the lawn stood a statue, a proper statue, none of your elves-on-toadstools variety. These came with certificates to say they were authentic copies of ancient, classical deities, complete, or rather incomplete with the obligatory damage – missing arms, busted noses and snapped off genitalia – and they all faced into the centre of the lawn, straining their vacant, blind eyes towards the mermaid.

No. 11 Damhope Road, on the other side of the Maitlands was a warm looking red brick house, the sort of house that looked like a family home, but there had been no children in it since the Misses Reynolds had grown up. There were either three or four sisters. Jane had been sure that she had seen four when they first moved in, but for some time now, for well over a year, only three had driven off in the mornings at the same time as she chivvied the children into the car behind an impatient John. The Maitlands' upstairs windows overlooked part of the Reynolds' garden and the Misses Reynolds, stocky brownish-haired women in trousers, could be seen working in it, digging, hoeing, raking and watering, but they could never be heard. Even when Jane, pausing in her efforts in her own garden, could hear from the other side of the stone wall the scratching sounds of raking or the play of the hosepipe, she never heard the sisters speak to each other. Most of the year they seemed devoted to growing straight rows of equidistant vegetables but in early autumn, their garden was alive with a latent, repressed colour that would out in the form of dramatically vivid dahlias. Two different Miss Reynolds had on two separate occasions called round at

No. 10: the first time with a misdelivered parcel; the second with a school-book which Ham had dropped out of his bag. They had both smiled easily, both said , "Not at all," when thanked but both had declined to enter No10 and had never offered any invitation. So as neighbours they had never developed any individuality; they just remained bracketed together as the Misses Reynolds.

On this particular evening Moira and Patrick Paterson were to find themselves almost overwhelmed by the genuine warmth of Jane's reception. John had spent the time between the completion of the rocking-chair and their arrival alternately consulting Jennifer's biology text book and a medical self-help book which Jane frequently regretted having bought at a jumble sale because she herself could never refer to it without feeling the onset of alarming symptoms. However frightening, she had kept these to herself whereas John could not. His need for her reassurance put paid to his inhibitions about the children being privy to his unhealthy condition and Jane found herself striving to allay the anxiety of all three while following a rather complicated recipe for caramelising apricots.

"For heaven's sake," she said exasperated, one arm around a tearful Ham, the other stirring an ominously black-flecked syrup, "You've had a warning. Nothing more! Nothing worse! Just a timely warning. Now, Ham, if you want your father's health to improve, give him back his lawn-mower, force him to play football with you but don't put him in goals and if you still want to eat with us, go and wash your face and hands, please now – using soap and water! No dry-cleaning on the towel!"

At least John did wait for his son to disappear before summing up the situation with, "If the worst comes to the worst, you and the children are provided for and you won't need …"

At that point the Patersons rang the bell and walked in. Jane, meeting them in the hall, embraced them both fervently with, "How absolutely lovely to see you!"

Although the sitting-room of No.10 faced north, it was a warm, cheerful room, the furniture from John's childhood home fitting in comfortably beside the more modern pieces which John and Jane had chosen carefully together before and during their marriage. The solid rectangles of the long sash windows were softened by John's mother's rich brown velvet curtains and by the padded window seats which Jane had had upholstered in old gold. The old, low, unyielding horsehair sofa had been re-upholstered to match the window seats and the fabric was so thick that the itchy texture which John remembered from when he curled up on it as a boy was no longer a problem. The brown velvet of the high-backed, winged chairs almost matched the curtains and the sofa, the chairs and the window-seats were liberally scattered with cushions in vivid autumn colours and soft greens. On the mantelshelf, under a large mirror, slightly freckled and heavily gilt-framed, stood photos of the children in mock tortoiseshell frames, a small Lalique bird, a nineteenth century brass spirit kettle and a wooden candlestick which Jennifer had made for her mother at school and which still held last year's unlit Christmas candle.

Moira lowered herself onto the horse-hair sofa, settled back amongst the cushions, adjusting them to her comfort and arranged the evening's entertainment between sips of her gin and tonic- a rather strong gin and tonic because John was under orders to "deaden her palate for heaven's sake: the soup's from a can."

"We'll postpone telling you about our holiday until after the meal," she said. "If you can wait, that is."

They all felt they could.

"The thing is we've brought a whole album of photographs to show you. And we've got a DVD too if you'd like to see it. It's not very good. I was so excited that my hand shook and, although the camera's got that thing to counteract wobble, I wobbled rather too much." She exploded with laughter. "Anyway," she pulled herself together, "we want to hear what you've been up to. Don't we, Patrick?"

"Oh yes!" agreed Patrick over-enthusiastically. "Still slogging away at the schoolwork, old man?"

"Oh yes!" parodied Ham innocently without realising the question was not intended for him. "I always have millions of homework. Except I don't have any tonight," he added hurriedly, hoping to be included in the DVD viewing.

"John's been on a lot of in-service week-ends," Jane rescued. "It's not left time for much else."

"What do you do on in-service?" giggled Moira. "In-service? It sounds as though you were a butler or a chambermaid or something. You know. In service."

John fixed her with the how can you be so

ignorant expression he reserved for his silliest pupils before responding pompously, "*In-service* is a common term, particularly in academic circles for ..."

"Sorry to interrupt, folks, but it's time to eat or the food will spoil," Jane interrupted smoothly. "Do bring your gin through, Moira."

"Oh no! Just one quick slug left!" She knocked it back, accepted her husband's hand to pull her up from the sofa and brushed imaginary crumbs off her skirt onto the carpet.

Picking up the empty glasses before following through, John had time to compose himself. Moira's *in service* comment was just a silly throw-away remark, not even offensive really, and he felt angry with himself at his over-reaction, felt once again like the small boy in the school playground whom the teacher had had to rescue from the jeering of the popular boys, so that the shame of having to be rescued was even greater than the shame of having over-reacted at the teasing, at having cried in public.

"John, dear!"

"Just coming! Forgot to open the wine," he boomed cheerfully.

Towards the end of a meal, providentially unremarkable considering the climate of its preparation except for the gritty bits in the caramelised apricots which served as a conversation piece, Patrick said with studied casualness, "Actually, why don't you come over to ours for coffee? The DVD'll be easier to follow on our wide-screen plasma thingamebob."

Jane held her breath but John reminded himself that a small television set was a sign of intellectual superiority, a sort of inverted status symbol, and smiled.

"Why not?" he said.

The wide-screen, plasma television apparatus lorded it in the Paterson's decluttered sitting-room, a room so bland that to relieve its virginal monotony, it seemed to beg a scuff mark on its lacquered floorboards, a mug-ring on the nothingness of the glass-topped table or even the faint purplish haze of an old wine stain on the pristine whiteness of the enormous cornered sofa backed against two walls. Ham instinctively removed his shoes without being asked and perched on the very edge of the sofa to avoid indenting it.

While Patrick handed round bitter, dark coffee in bite-sized gold rimmed white cups, Moira snuggled girlishly into the corner of the sofa and tucked her feet under her, arranging her skirt fastidiously over her legs by plucking at it with her thumb and forefinger and frowning at it as though the arrangement displeased her. Then she smiled round.

"You'll need a wee bit of an introduction before we reveal all," she said coyly, pausing to invite a snigger and they simpered politely, in acknowledgement of the double entendre of Moira-speak. "We," she smiled archly at Patrick, "decided to sample water sports. I've always known that Patrick was a frustrated yachtsman at heart and you know me! Game for absolutely everything!" They simpered obediently again, "We also absolutely adore the north of Scotland – all that wild unspoiled wilderness." She waved an arm to embrace the whole unspoiled sitting-room and the conservatory extension. "Then we heard of this resort in one of *the* wildest, *the* most unspoiled parts where you can learn to water-ski, sail, shoot rapids, absolutely everything. They have massively good instructors too. It was all quite expensive of course, but, to quote James Bond, "'You only live twice' and ..."

"I don't think James Bond actually ..." John started but Moira was over-riding him.

"O.K.? Are you all comfortable. Anyone for more coffee? Better not! It'll keep you awake all night. O.K., Patrick? Shoot, man, shoot!"

Patrick pointed the remote control in the direction of the television and fired. A huge, bright orange rectangle electrified the blandness. Across it the caption read, *Moira and Patrick take to the water!*

"We thought that rather clever," Patrick boomed, "You know! *Take to* meaning start and *take to* meaning that we got to like it. Get it, Ham?"

"Yes, thank-you," said Ham politely.

The caption changed to *Arrival of the Water Babe.* Moira tripped up the steps of what was obviously the resort hotel, clutching a small red vanity case and tossing her neatly bobbed hair self-consciously. She paused at the top of the flight to turn and smile round at what was presumably the view. The smile was just giving way to a scowl of impatience when she was beamed up to the hotel bedroom. The camera had misadapted to the indoor lighting. The room was feverishly pink and a fruitily lipped Moira was burrowing into her case with sanguine nails. After swinging giddily round the room, taking in the swathed fourposter and the entire contents of the cocktail cabinet, the camera steadied as it focused on the view from the balcony. The loch below, impenetrably dark with its matt surface and its water, heavy with peat, undulating almost imperceptibly against the rich green of the early summer shoreline, narrowed into the distance and wound out of sight. On one side the remains of a white croft house, roofless and with brutallised window holes, crumbled onto an even green slope scattered with white lumps which could be stones or grazing sheep or both. On the other side regimented rows of dark grey-green forestation dressed the hillside to the skyline. It was a scene so typical of any Scottish loch that Jane was surprised to hear John's sharp intake of breath. She turned to him, placing a hand on his knee, but his face was expressionless in the orange glow from behind the next caption, *Wearing our L plates.*

The camera was now in less experienced hands. The wobble was more pronounced and Patrick and Moira appeared to shiver violently in their wet suits. They were standing on a brown coir-matted jetty surrounded by opportunistic ducks and a powerfully built young man with a white grin, broad shoulders and slim hips was assisting them with their life jackets.

"Our instructor," Moira elucidated, pointing an excited finger at the screen, "You should have seen the tan under that wet-suit!"

They all simpered co-operatively again and watched Patrick give a shaky thumbs-up before stepping warily from the jetty into the boat and over-reacting with spread-eagled arms as it rocked gently under his weight. The instructor handed Moira aboard and leaped in after her, rope in hand. With a spray of speed they were off, cleaving the water with their wake and setting up agitated ducks. The novice camera man obviously misunderstood his instructions, particularly regarding the manipulation of the zoom and as the nursery area for water-skiing was some distance down the loch, John, Jane and Ham found themselves screwing up their eyes to make out a boat the size of a pond insect with two minute tea-leaves, presumably Moira and Patrick, adhering to either side.

"We were holding onto poles on each side of the boat," explained Moira. "That's how you start. A rope isn't really rigid enough for you to learn to get your balance. Don't worry. You'll see us properly in a moment."

And the words were hardly out of her mouth before her crouching wet-suited buttocks lunged into focus, thrusting out from the screen and wobbling vigourously in the hands of the inexpert cameraman. After some zoom adjustment the field widened to include the sterns of the boat and of Patrick.

"Didn't you get to stand up?" asked Ham innocently.

"Later," snapped Moira. "Actually we found water-skiing a bit boring."

"Moira preferred the après water-ski," snorted Patrick.

With the sailing lessons the technique of the on-shore cameraman improved so that the limited success of the novices was recorded with grim accuracy. *Shooting the Rapids* was reduced to ten seconds of spray, drunkenly rocking river banks and other people's safety helmets because "We couldn't hang on *and* film!" The high point of the show, captioned *The Bird Man of Loch Foy* was definitely provided by Patrick dangling from a parachute, towed by the same speed-boat that was used for the water-skiing lesson. The camera was in Moira's expert hands and the lines of terror across Patrick's forehead were etched unerringly across the widescreen plasma.

The record of the après water-ski and the après other activities was instantly forgettable. Shiny, unfamiliar faces, most of whom were nameless even to Moira, grinned blearily at the camera over empty glasses stained with beer froth. *An Evening Walk* featured too much of Moira picking her way gingerly along a narrow nettle-bordered path, slapping herself frantically as invisible midges bit, and too little of the surrounding scenery. *Au Revoir Loch Foy* - the packing of the car by Patrick prior to departure – came not a moment too soon. Ham, slouched against his mother's shoulder' was yawning openly by this time and gave John and Jane the excuse they needed for a hasty exit.

"We're going again next summer," Moira's voice called after them as they trooped down the path, "and we'll have even more to show you. Promise!"

Ham went up to bed immediately. Jane and John cleared up the detritus of the dinner, loading the dishwasher, washing the silver and the glass, moving around each other without touching, restricting communication to the job in hand. Both were unwilling to pick up the frayed edges of their debate on John's health or lack of it; each was afraid that the other might attempt it. Jane left John to finish drying the glasses and escaped to a bath. She ran it deep and lay low, almost totally submerged, listening to his padding about in the bedroom, hearing the sounds of progress as the wardrobe door opened and shut and the lid of the wicker linen basket creaked. She gave him fifteen minutes to fall asleep after he shuffled off his slippers and then she surfaced and wrapped herself in a towelling robe.

John was sitting on the edge of their bed with the *Atlas of Scotland* open before him. As he poured over it, the heavy wedge of his forelock hung over his forehead and his glasses had slipped down to balance precariously on the end of his nose. His forefinger, tracing across the left-hand page veered off course as he looked up at her over the rim of his glasses.

"Loch Foy," he said, stabbing randomly at the page. "I knew it! I knew it! I knew it!" He smiled at her. "My father and I used to go fishing there."

"That must have been a long time ago." Jane settled herself comfortably into bed, adjusting her pillows to support her back. John's father had died when he was twelve and he was now forty-three. "Over thirty years!"

"Yes," he agreed, "it was."

Instead of joining her in bed, he moved across to the window, drew back the curtains and leaned his elbows on the sill. "Indeed it was!"

A robin, confused by the sudden shaft of light falling across his hawthorn bush, started up an early morning twitter, realised he had boobed and subsided into silence.

"Dad and I used to call it our escape," John's voice was muffled because his chin was resting on his hand but Jane could still recognise the emotional huskiness. It was the first time she had heard him express his need to escape from his overbearing mother to whose memory he was unwaveringly loyal and she understood his need to speak with his back to her, to confide into the long June dusk where shape and form merged and were unrecognizable. Even now his maternally fostered conscience forced him to modify. "Not sure from whom or from what we needed to escape. Well, not quite sure. Anyway, we used to take a tent and fishing gear and head up North for the lochs. Loch Foy was one of our favourites and we camped once just next to that ruined cottage. I can remember lying in the tent in the semi-dark listening to the water moving and the sheep bleating and nibbling. Sheep eat very noisily, you know. They sound as though they're munching corn on the cob. Dad and I never caught many fish and we usually threw back those we did catch – took one or two back with us just to keep the old girl happy." He paused, rubbed his elbow and leaned his chin on his other hand. "But you know, Janie, those were the happiest days of my whole childhood. I remember saying to Dad that when I was older I would go to all the lochs in Scotland. I said it one night when we were lying in our tent and I was almost asleep. And I could hear the smile in his voice as he said, 'Right, son, you just mind and do that.' It wasn't the sort of smile that meant he was laughing at me either because he wasn't like that. He sounded encouraging. 'You'll have a big job on your hands,' he said, 'but I'm sure you can do it.' He felt across my pillow for my head and patted it. 'But you'll do it with me, Dad?' I can remember this bit clearly because I was sure he would say 'yes' and I waited and waited. Then he said, 'My son, you'll do it just fine on your own.' Six months later he was dead.

'I kept up the idea of doing the lochs but Mum was dead set against it. She said it was out of the question and that my father's medication had impaired his judgment. Eventually it was just a dream that died as most dreams do."

Jane slipped out of bed and stood beside him. He put his arm around her, pulling her close and sniffing her after-bath soapiness.

"I'll do your lochs with you," she said. He smiled down at her but her face was serious. "I mean it, John. We'll aim to walk around all the lochs in Scotland. We'll be like Munro-baggers, only doing lochs instead of hills. After all, the exercise is what you need, John dear. In fact, it will do us all good."

He detached himself gently and returned to the atlas.

"It's almost impossible," he mused. "Some of them are sea lochs and …"

"We'll make up the rules to-morrow in the clear light of day," she said firmly, taking the atlas, shutting it and balancing it on the edge of her dressing-table. "We'll work everything out in the morning. Now come to bed!"

He was like a small child reluctant to part with a favourite toy, wanting to extend the pre-bed playhour. "Let's toast the decision," he whispered eagerly. "I'll go and open a bottle and …"

"We'll toast it in water," she said firmly, seizing the carafe of water beside her bed. "Calories?"

'And I'm getting just like his monster of a mother,' she thought, watching the brightness seep from his face. 'Why couldn't I just play along as I used to?'

She smiled at him persuasively, patting the bed beside her. "We have to toast it in water, darling. It's lochs we're talking about."

Sitting upright, side by side, they clinked glasses
"To the lochs," he said.
"The lochs," she echoed.

Chapter Two

A Cuckoo Idea

The Beak Taps on the Shell

As Jane reached for her hairbrush she nearly dislodged the *Atlas of Scotland* from her dressing-table. She grabbed it just in time to prevent it from falling and looked around half-guiltily for some obscure hiding place: it was an embarrassing reminder of nocturnal intimacy which had no suitable place in the daylight of practical family life. It was just a ghost of an idea which should have evaporated with the other spirits of the night at cockcrow - or at least when her alarm went off. But against all the dictates of her common sense she compromised by placing it under her pillow so that its dog-eared corner just stuck out. "For later," she whispered apologetically to herself and went to pick up her hairbrush again. John was singing in the bathroom cheerfully enough and Jane recognised the anthem which the choir had sung in church the Sunday before. *This is the day which the Lord hath made: we will rejoice and be glad in it.* "He must have forgotten he's on another in-service to-day," she thought wryly as she went downstairs.

John had not forgotten his in-service. He merely felt happy. "For no reason," he lied to himself because there were no words to justify his happiness, not even for an English graduate. He had not only shared a long dormant dream, but shared too the possibility of its fruition and he knew a contentment akin to a post-coital glow. Nevertheless, the whole loch thing was still only a dream, as fragile and ephemeral as a dragon-fly emerging damply at night from its lengthy pupation, and he hoped that Jane would not expose it too precipitately to the cruel light of rational day. This irrational sense of vulnerability forced him to keep the newspaper between them at breakfast. Ham, exhausted after his late night, did not come down to bridge the silence between them and Jenny did not believe in breakfast on Saturday, so he kissed Jane lightly on the forehead and left a good half-hour before he had planned.

There was only one other car in the round, gravelled car-park when John pulled in to *Hedges House* for his in-service and he drew up alongside it, carefully parallel. *Hedges House*, twelve miles or so West of Edinburgh, was one of those sad, old stone mansions in and around the city, abandoned as family homes because of the enormity of their upkeep and snapped up as bargains for commercial purposes – hotels, *luxury* apartments or conference centres. Only the walled kitchen garden remained as it would have been in the past and even it was being commercially exploited as indicated by a large notice *Plants for Sale* on the blue-painted door in the wall. The rest of the garden had been 'landscaped' into an easy maintenance, featureless lawn encroached by predatory rhododendrons and it did not invite lingering. John walked through the open front door, his footsteps sounding in the emptiness of the tiled vestibule, on one side sparsely equipped with rows of empty coat hooks and an empty umbrella stand and, on the other with a narrow table overlapped by rows of blue-grey conference folders. Over the table a sepia photograph of the family who had once lived in Hedges House, completely out of keeping with the present purpose of the building, had probably been allowed to remain because there was nowhere else to put it and because it was of insufficient interest to detract from any project in hand. At a glance, John took in the three generations posing in front of the house; the men expressionless behind their moustaches and the women with stiffly billowing bosoms seated with the children propped languidly against them; the stern grandmother upright and central and on her knee an infant with its long white gown spilling over her dark skirt and its small face puckered against its urge to scream; the servants on the periphery, maids capped and aproned and a gaitered game-keeper with a heavy moustache and a broken gun. John managed to edge out his folder without unsettling the pile and pinned his name badge over the logo on his blue sweatshirt.

Only after he had seated himself in the lecture-room did he remember that he had left his newspaper in the car. Tutting at his own forgetfulness, he put on his glasses and opened his folder to discover what he had let himself in for. The title of the course, *Fleshing Out Our Dreams Together*, held promise of being the sort of soul-searching, unbosoming in-service course he openly despised; the sort that began by extracting grudgingly muttered assurances of mutual appreciation from participants and climaxed by demanding flagrantly physical demonstrations of their support for each other – indiscriminate hugging and such-like. *Bonding* they called it. "Bonding is to team-work what fore-play is to sex," the new head had brazenly asserted during her opening remarks to the staff.

He read on to discover that the course was the brain-child of a certain Caroline Parry whose qualifications appeared to be in psychology and who would be conducting the course herself, in person. Caroline aimed *to search out the latent you, to resurrect those dead and buried dreams of your youth.* After this re-awakening he could apparently expect to emerge not only *with your goals clarified* but also *with a realistic plan for their attainment.* Good old Caro!. No, *he* could see through it a mile away. This was a course tailor-made for those who, sadly, had reached their professional peak and who should be diverted from attempting to climb any higher up the professional ladder;

for those with a penchant for sentimental retrospection and certainly not for John Maitland. No-one could seriously consider him to have peaked? The new head, of course, would not know how he had single-handedly completely re-structured the English Department when he took it over ten years ago. Since then …? He had dabbled in various extra-mural activities like … Well, he *had* helped with the Outdoor Education Programme until that unpleasant fracas with the idiotic McHarg woman maintaining that her daughter had been forced to share a tent overnight with two boys. It wasn't his fault that the girls had carelessly forgotten to bring their tent-pegs. "She needs to be properly equipped in future," he had responded coldly. This was duly translated in the daily rag as *Teacher Insists Students Carry Condoms*. …And he'd nearly died of boredom umpiring cricket when they were desperate. … And he'd run afternoon detention for years, and would continue to do so, despite the modernistic mutterings about infringing upon 'young citizens' rights heard among one or two of his younger colleagues. One of them – indubitably Jason Whatshisname with the ear-ring – the one who refused to sing the National Anthem at the school Speech Day – had stuck a leaflet about these liberties in his pigeon-hole. Looked like a home-made leaflet, with the odd misspelling too. Discipline! It had ceased to exist. The word *punishment* had become obsolete. It had been replaced by *sanction* and just as he had got used to hissing *sanction* at the insubordinates, it had been further watered down to *consequence* and discipline was a mushy mess. He'd certainly not peaked. He might have plateaued perhaps. He liked *plateaued*. If it implied absence of challenge, it also suggested that he could coast at a high level without difficulty; that he had a superior breadth of vision. It spoke of unhurried, easy evenness of life. The chair beside him creaked. Seated beside him, too close for comfort really, was the only other delegate from his school, the librarian, the Arbuthnot woman Shona, or was it Sheena? Something like that. He would not be able to read her name without peering and she had pinned her badge directly over her left nipple.

"Hi, Sh...," he smiled kindly, thinking that if he had been Ear-ring John, he would have added, "You're invading my personal space."

Sh responded with a brief, tight-lipped smile that suggested she could be self-conscious about bad breath and returned to examining her folder.

"A tad Mills and Boone, title-wise," he remarked laconically, thereby provoking another halitosis half-smile. Maybe she didn't want to be there either.

He leafed through to the list of delegates. His name was clear enough on the sheet and he discovered that *Sh* was actually Sheena. He would try to remember that. Mnemonics perhaps. Always recommending mnemonics to his students. "Sheena ...I've seen 'er" or "Have ya seen'er, Sheena?" or "I'm keener on Sheena" Never! Perhaps, "Ya could be leaner, Sheena"...

"Good morning and welcome!"

Caroline, presumably. Having separated herself out from the small group of people clustered round the table of leaflets, she stood smiling round the room, marker pen rolling between her hands while the leaflet-gatherers shuffled in a self-conscious flurry between the rows to their seats in the front row. Presumably the composition of the front row would be the same as in class, a mixture of the toadies who could be relied upon to laugh at your corniest joke and the late arrivals who couldn't see anywhere else to sit. Glancing round, though, he could see plenty of empty seats, which meant that the front row was probably solidly sycophantic. Lucky for Caro!

"My name is Caroline Parry, as I expect you will have gathered," her voice was as clear, hard and brittle as glass, "and I shall be providing just the framework for this one day course …"

Caroline's red marker pen exactly matched her lipstick which exactly matched her shoes. She had written a heading on the flip-chart and underlined it. The line was not very straight. The heading read, *Who and What Am I?*

"Now!" she was still smiling. Could it be that she actually enjoyed this? "You will all be paired up and to make sure you don't cheat by pairing yourself with a colleague, I have pre-paired you myself. *Pause for appreciation of the pun.* You will have fifteen minutes each to give your partner the clearest possible non-verbal information about who you are; what you do at work and at play; what makes you tick. After that you have five minutes feed-back, talking this time, to find out what your partner has concluded about you. Any questions? Every-one ready?" There was an apprehensive silence, during which she ferreted in her brief-case. "Now, let me introduce you to my cock-a doodle-do." Some imbecile behind John sniggered and he just stopped himself from automatically turning round to glare punitively. Caroline produced a rainbow-hued ceramic cockerel with a clock-face on his puffed out chest and flourished it aloft. "This is Chanticler and he will crow for you at swap-over times – like this" Chanticler emitted an unearthly braying noise and she placed him on the front of her table. "To make it easier for you," she added "I *will* tell you that we have many and varied occupations present today so just don't assume that your partner's occupation will be like your own. To make it more difficult the rule that all communication will be non-verbal is very, very strict! Got it? No words! You may mime. You may draw – use sketches, symbols."

"If we have to play party parlour games, I prefer charades!" Jasper confided to Sh …*seen 'er was it*? …Sheena. "I'm afraid it looks as though you and I won't be a pair."

This time she actually showed her teeth as she smiled

back at him, obviously warming towards whatever final intimacy would be demanded.

"Well, hi, John! I'm Katie as you can see!"

Katie was in her early twenties, he guessed, round about twenty years younger than he was. Unlike most of the other delegates who appeared undressed for in-service, as though ready for a day's gardening, she was buttoned tightly into a formal, double-breasted navy-blue suit with a froth of white blouse at the neckline. But she smelled of jasmine, or perhaps mimosa, and an armoury of bangles jingled round her brown wrist as she tapped her name-plate.

"Hi," he replied awkwardly, straightening the tie that wasn't there as she, perched on the seat opposite him and pushing her thick dark hair off her face, offered like one who was used to dealing with the tongue-tied and awkward, "Would you like me to go first or would you rather get it over with?"

"Please, madam, after you!" He took refuge in mock formality and then wished he hadn't because her generation was often suspicious of sexist gallantry.

But she smiled.

"Just give me a minute to think how I'm going to do this and I'll start!"

Wrinkling her nose and pushing her pen between her lips, she looked as though she was waiting for a prompt. John took out a notebook, shutting his brief-case with exaggerated quietness, and fished his pen out of his pocket.

"Job first!" she mouthed.

"No talking there!" called out Caroline, wagging a finger at her.

Katie blushed self-consciously and pulled the sort of

face John saw on schoolgirls he was telling off for passing notes or chewing gum. Come to think of it, Katie seemed to be chewing gum too, but the chewing ceased as she suddenly composed a serious face; sat up very straight; cast her eyes heavenward and clasped her hands as though in prayer.

He had to scribble with his ball-point pen to make the ink flow. Then *nun* he wrote, stared at the word as though it was misspelled and added *novitiate.* That would give her time to change her mind before taking her final vows. He then added *priest?*

She was standing up now and bending over the small table placed against a wall. She slipped the rings off her fingers, stretched imaginary gloves up over her bangles and occupied herself with mixing substances together. She was probably working with food, but why the gloves? She must be ultra-hygienic and the nails that had tapped her name badge had certainly been on the long side. Now she seemed to be peeling potatoes. He wrote *chef* and then *housewife?* And then wondered if she was describing cooking as a hobby.

"Are you still on the job?" he whispered.

"John!" remonstrated Caroline from somewhere behind him. Irritating woman!

Katie nodded and stood up straight for a moment's indecision. Then she marched slowly up to the table, stroked something on it with unbelievable tenderness and, leaning over it, kissed what she had just stroked.

John decided not to record his thoughts.

She straightened up and cast him a pleading, questioning look as if to say, "Isn't that enough."

Though clueless, he smiled benevolently and nodded.

Flushed from the stuffiness of the room rather than from her exertions, she took off her jacket and hung it very carefully around the back of her chair before glancing furtively in Caroline's direction and mouthing, "Hobbies now."

He nodded conspiratorially.

This was easier. She rose up and down astride her chair, while holding imaginary reins. She held a "book" in her hands, pursing her lips demurely as she turned the pages. She scattered seeds and pulled up weeds and she had just held binoculars up to her eyes and was arching her back to peer upwards through the trees when Chanticler crowed.

Katie stretched back in her chair, clasping her hands behind her head so that her breasts thrust against the soft thinness of her blouse.

"You're on now!" she grinned,

John got through the teacher bit quite easily with Katie smiling encouragingly as he wagged his finger at imaginary students, marked "jotters" with flourishing ticks and wrote on an imaginary blackboard.

At hobbies he found himself panicking. As he copied her reading and birdwatching slavishly she nodded in comradeship, but when he indicated, by drawing the traditional square with his finger, that he watched television, she pouted. Obviously, the outdoor type! Anxious to redeem himself, he mimed pulling on boots, tugging the laces fiercely to indicate tough walking boots and strode across the carpet, shading his eyes as he peered into the hinterland. Katie smiled, impressed, and scribbled something on the back of her hand.

Another bray from Chanticler brought a lifting of the ban on verbal communication. "And now you *may* talk! Tell each other what you have discovered about them. I'm looking forward to eavesdropping!"

Katie leaned forward expectantly like a pupil awaiting a test result, "You go first. What am I?"

Was she eager or anxious? John was unsure and he hesitated before beginning slowly, "It's difficult to say, really. I've written a couple of ideas down but I could be very wrong…"

"Not your fault," she interrupted giggling nervously and pushing her hair back again. "My miming's outrageous. You should have seen me at Drama at school. I got chucked out of the class regularly. Look, let's get it over with before she comes to listen in."

She jerked her head towards Caroline who had begun circulating, hands clasped behind her back, pausing to lean over couples to listen in, smiling inscrutably.

"Well, I thought at first that you could be going in for something religious – like a nun – or training to be a nun – or training for the ministry?" He looked at her questioningly.

"And then? Do go on!"

"I thought you could be cooking? Nothing wrong with that. I'd be the first to say that being a housewife is a career in itself. My own wife … Well never mind. Let's just say I thought you were cooking. And, frankly, I haven't a clue why you kissed something or some-one on the table …"

"Oh that bit? Sorry! The kissing bit wasn't actually my job. I was just setting the scene sort of."

'Don't say 'sort of!' went through his head. "I'm afraid that I haven't come to any firm conclusion," he finished shaking his head wryly.

"I'll tell you right at the end." Her eyes were dancing. "If I tell you now you'll probably freak out! Go on and do my hobbies and then I'll do you."

He got them all right and she clapped her hands so that her bangles jingled like a Salvation Army percussion band and attracted Caroline's attention. She wound her way slowly towards them as Katy began to interpret John.

"You are a teacher!" she announced triumphantly. "You're quite a strict teacher from the way you wagged your finger … but I'm sure you're very kind!" He felt himself blushing and ran his finger around the inside of the neck of his sweatshirt. For heaven's sake! He hadn't reached the stage of mid-life crisis hankerings yet! "I don't know what you teach. Not English I shouldn't think. The English teachers at my old school were all barmy. Maths?"

"No, English I'm afraid!"

She was unabashed, "At least it wasn't Geography. I hated Geography," she confided in a whisper.

Caroline had taken up position right behind him, ready to become privy to what made him tick. He was glad that he had fabricated so much of it.

"John and I share quite a few interests," Katie addressed Caroline directly over his head. "Don't we, John?"

He nodded all the more emphatically because Caroline made no attempt to disguise her surprise.

"We both like to read. And birds too!" She addressed him directly, "You and I both love watching birds. Interested in any particular sort of birds?"

"Just birds! All birds, actually. We feed them." Well Jane did and, even though he had grumbled at her to stop because of the bird mess on his car, she still went on.

"Sometimes you like to watch television …

"Not all that much," he interrupted hastily. "I just have to endure it when the wife puts it on. I don't really enjoy it at all … disturbs my reading … drowns the bird-song …"

"Oh. I love the telly!" she sighed. "My television's not working properly and when you mimed it I remembered I'd forgotten to phone the repair man before the course this morning. Never mind, I've got my mobile and …"

"Is that all you unearthed about John?" Caroline sounded vaguely critical.

"Oh no!" Katie started, obviously having forgotten Caroline's presence. "It gets much more exciting! John is an explorer. You are an explorer, John? I'm sure I got that right."

As John hesitated, she prompted encouragingly, "What,

where do you explore, John?"

Her question sounded very loud above all the background chat and tittering. Caroline was still hovering behind him and, looking round, John spotted Sh … seen ya … whatever only two tables away He dropped his pen and bent to retrieve it, managing to knock it under his chair to give himself more time. Caroline tried to help him and they bumped heads. Her head was unexpectedly hard under all that fair fluffiness and he rubbed his own ruefully as he emerged. She was still smiling as she shifted on towards the next couple.

"Lochs," he gulped reluctantly. "You see I'm fascinated by lochs. Always have been." She was transfixed. "Go round them … collating various data. I'll not go into the details now." He spoke very finally and would not be drawn, even when Katie pleaded with him.

"You haven't told me yet what your job is?" he countered.

Caroline was absorbed in the next couple now but, even so, Katie leant right forward to whisper in John's ear, gasping breathily so that he could not make out what she was saying.

"Come again?"

"I'm an embalmer." Her breath was hot and anxious on his neck.

"Come again!" He could not have heard correctly.

She pulled the told off school-girl face again and spoke quickly and fiercely,

"You heard right the first time. I work for my father's undertaking business. I'm not really strong enough for the lifting jobs so I concentrate on the embalming. It's better than the office work, but it's still well *doh*! I want to find another career and I feel bad about that, but Dad understands. He paid for me to come on this course."

"That's very interesting," managed John.

"I was being a mourner coming to pay respects to a

departed with the kissing and stuff. I thought it might help if I set the scene a bit, but I think I made it more difficult."

"Not at all."

"You seemed to be enjoying yourself!" Sheena accused as he sat down beside her again.

"You seem to have found your tongue," he countered defensively.

"Oh ..," she fidgeted slightly, "I'm never very good first thing in the morning. It takes a bomb to get me out of bed. Biorhythms you know. I'm low in the morning, go up during the day and by the evening ..."

"If you're ready every-one..." The honeymoon period was over and Caroline, tapping her marker pen against her flip-chart, was obviously waxing bossy and controlling but at least he didn't have to listen to what Sheena did when her biorhythms peaked.

Caroline swung towards the flip-chart and wrote energetically with her red marker pen. *Lies Speak Truth!*

"Now, it is a well-known fact that it is much easier to mime a lie than to articulate one and the chances are," she pontificated, "that you have, or most of you have, been miming a lot of porkies. You probably told the truth about your job, but my guess is that a lot of fabrication went into the rest." John was studying his folder but he was sure that her voice was directed at him. "Some of you selected what you felt you could mime easily. Some of you wanted to make a good impression on your partner and deliberately chose hobbies that you thought would elevate you in their eyes. Some of you mimed what you would like to do or be involved in, rather than what you are actually involved in." John attempted a *how preposterous* expression as Caroline expanded with unnecessary accuracy. "We all carry with us an image of ourselves that we would like to be able to project – an image of our physical appearance, which I am not concerned with - and an image of possible successful achievements which is our business today. I am not talking about the field of work but rather of the creative side of us, the interest and hobbies side that is so intensely important for our well-being and self-respect and tends to be pushed behind the demands of a career. Why have we never achieved these goals and what obstacles are preventing us from achieving them now?" She paused. "We will break for coffee now and consider those obstacles after our break."

John took his coffee outside and breathed in the freshness of the air to clear his lungs, his mind and his conscience. He was alone except for two smokers, skulking between cars in the car park, flicking their cigarettes onto the gravel and toeing the ash in between the pebbles, and a wary blackbird - he *could* recognise a blackbird – hopping gingerly across the lawn and pausing after every third or fourth hop to glance suspiciously at the smokers. He didn't want to discuss whether or not he had lied with Sheena or with anyone else. The blackbird was tugging at a worm, probably trying to stretch it to impress either Mrs. Blackbird or his bit of fluff on the side or whatever. Lying? Perhaps. He had always been bad at owning up, even after cheating at Monopoly, although that had been just with his younger cousins, which didn't really count as cheating. The blackbird flew off with its elongated worm and the smokers stubbed out in unison. Eventually, he followed them in and was the last to regain his seat, thereby drawing Caroline's fixed smile.

"Now that we're *all* here," she really was getting her horns out, "we'll make a start on the second part." There was a pause while she adjusted her tone to a more friendly level. "It won't surprise those of you that I was talking to at coffee-time (an appreciative rustle of her recognition of them from the front row) that you will be back in your pairs again. This time there is a definite plus: you will be allowed to talk. In fact, you can talk as much as you like. On the minus side, however, you have to tell the truth. Yes, you do! In fact you have to go back through all the hobbies and interests that you mimed to your partner and tell him or her which were true and which were either exaggerated or complete fabrications. When you've recovered from that, try to think why you lied or exaggerated. I am sure that you will find that some of your fabrications are leisure pursuits you would really like to have followed. What's stopping you now? I want you to discuss what on earth is preventing you from doing so. Now," and the pitch of her voice was rising like a teacher's giving final instructions at the end of one lesson to a class who had already started to pack up, "I want to see everyone with pen and paper, noting down the obstacles which prevent them from following what could be genuine interests."

"It's beginning to get over-complicated," whispered Sheena.

"They always do."

"What if you weren't lying? We're not all deviant, are we?"

"No, of course not," lied John, wishing she would return to her early morning vegetative state, "but I did leave some of my interests out. I've just got too many."

"Think I got all mine in. No! Come to think of it I left out my kick-boxing. How could I?"

"Take it that's an evening pursuit." And John picked up his folder and went to find Katie.

"O.K.! Who goes first?"

She was definitely less self-assured and masticating furiously at her gum.

"Why don't we alternate?" He couldn't stop himself from elucidating. "That means you do one and I'll do one and so on until we've covered them all."

"Right!" she hesitated. "O.K.," she said slowly. Then in a burst, "Well, I do read, but not as much as I used to. In fact weeks go by without my opening a book. I do enjoy reading, but the thing is …Well, I suppose I have to be relaxed, sort of, if I'm going to lose myself in a book …and I haven't been able to relax recently …"

"Do you know why? You don't have to tell me if you don't want to, but if you know why …"

"Boy-friend trouble!" she blurted out and studied his face for a reaction before going on. "Thing is it was really serious. He's at Uni. and he was looking for a part-time job and my dad gave him a job in the firm and everything. That's one of the reasons I want to leave. Keep remembering him about the place even though he's left. He two-timed me. Got stuck on the girl from the florist who delivered the floral tributes. Always hanging around when she was due to appear. As though I wouldn't notice and I'm not the jealous sort. So I ditched him and … that's it really. Drives the florist's van now.

Anyway, I can't really settle to read much at the moment."

"Presumably, once you're through all that, the reading'll start again though." He couldn't think of anything else to say.

"The reading? Oh … yes! Well probably," she sighed and rested her chin on her hands. "Your turn now."

"I do read, but," and he took a deep breath, "the bird thing was pure fabrication."

"And why did you lie about it then?" She attempted severity.

"I couldn't think of anything else to mime at the time. And it looked good, the way you did it. I don't like birds all that much. The wife keeps feeding them and they cr… mess on my car."

She tossed back her hair and laughed. "I *do* watch birds," she said, "and I particularly like raptors. Mark, that's the ex, and I went up to Loch Garten to see the ospreys just a month ago and last year we went to a raptor centre and I flew an eagle owl. It was so amazing! Such a big bird and yet it felt so light! They gave me a day-old dead chick to lure it with. I had to dangle it from my hand." She gave an expressive little shudder. "But it was great! Funny to mind a dead chick when I'm so used to dead people …Isn't it?"

He smiled indulgently and she forgot about turns and went on.

"My biggest lie was the riding," she confessed. "I've only ridden once – on a friend's pony *and* I fell off. But I've always really wanted to ride. Read all those pony books when I was a kid and imagined myself galloping over jumps …"

"You shouldn't try galloping over jumps," he smiled.

"Do you ride then?"

"No, not I! But my daughter does. She's quite good – so I've picked up a few tips. What stops you?"

"What stops most people. Money! Something she" and she jerked her head towards Caroline, "probably doesn't have to worry about. I tried to persuade Dad to have a horse-drawn hearse. I think that would really increase our business, don't you? But he said that he didn't mind increasing our business, but he didn't think we ought to make it and that if I were to be driving the horses through traffic, we would be making business. Thought he was *so* funny. He squashes all my attempts at innovation!"

"To get back to your riding," John prompted her, much more gently than if she had been one of his pupils rambling off at a tangent, "how do you think you could have more contact with horses?"

She leaned forward, elbows on knees, cupping her chin in her hands and thought.

"Well, now that Mark's away, I have most week-ends free and Wednesday afternoons as well. I suppose I could see if I could work at stables – livery stables or perhaps a riding school, but I'm a bit old for that. That's the sort of thing kids do. Still, perhaps I could. Or I could cut down on what I spend on clothes – which, admittedly, is quite dreadful. But I tell you what. I'm going to try. I really am. I'm going to try. "She grinned at him, "You're doing me good, you know."

"Well, you never know, perhaps when I pick Jenny up from the riding-school, I'll see you there…"

"Now you!" she sat up eager to repay him. "I've got to help you too."

"Well, I do watch television, which is probably why I'm square-eyed and paunchy, but I lied about the lochs …"

"Oh you didn't!"

He nodded

"Do you really mean that?" she frowned. "Really mean that it was a complete fabrication, that you really have no interest in exploring lochs?"

John felt irritated. What did this kid with her gum and her jangly bangles and her anecdotal waffle about her love-life think she was doing criticising him? He never tolerated impertinence.

"I've come clean." His reply was crisp and his foot was tapping. "I fabricated that bit."

"Why?"

"Because, I suppose it's probably the sort of thing I would like to have done years ago – except that I had other commitments."

"Like what?"

His thin lipped smile was intended to prove to her that he found her questioning vaguely amusing; that she tickled rather than ruffled him. "Like … studying" he drawled. "Like… working; like … raising a young family. Do you really want me to go on?"

"I'm sorry," she laid a hand on his knee soothingly. "I didn't mean to get on at you. It's just that it was such an interesting idea. Everyone in Scotland goes up hills and I'd never heard of anyone going round lochs."

"Actually," he found himself relaxing again, largely because of the warm hand which was still on his knee. "You know, when I was a small boy I did decide that I would walk round all the lochs in Scotland. Loved water. Fascinated me. It first started, I think, at my grandmother's fish-pond. She had a large fish-pond, very large, and I was forbidden to go near it."

"They're so dangerous for small children," put in Katie wisely. "I was reading in the paper – just last week I think it was – that a wee ..."

"Oh! It wasn't the danger!" he interrupted. "It was the flower-beds round the pond. Grandma was very keen on her garden. Anyway, I suppose I was pretty disobedient and willful and all that and my happiest hours at Grandma's were certainly spent at the fish-pond, sailing paper boats, watching the fish and the water-skates and the water-boatmen, dangling my arms in it to make waves. I even tried to swim in it once – caused a lot of damage and retribution was very violent."

"It would have been in the old days," she sympathised.

"Now, I did used to imagine I was an explorer then, but the fish-pond wasn't a loch: it was a tropical lagoon with piranhas lurking. Never felt the same about piranhas when I discovered they were fresh-water fish and couldn't live in lagoons."

"You could have sharks instead," she suggested helpfully.

"Then a little later on, I would go with my dad on his fishing expeditions. Just him and me. Didn't like fishing much. Just liked ploitering around the edge of whatever loch we were at. Sometimes we would take a tent for overnight expeditions and we'd go to sleep, embalmed in anti- midge spray, listening to the steady pulsing of the waves. Throb, throb, throb! I still love the smell of anti-midge spray. And, you know, I can remember saying to my dad one night when we were lying in our sleeping-bags that I wanted to visit all the lochs in Scotland."

"But you didn't!" she laughed.

"No, I didn't. But I made a start. I got out the road atlas and started trying to count the lochs. I did! I even tried putting them in alphabetical order, but I didn't get very far. Anyway, after my dad died, we stopped going up North. Tended to spend our holidays at my mother's relatives, with hordes of nauseating cousins. Though, recently, my wife and I have been thinking about it again – vaguely. About exploring lochs that is."

"Never taken your own family up North?"

The idea surprised him.

"Well … I don't fish … and the wife likes to go overseas. Good for the children's education. Broadens their minds and so on," he said lamely.

"You're so unselfish, John," she murmured and the hand patted his knee before she withdrew it.

Chanticler crowed hungrily.

"Doesn't time fly when you're enjoying yourselves! We'll now break for lunch and resume at two thirty very, very promptly!" Caroline again.

"Listen, old chap, the course may well be a load of bollocks, but the food will be tremendous. It always is there!" had been the recommendation of Harry Aitcheson, the classics master and a member of his staff-room clique, when John had moaned to him about the course. "Bring back a doggy-bag, won't you."

At school Harry was regarded as a bit of an anachronism, the demand for classics having dwindled progressively over the years, and he had had to pad out his timetable with *Religious and Moral Instruction* and *Good Citizenship* which seemed to be a euphemistic umbrella for drugs, sex, local politics and healthy living. Little wonder that Harry attended more out of school courses than any other member of staff and had become a reliable judge of venues and catering arrangements. He was spot on about the buffet and John was unexpectedly hungry. By the time he had piled his plate, Katie had found a table in a corner and was drawing up a second chair. She waved to him and he attempted a thumbs up with his knife, fork and napkin hand.

"*You've* a good appetite!" she smiled as he laid his plate on the table. "I never eat much lunch. I think it's the smell of the stuff I work with that takes away my appetite. The smell sort of stays in my nose and affects my taste-buds. You've no idea how strong it is."

"I can imagine," agreed John, trying not to.

"I'd really like to work with people," she said, stabbing a sliver of avocado with her fork and studying the four little holes in its slippery surface. "I know I work with people now, but they're not exactly responsive. On the plus side, you can tell them anything, really get it all off your chest. But when you've finished what you've got to say and you'd like a comment or some sympathy or something there's just this ghastly silence. It's quite off-putting."

"I can imagine," said John again, "but there are plenty of other jobs with people who are rather more pro-active than your clients."

"I've got quite good Highers," she remarked brightly, chewing unnecessarily at the avocado.

"Not Geography!" he smiled

"'Fraid not. Our Geography teacher was a right nutter. I've got History, English, Chemistry, Biology … and something else." She paused, narrowing her eyes in an attempt to remember, "Oh yes! How could I forget? Maths. Scraped it by the skin of my teeth. Got a C after an appeal."

"Well, there you are!" he said. "And universities look favourably on older students, too. Sometimes make it easier for them to get in."

"I'm really not sure that I want to go to uni," she said slowly, arranging and re-arranging the food on her fork. "Thought I'd quite like to do nursing. Or midwifery perhaps. That would be good. Bringing people into the world instead of sending them out."

He laughed. "If you already know that's what you'd like, go for it! What's stopping you from applying?"

"Cash again, I suppose!" She pulled the school-girl face again. "I'll be awfully poor while I'm training and I won't even be well paid when I've finished. Not like you teachers!"

"We're abominably paid!" he retorted with his mouth full. "You've got to decide whether you want job satisfaction or money. And my advice is, if it's money you're after, try plumbing. The only time we had a Rolls parked outside our house was when the drains were blocked!"

"Yuck! You wouldn't catch me fishing around in all that sewage. You putting me off my lunch making me think about it?"

"Our John? Putting you off your lunch? Never let it be said!"

Sheena laid a spidery hand on John's shoulder. It tickled irritatingly and he felt uncomfortable with her standing behind him.

"John has been most helpful!" pronounced Katie. "He's helped me find a new career!"

"Oh! What is it you do now?"

"I'm into preservation," replied Katie airily, after only the slightest hesitation, "and I've finished my lunch so I'll fetch the coffees. Would you like some coffee … I'm afraid I don't know your name …?"

"Sheena," supplied Sheena while John was still wrestling with his mnemomics. "No thank-you!" She emphasised all three syllables. "Caffeine at this time of day and I'll be zinging all night."

After lunch, John hoped that they might be paired up again, but Caroline had other plans. She stood with her feet placed wide apart, as though balancing on a listing boat, and gestured towards the flip-chart on which she had scrawled in block capitals, *"OBSTACLES ARE CHALLENGES."*

"By now everybody in this room should be aware of at least one unfulfilled pursuit – some creative goal that she or he would like to have fulfilled. You *should"* the admonishing finger again, "have made a note of the obstacles which are currently preventing you from achieving this goal. I am not going to ask who has done as they were told. We shall move on rapidly. Look around you. There's plenty of room in here. Space yourselves out so that nobody distracts you from the task in hand. Take a clean sheet of paper and fill in under these headings." She flipped the chart over dramatically to reveal them. "I don't think I need to explain any of them. I'll give you twenty minutes to draw up your plans. Anyone want a pen? Paper? While you are doing that, I'll circulate the course assessment sheet, because I expect you all want to leave pronto at the end of the day."

There was a general movement around the room. The front row brigade dragged chairs to remote corners on tiptoe and sat with their backs to the rest of the room. The smokers both retreated outside onto the verandah. John moved two seats away from Sheena. He took out a sheet of paper and copied the headings off the flip-chart, *1) Goals. 2) What is preventing me?. 3) How I **am** going to overcome them.* without underlining the *am*, because he disliked over-dramatisation. For a long time he doodled. He doodled leaf shapes and attempted a rather wonky treble clef. He looked out the window. There was an irregularity in the glass so that when he nodded his head slightly, the lawn outside appeared to ripple. He wrote *Goal* and underlined it. Underneath he wrote *To walk round all the lochs in Scotland! Ha! Ha!* Then he scored that out and wrote *To walk around all the lochs in Scotland named on the Ordnance Survey map.* That was more feasible – would eliminate a few hundred. Under *What is preventing me ?* he wrote quickly and easily *enormity of task, time, absence from family* and left a blank space to fill in all the other factors which made the proposition a near-impossibility. He only had five minutes left for *How am I going to overcome these obstacles.* He wrote *I'm not!* Then he scored that out very carefully so that no-one would be able to make out what he had written and wrote *Plan routes carefully to combine lochs and maximise time, not just walk – cycle, boats, horses etc.* After writing *horses* he glanced in Katie's direction. She appeared to have finished writing and was chewing the end of her pen and studying what she had written. He continued *use week-ends, holidays. Get family involved.* He was feeling suddenly inspired. *Organise expeditions to lochs with school students.* The ideas were flowing. *Use the internet to motivate others who might be interested – web page - might call it Loch Netting* ...Caroline's timer crowed triumphantly.

He was still flushed with success when Sheena plumped herself down beside him and craned her neck to read his sheet of paper.

"Lochs!" she said before he managed to turn the sheet over.

"Sh!," he warned curtly. "She's trying to talk."

Caroline closed with a homily on commitment which went largely over John's head because he heard the same sentiments most speech days, except that this sermon contained muted warnings for the benefit of *one*: how *one's* life could become meaningless after retirement if *one* neglected *one's* outside interests – if *one* allowed *oneself* to stagnate. "But life breeds in stagnation," mused John dreamily as he perfected three perfectly formed treble clefs. "Decay is a marvellous source of life- even if it is a maggotty old sort of life." He drew a plump, thriving maggot with an enormous grin on its face.

"…and I *do* hope you have found it helpful." Caroline was smiling round the room. "Please leave your assessment forms on the chair by the door.

"Done mine!" he said to Sheena during the applause which followed the vote of thanks proposed by one of the front row. He hadn't, but he wanted to escape before she asked any more questions. Out on the verandah he felt half-guilty about not having said good-bye to Katie. Still it couldn't be helped.

He had turned the key in the ignition when she tapped on his window.

He switched off the engine and ran the window down. "Want a lift?"

"Oh, no thanks! I've got my car." She held up her car keys in evidence. "Just wanted to say thanks for all your help." She hesitated before leaning forward and resting her arm along the sill of his window, "Actually, when I first saw you, I nearly freaked. Thought you'd be totally up yourself and all that! Well, how wrong can you be? You were great!"

"Pleasure," he managed and smiled at her, "and thanks for your help too."

"For mine? Why? You mean you *are* going to do your loch thing?"

"Yes, I am!" He surprised himself by his own conviction. "What is more," he added, "some of those lochs are crying out to be ridden round on horseback so just you brush up your riding skills and come along too!"

"O.K.! Will do!" She grinned back and waved him off.

Chapter Three

A Cuckoo Idea

The Family Feed The Foster Chick

As soon as Jane heard John's car start up to leave for the in-service, she dispensed with the breakfast clutter and escaped into the garden. Although the hour was early, the air was sultry, heavy with the promise of a storm brewing, and she passed swiftly through the flower garden where the colour and scent were disturbingly provocative, taking the steps down to the lowest level and the precise orderliness of the vegetable beds. Apart from the few square metres of mud-washed strawberry bed, the vegetable garden was at its functional best. Getting the most disagreeable job out of her way first, she emptied her slug-traps, shallow dishes in which the bloated black bodies of drowned slugs floated in mud-flecked beer. She didn't believe in slug-pellets.

"I don't care how safe they say they are," she had retorted when John had expostulated over his favourite lager being imbibed by slugs. "To kill the slugs the pellets must be toxic and the toxins must be passed on to the birds that eat the slugs. I'm not going to be responsible for releasing toxins into the food-chain."

"And if the birds eat the slugs-in-beer, they'll probably develop a liking for alcohol and just how good is that for them? Before you know it they'll probably all have become seasoned alcoholics."

The next day she had found a notice propped up against one of the slug dishes, penned in John's best black-board printing style. It read *Don't Drink and Fly.*

She smiled at the memory, frowned trying not to remember when since then they had laughed together and tried to concentrate on hoeing between the lettuces in the catch-crop row, noticing with satisfaction their perfect gradation from tight pale green buds at the far end to the open-hearted blowsiness at her feet. She took a knife out of her pocket and cut one for lunch. Straightening up, lettuce in one hand, knife in the other, she was dismayed to see Moira negotiating her way down the garden, placing her feet sideways on the narrow stone steps with great care so as not to jam her heels in the cracks and pressing her red-nailed finger-tips against the stone wall to steady herself. Jane waited until she was on level ground before greeting her.

"Good morning?" Jane could hear the question in her own voice; the *what on earth?* and *why so early?* inflection.

Moira did not return the greeting. She glanced anxiously around from one high stone wall behind which the Misses Reynolds might possibly be skulking, presumably with tumblers pressed against the wall the better to eavesdrop the conversation, past Jane's peas, beans and cabbages , to the other wall, bordering her own property and over which her own Aphrodite's preposterous spaghetti coiffure gleamed whitely and she shuddered.

"Could we go inside for a minute?" she mouthed through lips pallid for want of lipstick. "Please!" she added urgently and without waiting for a reply she started gingerly to remount the steps.

Passing through her kitchen in Moira's wake, Jane found her son and daughter apparently amicably united in preparing their breakfast. Ham, barefoot, tousle-headed and still in the T-shirt and boxers in which he had slept, was leaning on the counter, chin on hand, mesmerised by the toaster. Jenny, surprisingly fully dressed and, even more surprisingly, smiling, was filling the coffee machine.

"Coffee, Moira?" she offered sweetly to Moira's retreating back. But Moira appeared not to have heard her.

Over the years Jenny had derived considerable entertainment from Moira's crises and this had all the hall-marks of being a good one: the hour was unsociably early and Moira had obviously left home without preparing a face to meet the world. "Reckon it's the Big D this time," she remarked cheerfully to Ham, but he was too intent on smearing peanut butter thickly on his toast to reply. Leaving the coffee to percolate she tiptoed into the hall and seated herself on the lowest step of the stairs just outside the sitting-room door, leaning forward on her elbows to listen. She heard the wooden legs of the old sofa creak as the two women sat down, heard her mother say, "Moira, what on earth…"

"It's Tilly," Moira moaned.

"She's not ill?" Jane's voice sharpened with genuine anxiety and Jenny strained to catch the reply. They all liked Tilly, the youngest member of the Paterson family.

"Oh no! *She's* fine!" Moira snapped bitterly. "She arrived at half-past seven this morning. Off the sleeper, if you don't mind!" Moira preferred her offspring to fly: trains were for lesser mortals. "Took a taxi from the station," she added, her tone suggesting that this compounded Tilly's indiscretion. "'Surprise! Surprise!' she shouted. Shouted it. Through the letter-box! 'I've brought a friend!'"

"She's engaged," thought Jenny. "She's going to marry unsuitably. Or is she married already? On the sly and …"

"A friend!" Moira blew her nose long and loud. "A friend?" she repeated. "It's a dog! I thought Tilly had sense. A dog! In a flat! In London!" Her voice was loud and high with anger. Jenny leant back against the second step and relaxed because she could overhear without difficulty. "What is more, she is wanting us to have it because she's got some fancy job in France, very highly paid, of course and she says she can't take the dog to Paris. And when Patrick said, and said quite rightly in my mind, 'No way, Jose!' do you know what she said? I never thought my Tilly could be so unkind, so ungrateful after all the sacrifices we've made for her …"

Ham joined Jenny on the bottom step, the corners of his mouth flecked with toast crumbs, and whispered, "Is it the Big D?" She placed her finger over her lips and scowled, daring him to interrupt.

Jane had obviously been unable to fathom what Tilly's reply had been and Moira was continuing, "… actually had the nerve to say , 'This is the only thing I've ever asked you to do for me and if you can't do it, just forget I'm your daughter."

Jenny smiled to herself, the embryo of an idea gestating in her mind and retreated to the kitchen to fetch the coffee and prepare her intervention. Ham followed her. She arranged biscuits on a plate and handed him the remainder of the packet. He accepted the unspoken bribe and stayed in the kitchen demolishing them as she carried the tray through, pausing outside the sitting-room door for an appropriate cue.

Her anger spent, Moira was keening pathetically, "How can we? He's a mongrel. And he'll go lifting his leg round our statues and he'll mess on our lawn and, you know, if you walk dogs these days you have to pick up their poo."

Jenny bumped the door open, her eyes on the tray to avoid her mother's level look. Moira blew her nose again and provided Jenny with the opening she needed by summing up the situation with a resigned, "Anyway, we'll just have to lose a daughter because we can't possibly have a dog!"

"*We* could," remarked Jenny innocently. "I've always wanted a dog. Know where we could get one, Moira?"

"Oh, Jane!" Moira ignored Jenny and turned to her mother, screwing her face into furrows of angst and her damp handkerchief into a tight little ball. "Oh, Jane, that would solve *everything* !"

"What would?" Jenny's ignorance rang false even to her own ears and neither Moira nor Jenny bothered to elucidate.

"I don't think ..." Jane began slowly, trying to pinpoint just one half-rational excuse."

"Oh, Mum, please! Please! You know how I've always wanted a dog. You know I have. And I'll even share it with Ham!"

Jane, stony-faced, bought time by concentrating on pouring the coffee and handing Moira a mug with exaggerated care as though she was afraid of spilling it. "Sugar?" she said, knowing full well that Moira used sugar substitute or nothing.

"Mum!" Jenny was becoming desperate but the ritual of the coffee pouring had given Jane the time she needed.

"The thing is, Moira, we are going to be away for quite a few week-ends on a project John is developing and ..."

"First I've heard of it!" stormed Jenny, "What project?"

"Research work on Scottish lochs, dear," Jane replied smoothly.

"Well, count me out! If I can't have my dog, I'm not coming. Why should I co-operate when you won't?"

Moira raised her eyebrows at this show of blackmail and insubordination and sipped her coffee through pursed lips.

"Jenny, this is the first we've heard of your even wanting a dog," stated Jane reasonably.

"It's the first you've heard because you never listen to me," wailed Jenny. "If Ham asked you, you'd say 'Yes, *dar*ling!' or 'Of course, *dar*ling!' but I count for nothing."

"When you start speaking sense I'll listen," said Jane evenly.

Moira, feeling her own problems diminish in the face of this histrionic display of petulance by somebody else's daughter, was almost overcome by gratitude to Jenny for restoring her perspective and felt compelled to offer at least help, if not advice. "I could look after it for the odd week-end," she offered, "provided it stays here. I'd just pop next door and ..." she met Jane's eye and tailed off.

"Better still, we could take him with us!" Jenny's face was alive again. "Dogs love water. All dogs love water. Don't they, Moira?"

"Oh yes!" obliged Moira.

"What does Tilly call him?" In her eagerness, Jenny forgot that she wasn't supposed to know the history of the situation but Ham's timely entry saved her from her mother's rebuke and provided her with extra ammunition. "Ham," she beamed at him, "we're getting a dog and we're going to take him up north some week-ends to help Dad with a project on lochs!"

"Is it a rottweiler?" Ham sprayed biscuit crumbs as he spoke. "Ian's got a really cool rottweiler."

"No, I don't think so. I don't know. What is it, Moira?"

"Labrador-cum-collie," supplied Moira. "I think."

"And his name is …?"

"I don't know, but I'll go and find out right now." She put an arm around Jane and hugged her and, finding her unexpectedly stiff and unresponsive, knew instinctively that she should leave while she was ahead. "You're wonderful, Jane. I knew you'd help out." She turned at the sitting-room door. "I knew you'd help!" she repeated. "I said to Patrick, 'Jane will help us out!' and I was right! You have! I'll just go and find out what his …" Her voice faded down the hall and out the front door.

When Jane found her tongue, she vented her frustration on the unfortunate Ham. "Just you go and get dressed this minute! Fancy appearing in front of people like that! And," she waved the empty packet at him, "you've obviously eaten all the biscuits. You're nothing but a little pig!"

Jenny curled up on the sofa contentedly and reached for the remote control. "Mum, has Dad really got a project on lochs on the go or was that just a lie … I mean an excuse ….for not having the dog?"

"I do not lie, my girl," Jane snapped as she replaced the coffee mugs on the tray as firmly as she dared without cracking them, "He does have a project and having a dog is going to be massively inconvenient. And, just for the record, may I remind you that listening in to other people's conversations is completely out of order. Do we listen in to your prolonged phone calls? Well, do we?"

But Jenny was too busy flicking through channels, her eyes narrowed with concentration, to reply.

Ham sat in a forlorn huddle on the cold, stone steps leading down from the front door awaiting his father's return and alive to the pathos of his voluntary exile from the warmth and brightness in the garden at the back of the house where Jenny was playing with their new dog. "I am staying here," he informed himself with bitter self-pity, "because if anything else goes wrong, I'll get the blame for that too. I hate my sister and," he added with only a modicum of guilt, "I hate my mother too!"

As he leaned forward and tore off a leaf from one of his mother's favourite hostas, shredding it with his thumb-nail along the deep veins etched into its smooth surface, he compiled a mental catalogue of hardship with which to regale his father. First thing this morning, his mother had shouted at him for not being dressed when it was really Jenny who had annoyed her. Then, after lunch, a blotchy-faced, red-eyed Tilly had brought her dog round, a dog that had turned out to be a girl-dog called Jelly "Her name begins with 'J' just like the rest of the family except for him over there," Jenny had said to Tilly, gesturing towards Ham. Together with Jelly, Tilly had brought her feeding-bowls, a supply of her favourite dog food and a three page list of her habits, preferences and requirements. His mother had scanned the list, frowned and promptly given *him* a row for not having cut the grass. When he had tried to remind her that she had said only the day before that Dad was to take over the mowing in future to improve his fitness, she had given him yet another row for arguing and talking back. While he'd laboured, Jenny, stretched out on the lawn in the sunshine with Jelly lying alongside, had screamed

at him for 'nearly cutting *my* dog's paws off' with the lawn
mower, and he had barely finished when his mother, without so
much as an appreciative glance at his handiwork, had whisked
them, dog and all, off in the car to the pet shop, declaring
fiercely that in her house dogs slept on dog-beds whether they
liked it or not. Jenny, for once in the back, and with her arm
possessively round Jelly, had said that in her opinion this was
'barbaric' and his mother had reacted by slapping *his* bare leg
hard merely because he was tapping his foot in time to the
music and she found it 'irritating'. The beds in the pet shop had
been labelled for various breeds from Great Dane down and
because Jelly was what the pet shop assistant called 'a
composite type', his mother had had difficulty in deciding on
the right size. "Bring her in!" suggested the friendly assistant
and Jenny was given the car-keys to fetch her. Jelly, elated by
the heady scents of dog food, live rabbit and other tempting
edibles had not been able to stop wagging her plumy tail and
had managed to dislodge a pyramid of packeted bird-seed ,
bursting the contents of at least three packets. Ham had realised
too late his error in laughing. His mother had harangued him
publicly and banished him to the car where, without the keys or
the dog, he had to stand and wait for forty minutes while she
helped the less friendly assistant to clear up and Jenny
fossicked for dog brushes, fancy collars, toys and other
essentials. He had not even tried for the seat beside the dog on
the way home: had concentrated on keeping his feet still and
trying not to hear Jenny's murmured endearments or the soft,
rasping sound of the dog's tongue as she licked her. He carried
all the equipment in from the car in silence. In the kitchen, his
mother had given him a hug. "Tell you what, Ham," she'd said,
"you can give Jelly her first meal. I'll help you put away the
lawn-mower and rakes first." It had taken time, winding up the
electric cable and fiddling with the rusty padlock on the garden
shed and when they returned to the kitchen, they found Jelly

licking the last of her supper off her whiskers. "Sorry," said Jenny casually when his mother had given her what seemed to Ham to be a totally inadequate rebuke, "I didn't realise Ham was to do it. You can wash her dishes, Ham," she had added kindly.

At that point he had taken himself round to the front of the house, to the discomfort of the stone steps. He could hear Jenny laughing and Jelly barking excitedly as they played on the lawn he had had to mow. And then he could hear the crunch of his father's car tyres on the gravel. He stood up, throwing the shreds of hosta leaf into the shrubbery.

"Hello, son!" his father looked happy, excited even, and he bounded towards the steps and hugged Ham. "Why the long face?"

Suddenly Ham forgot his long tale of misery as he realised that he could be the one to break the news, to tell about Jelly.

"Guess what, Dad?" he began. "Just guess what ..."

The front door burst open and Jenny's voice shrilled past him. "Dad! Dad! We've got a dog and we're going to take it round the lochs with us. What d'you think of that?"

Chapter Four

A Cuckoo Idea

The Chick Fledges

That Saturday night the air was still and heavily congested, ideally fetid for the breeding of midges and worry. Carefully Jane dislodged John's encircling arm, detached herself from the clinging sheets, pushed the sash window up as far as it would go and leaned out. The lowering cloud, underlit by the lights of the city, hung overhead in cumbersome swathes, the ceiling of a huge marquee, and reflected the light back downwards so that she looked out onto an indistinct dimness rather than onto dark. Down on the right a rectangle of light thrown from the Misses Reynolds' kitchen window imposed yellow squares on their neatly buttoned cabbages. On the left the Patersons' statues gleamed and postured grotesquely. Down across the stream the brittle, white plates of elder leaned ponderously across the stream to face her out. Between these three brighter reference points her own garden seemed to have shrunk into darkness, sandwiched between the enclosing walls that wrung the scent out of it, pressing it upward.

"I'm needing space," she whispered into the thickness, "space to breathe, space to think, space to know what I really want."

She wrapped her self-pity and her thin dressing-gown around her and slipped silently downstairs to make herself a cup of tea. Having forgotten about Jelly, she was momentarily startled by the tentative thumping of the plumy tail on the kitchen floor. The new dog-bed was empty. Jelly had dispensed with it and was lying with her head on Jane's apron, having pulled it off a kitchen chair and trampled it to form a pillow. Although she thumped her tail slowly, she did not raise her head. Lying with her chin on her paws, she looked dolefully at Jane. Jane knelt beside her while the kettle boiled, stroking the satiny smoothness of her head and then running her fingers through the long shaggy coat on her back, feeling the sharp narrowness of her frame under her thick coat. Jelly licked her knee.

"Poor thing," murmured Jane, "You've not been able to make many choices either. Heaven knows your history before Tilly took you out of the dogs' home. Now Tilly's moving on to better things and can't have you. Moira and Patrick certainly don't want you and, to tell you the truth, I don't really want you either, but I don't seem to have any more choices than you do." Jelly raised her head and licked Jane's hand sympathetically. "No, I don't," Jane went on hard-heartedly, "and what is more I seem to have let myself in for this loch business good and proper. John's come back from the in-service keener about it than ever and I know that he does need to do some physical activity. The children now know about it and are all for it … at the moment. I just feel overwhelmed and pressurised. I know I agreed. I even encouraged John last night, but somehow I thought …"

The kettle reached boiling point and switched itself off with a click. Jane glanced up momentarily only, absorbed in pouring out her woes to Jelly.

"Nobody's even considered what it means. We've only got week-ends to do it and we've all got week-end commitments. We haven't thought it out at all. Where will we stay? What about you?" She paused, knotting her fingers tightly in the thick fur. "And it's all just typical! Typical of the way I let myself get roped into things. Why did I have to bring up the loch business as an excuse this morning? Why couldn't I just say, "No" to Jenny and "No" to Moira without giving a reason. Why couldn't I say, 'No, I don't want a dog! I want to be left in peace!'"

Jelly sat up and yawned as though she'd had enough, shook herself and suddenly pricked up her ears. Jane followed her gaze towards the kitchen door. No-one. Then, soundlessly to Jane's ears, John appeared, rubbing his head, blinking his eyes and frowning at the light. Instinctively Jane felt guilty: had he heard what she had said about the lochs? Apparently not. He had just overheard the last outburst.

"If you don't want the dog," he said, "we'll find another home for it." Having settled the problem, he switched his attention to the steam rising from the kettle. "Are you making tea?"

Irked by his swift dismissal of her problems, the way in which his easy solution minimised them, Jane ignored the question. "It's not just the dog," she said slowly, holding the spout of the kettle high over the teapot and watching the smooth shaft of water plummet downwards. "It's ..."

For once he waited. He didn't try to finish her sentence for her or prompt her to hurry up. He waited.

"It's just that I feel rushed into things without being given time to decide whether I really want them or not." She hesitated. "It's this loch business too." He sat very still and she looked straight at him. "On the one hand I do think, in fact I know, that it is a really good idea. We could both do with being fitter, not just you. It would do me good to have regular physical activity too. I love the idea of spending week-ends up north and I do, I really do want us to start doing something as a family. I also know that if we don't have a project with aims and objectives, any plans we make to go up north will just de-materialise in the face of other commitments." Surprised at just how many positives there were, she was almost reluctant to switch to the negatives. "On the other hand we do have those other commitments. You know there's your choir, Ham's football, Jenny's riding and my cricket-teas which, incidentally, I'd be only too happy to give up. That's just another thing I agreed to because I can't say no."

He still remained silent, staring intently into the mug of tea in front of him and blowing softly at the threads of steam, but she knew that he was listening. Jelly stood up, re-arranged the apron by scuffling at it, circled it and lay down yawning. Jane thought very carefully.

"What I'm really saying is that I'd like us to have a trial run at the lochs. For six months say?" She looked at him questioningly. "I'd like us to give up no more that one week-end a month. And I want it to be carefully planned. I want us to decide exactly what our aims are and I want each trip properly organised at least ten days in advance. After six months we can all decide whether we want to go on or call it a day."

He spoke at last. "You're one hundred per cent right." He slapped his hand gently on the table in applause. "Actually I think you're pretty marvellous agreeing to give it a try at all."

Jane stirred her sugarless tea briskly to hide her inner glow. Behind the bright pinks and reds of her potted geraniums on the windowsill the window reflected and framed her kitchen at its brightest: her shelf with the jars of preserves glowing warm reds and oranges; the gleaming handles on the Aga which she had polished the day before; the floral calendar with this month's picture of a box-hedge maze which she had studied so often that she felt confident of her ability to direct herself faultlessly through the real thing. The clock was smiling at ten to two, ticking so softly it could almost be purring. She took a ginger-nut from the biscuit tin, broke it in two and gave half to Jelly. "Tomorrow," she promised," we'll draw up plans."

"What's to happen about the dog then?" asked John.

Jane misunderstood, mainly because Jelly was suddenly

no longer a problem. "Well, I do feel a bit sorry for her down here alone on her first night with us," she said. "We could take her bed up to our room just for to-night. After she's got to know us I'm sure she'll be all right down here."

Jelly understood at once. She stood up, stretched and preceded John up the stairs as he staggered upwards under the weight of the de-luxe bed with canopy bought to satisfy Jenny and appease the shop assistant. She was already sprawled on the double bed when they entered the bedroom.

"Down, girl!" hissed Jane firmly and Jelly dropped obediently to the floor and remained awake in her dog-bed until they were sound asleep and she could wriggle up gently in between them. Outside the storm broke and the heavy cloud canopy splintered petulantly into shards of rain which fell gently on the garden, easing around roots.

"Planning can be more than half the fun!"

After a soporific Sunday lunch John needed to convince himself as much as the rest of the family. As a concession to Jenny who needed to be propitiated after the discovery of Jelly asleep on her parents' bed that morning, the planning meeting was being held outside on the lawn so that those who wished, namely Jenny, could lie in the sun. The rest were to draw up their deck-chairs in her vicinity under the shade of the larger apple tree. The lawn was soft and mushy after the heavy rain and, as their wooden legs sank easily and unevenly through the sodden topsoil, the deck-chairs listed, offering lop-sided seating accommodation on which John, Jane and Ham leaned at varying and uncomfortable angles to counterbalance the force of gravity.

"Spoiling my grass!" pouted Ham, glaring at the skid marks made by the opening of the chairs.

"You shouldn't have cut it anyway. That job's reverted

to me now," replied his father unsympathetically.

Red-faced and speechless with indignation, Ham could only stab with an accusing finger in the direction of his mother.

"It *is* my fault," she said quickly. "He *did* remind me that it should be you when I made him do it. I'm sorry, Ham."

Ham, who had yet to master the art of accepting apologies graciously, sniffed, withdrew the accusing finger and picked his nose.

"Well, if we've got to do this, let's get it started and over with," Jenny, her jaw on her hands, muttered indistinctly. She was beginning to feel the dampness seeping up through the towel and was wishing she hadn't been so quick to scoff at her mother's suggestion of the waterproof picnic rug. It would have meant fetching it from the car and she couldn't see her parents or Ham doing that for her.

A little self-consciously, John opened up an old jotter he was recycling and wrote a heading, *Plan*.

"We'll start with your mother's idea," he said, neatly deflecting any criticism. "She feels that our loch visits should have definite purpose and that we should do one loch a month for the next six months and then review it." Ham was screwing up his face in puzzlement. "That means decide whether it was a good idea and something we want to go on doing, or whether we want to pack it in."

"We're not morons," mumbled Jenny. "Oh well! I suppose I can only speak for myself."

"Your mum also feels," he went on, wishing that Jane would back him up instead of lying back, half out of her chair with her eyes closed, "that we should plan each trip really well. I think you said at least a week in advance, Jane?"

"Uh-huh," was the disinterested reply of the one who had more or less prised him out of bed to discuss it the night before.

"What I don't understand," said Ham slowly, "is what

exactly we're going to do at all these lochs. I mean are we just going to sort of sit down and look at them or what? 'Cos it could be quite boring if that's all!"

"My original idea when I was your age was that I wanted to walk round all the lochs in Scotland." He ignored Jenny's derisive snort. "Now, of course, I know that that's not possible. For one thing some of them are sea lochs. For another, it's not really in the interests of loch wild-life or vegetation if people go tramping around them indiscriminately. I now think that our aim is to explore the routes around them as far about each loch as possible and try to assemble as much information as we can – size, depth, birds, wild-life, plants. A certain amount of physical activity will have to be undertaken at each loch if we're gong to explore properly. It could be walking or cycling or boating and so on. On some lochs there's the possibility of water sports; on others that could be most inappropriate. We might," his eye was on Jenny, "be able to ride round some."

"*You* on a *horse*!" Jenny started to giggle but at least she was listening.

"Exactly!" John was finding it easier. "It will sometimes be a laugh. Sometimes, I expect it will be quite hard. We need to record all our experiences and make recommendations for future visits by ourselves or other people. The lochs will change with the weather, the seasons and the climate and there will always be more to add. Our findings will continually need to be updated and modified. Once we've got this thing of the ground, I'd like to stick it on the internet and hopefully interest other people. After all there are over two hundred and seventy lochs in Scotland. Then these other people will record their findings, making it more and more comprehensive …"

"So we're going to blog?" Jenny sounded interested.

"Er…yes." It was suddenly moving too quickly. "I

suppose we are."

"I could do the computing bit for you," offered Jenny kindly.

"So could I!" said Ham.

"Fine!"

Jane straightened herself and leaned forward. "I'd like to make a suggestion," she said. "I think we should do a day trip to a small loch nearby and that should give us a better idea of what we might do ..."

"Which loch?" interrupted Ham before his mother went too deeply into boring detail. "Which loch are we going to do? And when?"

"Next Sunday," decided Jane unilaterally, "and seeing that Ham had such a rotten day yesterday, we'll let him choose the loch. We'll give you the *Atlas of Scotland* to plough through, Ham. Remember it's got to be near – and small, just a pinprick of blue water on the map."

Put off his stride by this take-over of his authority, John opened his mouth to make some finalising executive statement, couldn't think of one and closed it again.

"I'm riding next Sunday afternoon," objected Jenny automatically.

"Suit yourself," said her mother shortly. "You'll have to make your own arrangements about getting to the stables."

Before Jenny could voice her usual about being the last member of the family to be considered, a bark and a "Coo-ee" announced the return of Jelly and Tilly who had asked to take the dog for one last walk. Much to Ham's delight, Jelly flopped down at his feet.

"She's only chosen you because you're in the shade," pointed out Jenny.

Tilly laughed. "I'm sure she's going to love you all. She's not really attached to me yet. Don't tell Mum but I've only had her for a week and I knew the job in Paris was pending when I went with Sam to the dogs' home, but when I saw her there she was so miserable looking. You don't mind having her, do you?"

"Not at all," said Jane. "We love her already!"

John muttered under his breath and closed the notebook in which he had recorded nothing under his heading. They'd covered the main points, he supposed.

An hour or two later, at Ham's request, Jane brought the *Atlas of Scotland* down from their bedroom and laid it on the kitchen table so that he could choose the very first trial loch. It was very peaceful in the kitchen she thought; just the odd rustle from John reading his newspaper or from Ham flicking through the atlas. Jelly was under the table, whence she had fled when she had seen Jenny advancing on her for the third time that day with the new dog-brushes, and was asleep and snoring gently. Jenny herself had retreated to her bedroom to "finish off", a euphemism Jane felt, her homework. She opened the kitchen door to smell her garden growing in the warmth and wetness.

"Hen Poo!" said Ham distinctly.

"No, dear, not this year. I bought a couple of sacks of horse manure from Jenny's riding stables, but it's so well rotted you'll never be able to smell it."

"Bought? I'd have thought they'd have given it to you after all the money we've spent there over the years." John's after lunch contentment was on the verge of souring into indigestion. "And what is more…"

"No!" Ham irritated by their permanent inability to comprehend him, stabbed his grubby forefinger repeatedly at the open page in front of him. "Hen Poo Loch! Here it is! We're going to Hen Poo Loch!"

"There isn't really a loch called *Hen Poo* is there?" Jane went to look over his shoulder at the book on the kitchen table.

"Well there's a little drop of blue and next to it it says *Hen Poo L.* and *L.* stands for loch, doesn't it?"

John joined Jane at the table. Unable to make out the minute lettering he took his glasses out of the breast pocket on his shirt and leaned forward.

"You're quite right, Ham," he said. "Well done, lad! And it's only an hour or so from Edinburgh. Well done indeed!"

"When's supper?" said Ham taking success in his stride. "And don't forget it's my turn to feed Jelly tonight!"

If the maxim that a bad dress-rehearsal guarantees a good performance runs true then the trial expedition to Hen Poo certainly augured a brilliant future for loch-netting, an initial lack of success felt keenly by John who had spent the week prior to the expedition indulging in daydreams in which the future of loch-netting became ever brighter and he, as its founder, ever more a figurehead. Under the eye-catching title, *Lochnetting,* of the lochnetting manual which he saw himself pressed by public acclaim to produce, would loom his own head and shoulders, transformed with just the right amount of designer stubble on his lean jaw and with a deep tan reaching down into his open-necked shirt. Just visible over his shoulder would smile the minute figures of Jane-Jenny-and-Ham; Jane at the apex of a triangle with a shielding/restraining arm around each child. A few days later, when the dream developed and mobilized onto the small screen, they would still be there, happy to be in the background and absolutely safe which was important for his peace of mind, playing their subordinate roles contentedly. In their homogeneous, biddable little family group they would be following him at a respectful distance as he headed along rain drenched paths, sniffing the bog-myrtle or the heather at his suggestion. Or sometimes they would be relaxing, tucked way down in the prow of the boat, trailing their fingers in the water and marvelling at the powerful wake he would create as he dipped and pulled at the oars in effortless rhythm. By the end of the week his dream had expanded and he had felt able to control more than just the family group as he envisaged the loch-netting bug spreading rampantly via the internet perhaps, drawing more and more disciples. Still he remained ahead, his now large and faithful band of fit and active enthusiasts acknowledging his authority, following behind him at a comfortable distance, but still clearly visible in their bright T-shirts displaying the lochnetting logo. Eventually, he saw himself, forced to give up teaching to handle the continual need to update his manual and to respond as even-handedly as possible to the demands of competing media requests. Those were just his daydreams. In the ones at night, which he could not control, he did not always lead his flock. More often than not he was about Ham's age, trotting contentedly behind a bald-headed man with a flat-footed stride, whose shirt, away from his mother's watchful eye and even keener nose, stank of stale sweat. And in those dreams he smelled sweat and wood-fire along with bog-myrtle and heather.

In his dreams John forgot to cater for Jelly who provided the first opportunity for disunity when on the first trial expedition, contrary to John's expectations and wishes, he discovered that his followers had no intention of leaving her behind. Ham on his mother's directions, had filled an empty lemonade bottle full of water for Jelly and asked him for the car-keys so that he could put the bottle and Jelly's water-bowl in the boot.

"Hang on, old man," he said in a jolly voice appropriate for family expeditions. "We're not taking the dog."

"Mum thinks we are," said Ham shortly and continued to hold his hand out for the keys.

While John recognised that as self-appointed leader he

had to establish authority, he also had a sneaking suspicion that the homogeneous little family group might just mutiny. The result was a flat command that tailed off into a placatory wheedle, something which, he later privately admitted to himself when reviewing his role, could have been viewed as a mixed message.

"The dog is not coming," he started firmly enough. "I don't want hairs on my seats. You know I'm not fussy. You know I love Jelly but I have to use my car to give people lifts and some people are really allergic to dog hair. I hate leaving her behind." He could see they didn't really believe him. "It's just that some places are not meant for dogs."

"Like your bed," said Jenny bitterly. "Well, I'm not coming if she's not."

"Neither am I," muttered Ham.

"You'll both do exactly as you're told!" he roared, losing control.

Jane took over, using the honeyed tone he recognised from when the children were small and fractious, but now using that tone to *him*, "We'll all go in my car. I know it's small but we can all fit in and I'll put the picnic rug under Jelly."

"I can't drive your car," he objected untruthfully.

"I can," she said firmly. "Have you been to the loo, Ham?"

That was the wrong picture: Jane leading the group; Jane making the decision; Jane driving.

"You'll need to direct me," she offered, just as though she could actually read his thoughts and was trying to put him back on his plinth.

"You know where Duns is!" he snapped.

The very first journey to the experimental loch was not entirely enjoyable. John, in accordance with his intention to preface the exploration of the lochs with a brief guide to routes to each loch, alerting the would-be lochnetter to places of scenic interest, bad road conditions, ideal picnic spots etc., had meant to cook up a trial lochnetters' guide to the route to Hen Poo, but the blackness of his mood prevented him from thinking creatively or even positively. He sat wooden as a tailor's dummy on the front passenger seat, moving only to twitch his feet involuntarily at phantom clutch or brake pedal or to flinch spasmodically and whistle through gritted teeth when he thought Jane's driving merited criticism. Sibling tension in the back of the car was reaching its elastic limit. Ham had amended "We're all going to the Zoo tomorrow" to "We're all going to the Poo tomorrow" and was singing it challengingly, determined to provoke a reaction from someone. Jenny responded by turning up the volume of her head-phones so that the rhythmic scratching was like dry windscreen wipers on a dry windscreen. Jelly, having finished licking the bits of her anatomy she had missed earlier, attempted to stretch her full length on the back seat by digging her forepaws into Ham and her hind into Jenny.

Unwilling to blame the dog for her discomfort, Jenny accused her brother, "Ham, you fat slob, you're taking up too much seat."

"Am not!" retorted Ham stopping in mid-song. "You are with your big, fat bum. And you are squashing poor Jelly."

"We're nearly there," soothed Jane automatically. "Just another twenty minutes."

A very long twenty minutes later Jane pulled up the handbrake outside the castle gate entrance to *Hen Poo* **Lake.**

"*Lake,*Ham," hissed Jenny. "*Lake* not *Loch*! Doh!"

"Now it is important to make sure that you have everything before leaving the car." John used the voice that penetrated to the back row of his biggest and most disruptive class as he put his pen inside his notebook and pocketed it, but he was speaking to an empty car and the closed windows threw his voice back at him

"Hurry up!" Ham who had won first shot of Jelly rapped on the window. "Jelly's desperate!"

John got out of the car, deliberately not hurrying. "I've still to change into sensible footwear. It is important to have your ankles properly supported and also important to do stretching exercises before walking any distance, especially after sitting in a cramped position."

He knew as he was speaking that he was just separating himself still further from the three trainer-clad members of his family standing in a small close-knit group on the other side of the car, eager for the off and was as irritated with himself as he was with them. He hid his irritation in the car-boot as he searched for his walking-boots.

"We'll start off very slowly," Jane's soothing voice again, "and give you time to …"

"I don't need you to walk slowly," he forced out a laugh as he spoke. "Just walk normally. I'll soon catch you up."

Jenny almost choked as she tried to suppress her giggles, "But it is *important* to walk slowly."

"Come on!" said Jane sharply.

John's hands shook slightly as he attempted to thread a fraying lace through the eyelets of a walking boot that smelled of mould. Whose stupid idea had it been that this whole project should be a family venture when it had been his idea. The whole loch thing had been his idea. His and his alone. He looked up from tugging at the fraying lace at their three receding backs, neatly framed in the archway through the outer wall of the castle grounds; Jane in the middle, child on either side in a parody of the symmetrical grouping he had envisaged on the dust cover of his book, a parody because now they were ahead of *him*, leading *him*. He could hear them laughing at some shared joke, probably against himself. Was it that long ago that he and Jane, still blissfully childless, would have been walking through the arch hand in hand, even perhaps with their arms around each other? Or, later, taking it in turns to push the buggy and smile down into it? Or later still swinging a toddler between them or steadying a nervous excited child on a wobbling bicycle? Somewhere along the line the stabilizers had come off – and consequently their need for him. His role had been increasingly to wave them off on family outings and less and less, as they came home afterwards, had he heard about what they had done, highlights being more and more strictly edited as they had chosen to imagine his capacity to share with them dwindling. The lace of his boot broke and he changed back into his trainers. They probably wouldn't notice.

The others had stopped near the entrance proper to the castle on a small triangular patch of grass on which a monument to Duns Scotus had been erected. Jane was attempting to interest them in the life and works of Duns Scotus, but only Jelly appeared to have any real interest in the monument, sniffing eagerly around its base where there were some interesting yellowish stains.

Jenny was interrupting her mother's account as he caught up.

"Private this and private that!" She gestured dismissively towards the notices banning stray visitors from the castle grounds. "When I have the vote, I'm going to vote Communist! I believe in sharing!"

"You do not!" countered Ham bitterly.

Jenny ignored him. "I shall vote Communist whatever you say!" And she glowered expectantly from parent to parent.

Somewhat out of breath, John did not take up the challenge.

"No-one said anything, dear," remarked Jane mildly. "Let's all move on."

"I'll take the picnic basket," John relieved her of it masterfully and felt his shoulder sag under its unexpected weight, "and next time we'll each be responsible for our own food and carry it in backpacks. Hang on! Let me make a note of that!"

At last he led them, striding down the narrow path skirting the walled private grounds towards the cattle grid at the entrance to the park surrounding the lake and picked his way gingerly across the grid, feeling the imbalance of the weight of the picnic basket. They stood and watched him.

"You need to be careful here," he cautioned. "Try to stand on two bars at a time like I have done."

"Dad, there's a gate for people," Ham hissed when he was just over halfway across.

Jenny was doubled over with mirth and Jane was grinning treacherously.

"A gate's fine for those who don't like a challenge!" he retorted, turning a deaf ear to the sniggering."

"It looks good here," Jane smiled encouragingly at him as he caught up with them again, "Peaceful and pastoral."

Before them the hillside sloped gently down towards a reed-fringed stretch of water, modest in size and seemingly over-populated with ducks. More ducks, with their feet invisibly tucked beneath them appeared to be floating on the sloping grass banks– some of them mere feathery mounds with their heads under their wings.

"Honestly, I don't know why we're here," sniffed Jenny, stepping with fastidious care along the path on which there was faecal evidence of duck. "I don't know why we didn't just walk round Blackford Duckpond. Trust Ham to pick a loch that isn't even a loch!"

Ham ignored her because his attention had been drawn to a settlement of cattle lying in a sociable group on the hillside above, flicking odd ears at invisible flies as they gazed incuriously down at their visitors with their mouths working languidly.

"Are those cows or bulls?" he asked, twisting his neck sideways in vain attempt to focus on their undercarriages. "Because if they're bulls I reckon we're for it."

"They usually put only one bull in with a herd of cows," replied John quickly as Jane opened her mouth in reply. "One bull is sufficient to serve the lot."

"Serve?" Ham was puzzled.

"Bring them tea and cakes on a tray," spluttered Jenny.

"There's something about horns isn't there?" mused Jane. "I think with Highland cattle a bull's horns go out to the front and a cow's horns go out sideways and those seem to be going out sideways don't you …"

"Sounds like an old wives' tale to me."

Far from being disturbed by Jelly's presence, the ducks clamoured joyfully at their approach, waddling to meet them and alerting their brothers and sisters on the water to scramble ashore, shaking their wings and flicking their tails as they joined in the procession.

"I'm hungry too," remarked Ham. "Let's have lunch."

John considered commenting that they had yet to make a quarter of their distance, considered the heaviness of the picnic basket and acquiesced with a kindly "Can't have you hungry, lad."

Munching sandwiches on a slatted wooden bench with Jane and Ham while Jenny, a comfortable few metres away, shared hers with the ducks and struggled to distribute them fairly, John felt more contented. The sky was overcast, blurry outlines of clouds nudging each other gently with no apparent sense of direction and, with the absence of bright light and sharp reflection, the loch/lake lay dark and turgid, the wakes of waterfowl forming low, V-shaped ridges widening slowly across the viscous surface. He stretched his legs and closed his eyes. Jenny finished distributing her sandwiches and thoughtlessly wiped the palms of her hands down the sides of her jeans. The ducks around her feet were still stretching their necks towards real or imaginary crumbs and disputing their claims noisily. A few satiated customers had settled on the bank and were preening themselves in preparation for a post-prandial nap. She stepped through them carefully and John felt the jolt along the bench as she slouched down hungry and disgruntled and kept his eyes firmly closed through, "Shove up, Ham! Big bum! What else is there to eat? No, I don't like those chocolate wafery things. They feel gritty between my teeth. What else is there? Thanks!" With her mouth full, "What are we going to do now? Just sit here all day?"

Jane bit the bullet. "I have been wondering," she started tactfully, "if it would be a good idea to split up. There seem to be different walks in different directions and we don't all have to do all of them do we? How about if Jenny and I pick one route, John, and you and Ham another?"

"Seems reasonable," said John with his eyes still closed in an effort to shut out distractions and concentrate his efforts on composing a suitable *Introduction to Hen Poo Lake* for *John Maitland's Guide to Lochnetting*. He floundered as he struggled to manipulate the slippery, cliché-ridden language of the travelogue into something fresh and innovative. *Hen Poo Loch ...Lake*, he might begin, *is a well-hidden secret known only to the good people of Duns and* he screwed up his closed eyes in frustrated effort *to those who stumble upon it accidentally?* Too random!*...to the discerning few?* A steady trickle of *the good people of Duns*, or perhaps of *the discerning few*, had begun to filter through the gate beside the cattle grid and the ducks set up their noisy clamour at their approach.

"Let's go then!" Jenny stood up. "My turn with Jelly. Mum and I'll take the Captain's Walk thingy to give Jelly a proper walk and you and Ham can go the short walk to the hide."

John remembered the weight of the picnic basket and stifled the urge to quash Jenny's attempts at control.

"Fine by me," he replied, earning an approving smile from Jane for his co-operation.

No-one had consulted Ham. Furthermore nobody had apparently noticed that he had not been consulted. He loitered just behind his father, kicking at stones.

"Wish I'd brought a ball," he muttered. "Could've dribbled it."

This drew no response.

"Not that anyone'd bother to kick around with me.

Still no response. John, not listening to his son, was wondering if he could risk *loch becomes a platform of water-lily leaves*. He rather liked that.

Jane, Jenny and Jelly had turned off at the signpost to the Captain's Walk. Looking after the jubilantly scampering Jelly, Ham wondered if he might be permitted to go with them. Dad wouldn't even notice. Looking up from his kicking, he noticed for the first time that the man beside him had grey hairs showing at his temples. He must be getting old, old and weak. Ham felt sudden inexplicable guilt and shouldered filial responsibility.

"Dad," he suggested tentatively, "there's no-one around. Why don't we hide the picnic basket behind some of these really thick bushes and pick it up on the way back?"

John had just rejected *tantalizing glimpses of the loch between the trees*. He looked down at his son with admiration and pride, "Well thought out, lad."

Together, almost conspiratorially, they explored the undergrowth at the side of the path for an appropriate place to conceal the basket and eventually agreed on the ideal spot. Ham placed a piece of brush over it for extra camouflage and stood back to admire his handwork.

"Dad," he smiled, "know what it looks like? Remember how Grandma used to hide a basket of eggs in the garden at Easter?"

John nodded

"And you used to tell us not to find them too quickly or she'd take the huff."

They were back on the path continuing their journey at a faster pace. "And I remember the first time we found it and Jenny cried because it had real eggs in it instead of proper chocolate ones 'cos Grandma said that chocolate was bad for our teeth."

"I seem to remember your being none too pleased either," John felt he had to put the record straight, "and after that we had to bribe you with an extra Easter egg each if you looked for the basket without making a fuss."

They laughed together.

"But I didn't like going to Grandma's," confided Ham soberly, shaking his head. "She was always taking the huff about something and," he lowered his voice, "I didn't like Grandma much either. She was bossy and strict."

"She was not! You were just thoroughly spoiled!"

Ham hung his head at the sharpness of John's tone and fell out of step with him, kicking at the stones again. Though John had felt himself flush with indignation at the criticism of his mother, he regretted his words as soon as they were spoken. Defence of his mother was a habit he had formed during his school-days when the boys in his class had laughed at his carefully protected lifestyle, at the fact that he always had to wear a vest, summer and winter, and in winter it was a thick, woolly one, yellowish, pock-marked from much washing and itching uncomfortably; laughed when they saw his school lunches with the hand-wipe for him to remember to use before he started eating ; laughed hysterically at the brownish-red thermos of home-made soup; pitied him, worse than laughing, for his curfew, weekdays nine o'clock, week-ends ten o'clock, even when he was in sixth year. Flouting of her rules brought swift punishment and, worse than the punishment, the knowledge that he had disappointed her deeply. Her deep, sorrowful silences followed even the most minor indiscretions. Although he longed to be as the other boys – to eat chips in the street, walk in the rain in only his T-shirt and stay out late without risking the reproachful tooting of his mother's car horn somewhere outside, the hooting which always seemed at its loudest when he was in the company of the truly free and easy, his mother had become his conscience: she made the rules of right and wrong and his biggest sin from earliest childhood was incurring her displeasure. Fear of this had cramped his style as a boy and now, even now, it seemed to be coming between him and his son. He took a deep breath.

"I'm sorry, Ham," he managed finally, rumpling Ham's hair as he spoke. "You're not really a spoiled brat at all. It's just that I find it difficult to hear Grandma being criticised."

Ham flushed, more embarrassed by the huskiness of his father's tone than by his apology. "S'all right," he mumbled and was thankful to change the subject. "Look! There's the bird hide!"

A wooden sign directed them down steps cut into the bank towards a green wooden hut, just visible amongst the thick vegetation around the river bank. Ham ran on ahead and disappeared behind the hut. John could hear him rattling at the door.

"It's locked!" he announced as John rounded the corner. "What's the point in having an observation hide and keeping it locked?"

"Must be worried about vandals."

The disappointment in his voice was less the result of finding the hide locked than because he felt keenly the incongruity of the possibility of vandalism in *a well-hidden secret of a place,* frequented by *heritage-proud locals and the discerning few.*

Ham misread his father's disappointment and came up with a solution.

"If we were to go right down to the water's edge we would probably see just as many birds as we would have been able to from the hide."

"Yes, and they'll all see you and …"

But Ham had already started pushing his way down through the undergrowth. He leaned too heavily on a small flexible birch, lost his balance and yelled as he rolled down the slope. John waited for the splash but it never came: there was just the squawking of horrified ducks and a squelchy, sucking sound as Ham pulled himself up out of *the rich sediment providing the growth of water weed on which the ducks feed.* He scrambled up the slope, the exact composition of the sediment with which he was coated obvious to anyone with a nose and stood shivering from shock, sheepish and indignant. John's first instinct was to absolve himself from any guilt. Ham had run down before he had time to stop him. But then hadn't he too fallen into a loch in much the same way when on one of his fishing trips with just his father, not his mother, and hadn't his father laughed? "No big deal," he had said.

"No big deal," he said to Ham. "We'll get you back to the car for a dry up and clean up."

On the way back Ham attracted curious stares from many. The incurious exception was the succession of male joggers, mainly unshaven and with sweat plastering hairs to their legs. They ignored Ham, clutching their water bottles and staring fixedly ahead towards the goal of the body fit and beautiful. From the others Ham found himself the subject of much curious questioning and explained over and over again how he had fallen in and where he had fallen in and he did so with a good-humoured grin and a complete lack of self-consciousness which his father had to admire.

"Dirty boy!" admired one toddler wistfully pointing at him.

"That's what happens to boys who go too close to the edge," triumphed his mother. "He's lucky the ducks didn't eat him."

"Horrendous parenting skills," observed John smugly. "By the way you're doing well, Ham."

"How?"

Back at the car Ham found that he was expected to strip off and wrap himself in the picnic rug and his good humour evaporated. "I'm O.K. as I am. I'll take off my trainers and socks if you like. I don't smell that bad. I've dried off a bit on the way home. It's warm." By this time he had been forcibly divested of his sodden and stinking garments and had the scratchy picnic rug tucked around his nakedness. "I want a drink," he added sullenly, "please."

"Right you are," said John as he spread the soggy clothes across the back bumper of the car as a temporary measure. Then, after searching in vain for the picnic basket, he remembered that it was still hidden somewhere along the path. H e retraced their steps but couldn't remember exactly where along the path they had hidden it which necessitated a fair amount of fossicking among the bushes. His intentions were misinterpreted by a pair of female dog-walking ladies. One of them hurried past the shaking bushes, calling to her friend, "Don't linger, dear." The other, a woman of metal, stood still in her tracks and observed loudly. "If he parades it in front of us, dear, I'll set Miffy onto him."

"John parted the bushes and enunciated slowly and clearly, "I am just looking for my lunch basket."

"As one does," she replied tartly. Her Skye terrier aghast at the sight of the head emerging from the bushes, uttered a yelp of dismay and shot off after the companion.

Two minutes later a furious John, back on the path, yelled after them, "I've found it now. If you don't believe me, would you like to see it."

But inexplicably they both quickened their pace.

Although encumbered by the lunch hamper, John was so spurred on by his indignation that he reached the car ahead of Jenny and Jane and was standing by the open boot, shaking his head at Jane's overcatering and pouring a drink for Ham, when they arrived back.

"We saw you coming up the hill on your own and decided you'd seen the light and got rid of Ham once and for all," Jenny remarked cheerfully. "Oh, there he is!" She affected a disappointment which gave way to uncontrollable delight. "Mum, look!" she squealed, pointing at her brother and shrieking with laughter.

Ham smiled wanly and bravely, concentrated on his drink and left it to his father to explain his condition.

"We'll get you home quickly," comforted Jane. "You can have afternoon tea as you travel."

"Do you mean I lugged afternoon tea as well as the remains of lunch?" muttered John, eying with distaste the low-cholesterol, low-fat wholemeal bread and salad sandwich with which he had been issued.

"Brilliant! Eh, mum?" Jenny spoke with her mouth full of the same chocolate biscuit she had spurned at lunch and didn't wait for her mother's corroboration. "Woods with red squirrels and enormous glades – well one enormous glade. Telling you, it was like walking underwater in a green sort of underwater light. Even Jelly liked it and …"

"Trust you to get the best part," Ham said almost bitterly. "You always do."

"I know," agreed Jenny smugly.

Her good mood lasted the length of the journey

allowing for a peaceful passage home. John took out his notebook, scribbled a heading, *Lessons to be Learned*, underlined it and promptly fell asleep.

The expedition review scheduled for after supper also passed amicably, largely because Jenny excused herself, having remembered a "wee smidgen" of unfinished homework which seemed to take her the rest of the evening to complete. John's point about everybody being responsible for his or her own provisions was unanimously agreed with Ham merely stipulating that the backpacks should be *cool* ones and also demanding that the outdoor clothing and boots John insisted upon should similarly be *cool*.

Later in bed, after flailing around like a spawning salmon in an attempt to settle his tired legs into a position in which they could relax, John began a second review.

"Went well, I thought."

He placed a pillow under his knees.

Jane closed her book. "Yes," she agreed hesitantly, "but Jenny is difficult. I know it's just her age and that all teenagers are moody because of their raging hormones, but she really can make the atmosphere unpleasant when she's in a bad mood."

"Mothers and daughters," sighed John, removing the pillow and went on to concede, "and I do find her difficult sometimes. Believe it or not, in school they think she's charming."

"She is sometimes," said Jane, "and she can be really kind and helpful. Perhaps the answer is to include other people. I know we planned to keep the lochnetting to ourselves for the first six months, but Jenny is so much easier when there are other people about."

"Yes, but who?" John threw the pillow impatiently to the floor. "We don't want bossy so-and-sos who'll take over our idea and start running the whole show."

"No, we don't. We'll be very careful," soothed Jane.

"We'll just sleep on the idea." She switched off her bedside light conclusively. "Today was a really good start."

Long after she was asleep, John lay listening to her regular breathing and trying to think of one suitable person whom they could include. Jelly, sensing his anxiety, leaped softly onto the bed and curled up in the crook of his knees.

"Today," he whispered so that only Jelly could hear, "was a complete farce!"

Chapter Five

The Team

No. 11 Damhope Road

On the Sunday morning upon which her neighbours at No. 10 set out on their first trial loch-netting adventure to Hen Poo Lake, Miss April Reynolds was drawn to the window of her large, dark, north-facing bedroom by their shrill arguments as they packed themselves and ... could it be a dog? ... into the small car which they did not usually use for family outings. She stood slightly back from the window despite the fact that she was more than adequately screened by the heavy white veil of net curtain and, safe in the knowledge that they could not possibly see her, waved as they drove away. Then she suddenly noticed with a frown that the folds of the gathered curtain were as evenly spaced as rigid bars, adjusted their hanging into something more relaxed and, in looking upwards to do so, dislodged a speck of dust into her eye. She drew in her breath sharply at the discomfort of the gritty little mote and groped her way towards a mirror so that she could remove the speck with the corner of her white cotton handkerchief.

Pulling down her lower eyelid and prodding at the reddening rim, it struck her that the mirror hanging on the wall above her chest of drawers was not at a convenient distance or height for minute examination of her facial features for any purpose. Her father had of course been much taller and she herself had never used it for more than a cursory glance to satisfy herself that her short hair was neatly combed into place. She recalled her youngest sister, Prudence, the one who had had the leisure to dabble into magazines on interior decoration, fashion and such-like, had years ago laughingly identified the only possible purposes of the glass; to reflect light into the darkness of the room and to maximise the potential of any divergent sunbeam which at the height of midsummer might manage to circumvent the twin pinacles of conifer and penetrate the north-facing room. As the eldest sister April had unavoidably inherited the position of the mirror together with the chest of drawers beneath it and every thing else in the large, cold bedroom after her father's death. She had moved into the room a discreet interval after his funeral and, despite encouragement from Prudence to adapt it to her own taste, had left it completely unchanged. In any case, she had not been at all sure what her own taste might be and was nervous of having her artistic sensibilities unleashed by Prudence. She had merely bagged the trivia from her childhood bedroom into two heavy duty black bags, then for some bizarre reason granted them a reprieve from the bin by putting them in the attic instead and, having transferred the physical necessities of her adulthood into her father's bedroom, had spent the first few nights shivering nervously on what she surely remembered as her mother's side of the bed.

Now, having satisfied herself as far as was possible, given the inadequate lighting and the position of the mirror, that there was no longer any foreign body in her eye, she stepped back, at first blinking at her reflection and then narrowing her eyes to scrutinise the face that she knew very well in passing. It was still very much as her mother had analysed it for her almost forty years earlier. "Handsome is as handsome does," she had remarked, brushing April's long, dark-auburn hair vigourously before plaiting it so tightly that April felt as if her ears were being wrenched backwards. "Your face may be too round, your nose too short and your mouth too big, but your hair is magnificent. Always make the most of your hair."A few years later when April was eleven and a half, before teaching April how to make the most of her hair, she had died shortly after the birth of her fourth daughter, Prudence.

If April's father had seen it as his duty to teach April to make the most of her hair, she would undoubtedly have had the most amazing coiffures because he was punctilious about his duty but unfortunately for her he saw his duty as lying elsewhere: firstly to nurture and expand his jam-making business, thereby providing security for his family and, secondly, to leave a lucrative inheritance for the son and heir he hoped to father. The fact that he succeeded in the first aim but not the second was not through lack of effort on his part. April, his first child was born exactly a year and a month after his marriage to April's mother, Eleanor, herself one of six children – surely good breeding stock. He celebrated April's arrival, even though she was not gender perfect, by entertaining the entire staff of *Reynolds' Superior Preserves and Marmalades* to a champagne lunch provided by outside caterers but served during the lunch-hour in the canteen, thus avoiding too much interruption to the working day. The birth of the second daughter, May, arriving just thirteen months after April, was marked by the provision of wine with the normal canteen lunch and when, after a further thirteen months, June was fetched into the world by Caesarean section another case of wine was dutifully ordered but returned to the wine merchants unopened when Eleanor's obstetrician gave his unsolicited opinion that any further births would put both mother and baby at risk

The fourth baby, Prudence, born in October eight years later, had been named by her mother..

"Why 'Prudence'?" June had asked. "Why not 'October'?"

"Because *I* like the name," her ashen-faced mother had replied, adding so quietly that only April who was standing at her father's shoulder could hear, "and because for once in my life, William, my dear, prudent is what I was not."

Eleanor Reynolds had never come home from the hospital. For a long time after she had been told that her mother had died, April fancied that *They* were mistaken , that her mother was still there in the hospital, behaving like all the other new mothers, the ones she had seen during her one and only visit after Prudence's birth and who had not been confined to bed like *her* mother. Her mother too, she believed, would now be out of bed and also either shuffling along the disinfectant smelling corridors in her slippers, grimacing and clutching her back, her dressing-gown hanging open as though she was too tired to tie it properly, or sitting precariously, uncomfortably on the very edge of her bed. She went on imagining this for a long time after the funeral from which she and her sisters were excluded because her father felt that it would be inappropriate for them to attend. It was not until after she had been taken to see the black marble headstone in the graveyard by Aunt Margaret, her mother's youngest sister, who had come to look after them very temporarily, that she faced up to the fact that flesh and blood could be petrified to black marble and stopped peering hopefully into the windows of the maternity wing of the hospital when she passed it in the bus on the way home from school. Eventually Aunt Margaret had left, taking baby Prudence with her "until she is old enough for your father to manage." She took with her too all the baby things which April and her sisters had helped their mother to look out. She took everything up to Aberdeen, just sending them the odd photograph to let them know what they were missing.

A small cough ascended from the bottom of the stairs, more a slight clearing of the throat than a cough, at the same time apologetic and reproachful. She responded automatically, "Just coming." Their father had used dedication to routine to control their lives, both insidiously and overtly, seldom remonstrating or punishing, never raising his voice, merely enforcing a framework in which he expected them to play the roles of obedient daughters and co-operative sisters. This technique had proved so successful with his three elder daughters that it still dominated their lives. By this time April should have been half way through the egg that May would have boiled for her. Neither May nor June would dream of starting breakfast without her and neither would reproach her for the fact that all the eggs would be hard. April felt the first stirrings of a delayed adolescent rebellion. Instead of scuttling downstairs in an apologetic fluster, she took a final look in the mirror and, standing on tiptoe, ran her comb slowly and carefully through her hair.

For the last two minutes, ever since the cockerel egg-timer had crowed its three and a half minute soft boiled deadline, May had been miserable in her indecision. June, already seated at the table was passively and quite justifiably expectant. April, the senior sister was absent. And, even if she were to fish out June's egg, just June's, June would not dream of cracking it until they were all assembled. So May stood nervously tapping her slotted spoon against the rim of the saucepan until, irritated both by the tapping and the wait, June frowned almost imperceptibly, forcing May to take drastic action. She went to the bottom of the stairs and coughed.

Since her childhood, indecision and uncertainty had featured prominently in May's concept of hell. As long as the male heir remained unborn, April, as heir presumptive to the preservation business, had been groomed by their father for management. June's flair for working with numbers had early been recognised, all the more easily because it stood out in sharp contrast to May's own numerical weakness and it was naturally expected that June would grow up to handle the financial side of the business very competently. As for May, her possible contribution to the family business had remained undefined. Her mother had encouraged her artistic streak, had hung her childish paintings on the kitchen wall, leaving them there long after they had grown limp and blurred with steam. Her floral arrangements had been placed where all could see and admire. On her mother's death, her grief had been immediate and when her father, gently he thought, had rejected her lop-sided wreath of garden flowers in favour of a florist's creation of tight pink rosebuds, thinking the latter to be a more suitable tribute from her and her sisters, she had grieved too for that creative part of her own short life which, even at ten, she had sensed to have died with her mother. Her mother's death threw her artistic ability into perspective, her father's perspective: it was a talent, not a skill, nice but not necessary. It could not define her roles in the family or in its business and both remained undecided through her teenage years. Any adolescent dreams which might possibly have filtered through the work ethos, dreams perhaps of becoming like Shelley, *a beautiful but ineffectual angel,* were quashed by the sudden return of her sister, Prudence, who seized that role for herself and filled it to perfection. Even now, she had no job title at the factory. She simply filled in as and when necessary and strove to compensate for what she knew to be her inadequacies at work by taking on more than her fair share of the housework, the shopping and the cooking, adhering closely to the domestic timetable they had followed during her father's regime and finding a measure of self-approval and security in completing tasks within his timescale; just a small measure of self-approval, security and relief.

April's footsteps on the stairs sounded not only slow, but evenly spaced as though she was making a deliberate attempt not to hurry. She took her seat at the head of the table with a crisp smile and no word of apology for her lateness. But May was still unprepared for what followed.

"I rather think that in future we should boil our own eggs on a Sunday, May," she remarked casually as though it meant nothing. "Then we can do things in our own time. Besides I'm not sure that I always feel like a boiled egg."

"Good idea!" June thumped a fist on the table in approval.

May felt the onset of panic at this executive decision, as though the kitchen was closing in on her, squeezing her out of justified existence. She took a deep breath and started tapping at her egg. Twelve taps meant a perfect circle of cracks around the pointed end. June sliced hers off with one blow of her knife, leaving an uneven, jagged edge to the shell. "Why do you always do that, May?" she asked crossly because she was hungry. "That silly tapping business I mean?"

May looked at the egg and then at June and then back at the egg. "I don't know," she remarked and giggled. "Silly isn't it?"

But neither sister reassured her; June because she was already concentrating on the *Money* section of *The Sunday Times* and April because she was staring out the window at the garden with her eyes screwed up as though she hadn't seen it before.

Apparently taking her cue to be nonconformist from April, June left the table as soon as she had finished reading the column which interested her without excusing herself formally. She simply pulled her napkin untidily through her napkin ring and announced abruptly, "Going to spend my vouchers."

She usually made an excuse to take the car out on her own after Sunday breakfast. That activity never varied, only her excuse for so doing. Once a week, on these Sunday morning excursions, she sang loudly as she drove, releasing lungfuls of her rich contralto voice at the world, at a deaf world because she was careful to keep the car windows closed and at traffic lights she lowered her voice and tried not to move her lips She had sung in the choir at school, often performing solos. In fact the music teacher had been keen for her to take Music as a subject, but it had been in the same choice column as Accounting. During her university years in Glasgow her degree in Business Studies had not proved stressful, allowing her leisure to devote herself to her twin passions of women's rugby and singing. Whereas the former, in which she played hooker, fanned yearnings which she knew she had to suppress in the interests of the family business and its reputation, the latter had provided nothing but release. Since returning home after her education was completed this release was restricted to her hour's driving on Sunday mornings. When she listened to music at other times it was a private experience for which she used headphones, and never sang along. April knew of her love for music, even knew of her preference for opera, even if she did not know that June's main purpose in listening to arias was to be able to belt them out herself with all their unrequited agonising. Knowing this, she always gave June music vouchers for her birthday. It had been her birthday the Monday before. As usual, April had supplied vouchers and May had baked the customary chocolate sponge and had taken it to the factory where, in front of the entire work force, June had been expected to pucker up graciously and blow out her forty-seven candles. "Wait!" May had urged anxiously. "Wait until we're all ready!" And June had waited, feeling increasingly irritated, while May had fussed round, handing out pink paper plates and matching pink napkins. And as she waited she had imagined May in the kitchen at home, spacing out the candles evenly, "one yellow, one pink, one blue, one white, one yellow ..." and had had to subdue a sudden urge to seize the fire extinguisher from the wall and do the job with that.

June had never rated birthdays. As far as she saw it the sensible thing was to buy for yourself as need or desire arose and not to be at the mercy of other people's taste as an accidental date might dictate. Even as a child she had disliked all the birthday fuss. Childhood photographs showed how ill-suited her small square, chunky frame had been to the long, elaborate party frocks beloved by her mother and her sisters. On the morning of her tenth birthday, four months before her mother's death, she had taken her mother's sharpest dress-making scissors, forbidden to her and her sisters, and slit the skirt of her new party dress from hem to waist, spacing the slits close together so that the skirt hung in irreparable ribbons. She then replaced the dress on its hanger in her wardrobe so that it was not discovered until just before her party. Her mother, her belly ballooning, pink balloons in one hand, sabotaged dress in the other, had stood over her as she rolled on the floor among the detritus of tissue paper and ribbons from her presents, giggling uncontrollably. She had thought herself invincible, thought that no punishment, however severe, could obliterate the triumph of the moment. But she had been wrong. Her father, summoned to pronounce sentence, had sighed wearily and said, "Very well! She will have to wear it as it is!" and held her squirming in protest in a grip of steel, while her mother had pulled the dress over her head and zipped it up.

So, on her tenth birthday, June had learned that her father's authority was absolute, to pit herself against it amounted to self-harming and from then on had pruned her considerable range of skills down to those he deemed to be useful.

Arriving at the car park at Johnston Terrace while she was still midway through *He shall feed His sheep*, she decided to circle the block to allow herself time to finish. She drove up Cambridge Street, very slowly passing the front of the Usher Hall so that she could examine the posters, picked up speed past the glass-fronted Lyceum Theatre and timed her entry to the car-park so that she pushed the button for the entrance barrier on her last note. Having manoeuvred the car into a perfect parking position, she felt for April's envelope in the glove compartment. It was pink. Unlike April to choose pink. Then, as she flipped it over, she saw that it was stamped, franked and addressed to her in the flamboyant handwriting she had recognised immediately on receiving it, although Prudence had not remembered any of their birthdays since she had left well over two years before. Fortunately, as it fell to her to sift through the post in order to pick up any bills, she had been able to rescue it before either sister could see it, before April could draw her lips tightly together or May become watery-eyed, and had secreted it, still unopened, into the desk drawer she had labelled *June-Personal*. Later it had been joined by April's identically shaped envelope and this morning, in her eagerness to escape, she had snatched up the wrong one. She opened it now, experiencing the usual conflicting emotions which Prudence aroused in her.

Happy Birthday, Sis! See you soon! Hope all are well! We are both blooming! Lots of love, Prue XXX.

June dwelled on each phrase, analysing it hungrily. "Sis!" Prudence had always called her and only her, *Sis* in recognition she was sure of the peculiar intimacy which had developed between them. *See you soon!* No doubt for Prudence with her restless whirl of activity, the two years had passed swiftly and the *soon* was probably still a decade away. *We are both blooming.* The *we* would of course include Hans. June could recall him only too clearly with his rubicund, cherubic face and his easy grin. Hans had been the night watchman at the factory. Privately, just to June, April had congratulated herself on his appointment, remarking that his bleary-eyed, hang-dog appearance in the morning was absolute proof that, unlike old Bob, he didn't sleep on the job. He didn't. It had been common knowledge among the work-force that Prudence often shared his watch; common knowledge for some time before the sisters found out. Even June, who knew that Prue often slipped out at night and covered for her without ever asking where she went, remained in ignorance until the morning that May, filling in for an early morning cleaner, was horrified to hear moans and gasps coming from Reception, seized the First Aid Box and burst in on Prudence and Hans, stark naked on the sofa, initially oblivious of her presence and entwined in a coital position she had later been unable to describe to her psychiatric counsellor. April had primly informed a widely grinning Hans that it would be in the best interests of the factory if he left immediately. Then she paid him off generously and, at his request, topped up his severance pay with his return fare to Germany. He only went as far as London. She also reminded Prudence that, as a member of the management team, even as a largely parasitic member, it did not do to become over familiar with employees. Prudence retorted, "Oh, get a life!" packed her bags and followed Hans on the next train. It was June, who had run her to the station, paid for her ticket and helped her lug her cases across the station. Then Prudence was gone with a hug and a "Look after yourself, Sis!" June had not sung on the way home.

Well, at least she - and Hans- were *blooming*. Nice to know.

Realising that she would have to pay for an hour's parking anyway, she shoved Prudence's card deep into her pocket, locked the car, tripped amazingly lightly down the steps and strode off across Princes St. Gardens to lose herself in the cosmopolitan crowds.

"Look!" Prudence picked William up out of his buggy and held him in her arms. "Look! The birdie is coming out of the clock! Look! In that little bush there!"

"Cow!" pronounced William obligingly. "Moo!" But then his attention was diverted away from the floral clock in Princes St. Gardens by the flashing cameras and hasty directions in multiple languages coming from the small crowd that had gathered to watch the cuckoo making its noon appearance. His head moved from side to side following the voices.

"Stand there!"

"Excusez-moi!"

"No, you're blocking it now!"

"Got it!"

"Shit! The thing's jammed!" The last by a tall American, frustrated in his attempts to capture girl-friend beside cuckoo. He leaned towards William flashing a wide, white grin.

"Hi Cutie! I'm teaching you bad language and your mommy's gonna thump me! How old is she? Or is she a boy?"

"Yes, he's a boy. He's eighteen months and he's heard worse most days on the tube," smiled Prudence. She squatted down to fasten William into his buggy harness and started wheeling him away before he could start grizzling at being confined.

William had not slept since they had left King's Cross. He had spent the time loudly exclaiming; first at the arm-rests on the seats that moved up and down; then at the dog under the seat across the aisle who had not grasped that his "woof-woofs" were friendly overtures and bared its teeth in the most exciting way; then at the man seated opposite them who had smiled at first and who had a newspaper which you could stick your finger through. His head had drooped promisingly just before Newcastle, but his spirits had soon been revived by the intermittent ringing, an upbeat version of *Greensleeves*, of the mobile of the girl who had joined them at Newcastle and slumped into the vacated seat of the newspaper man who had transferred to the quiet coach. Now, as they trundled along, he yawned and snuggled down into his buggy. By the time they reached the tiers of the Ross Bandstand he was fast asleep. Prudence parked the buggy next to an empty bench, shrugged the heavy rucksack down from her shoulders and, keeping one hand on the handle of the buggy, sank wearily down onto the wooden seat, stretching her long legs in front of her, throwing back her head and closing her eyes. If June had been given to cooing over babies she would surely have spotted her as she strolled past on the way back to the car park, deep in her private world of thought.

Although Prudence's eyes were closed against the world, she could not shut out the nigglings of her conscience. She *should* have phoned them. She should have told them about William. She should have asked if it was all right to bring him home. Well, it *was* her home too! She had a quarter share of it just as she had a quarter share of the business. And she would remind them of that too if necessary. She would fight for William and his rights. That was why she had come after all: she had come to take William out of the poky basement apartment where traffic fumes seeped thickly through the rusty contortions of the iron railings and sank, lead-laden, down through her window. She had planned it last month when the little guy had been so ill and she'd sat up with him, hot night after hot night, with the panes of the closed windows vibrating from the traffic heaving above and from the tubes worming their way underneath. The rent for that flat was all she could afford out of her share of the profits, especially as she had had dependants to support; first Hans and, after he had departed on suddenly recalling that he had a wife in Germany who might be able to provide for him more comfortably, William. Hans had never seen William. He was all hers – her hand tightened its grip on the buggy – the first human being she had ever totally belonged to.

Although Aunty Margaret had been as kind as she knew how, motherhood had not come naturally to her. Her principal parenting resource had been a weekly periodical, *Just for Women*, with cosy knitting patterns, short stories with happy endings and a matt, blue cover, the colour of which reminded Prudence of Aunty Margaret's other principal resource – the Milk of Magnesia bottle. At the time Prudence hadn't known that she suffered but much later she described her early childhood to June as having been *all smocking and smacking*. After she had started attending the small private girls' school of which Aunty Margaret was a former star pupil, she discovered that all the other girls had "Mums" and had asked Aunty Margaret if she could, at least in public, call her "Mum." Aunty Margaret had slept on it and then explained that this would not be fair on Prudence's own mother who was in heaven with the angels. She had then capitalised with deplorable self-interest by assuring

Prudence that if she was good and did as she was told without arguing *and* kept her bedroom tidy, she too would get to be an angel one day and would be able to see her mother. Although this had not relieved Prudence's embarrassment at being motherless, it had been quite an exciting idea and had given her something to look forward to until on one of her father's infrequent inspections, he had seen fit to confront her with a photograph of the black marble headstone. "Cheer up!" she had said to him gaily. "She's not really there. She's waiting for us in heaven with the angels." Whereupon her father, who referred to himself as a 'free thinker' rather than an atheist, had told her briskly that she was to obey her aunt in all respects but was not to be 'misled by her Victorian sentimentality'. By the time Prudence had worked out what she thought this meant, adolescence had kicked in. She interpreted his advice as licence to disobey Aunt Margaret whenever she chose and blossomed into a riotous display of garish teenage colours. The detritus from Prudence's bedroom began to spill liberally over the rest of the house; the rosebuds on her walls wilted in her tobacco fumes and Martha McAdam, who glibly solved four problems a week for the other distressed women who wrote in to *Just for Women* for guidance, failed Aunt Margaret. The long-standing if tacit arrangement between Aunt Margaret and William Reynolds had been that Prudence should be returned home once she had proved herself fully able to cope unaided with the paraphernalia of menstruation. Aunt Margaret had had no compunction in putting her on the Edinburgh train home on the day after her first period.

When Prudence joined her family she had been ready for a fresh start, eager to please and to belong, but William Reynolds had already organised his three elder daughters to cope with the demands of the business and an appropriate role for Prudence had not immediately presented itself. He had bought time by packing her off to boarding-school where she proved herself multi-talented as well as beautiful, but after her return from school there had still been no place for her and he had felt guilty enough to allow her to follow her own volition. She had chosen to study at a well-known drama school in the south of England and to top it up with a post-graduate course in mime in Paris. June, who by the time of the Paris excursion had been solely responsible for the family finance and known exactly how much it cost to cover Prudence's education and lifestyle, had been the sister who resented Prudence the least, if at all, enjoying on her increasingly few visits home, her chatter about her occasional theatre work, celebrities she had brushed against and frank disclosures about her love-life on which she sought June's opinion. The gap between Prudence and her two elder sisters had widened and when, after eleven years of intermittent employment, lengthy resting and two broken engagements, she had come home pale and hollow-cheeked, the emotion that April had admitted to was impatience. She had not admitted to her irritation that Prudence's hair, as richly beautiful as her own, had been looked after by Prudence in accordance with their mother's standards. For May it had been worse: her sisters, prompted by her obvious lack of self confidence rather than their appreciation of her latent artistic sensibilities, had always pointedly consulted her on colour schemes, interior furnishings etc. and implemented her suggestions wherever practicable. Prudence, not being in the know and having very definite artistic likes and dislikes of her own, had criticised the décor both of the home and of the factory, using words like "dated" and "lifeless" to do so and their father had listened to Prudence and agreed with her. This coupled with her inclination to act as the spirit moved her rather than to fit in with the domestic routine had unsettled May. Unwilling to confront Prudence, she had punished her in little ways which Prudence hardly noticed. But when she deliberately left Prudence's egg to hard-boil and Prudence casually dropped it in the bin and cut herself a generous slice of fruit-cake – fruit-cake for breakfast! – and munched it slowly, savouring every mouthful before congratulating May warmly on its excellence, May had fled from the table , gulping back sobs.

"Leave her alone!" old William Reynolds had advised from behind his paper as Prudence had risen in distress to follow her. "Sit down and leave her alone. She's touched!"

Old William, now in full retirement and thoroughly enjoying his leisure, had been delighted to find Prudence entertaining rather than useful, had acted on her every suggestion and died happy six months after her return leaving her an equal share in his estate, but no niche of her own either in the business or the home. She had taken on a succession of temporary part-time jobs from florist's assistant to trainee librarian to supplement her income and had spent a good deal of leisure at the gym where, at her suggestion, her father had given automatic membership to all his employees. It was at the gym that she had met Hans and they had been instantly drawn together by admiration each of the other's physical excellence and by boredom.

Prudence looked down at the sleeping child beside her and managed to ease the thumb gently out of the small, moist mouth, but William, though fast asleep, gave a small spasmodic jerk, re-inserted it and began sucking vigourously.

"Oh, William," she whispered, "your mum's been so stupid, such a ...doh!"

But to make such an admission to the unconscious William was one thing and to make it to the sisterhood quite another. She had deliberately chosen to waste time in the Gardens rather than to take a taxi straight home to Damhope Road to give herself time to prepare for the meeting. She frowned now as she struggled to compose her introductory speech. Since William's birth she had found it difficult to rely on her acting ability to carry her through awkward situations partly because she didn't have the energy to adopt another persona and partly because it seemed more honest, more worthy of her position as William's mother, to be strictly truthful.

"I know this is a shock," she might begin, except that to use the word 'shock' seemed disloyal to William. "I know this wasn't what you were expecting and I'm sorry to arrive unannounced but ..."

She and William lingered over lunch in a child-friendly restaurant in George Street. They had had to wait for a table but that didn't matter: she was in no hurry. William insisted on feeding himself. As she steadied his plate with one hand and watched him mashing his custard with his spoon, she imagined her sisters busying themselves with their Sunday afternoon gardening routine, working silently and separately at their complementary tasks: June, with her headphones, hoeing in time to her private music and lost in her private thoughts; April driving the lawnmower with executive ruthlessness over the daisy heads and May concentrating on her watering, her lips moving as she counted the seconds in order to make sure that each plant received an equal measure of watering time.

"And you can make mud-pies," she said defiantly to William. "Nice, gooey ones like I never got to do."

An hour and a half later she stood on the pavement outside No. 11. The taxi driver, having unfolded the buggy and deposited at her feet her London life condensed into a rucksack, pocketed his tip and deserted her. A small car drove through the gate at No10 next door. Car doors slammed and a girl's voice whined, "Does he get off carrying things in because he was stupid enough to fall in?"

A dog barked.

"Woof woof!" said William suddenly and she kissed his soft cheek.

"Come on, then," she sighed and let herself and William through the side-gate into the back garden.

April and June appeared to have exchanged jobs. June, still with headphones, was mowing the lawn while April hacked away spiritedly with the hoe. May, looking her bewilderment at her sisters' departure from the norm, was playing her hose haphazardly with little sense of direction and was the first to spot Prudence and William, swinging round so that an arc of hose water caught the hint of a rainbow in the sunlight as it swung with her.

Prudence couldn't remember her speech.

"Are my dahlias up yet?" she asked.

Chapter Six

The Team

The Team Composes Itself in Two Days

Norman Paterson's ten o'clock appointment had yet again failed to turn up. This was not unusual. Patricia Edwards dipped in and out of his psychiatric counselling services at whim as the ups and downs of her love-life dictated. She always paid anyway, but she was one of his more interesting clients – lived life to overflowing and didn't spare him the details so he was always rather disappointed when she didn't materialise. May Reynolds, who followed without fail at eleven, was, in sharp contrast to Patricia, definitely the most boring client he had ever taken on. He had tried on a number of occasions to persuade her that she no longer required his services and her response was always the same: a slight bemused frown, a quiver of the lips and "But we all think it's such a good idea." He glanced at his watch, saw it was five to eleven, folded his newspaper to the sports section and placed it strategically under his desk where he could glance at it surreptitiously from time to time. Then he pressed the button of the intercom which his predecessor had had installed forty-five years earlier and which was now so obsolete that it had become a valuable antique.

Gillian's voice, nasally distorted, vibrated under his finger-tips in response. He pictured her leaning forward to reply, the gold heart round her neck falling forward from her cleavage and swinging hypnotically, the hand not on the intercom feeling for the heart and tucking it to one side of the V of her blouse.

"Coffee for Miss Reynolds, please Gill, and for pity's sake put something strong into my cappuccino."

He switched Gillian off while she was still in the middle of her obligatory sympathetic chuckle and dismissed the thought that she would not be so responsive if he were not the one who paid her wages.

He always drank coffee with May. She was happy with the arrangement. Drinking coffee was what one did at eleven o'clock and it gave her something to do with her hands; stopped her from the fidgeting which she sensed irritated people sometimes. This morning he watched her patiently as she stirred her sugar three times clockwise and three times anti-clockwise, sipped his own strong brew, licked the foam off his moustache and waited. The session usually opened with May relating the events of the week and he sometimes entertained himself by mentally recounting the inevitable pattern just ahead of her report. This morning she forestalled him by blurting out while still sipping, so that it came out in a hot bubbly hiss, "Prudence is back!"

Disconcerted by this lapse of routine, he was unable to nudge her gently on. She looked at him, worried that his silence might mean that she had blundered, and faltered apologetically, "Prudence ... she came back yesterday ... she came from London ... yesterday ..." Then she burst into tears, not the timid sobbing he might have expected, but a harsh, dry keening sound.

He collected himself and raised his voice above the wailing, "Prudence ... the one on the couch? The one you found on the couch with ... whoever?"

"Sorry!" The keening subsided into apologetic sniffs. May took a swig of her coffee, hesitated as though waiting for it to have some medicinal effect and took a second gulp before clattering her cup clumsily back onto her saucer. "It's not just that she's come back," she said slowly. "Everything's confused. The others are different. They had already started to be different. And Prudence has got William with her which make things even more different and I don't know what to do."

'William?' he thought. 'Was it William on the couch? Must have been.' Out aloud he said, "Presumably they've got their own bedroom?"

"Yes, they're sharing just now. But that's another thing. Prudence wants to do up the boxroom so that William has a room of his own. It's got a window, but it's always been the boxroom." She was starting to look tearful again. He handed her a box of tissues. "The boxroom is right next to my room and if he starts his carry-on at night, the others might expect me to be able to cope with him and I don't know how…"

Norman leant forward and phrased his next question with the utmost sensitivity. "Doesn't Prudence … provide for his needs?"

"Oh, she does! She does!" May laughed ruefully. "But he's got a lot of needs."

"Such as?" The sports section slipped to the floor unnoticed

"Well, whatever babies need. I don't know." She was irritated more by her own inability to itemise these needs than by the apparent fatuousness of the question. "His food and …"

"William is Prudence's *baby*?"

"Of course," she giggled coyly. "The rest of us aren't married. Actually," she started, "I don't know that …" She frowned and the sentence hovered in the air unfinished.

Norman felt suddenly so tired that he forgot not to be directive.

"May," he said, looking so deeply into her eyes that she blushed, "you *must* take a holiday. There are *no* 'buts'. There is *no* argument. It is *imperative* that you take a holiday and I shall inform all your sisters accordingly."

Sitting at her kitchen table with her legs wound round the legs of one of the wooden chairs they had bought at Ikea to go with John's mother's old kitchen table, Jane finally finished the letter she had been composing, tucked it into an envelope, absent-mindedly licked it although it was one with a self-adhesive seal and said to Jelly, "Now that that's done would you like to come with me to post this? I think we'll just make the eleven o'clock collection. Anyway, they're always a few minutes late." She took the lead down from its peg and clicked it onto Jelly's collar. "I just hope I've done the right thing."

Jelly wagged her plumy tail encouragingly but Jane was still frowning as she slipped the envelope into her pocket. She knew that the penalty of acting on her own initiative was to invite criticism from each and every member of the family.

"But we did agree," she said defensively to Jelly as she turned the key in the back door lock. "John and I agreed that we need other people to come loch-netting with us. Jenny's always so much easier when she's not alone with us and Ham and Chris have always been good friends."

Jane had woken from a strange dream of lochs and ducks and lain awake puzzling sleeplessly about who would be best suited to join them until inspiration had come with first light. Her cousin, Julia, and her family would be ideal or so it had seemed to her tired mind. As soon as she had waved the family off to school she had picked up the phone determinedly but had hung up in mid-dial, unable to think how she could present loch-netting invitingly to Julia. If Tim, Julia's husband were to answer it would be worse. Tim was everything that was nice, solid and dependable but was entirely without imagination. Clearing away the breakfast things had not helped her to clarify an explanation of loch-netting to her satisfaction and she had eventually decided that it would be easier to write, to invite the family for a week-end and mention that they intended to spend some of the time exploring a loch – as one does. The task had not proved easy but after an hour and a half the letter, including polite preliminaries regarding their health and other irrelevant family news, was finally finished.

"I know I've done the right thing," she convinced Jelly as she pushed the envelope irrevocably through the pillar-box slit into the darkness, "and I'm not going to worry about it."

"Cow!" pronounced a small voice triumphantly behind her. "Cow! Moo!"

"No, William, it's a dog. You know dogs! Remember the one on the train yesterday?"

"G-r-r-r-r!" said William with relish.

Jane turned to see, as she had expected, a mother with a toddler in a buggy. There was something familiar about the mother but she was bending over the buggy now to adjust a blanket and her long bob of dark auburn hair obscured her face.

"Hello!" Jane said tentatively, addressing the baby. "Do you like my dog then?"

William replied by removing his fist from his mouth and pointing a wet finger in Jelly's direction.

"Loves dogs," supplied his mother looking up and smiling. "I don't know if you remember me. I'm Prue Reynolds from next door. At least I've just moved back next door again. And this is my son, William. You're Mrs. Maitland?"

"Jane," said Jane.

The dark auburn hair was the same shade as the hair of one of the sisters but this Miss Reynolds was beautiful.

"I've been in London for a couple of years so you won't remember me but we're back now, aren't we William?"

They walked back up the road together laughing as

William recited his limited repertoire of animal noises. When she reached her gate Jane said impulsively, "Do come in for a coffee? Just a quick one if you're busy."

Prudence hesitated. "I'd really love to but I'm nervous of visiting with William. He's a demolition expert as my sisters will tell you. I'd better not, but thank-you."

"No, come on," Jane urged, "and we'll take our coffee into the garden where William can do his thing without your worrying."

In the garden they lay back in deck chairs with the warmth settling down on them from the sky and rising up around them from the earth. After Jelly, panting, had sought refuge for herself and her fascinating tail in the cool of the house, William contented himself with fingering daisies and eating their petals experimentally. Jane listened to a lively account of Prue's London adventures and heard her loneliness threading through it and Prue made encouraging noises about the loch-netting project and saw how Jane was torn between her qualms and her need to support John.

When Ted Warburton (Economics) took out his lunch-box before he opened his newspaper it meant that he was going to talk, not listen, talk. John, recognising the signs, slid down into his chair and concentrated on the contents of his own lunch-box, a dismal selection of salad sandwiches on low calorie bread, a pallid strip of low-fat cheese and an apple.

"It's amazing." Ted might sound laid back but it would have been carefully prepared, "just amazing how just a few hours back at school can snuff out any pleasurable sensations one might have enjoyed at the week-end."

"Uh-huh," agreed John, hoping that his response held no invitation for Ted to expand and that the three members of his lunch group currently skulking round the school's "arboretum" with their cigarettes would return imminently.

"Did you have a good week-end then, Ted?"

Trust *Should-be-leaner Sheena* to encourage him.

"Not bad," replied Ted with his mouth full. "Wife and I thought we'd try out that new hotel in the Lake District. Name escapes me, but it's the one that's supposed to be gastronomically tops. Thought it might teach the old trouble and strife to cook. At present she's stuck on a hundred and one things to do with fillet steak. Food was very good. Facilities definitely O.K.! Worked off all the pounds I probably would have put on."

He pulled in his flat stomach, puffed out his substantial pectorals and snatched a neat bit of a sandwich which could not possibly be salad on low calorie bread.

"That's the one with Pat Roberts as chef?" Sheena yet again. "We've got his autobiography here in the library. *My Ingredients* it's called. His early life was quite horrific. Both his parents and his mother's boyfriend were on drugs. Really on drugs! And he had to cook all the meals for himself and for his two little sisters at the age of ..."

Ted frowned peevishly. This was leading nowhere.

"What about you, John?" he interrupted. "Any fun? Or did you have yet another wholesome family week-end?"

"Oh, John goes loch-exploring," said Sheena eagerly. "Don't you, John?"

John smiled coldly and shrugged. He didn't know which he resented more: the disclosure of his loch-netting plans or the implication that Sheena was conversant with his private life.

"Something like that," he drawled vaguely. "What did you say your hotel was called, Ted?"

Ted still couldn't remember, but he expanded on his week-end, managing to drop in his single figure handicap in his description of the golf-course and reference to his near inclusion in the Olympic swimming team in his estimate of the size of the pool. He was on the size of the week-end wardrobe which his wife had crammed into the boot of his Lexus (this year's model) when John packed up the remains of his lunch and took himself up to the library where, without Sheena watching his every move from behind the counter, he would feel free to explore the geography of Scotland section. On his entry Pete, the assistant librarian, merely looked up to make sure that he wasn't one of the school students, banned from the library during lunch in case they ate over the books, grunted and returned to his crossword.

John spread a class-size map of Scotland across one of the library tables, smoothing the fold-creases gently with his flattened palms and leaned over it. He looked at the brown of the high ground deepening into purple as mountain ranges rose up and peaked into blue rimmed whiteness. The largest lochs sank long, pale-blue wedges into the faded green on the lower ground but there were some small ones curling amoeba-like round the purple heights before plunging downwards, spilling into streams and waterfalls. In their depths they would be impenetrably blue, solid little sapphires deep set into claws of hills, the fringing waters of their shallow reaches as sharply clear as glass, magnifying the water-moulded, rounded pebbles of the water-bed. He could almost taste the icy sweetness of the melted mountain snow, so shockingly cold to the palate that you caught your breath. He had thought that they should perhaps include only those lochs of above a certain circumference and this would mean too that they would probably be exploring the more accessible lochs. But should you discriminate in this way and risk sacrificing diversity? There was no doubt about organisation being a problem. With his index finger he traced some of the worm-like threads of roads which ended abruptly where crofts marked the furthest point at which a living could be coaxed form the hills, presumably from grazing black-faced sheep or perhaps goats or both. He could always group them according to their accessibility; could categorise them as Easy, Medium and Difficult Accessibility. Bearing their position in mind he could also put lochs into convenient week-end groupings: some of the bigger ones would need a whole week-end or longer; some of the smaller ones could be grouped together into neighbourhood groups. He would also have to decide which should be cycled or ridden round, which explored by foot and where the hiring of a boat would be necessary. Accommodation would be another factor: small towns near lochs might easily offer hotel or bed and breakfast accommodation; elsewhere they might have to camp.

Scribbling happily, he was startled by a voice at his elbow.

"So our Sheena was right about your lochs?"

It was only Harry Aitchison.

"She hasn't been talking to you, too?"

"She mentioned it – along with other items of interest such as the library poster competition and the need to worm her cat. I only remember it because I thought it such a good idea. What exactly do you plan to do?"

John didn't mind filling Harry in. Although he was bitterly cynical about the way his teaching of Classics had become diluted by Good Citizenship classes, Harry was fundamentally kind and very discreet. He outlined the project, ending by recounting the experimental trip at the week-end and laughing ruefully.

"We've all got a lot to learn and Jane and I think that it would be better to include a few other people – less family bickering!"

Harry smiled," Well, let me know in advance. I might be able to come sometimes. Sounds interesting."

John hesitated. Harry was fifty-nine, just the age for heart attacks. Then he remembered his own lack of fitness and also that Harry had been the one to introduce the Duke of Edinburgh scheme to the school and to organize the expeditions involved.

"Perhaps you're looking for families though." Harry had noticed his hesitation. "There are just the two of us and it could even be just me. Don't worry!"

"No! No!" John hastened to reassure him. "Love to have you along. It's just that we need to clarify it all first. You know! Put the lochs in some sort of order and look at their suitability for different modes of exploration and all that. That's what I'm trying to think out now."

The bell rang as he was speaking

"Let me know if I can help then."

Harry helped him fold the map and they left the library together before the return of Sheena.

In the gently palpitating heart of Morningside, May Reynolds was experiencing a less than comfortable lunch-time session in *The Brown Lizard*. Monday was her Personal Space Day. They each had a Personal Space Day and May habitually filled hers to capacity to leave no room for a personal vacuum, her fear being that where nothing happened, anything might happen. Her routine was quite simple. She only had to follow the hands of the wrist-watch her father had given her for her eighteenth birthday: the washing was hung up by half-past eight; by half-past nine Mary would be massaging shampoo into her scalp in *Headfirst*; after paying the papers, she would take the 23 to the New Town for her counselling session at eleven; by half-past twelve she would be in *The Brown Lizard* studying the menu before choosing her regular meal; after lunch she would walk the mile and a half to the supermarket by way of the Braidburn Park and by three she would have left a trolleyful of neatly packed groceries for April and June to collect by car on their way back from work; after an early afternoon tea at *Lucy's* she would take a taxi and be home by four in time to do the ironing while listening to Radio 4.

But this Monday lunch-time she was sensing threat to her routine. She had entered *The Brown Lizard*, wiped her immaculately polished shoes on the mat, three times each foot, and pushed the door to behind her, feeling its reassuringly customary resistance to her effort because it was one of those automatically closing doors, before turning in the direction of her usual table. It was a small table, for two just, in the far corner beside the semi frosted windows. If she sat as she usually did with her back to the wall, she could watch what was going on inside *The Brown Lizard* and through the clear etching of *The Brown Lizard* lettering into the frosted glass catch reassuring glimpses of the normality of the outside world: the queues of traffic behind the inevitable roadworks; the traffic wardens weaving between parked cars; the mothers pushing against the handles of buggies laden with toddlers and with shopping and she felt safe in the knowledge that none of the problems of the outside world were currently hers. This lunch-time, however, she had nearly reached her table before she realised that it was occupied. A uniformed schoolgirl and schoolboy were sitting there, their heads bent low in mutual enjoyment of glasses of pink frothy stuff.

"Should be in school," she muttered to herself, so quietly that no-one could possibly hear, and took her place apologetically at a table for four, placing her bag on the empty chair beside her to justify her choice.

Her usual waitress, the one with the blonde hair slightly streaked with grey and kirby-gripped off her forehead, was not there and the substitute did not know that May always took a glass of water with her soup so that she had to ask for it, sending the waitress back on a special trip and causing her to worry about whether she should therefore increase the usual tip.

"I don't think you need worry," April would reassure.

"Of course not!" Joan would frown.

But now there was Prudence in the equation and Prudence would smile and say, "Please yourself!" leaving her unsure, disturbed.

The school students had finished their pink drinks and were running the ends of their straws through the residual foam and licking them. Suddenly, after no audible or visual communication between them, they rose together, picked up their school-bags and hovered round the till.

"No charge!" called the proprietress, a tall dark woman whose name after all these years May still didn't know.

"Oh! Thanks, Sadie," smiled the girl. With her hand in the boy's hand, she allowed him to tow her to the door, walking backwards as she called, "And I'll be round at eight o'clock sharp to baby-sit."

May looked at the empty table longingly, but the waitress, the new one, had already removed the glasses and was wiping it down for a new customer. Without the distraction of the outside world through the lettering, her thoughts strayed back to the frighteningly uncharacteristic urgency with which Mr. Paterson had advised her to take a holiday.

"We'll be going next month," she had replied brightly, happy to comply with his suggestion. "We always go away during Trades. The staff like to be able to take their children away during the school holidays and we have a little cottage up North where ..."

"Where you replicate the same routine as you follow at home no doubt."

She was sure there had been criticism in his voice.

"Not quite," she said slowly, thinking as she spoke.

"There are no shops close by so April and June …

"For pity's sake spare me the details!"

He had actually said that, almost shouted it, before continuing more gently with, "May, everybody needs a change. Believe me, they do! Find something different. Anything. Just get yourself out of your predictable rut."

Then he had leaned back in his swivel chair, run his fingers through his hair and, clasping his hands behind his head, gazed up at the ceiling as though she wasn't there. After a prolonged silence – silence except for the gentle clicks as she clasped and unclasped her handbag, he apologised for his outburst and ordered more coffee for both of them. She had drunk hers obediently even though she knew that it meant that she would have to pay a visit to the lavatory before leaving and it was a unisex lavatory, not a *Ladies*, and while she sipped he had talked to her in a gentle wistful tone about England's chances of winning the Ashes which she found impersonally soothing. As she was leaving he repeated firmly but kindly, "Remember, May, something different, please. Please! "and the way he said it had made her feel a little embarrassed because he had made it sound as though she would be doing *him* a personal favour rather than *herself*. Why?

She tried to concentrate on the remainder of her soup, tried to remember what it was supposed to be. "Soupe du jour" she always ordered, liking the French sound of it. The colours varied from reddish-brown through brownish-yellow to yellowish-green but she could rely on a constant epicentre of cream, invitingly cool and still, like the eye of a storm and she always tried to take her soup by swirling round the edges and leaving the creamy centre till last.

The substitute waitress pocketed the tip without seeming to appreciate that it was more generous than usual, but on the way out Sadie came across and spoke to her.

"I'm sorry that you didn't get your usual table," she

smiled. "Would you like me to put a reserved sign on it for you on a Monday?"

In the throes of a decision about whether or not this would be a good idea, May murmured an ambiguous "thank-you" and escaped.

The supermarket shopping took longer that usual because they had re-arranged the shelves yet again. June said it was a marketing ploy. The cream was where the bacon should have been and the gingernuts failed to materialise.

"Keep calm! Keep calm!" she repeated to herself soundlessly as she manoeuvred her trolley along the aisles with difficulty because she had picked a trolley with a crooked wheel and had not liked to exchange it. Eventually she found everything except the gingernuts but she was five minutes later than normal for her afternoon tea after which she had to wait fifteen minutes for a taxi. This meant that it was well after four o'clock when she arrived home. Putting her key in the lock, she was initially shocked to find that it wouldn't turn because the door was already unlocked. Then she remembered that Prudence would be at home.

And Prudence forestalled her entry by meeting her in the hall with William on her hip. He seemed to fit snugly around her almost like a garment, his arms looping round her neck, his head on her shoulder.

"Say hello to Aunty May," coaxed Prudence.

But William just looked at her unblinking and unsmiling without raising his head from his mother's shoulder.

"He's just waking up," said Prudence, kissing the top of his head, "and while he was asleep I managed to finish all the ironing."

"No!" gasped May. In her purposelessness she felt suddenly light-headed, giddy almost. She put out a hand and propped herself against the wall only to find that Prudence had deposited William on the floor and was holding her up.

"Come and sit down," she commanded. "You're just worn out!"

Sitting on the sofa with William screaming his neglect from the hall and the alien sensation of a warm arm around her, May felt the dizziness subside and knew that she should offer some apology but she could not find the words to excuse her behaviour because she couldn't understand her feelings herself.

At No. 10 Jenny, up to her chin in the foam of her mother's most expensive bath oil, trusted that her lengthy occupation of the bathroom was bringing the rest of the family to a standstill. She sniffed deeply, self-pityingly and the pungency of jasmine caught the back of her throat. She had ladled in at least twice the amount recommended for smoothing out the creases of advancing years, not because she had any creases, but because her mother owed her. They all owed her. Selfish lot!

There was a knock at the door. Good! Perhaps some-one was afraid that she'd slit her wrists. If she were to remain silent they'd be even more worried. On the other hand she didn't want anybody barging in to rescue her when she was naked. Well, not one of the family anyway.

"What?" she said crossly.

"I've left my watch on the shelf," bellowed Ham, loudly enough to be heard in the bathroom next door, "and I need it for Cubs."

"I'll be out soon," she lied, heard his footsteps retreating and settled back into wallowing.

To be fair, and she was always fair, Ham hadn't done anything wrong this time. He was just genetically annoying. Her parents, however, had acted despicably: they had been deliberately sneaky, selfish and underhand. They knew that she had been looking forward to loch-netting with them. She may not actually have said so in so many words but they were surely not so thick that they had been unable to deduce that from the fact that she had sacrificed an afternoon's riding to accompany them to that experimental trip to the duck-pond near Duns. And how many times had her mother not said that they needed to do things as a family? To bring them closer? Or something equally naff? So why invite Julia and family? O.K., they were sort of family. Unfortunately! Extended family who had recently extended themselves as far as Newcastle and to *her* mind, Newcastle was not far enough. Admittedly, there was nothing much wrong with Julia and Tim might be quite boring but he did have his looks, but as she had assured her mother, not half-an-hour ago, their children would make a horse barff. "Why a horse?" Ham had asked. "Because biologically they can't vomit, ignorant pig," she had snapped before slamming into the bathroom. Chris, just a few months older than Ham, made Ham seem like the ideal brother and while he paired up with Ham and the wrinklies followed pursuits suited to their mid-lifestyle, she would be expected to entertain eight-year old Alice who, according to Julia, "adored" Jenny. If adoration meant mucking around with other people's make-up, smashing other people's china horses and being car-sick on other people's jeans as she had been on the last extended family outing, then Jenny did not do adoration and she didn't expect it done to her.

She stretched one arm up out of the lather and the way the whiteness of the wads of foam slithering down it enhanced its brownness almost lightened her mood. She had to concentrate systemically on how she had been wronged.

Mum's having written to Julia without any prior discussion with the rest of the family was betrayal enough, but how could Dad have invited old Hairy Aitchison along? Nicknamed Hairy because of his incipient baldness, he had never made her black list of least desirable teachers: teaching a subject like Good Citizenship (non-examinable) and being past the age of being noticed, let alone liked or disliked, made him a sort of non-person. But person or non-person, he was a teacher at her school and it was bad enough having to be a model of good behaviour in school to save Dad embarrassment without having to carry the same standards into her leisure time.

"He won't come on all the outings." Dad had tried to soften the blow.

"Neither will Julia &Co!" Mum had added brightly

"It's the principle," she had stormed.

Looking back, she was quite proud of having said that. It must have sounded really mature.

There was another knock on the door.

"Ham, I've told you I'm coming. Now go away!"

"Jenny?"

It was her mother's voice so she did not reply.

"Jenny, Dad and I have been talking."

Sneaks! Talking about her behind her back! Again!

"We think it would be a good idea if you were to invite one of your friends to come along."

Jenny opened her mouth to say coldly, "I can't see any of my friends being remotely interested," but then there could be some merit in her mother's suggestion.

"Think about it," she muttered indifferently. "I take it I don't have to consult you about whom I decide to choose."

Jane thought of Ham's need to get his watch and of their being an increased chance of a peaceful family supper and stuck her neck out.

"Of course not, darling," she called gaily. But to level the score a little in her favour added, "Is that my bath stuff I can smell?"

At a quarter past eight Jane reminded John that he was walking to fetch Ham from Cubs , not taking the car.

"You could take Jelly," she added by way of an enticement, having registered the fact that he looked less than enthusiastic at the prospect of exercise. "She'd love to go with you."

John was the only member of the family yet to walk Jelly. He looked at her uncertainly. She was thumping her tail gently to indicate a modest degree of anticipation.

Jenny, her bitterness having trickled away with the bath-water, leaped in encouragingly. "It's really easy, Dad. She's ever so good on the lead. Just don't let her see the cat on the corner. It's usually sitting on the wall. Oh, and you'd better take a pooh-bag incase she does you-know- what on the pavement."

"I don't think …," he began.

She'll not do a thing on the pavement or anywhere else," reassured Jane hastily. "She had a complete clear-out this afternoon."

John and Jelly emerged onto a Damhope Road slightly distorted by the low-angled sunshine: the pot-holes pock-marking the crumbly, grey road were enlarged into deeper, darker, jagged edged craters; the parallel rays interleaved the green layers of the oaks, giving them sub-acqueous depth rather than height, and traced down the fissures of the grooves on the trunks, exaggerating their roughness; the slightly undulating greenness of the golf course was semi-shadowed into a static billowing over which tiny, brightly coloured pairings trailed grotesquely long shadows towards the club-house. At the corner the cat on the wall dangled a front leg, fishing languidly at the shadow of its paw. Jelly ignored her and John relaxed and allowed himself to concentrate on the thoughts and plans that threatened to become the A.O.C.B., to be fitted in once the agenda of life at school and life at home had been worked through.

He was beginning to feel that loch-netting was less and less his own brain-child and increasingly some external magnetic force which he had unwittingly liberated out of a sort of Pandora's box and which would develop and ramify along lines over which he had no control as it sucked in more and more devotees. He felt the urgent need, responsibility almost, to discipline it, give it shape, impose some parameters. He could do that. He would do just that.

Now that the group was almost certainly enlarging, the stamina of those taking part would be another factor for consideration. Julia's youngest, whose name escaped him, was only about eight and, whereas Harry Aitchison himself was probably fitter than anyone in the Maitland family, he had said "we" and John had no idea who this other person might be. Surely not a wife! He remembered Harry, who was of course somewhat of a gastronome, remarking only a couple of weeks back with that twisted smile of his that he had never married because the mere idea of a woman in his kitchen was too appalling to contemplate. Harry had never mentioned a male partner but that seemed the most likely scenario and, given that, the partner would presumably be close to Harry in age. That would mean grouping the lochs, not only according to accessibility, proximity to each other and size but also according to the collective physical stamina of the lochnetters engaged on each excursion. His first task then would be to list the lochs and then to arrange the groupings. It could be one of those family activities that Jane was so keen on. He could use the *Atlas of Scotland* while Jenny and Ham researched other details on the internet. It would be wisest probably if the earliest excursions were to the most accessible lochs. He felt more in control, more optimistic already. He liked lists. Even the idea of drawing up a list was vaguely settling.

The cubs were already out by the time he arrived puffing. Two toggled boys were kicking a football on the patch of grass beside the hut. Ham, oddly, was not with them He was standing outside the door of the hut deep in conservation with the cubmaster, a fit-looking thirty-year-old whose pectorals swelled under his flimsy shirt..

"Sorry I'm late," John gasped, trying not to pant. He gestured towards Jelly by way of an excuse. "I had the dog."

That's fine," said the cubmaster in a really friendly tone although John had only spoken to him once before when delivering stuff for the jumble sale and had thought him insufficiently grateful if not distinctly off-hand. "Ham has been telling me about your loch thing. Sounds really interesting."

John felt inexplicably nervous.

"Well," he responded hesitantly, "we're only just starting to get it underway. Aren't we Ham?"
He needed support from somewhere, from some-one.

Ham was crouching down making a fuss of Jelly. He looked up at his father, almost as though he were proud of him and grinned.

"Sounds like the sort of thing we'd like to get involved in," pursued the cubmaster remorselessly.

John had a sudden vision of a pack of howling cubs with a leader fore and aft bearing down upon the loch in the wake of Julia &Co., Harry and partner, Jenny and friend and the rest of his own family and the need to get things properly structured with rules and, more importantly, with an exclusion clause became even more pressing.

"I've got some groundwork to do first," he said firmly, "but I will let you know when I think it would be suitable for you to come along."

"Fine! Cheers then!"

They were dismissed.

Ham took over management of Jelly and they walked

home in silence, each occupied with his own thoughts until they reached the cat's corner when John suddenly looked down at his son and said, "Going to help me list the lochs and plan the outings, Ham?"

"Yes," said Ham eagerly without a moment's hesitation and John was in no doubt that his son did not share his reservations about the cubs. "Can we start now?"

John consulted his watch. "It's almost your bed-time," he said, "but if you get your homework done before supper to-morrow, we'll start straight after we've all cleared up."

Plans for tomorrow were always so graphically clear, carrying none of the amendments of today: the grubby last minute erasions of what had been neglected; the emergency stretchmarks of unforeseen interpolations .

Walking in the garden at the close of day ...

April Reynolds, doing just that, walking in the garden, could not remember where the line came from. She felt it had a hymnal ring about it but she could not be sure. After her mother's death her church-going had ceased abruptly in accordance with her father's humanist philosophy, snatches of her child-like interpretations of faith lingering in her mind like the scent of lilac in December. Her father had cut down all the lilac trees after her mother's death. She had not known why. Presumably this had been in accordance with his humanist philosophy too.

She walked the invisible plank between the neat green rows of rippling lettuce, stooped to pick a slug off a lettuce leaf and flicked it absent-mindedly onto a cabbage. Through an open upstairs window she could hear Prudence singing soothingly to William who had taken his lifestyle changes in his unsteady stride during the day, but at night was overcome by a homing instinct, a need to return to the noises and smells of the only home he had known. With the arrival of Prudence and William, change suddenly seemed to have engulfed the house. Was it a presentiment of this change she had experienced the morning before when she had felt stifled by routine and expectation, remorselessly upsetting May? She had almost laughed down the phone a few hours ago when that Paterson chap whom she paid exorbitant sums to preserve May's status quo had insisted that it was essential that May's pattern of life be disrupted.

"Believe me," she had assured him, "her life has indeed changed and it's going to be ..."

He had interrupted her rudely. That sort of disruption was apparently not what was needed. "Passive disruption" he had termed it disparagingly; disruption in which May would merely see herself as the victim of circumstance. May, he had prescribed, needed to be put in a situation where she had to make her own decisions and engineer her own change. That was all!

She had tried to discuss the problem of May with June when they were alone together because she had not felt that May's private business was Prudence's concern. After having packed May's supermarket shopping into the car they had remained in the car-park for the best part of half an hour without making any practical decisions. June was always so buttoned up, so closed in some ways, even without her ear-phones, her face so carefully devoid of any expression that April could not tell if she shared her own feelings of guilt about May: guilt because she knew that it had suited her personally to allow May to become firmly wedged in her rut and less dependent on her elder sister for reassurance and support. That uneasiness had stayed with her all the way home and into the house so that at supper she had welcomed the distraction of William banging his spoon on the almost paintless wooden beads strung across the tray of the high chair that Prudence and June had unearthed from the attic.

"Aunty Ape!" William had dubbed April.

"Aunty Jew!" he had christened June who for once had not attempted to hide her delight at being thus hailed.

But he had had no name for May, averting his eyes from her when she bent low over him with exaggeratedly mouthed endearments. May would feel this. The least April felt she could do would be to speak to Prudence about it, encourage her to coach William in "Aunty May." She could make May's sensitivity her excuse without being as disloyal as to mention her latest concerns.

Suddenly Prudence was beside her in the garden.

Without preamble she was demanding, "What's up with May?"

April found it easier to remain silent. Prudence's hair was even warmer and richer in the mellow evening light and it had been beautifully cut too. And that without their mother's having been able to say to Prudence what she had said to April so long ago.

Far from being discouraged by April's lack of response, Prudence pressed on.

"Today I did the ironing. I felt I ought to do something to help and when May came home and found it done she was nearly ill."

April remained silent.

"I'm not exaggerating. She just looked at me and went so white I thought she was going to faint. Honestly, April, she needs help."

They had reached the old wooden bench beside the dahlias which were growing vigourously, unevenly spaced. It creaked as they settled down together. Starting slowly because of her initial reluctance, April repeated to Prudence almost word for word what she had said to June in the car-park.

"A holiday!" Prudence was aghast. "She wouldn't cope on her own."

"No."

"Let me think," Prudence frowned with concentration. "Let me think about it. It's all very well that Paterson chap pontificating from his ivory tower but change takes time. We'll have to work slowly. I do have a sort of idea." She hesitated. "Look, I'm sorry I haven't helped with any family problems you know. I've been selfish."

April did not say, "But you are not really one of us." She laid her hand on Prudence's knee and she did say, "You have beautiful hair. Always look after your hair."

"It's exactly the same as yours," laughed Prudence. "You should let yours grow a bit. Show it off!"

April smiled despite the fact that she was wrestling with the suspicion that in some ways Prudence might be wiser than she herself was.

Ham attacked his supper with a speed that his sister said made her want to puke, but as this was a reaction he was constantly provoking, apparently, according to her, it didn't worry him unduly.

"Got to!" he answered her cheerfully, with a mouth full enough to turn her gills emerald, "Dad and I have work to do on the lochs, eh Dad?"

"Indeed," John welcomed his enthusiasm but felt the need to caution him, "and I'm, hoping every-one will join in."

Ham tried to console himself with an extra dollop of mayonnaise over the green, slippery stuff with which all their plates seemed to be smothered these days so that you had to excavate for the proper food underneath it. He hoped that

Jenny would come up with her usual, "Count me out!" but she didn't. In fact even before the remains of the meal were disposed of and the dishes stacked and the kitchen table wiped clean in preparation for the spreading of the big old map with fraying tears along its creases which Dad had borrowed from the Geography Department, Jenny had taken her place at the table. She was tipping her chair back in the forbidden manner, something they seemed to avoid noticing when *she* did it and was swinging her long legs under the table so that if he sat opposite her she could accidentally kick him.

He felt his father's hand on his shoulder.

"We need some-one to jot down our decisions. That's very important. Could you do that, Ham?"

"Can it write?" asked Jenny innocently but everyone ignored her.

John scribbled on the back of the re-cycled jotter which already contained his notes on the experimental trip to Hen Poo to make sure that the red ball-point pen was working and then slid both pen and book across the table to Ham. Ham turned to a clean page.

"Shall I put a heading?" he whispered to his father.

"In a bit."

John felt ready for this meeting.

"First of all, I am thinking that we should make a slight change to the programme before we decide on dates and lochs etc. You know we said we'd try one expedition a month for six months? Well that would take us into the coldest part of the year so I'd like to suggest that instead we have four monthly expeditions, the last one being in October, and after that we could plan another couple for the Spring. Is that O.K. with everyone?"

"Fine!" said Jane and looked round pointedly at the children in a vain attempt to engender a response.

"Do I write that down?" worried Ham

"Not yet," said John. "I'll tell you when?

There was a brief pause while John looked questioningly at Jenny, awaiting some sign of approval.

"It's like at weddings," observed Ham who, as a member of the church choir before the mobile phone incident for which he had not been to blame but had been unconvincing in his own defence, was fully conversant with the wedding ceremony. "Like that bit where the priest says, 'Speak now or forever hold your peace' and when nobody says anything it's O.K. and …"

"Wish you'd forever …" started Jenny.

"Well," interrupted John smoothly, "if that's all right with every-one I think we should plan two months ahead at a time. Ham, you could write *July* at the top of one page and *August* at the top of the next."

Ham, with the tip of his tongue protruding as he tried to swell out the letters into bubble-writing for the headings, picked up shreds of the discussion.

Julia had phoned. Probably gassed on for hours about the marvellous accomplishments of Chris and Alice, Mum might be taken in but he'd get the truth from Chris next month. Except it wouldn't be next month. Because of school holidays they weren't coming till August and were *so* looking forward to it. Mum said the *so* just the way Julia would have said it: a big rainbow-coloured, bubble-lettered, black- rimmed *SO* like the graffitti in the tunnel at Waverley Station which he much admired. He'd missed what Jenny was arguing about. Oh right! She was *not* telling them which friend she was bringing. Well, apparently eventually she'd have to because Mum said she'd have to speak to the girl's parents. Jenny said she wasn't bothered but still didn't say who and kicked her leg so high that she stubbed her bare toe on the underside of the table and they had to have a pause for First Aid. Dad didn't hear him asking about the cubs and moved on to say that Harry

Aitcheson and some-one else – Dad told him to write
A.N.Other, just like that as though it were a name- were on.
On what? Sounded as though they were on drugs or on
detention or something. You couldn't be just on nothing. Still
he wrote it down. Mum was talking about the Reynolds: the
ones next door; yes, the ones at No.11; yes, those Reynolds.
Yes, two of them *did* want to come along. Something about
one of them needing to get involved in something different.
Prudence Reynolds had been round about it and before Jenny
fell off her chair laughing would she just listen! He put his pen
down and listened too. The Reynolds had a house up North
near Loch Garry and could help with accommodation. There
could be beds in the house for two or three and the garden was
suitable for tents. A tent would be good if he could share with
Chris but Chris would not be there till August. "What about the
cubs?" he said really loudly this time. But did they listen? No,
they were still shaking their heads over the indisputable lack of
fitness of the Misses Reynolds.

"Thar's crap!" he said indignantly. "One of them is a
footballer."

"We're talking about No 11, doh!" said Jenny.

"Don't say crap!" said his mother.

Well," his voice was high in protest, "she may not play
it now but she used to. She used to play rugby too. I know
she's still good because if my ball goes over the wall at week-
ends, she kicks it back. She enjoys it. She says, 'Where do you
want it?' and it always land dead on target."

And having produced that crucial piece of information
all his mother could say was, "I've told you to be careful with
your football, Ham!"

But the Reynolds were 'on'. His father told him to list
them under July.

After the decision to include the Reynolds the pace
slackened as though his father was not altogether sure of the

way forward. He drew tiny match-stick Jellies in the margins of the jotter as they debated about which lochs to include for July. The Reynolds offer of accommodation altered things his father said. August apparently was easy, the Great Glen lochs were considered to be suitable for two families for a variety of reasons which he wasn't going to bore them with. It *was* beginning to be a bit boring. He had finished match-stick Jelly begging and was onto match-stick Jelly chasing a cat when his father interrupted his artwork with, "Ham, did you put that down?"

"What?" from himself.

"Doh!" from Jenny.

"Under July write *Loch Garry, Loch Poularyand possibly Loch Quoich and Loch Loyne.*" As he mentioned each loch, John jabbed his finger into the appropriate loch on the map. Following his finger, Ham noticed that Loch Loyne appeared to have a sort of road running through it. Interesting!

"We might just manage all three," John was saying slowly. Then he picked up pace. "Right now we're onto equipment. I can borrow tents and life jackets from the Outdoor Ed. Department at school."

"I'm not wearing a life-jacket!" Jenny was obviously wearying of the planning meeting too. "They squash your boobs and give you breast cancer."

"Shall I put down life jackets for the men only," suggested Ham helpfully.

"And let us women drown? Thanks a bunch!" hissed Jenny.

He thought briefly of gouging her eyes out but went for the jugular instead with "You're getting very fat!"

"I think," said Mum in that slow quiet voice, "that we should make a separate list of equipment for each trip. So we could leave that list till nearer the time. You've done a good job, Ham and your little dogs are super."

"Sooper!" drawled Jenny. "You are so dated, Mum!"

His mum made hot chocolate and Jenny went into the hall to phone a friend, probably the mystery friend from the way she was burbling on about the expedition. Ham leaned over the table with his father, shoulder to shoulder, and watched the mountains rise up blue, dark blue and light, misty blue and clouded from out of the flat dark brown of the map and saw the lochs plummet deeply and darkly down through the kitchen table and the fact that he, Ham, had no friend on the first expedition ceased to matter.

Chapter Seven

The Team

The Launch Party

June slipped into July. June, with its end of term weariness of paperwork and valedictory functions disrupting school routine with minor inconsistencies and major confusions, sidled into July; long-day, languorous July with summer losing its edge and becoming a habit; with turgid stems flopping limp as warmth stagnated breathlessly to wilting heat; with the fresh stimulus of early summer showers replaced by skulking grey haars lurking in low places, sucking the warmth out of the days and damping down energy. John found himself surreptitiously questioning the wisdom of loch netting and indulging in a querulous internal whining about the fact that there now seemed to be too many people involved for him to withdraw. The pre-expedition meeting had been fixed for the 4th of July, departure for the first expedition for the 12th. He was looking forward to neither. Furthermore, under Jane's supervision, he was still expected to satisfy his hunger with flimsy fare which he ate without looking at it.

As his own enthusiasm flagged so, it seemed, that of the rest of the family grew. Ham, whose typing skills were still rudimentary, had devoted so much time to typing out the list of equipment on the computer that the patch on the lawn worn bare by continuous goal kicking was beginning to green up quite encouragingly. Jenny had mellowed amazingly. In fact over the past few weeks she had been almost frighteningly co-operative and although she had consistently withheld the identity of her mystery guest, they had thought it sensible not to press her on this. Most of Jenny's friends were "suitable" and in any case all would be revealed on the 4th. Jane had expended considerable energy in rifling through recipe books to prepare a post-meeting buffet supper for the loch-netters and John had resisted his first selfless impulse which was to tell her not to bother. The idea of one of Jane's party suppers held great appeal.

"I did think of a barbecue," she had sounded wistful because it would have been an opportunity to show off her garden at its best, "but you just can't count on the weather."

"Not a barbecue," he had agreed readily. "Too next-door." With that he had jerked his thumb in the direction of No. 9 who, judging from the frequency with which meat ingrained smoke wafted over the wall and the way in which the entire spectrum of coloured light played on the smug, plaster features of Aphrodite & Co. were at the peak of their summer entertaining. Besides, small portions of grilled meat and generous helpings of leafy salad had almost become his staple diet.

On the evening of the meeting the first potential lochnetters to arrive were two of the Misses Reynolds. May entered first with a straight thin-lipped rictus and a box of chocolates held propitiatingly in front of her. June, propelling her forward from behind, reached across her with a bottle of wine and a jar of *Reynolds's Finest Orange Marmalade* Shortly after them Harry Aitcheson rang the bell. He had not one but two young men with him: one, probably in his late twenties with the sallow-skinned, aquiline good looks of Southern Europe, was so tall and broad-shouldered that the evening light shrank behind him as he crossed the thresh-hold, hand confidently outstretched. "Pete," said Harry, the pride in his voice, not unlike that of a vegetable gardener indicating a superbly overgrown leek, belying the casualness of the jerk of his thumb in Pete's direction. The other, just a boy really, certainly comparatively nondescript, slipped in almost unnoticed and remained unintroduced.

John poured wine, looked at his watch and observed, "We've just got to wait for Jenny's friend and then we can start? She *is* coming, Jen?"

"She, I mean *he* is here." And Jenny tapped a proprietorial hand on the knee of the unobtrusive boy who had shadowed Harry in, who was now perched on the window seat beside her and who immediately sought to make himself more unobtrusive behind John's mother's curtains as attention was focused on him. "Aren't you, Lewis? This is Lewis by the way. …He's my friend."

John read Jane's face, took a deep breath and said simply, "Right …well… welcome, Lewis. Let's begin."

As the discussion gathered momentum John felt the

dormant spark of his enthusiasm rekindling. It was the same re-awakening he sometimes experienced when introducing a class to some once well-loved but half-forgotten poem. He unfolded the Ordnance Survey Sheet No. 34 on the coffee table and they drew chairs around it.

"There's our house!" squeaked May, suddenly forgetting herself. "Sorry," she added, peering round to see if her indiscretion had been observed.

Everyone ignored her. They followed John's finger as it wavered for a few seconds before smoothly tracing the route around the North side of Loch Garry. The red road to Kyle of Lochalsh branched into a yellow minor road with passing places which skimmed the edge of the loch, sending an off-shoot to span a bridge southwards over a narrow neck of the loch before continuing its westward journey through Inchlaggan to the Tomdoun area where the Reynolds had their cottage. There he tapped his finger on the map to indicate the spot and May shuffled her feet in silent, self-conscious pride.

"Easy cycling," he pronounced, safe in the knowledge that with Lewis beside her, Jenny would not demand to know when he last bestrode a bike. "Or walking? Anyway let's go South now."

His finger crossed the bridge to hover around the broken lines of paths and tracks which seemed to wind as randomly and purposelessly as snail trails around the brown whorls of hills. The most straightforward route appeared to trickle from the Forestry Commission car park at the Eastern edge of the loch to Greenfield at its Western limit. He placed his thumb sideways on the map to indicate the distance from the loch edge to the track.

"A pity this track doesn't follow the loch more closely," he observed, "but I do feel very strongly that in the interests of wildlife etc. we should be strict about sticking to the track."

"Mmm," they hummed in agreement.

"And I think that we should walk the South side and cycle the North. That means about eight to nine miles easy cycling and about ten miles walking over somewhat mixed terrain."

"We should perhaps split up, John," suggested Harry. "I, for one, haven't cycled for years but would be happy to do the walking bit. Is there anyone desperate to do both?" No-one volunteered so he continued, "As long as we pool our findings and experiences, does it matter if we don't all do everything?"

"No," John shook his head in grateful agreement. "No, not at all, I don't think. As you say, we'll compile out findings."

"Then *I* could put them on the web-page," said Ham happily and Jenny, handicapped by her proximity to Lewis, could only unleash a blood-freezing smile in his direction."

Within an hour the plans seemed watertight. The expedition would take three days. On the first day Peter, Lewis, Jenny and Ham, wearing hats and fluorescent jackets would cycle the North side. June, May, John, Jane and Harry would walk the southern route to Greenfield from where, at a pre-arranged time, Peter and A.N. Other would collect them by car. The following day would be comparatively leisurely: they would nurse their blisters, amble along the road to Loch Poulary and look at various ways of tackling Loch Quoich on an ensuing visit. On the third day they would attempt to explore Loch Loyne, lying to the North of Loch Garry .

"You don't want to take on too much first time round," warned Harry. "After all this *is* a leisure pursuit."

John smiled at him indulgently. "We'll see," he said.

Although Jane's buffet was everything he knew it would be, John's need to over-indulge seemed to have been temporarily suppressed by the emotionally warm satisfaction the meeting had engendered. Standing a little apart with her plateful and glancing out of the window with unseeing eyes, June was experiencing a similar loss of appetite. The conversation around her seemed disjointed: there was nothing she could hook onto. As the level of chat and laughter rose, she felt increasingly isolated, more uneasy as though she was being suffocated by a claustrophobia of noise with her own personal silence screaming loudest of all. She needed her headphones to quieten her silence with music. On the opposite side of the room, May was, to all appearances, happily chatting to Jane. *Am I more dependent on her than she is on me?* The suspicion was insidiously whining through the noise. *Do I need to push her in front of me to barricade myself? Do I need to despair of her so that I don't despair of myself?* The whining was becoming louder in her head. *Do I...*

"Will you play football with me at Tomdoun?"

She looked down into the inquiring face of the boy from next door. She didn't even know his name, had never bothered to ask. He had spoken with his mouth full and obviously felt that his question had been insufficiently distinct. He swallowed, wincing at the discomfort of the bolus of food forcing its way down his gullet and repeated the question, this time with a "please" appended.

"Good idea!" she responded, uncomfortable at the enforced heartiness she could hear in her own voice. "Maybe we could persuade the others to join in a team game?"

Ham gave the idea his serious consideration.

"Ye-es, I think most people would play. Except Mr. Aitcheson probably won't be able to move very quickly. And my sister will scream about breaking her nails. How 'bout your sister?" His voice dropped to a conspiratorial whisper. "I don't want to be rude or anything, but she doesn't look like she plays football. Would you like to see our dog?"

The change of topic was too sudden for June to be able to refuse his invitation even had she wanted to. She followed

Ham to the warm silence of the kitchen. Jelly, in front of the Aga, lifted her head at their entry, stretched lazily and thumped her tail. Ham knelt beside her.

"There you are, Jelly," he said proffering a vol-au-vent with a small bite taken out of it. "It's not very nice but it's all I have left. Anyway, if you have too much you'll be sick. She can play football too," he addressed June who was by now seated on a stool, hungrily attacking her supper. "I've taught her to go in goals ..."

And he prattled on.

It was dark – as dark as it gets in July- by the time the last loch-netting guest had departed. Jenny had seen fit to escape upstairs on Lewis' departure. Her door was shut; her light was out; her message was clear. She was unavailable for comment on the unforeseen gender of her friend. Ham reluctantly offered to help with the clearing up, his offer punctuated by loud attempts at dramatic yawns, and was released to bed. John hand-washed the glasses and silver and Jane dried as they reviewed the evening.

"Went well, I thought," said John. "We'll only be doing one loch properly which is less than I'd hoped, but I think Harry's right about aiming for a softly-softly start."

"His Pete's a bit of all right."

"Odd though! I would have expected Harry's partner to be more his age."

"John! Pete's Harry's *son!*" She rolled her eyes to express exasperation at his misapprehension. "Yes, I know what you thought, but he told me all about it while I was writing out my recipe for game pie for him. He went to Rome early on in his teaching career on a school trip and had a fling with an Italian teacher of English. Peter was the result but Harry didn't know anything about him until he was fifteen and his mother was killed in a car accident. Peter's his love-child.

Romantic isn't it?"

"An affair on a school trip!"

John tutted and a soapy spoon, the last one, clattered from his hand onto the draining board.

"Come on! I don't suppose he wrestled her to the ground while pointing out Corinthian capitals to the kids. I'm sure it was very discreet."

"Talking about kids," John moved swiftly on from ancient history to his present concern. "What are we going to do about Jenny's young man?"

"About Lewis? Nothing! He's terrified of her, wise guy that he must be. I'm sure he'll keep his distance and I wouldn't be surprised if he chickened out." She slipped her arms around him and untied his apron. "Not so long ago you couldn't have tied that round your waist," she commented. "You've done really well and I'm proud of you. Now leave the rest and come to bed!"

Chapter Eight

The First Expedition

Tomdoun

"Want to drive?"

Harry was standing at the open boot, mentally listing its contents to make sure nothing was forgotten as Peter locked the front door behind him and joined him. He asked the question without turning round.

"If you don't want to."

The response was of course all deference, all consideration. It always was, always had been. To Peter, Harry suspected, he had been benefactor rather than father ever since their first meeting; ever since he had flown to Rome and collected a dry-eyed, self-controlled fifteen-year old when he, Harry, had steeled himself to allow his newly-discovered son to weep in his arms. Peter was dry-eyed at the funeral, dry-eyed on leaving Rome. Back in Scotland he had tip-toed around Harry in his bachelor pad. Any murmurs of adolescent unpleasantness or insurrection, had they ever existed, seemed to have been buried with the ashes of his mother. He was no different when they moved out of the flat to a sprawling bungalow with a large garden where he was encouraged to bring friends home. Harry, at school himself most of the day during the school term, had sent him as a day boarder at an Edinburgh school renowned for academic and sporting prowess. Peter excelled at both, enjoyed popularity with his peers and in the course of time was inevitably crowned head-boy and school dux. Any pride which Harry felt in him was modified by the knowledge that he had played no part in his son's formative years. Classicist that he was, he compared himself wryly to Zeus who had given birth to Athena by having her spring adult and fully armed from his head. Peter had arrived perfectly formed and definitely armed. But then Athena's birth had caused Zeus an appropriately superhuman headache at the time which consequently subsided completely as birth pangs do. At Peter's arrival he himself had experienced just an incipient twinge of discomfort at the interruption to his lifestyle, but this discomfort had aged into a chronic, nagging guilt about the boy's past and an agonizing fear that Peter could never be truly his own. When he had dusted down the family photograph album to show Peter his paternal grandfather, his grandmother, his cousins in Australia, whom he might care to visit one day, and himself at Peter's age, Peter had shown the meticulously polite, disconnected interest of the perfect stranger. Harry had wanted sometimes to shake him and shout at him something like, "You are mine! I love you! All I have is yours!" Well, not those words exactly. Too melodramatic. Soppy, really. There never had actually been the right words for it. After school his protégé had progressed smoothly through a gap year of doing excellent work in South America, even more smoothly through a law degree at Edinburgh University and was now working for a highly respected law firm in which he was expected to rise.

"We'll share it, shall we? You start." He hesitated. "Peter, are you sure that you want to be involved in all this lochnetting? I've a feeling it's not quite your thing."

Peter smiled at him, "I'll be fine."

'Well he would be,' thought Harry. Out aloud he said, "Don't forget that we've to pick up those two youngsters from Damhope Road."

As they drew up outside No. 10 Jenny in a vermillion T-shirt and fashionably faded jeans came running out and was mouthing something inaudible at Harry through the closed passenger window. He slid down the window and caught the last of it "…for a quick coffee if you'd like to. We're all ready."

Lewis, a slight shadowy figure in black sweatshirt and black jeans, lurked in her wake.

"No thanks to the coffee." He stood up out of the car and waved at John and Jane who were coming down the steps with a slight, blonde woman whom they introduced as Anne, Lewis' mother.

"No thanks to the coffee," he repeated to Jane. "We'll just push on and meet you at Spean Bridge for lunch."

"Be good," said Lewis' mother awkwardly, proffering her cheek which he obediently brushed with his lips. "Thank-you for giving him a lift," she added. Standing in the warmth of a July morning with her shoulders hunched and rubbing her folded arms, she looked cold and nervous.

"Pleasure," said Harry.

"We'll all take good care of him," reassured Peter from the boot as he fixed Lewis' bike alongside his own. "What about Jenny's bag?"

"*We've* got *that*." John pulled a face. "Her majesty has yet to discover the art of travelling light."

Jenny, from the back seat, forgot herself sufficiently to lean over Lewis and hiss at him, "Just because I believe in hygiene and you …"

John closed the door on her and waved her off with a grin and Jenny, feeling the inappropriateness of completing the sentence in the confines of the car, subsided temporarily into silence.

Already at Tomdoun and awaiting the arrival of the two

carloads of lochnetters, Prue Reynolds was feeling the heat. In their own individual ways each of her sisters had managed to remind her, indirectly of course, that she was responsible for this intrusion into their peaceful refuge. The strain was telling even though they stoically repressed their feelings by, in April's case, making exhaustive arrangements to preclude mishap with particular reference to the emptying of the septic tank; in June's case, developing coping strategies, mainly in the shape of silver discs and ear plugs which rendered her almost completely incommunicado; in May's case by counting and recounting – twenty-four dessert spoons, sixteen dessert forks, nine soup spoons, seven cakes of carbolic soap – "They're not going to steal" (icy interruption from April)- nineteen pillow-cases, five torches, three garden chairs …

So Prue left the stew she had made for every-one's supper on 'simmer' and took William for a walk. It was a hot afternoon, almost sultry in its humidity and although the midges should long since have sunk to loch level, the swallows were wheeling about inexhaustibly with their mouths open, squealing ecstatically as the warm upcurrents washed around them. For the first quarter of a mile the road, cleft between dark walls of motionless Forestry Commission firs lined into amorphous ranks, was so breathlessly still that it was like walking into a landscape painting down one of those roads you followed with your eyes into question-mark. She thought she preferred the silver birches around the house, wind-writhed into individual reaches and leanings and with leaves that shook and shivered at the breath of a midge. She lifted William over a cattle-grid. He smelled of baby powder and his little arms were slippery with sun-block as he slid them around her neck.

"I am not going to feel guilty," she said to him determinedly, nuzzling into the warm curve of his neck. "There's not a lot of work. We'll all be eating at the hotel after to-night and I'm doing the cooking for to-night. And," she swung him back down on the other side of the grid, "we'll all just use your potty if the bloody septic tank overflows."

"Bloody!" pronounced William, clearly agreeing with her. He wriggled out of her hold, trotted back to the cattle-grid and dropped a pebble between two of the iron bars. It splashed into the invisible pool of water in the well of the grid. "Plop! Bloody plop!"

"Ignore it," Prue advised herself. "He'll forget."

She sat down on the fraying green verge, close enough to lift him off the road if any car approached and passed him pebbles to drop through the grating. They were still there when the two cars rounded the bend. She scooped William up and waved cheerfully as the first of the cars drew up.

Jane rolled down the passenger window.

"The barbarian invasion's upon you," she smiled.

"Rubbish!" Prue laughed. "Believe me you're the missionaries bringing hope and salvation to the heathen. You'll find my sisters prancing around in their woad in front of the first croft house on the right. William and I will follow you."

They set off for home accompanied by Ham and Jelly; Jelly ahead, delightedly darting from side to side as her nose dictated, and William weaving a zigzag course behind her.

April had watched Prue walking down the furrowed drive that curled steeply from the back of the house down onto the road, adapting to William's pace as he alternately ambled and trotted, holding his hand so that he didn't trip on the rough surface, and her conscience nagged her. She had, she knew, intended to intimate to Prue that this idea of hers, that lochnetting would help May, had only foisted unwanted hospitality on the rest of them. She also knew that Prue had willingly shouldered most of the preparatory work.

Furthermore Prue had tried to help May constructively whereas her own method of re-channelling May's energies had merely been to express her personal irritation and exasperation. At least she was no worse than June who hadn't done much either. She sighed, went to look for May and found her hovering around June who was seated on the back doorstep, dobbining her own walking boots and May's, the brush-strokes rhythmically following the beat of the Waltz from *The Merry Widow*.

"May," she called, "would you come and check the barn with me and then when our guests arrive, you could please show them round while I get tea for them."

She saw May's face light up after the first part of her suggestion and dim with apprehension at the second and felt equally guilty about both reactions.

The 'barn' so-called was a rectangular, flat-roofed, wooden building rather like an outsize garden shed, erected on the site of the old shearing-shed about twenty metres from the house. It had been painted dark green on the outside but was still rough and splintery on the inside with the occasional amber ooze of resin seeping from the walls and was divided into two interconnecting rooms. The original purpose of this arrangement was lost in time but now the Reynolds sisters used the larger room with the long, low windows as a summer-house and the small room as a spare bedroom. The summer-house part was simply furnished: a long pine table, darkly notched, scorched in places, ringed by countless mugs and glasses, bearing an old but well-polished tilley-lamp; an odd assortment of upright chairs acquired over the years, the cushions on their seats variably bright and faded, and a hard-backed sofa which was supposedly convertible into a double bed but had never been put to the test as such. Through the inter-connecting door the small spare bedroom contained a single bed with a faded patchwork cover, a very small, square table with a single drawer and a wooden chair drawn up against the table. A square, oak-framed mirror on the table tilted at an angle at which it was impossible to see any reflection other than that of the ceiling planks. Except for a narrow strip of rush-matting alongside the non-wall side of the bed, the floor was bare. A single curtain of bright red gingham with a sagging hemline hung to one side of the square window which was open top and bottom and fitted with a frame of mosquito netting speckled with the tiny corpses of adventurous midges which had tried unsuccessfully to tunnel through its holes.

April stopped herself from pronouncing, "Looks O.K.," just in time and deferred to her sister.

"Do you think it's O.K.?" she managed.

May looked at her quizzically.

"Would you say it was all right?" April re-phrased.

"May looked around her as one seeking direction in an impenetrable rain-forest. "Some flowers?" She hesitated. "Some flowers would be nice … if you think …"

"Fine!" denounced April. "The nearest florist is a good thirty miles or more!" She remembered her resolve. "Are there any around here?"

"Honeysuckle in the garden?" suggested May warily. "And there are some bluebells out and they do well in water?"

"Wonderful!" April hoped she sounded encouraging. "You go ahead." She consulted her watch and stopped herself from commenting that there was hardly time for such unimportant details. "I'll go and make a start on afternoon tea. All you have to remember is that the girl is to sleep here if she wants to. She'll be near the tents, but if she's nervous she can have the downstairs bedroom in the house. Somehow I don't think she's the nervous type though."

May carefully separated the fragile stems of the bluebells she had gathered and counted the number of paper-thin and paper-crisp bluebells on each stem before arranging them in a small glass vase, carefully interspersing them with stems of soft, purple-headed grasses. Absorbed with her arrangement, she forgot about her more onerous task until she heard the first car crunching up the gravel. As she stepped forward, looking beyond her guests to the house for support, she noticed that June must have vacated the back doorstep in a hurry, leaving behind one of the brushes and the tin of dobbin. There was no sign of April. Her tongue seemed to be sticking to the roof of her mouth. To her relief, though, any initiative she might have been expected to take was snuffed by the enthusiasm of the groups that spilled out of the cars towards her, their greetings followed by so many questions plied in such rapid succession that she could answer none of them and it seemed enough to smile and nod and point.

"All well?"… "The weather's been very settled here as well as with us, I believe?" …"You're still going to join us, I hope?" … "Is this really where I'm sleeping? It's gorgeous!" …"Look at the flowers! Did you do them?" … "Is it O.K. to put the tents up here on this flat bit?" …"Where would you like the cars?"… "A tilley-lamp! Ages since I saw one of these! Does it work?" …

And then Prue and Ham and William and Jelly arrived on foot and Prue said straightaway that she was gasping for tea and weren't they all? Everyone followed her into the house and May, bringing up the rear, realized that her ordeal was over.

Chapter Nine

The First Expedition

Loch Garry

Despite Prue's excellent supper and the fact that her bed was surprisingly comfortable, Jenny did not sleep well. She had insisted that Jelly's bed be placed in her room "to guard me against any intruders" which everybody else appeared to find comical. She realised her mistake when Jelly, after exploring her new bedroom at unnecessary length and then arranging and re-arranging her bedding with much humphing, grunting and scratching, had her sleep punctuated by exotic dreams which caused her to squeak and scuffle with excitement. Although the window was open, the mosquito netting intercepted not only the midges but any passage of air so that even after having kicked off all her covers, Jenny was uncomfortably warm.

It seemed to her that she had only just fallen asleep when she was rudely awakened by Ham thumping on the door and shouting unnecessarily loudly that breakfast was ready. Hot and sticky, she pulled on her clothes and scowled at the flushed and puffy fragment of face she managed to catch in the mirror. She smelled. She knew she *smelled* . And her hair was *minging*. According to *THE BATH ROSTER* which the bossiest Reynolds – April or March or July or whatever had pinned up and referred everyone to soon after their arrival, her bath time was fixed irrevocably for six in the evening. She hadn't even been able to whinge on about it then like she could at home, in case Lewis thought she was a moan. She had just had to draw a smile across clenched teeth and say, "Fine!" and "May I help?" and "Isn't William cute?"

She pushed the interconnecting door open with her foot and found everybody else being loud and jolly, stuffing their faces and looking more than a little silly because of the uneven heights of the chairs on which they were seated. When she couldn't manage her breakfast, her mother accused her of being over-concerned about her figure, accused her out aloud in front of everyone. Lewis all but ignored her. Having discovered the night before that his tent-mate, Ham, was also a footballing soul-mate, he gabbled away about football to Ham with barely a glance in her direction. Then Peter started to get bossy and full of himself. She'd felt fine the night before about her dad asking Peter to be responsible for the cycling. Peter had been really friendly in the car and was definitely fanciable even if he was old. But when, towards the end of breakfast, he started to issue orders, it was all she could do to stop herself shouting, "Heil Hitler!" and giving him a Nazi salute. They were all to report to him in the barn for a briefing after their chores and as soon as it was less midgey, he wanted them to check their bikes with him. Well, her chore would last as long as *she* wanted it to. Her chore this morning was to see to Jelly. That at least suited her – until her father started itemizing it, pointing out that there was a prodigious output of Jelly poo to be uplifted from the drive and Lewis, wimp that he was turning out to be, having completed his own clearing the table chore, opted to help Ham with the dishes rather than her with the poo!

"Wear a midge-net," called her father after her.

Like hell! And look a complete freak? She elected deafness.

Although her sleep had been undisturbed, June's mood was no lighter than Jenny's as she packed her rucksack to *La Traviata*. May poked her head into the room and June pulled one ear-plug out with a frown that ensured that May's body didn't follow her head.

"What do I need?" she asked, swinging the door slightly so that it creaked irritatingly on its hinges.

June, though tempted, limited her answer to "What's on the list," and May retreated.

She switched off her player, fingered it for a moment and then tucked it down into the bottom of her rucksack. The head-phones she put in her pocket where she would be able to finger them from time to time 'like William and his sucky blanket.' She thought.

The lochside walk held little appeal. Her fitness was unquestionable. She often walked further and over rougher terrain, without her music even, allowing herself to wallow in the silence of the hills that could only be intensified by the mewing of a buzzard, the scream of a rabbit and, when the heather crisped in the autumn, the belling of stags reverberating till the hills throbbed; allowing her creased, folded and pocketed needs to transcend this current lifestyle of hers which had been so severely manicured for the sake of the family *business* which was, of course, synonymous with the family *reputation*. Sometimes in the mist she felt that Matty walked beside her, a Matty still young and warm and soft as she had been during that last year they had enjoyed a university flat together. Though not a full year, just an academic year, they had stretched it to comprehend a lifetime of dreams about setting up home together, somewhere up in the Highlands. Matty had favoured a disused lighthouse with eye-level gulls wheeling and screaming and gannets plunging like sharp-nosed paper aeroplanes and June had indulged her dream. She had also indulged Matty's choice of interior furnishings and colour schemes for the imaginary lighthouse. She herself would be swinging from a rope suspended from an unspecified projection to paint the outside walls, buffeted by the wind and on the feather edge of the salt spray, knowing that Matty was safe and warm inside. When the sea was calm, she would launch the *Matilda* and fish the sea, afterwards gutting, cleaning and filleting her catch by the rock-pools, throwing the offal to the gulls and watching them swoop to catch the pieces in mid-air. At night the beam would still be sweeping the seas rhythmically because somebody somewhere had forgotten to switch it off, their private safety lantern, searching out danger while she and Matty would be curled up together between Matty's favourite pink satin sheets. The year-long dream had nose-dived like a gannet misjudging its plunge and breaking its neck against the granite surface of the sea when her father and April came to Glasgow for her graduation and put her life into perspective for her; when they sat in the flat and talked proudly and firmly about June's future in *The Business*, the great indestructible and unbending *Business* in which there was no role for Matty and she had been able to say nothing to stop them and Matty had released her saying brightly, "Well, I'll have to come and visit June, the Accountant!"

Of course she never had visited, never would.

Standing up and looking through her window, she could see the rest of the party scurrying round the cars, getting in each other's way with the apparently purposeless choreography of ants round dead beetles. She gritted her teeth and went down to join them.

John stepped out of the barn and took up an elevated position wobbling unsteadily on a lichen covered boulder.

"Walkers, ready to leave in ten minutes," he boomed. "Let's split up into our carloads. Say June, Jane and Harry go with Peter; May, Jelly and I with April. O.K., May? Trust yourself with me? All right about the dog in the car, April? You kids'll stay with Prue until Peter comes back. Prue, you and I have to synchronise watches for the pick-up."

"Any minute now he'll start a count down to blast-off," muttered June. She sighed picked up her rucksack and joined the edge of the group as John started ushering into cars and shouting, "Right! To the woods! To the woods!"

Jenny standing beside her confided darkly, "Dad is such an embarrassment!"

She smiled at Jenny, "I've known worse."

Lewis, being an only child, had no sisters and, because his mother had not wanted him "to grow up too soon" attended an all-boys' school where girls featured mainly in multi-thumbed magazines as folds of satiny flesh with sugar-pink nipples and coy, half-hidden crevices. He had had therefore little opportunity either to sully his innocence or to familiarise himself with the giddying mood-swings of the adolescent female. Yesterday, Jenny had almost suffocated him with her relentless mothering; he had come up gasping for air between her bouts of ensuring that everybody else was attending to his needs to the extent that to his intense embarrassment she had forced her father to drive the fifteen miles to the Well of the Seven Heads to buy him a toothbrush when, supervising his unpacking, she found he had forgotten his. He had been glad when night came and he could escape into the tent with Ham and talk football. Even then, he could imagine he could hear her prowling around his tent with predatory possessiveness. This morning over breakfast she had been sullen, grumpy, whining, complaining and a complete mess to look at. He had averted his eyes. Now that the bikes had been checked and they were ready to depart she was once again the bright, beautiful creature he had felt so drawn to at the *Praise for Young People Festival* organised by the church: her cycling shorts were merely an extra black skin over the neatly rounded buttocks, even dimpling when she hitched her leg across the bar of the bike; her T-shirt so skimpy that if he looked when she wasn't looking, he could make out the peak of each firm little nipple and, having to look away again, imagine the pink buds of them and wonder how they would feel if he…

"Time we were off," Peter was saying.

Too right!

They were to ride in pairs: he and Jenny in front; Ham and Peter behind at an initial distance of two passing places. The little road was quiet enough to allow Jenny and him to ride abreast for most of its length. The wind blew cool against his hot face and shadow was striated with light as they rode fast between the screens of dark pine, slashed at apparently random intervals by the sunlit corridors of fire-breaks, leaving behind them the sharp, belated alarm calls of unseen birds in the thick pine branches. When they reached the tiny village of Tomdoun, most of the pines retreated up the hill to their left. Those remaining became sparse and grew tall around the sturdy little stone church. On the right, opposite the church was a chunky red phone box, probably overlooked when others of its ilk had been phased out a few years back. Apart from the church and the telephone box, there were just two or three houses and below them sunlight poured down sloping fields, uneven with patches of lushness that suggested hidden streams, into the broad shallow reaches of the River Garry. Past Tomdoun a low white building bore a lopsidedly hanging sign, *The Reel and Rod,* and they caught a whiff of fried bacon before the road unwound and straightened through a wood of low, gnarled oak and naked birch with ferns sprouting from the fissures of the low, stone retaining wall to the left. The passing places all lay to the right and at one or two of them wooden gates indicated overgrown paths leading down presumably to the river. They slowed down round the bend where the road lapped on the doors of the croft houses of Inchlaggan where they passed neat gardens with hollyhocks and a collie lying on the warm surface of the road, indifferent to their passage, before gathering speed down the hill to the bridge that crossed to the Southern side of the Loch. Loch Garry opened before them like a post-card photograph in which the foreground is all clarity while the perspective of the background is blurred and improbable. Just a few metres out on the water, a pair of swans, melting into their reflections, turned their heads curiously towards them without changing direction. The opposite shore quivering in the heat, lacked definition; with their glaring whiteness, the few houses were indistinct in their brightness. Behind the houses pine mossed the hills and the lower slopes of the perfectly conical Ben Tee, an intrinsically Scottish little Fuji without snow. They followed the contour of the loch, swooping low under green-to-early-gold beeches before tunnelling through a birch wood where here and there in clearings brightly coloured tents sprawled low and round like the tops of open golf umbrellas. As the forest ended, they rounded a deep bend to where their minor road fed into the main highway to Kyle of Lochalsh, the point at which they were to wait for Peter and Ham.

"They'll be ages!" Jenny dropped her bike on the grass so that it lay with a wheel spinning, undid her hat and tossed out her hair. Then she sprawled on the grass, flat on her back, spread-eagled, with her breasts peaking and her face turned upwards to the sun. "Come on!" she patted the grass beside her and then clasped her hands behind her head, arching her back luxuriously.

"In a minute!" Lewis, straddling his bike and leaning forward on his handle-bars, forced himself to concentrate on the patches of dark sweat forming under her arm-pits. They must stink. Sweat did stink. Even on Jenny. Then he screwed up his eyes as though he was studying the far side of the loch and prayed for the imminent arrival of the other two. His prayer was answered. Ham in front, with Peter safeguarding his rear, was flushed with exertion and hardly had breath to hail them.

Jenny eyed her brother askance and stood up. "Right!" She brushed off stray blades of grass, smoothing her palms appreciatively over her own firm thighs. "Let's go!"

"Hang on!" Peter laughed. "An old man like me needs to rest! Let's have a drink here!"

He threw his jacket onto the grass that Jenny had obligingly flattened, spreading it so that it would accommodate both himself and Ham, and sat down. "See anything interesting along the way?"

"Didn't know we were supposed to be looking!" retorted Jenny.

"*We* saw swans," said Ham triumphantly, "*and* a pine marten on the wall. Didn't we, Peter?"

"Oh well, if you're going to count swans," shrugged Jenny and couldn't finish her sentence. She stretched her length on the grass again with an exaggerated yawn and drawled, "Well, wake me up when you're strong enough to continue," Peter, pressing his lips into a narrow line as though he was having difficulty in opening his water bottle, experienced a dislike that almost surged into an angry, crushing retort. He curbed it with difficulty because he knew that his anger had its source not so much in the provocative insolence of Jenny's nonchalance as in his own insecurities: insecurities which were all the more shameful to him because he recognised the fact that he, twenty-six and dogged unremittingly by success, should have left them behind him. He had known boys at school, both in Italy and in Scotland, who had in the same way aroused his angry jealousy; boys who felt safe enough to be moody, difficult and insolent as Jenny this morning, as Jenny right now. It was the same furious envy he had felt when the cousins who flooded his maternal grandmother's house summer after summer in Rome, flouted the rules of the house, shielded by the parental umbrella, while he himself, obliged to atone for the inconvenience of his shameful birth, was bound to strict observance. His grandmother's standards had towered above his early childhood, blotting out the light, and she had never ceased to make him fully aware that his attempts to repay her hospitality and protection fell far short of his debt. He had shared her displeasure with his mother, who apart from teaching him to speak perfect English, left his upbringing to her own mother and escaped whenever she could with her friends. He had become skilled at identifying those friends of hers by their shoes, usually expensive shoes hand-cut from the softest leather, because he seldom raised his eyes to their faces. Eventually she had escaped finally and forever with one of the friends in one of the friends'overfast cars and his grandmother had informed him that death was the reward of sin. Before he had been able to think up a sin which might lead him to the same happy reward, a previously unknown father had arrived offering an alternative, an escape, a sort of after-life on earth. "He'll be back," his grandmother had threatened herself audibly, "when his so-called father's found out what he's like." But he had made sure that he never displeased this "so-called father" who seemed so confusingly ready to be pleased that pleasing him rapidly became a habit rather than an effort. That same father, he now recalled had said something about this trip "not being quite your scene, Pete," and he wondered fleetingly if Harry had known that he would find Jenny so unbearably self-assured, had suspected that he would not be strong enough to cope. With the need to prove himself, he leaped to his feet and fixed his water-bottle to his bike.

"Ready to move on?" he addressed Ham. "It's downhill all the way now." Ham nodded and Peter went on, looking at nobody in particular. "We'll go in single file: Lewis, then Jenny, then Ham and then me. Everybody wears a luminous jacket on this stretch." Without looking at her, he felt Jenny pull a face. "Come on, Jenny! You've no idea how well yellow suits you!"

Jenny blushed and scowled concurrently, but she donned her jacket in silence and they free-wheeled lazily down the smooth, black surface, catching glimpses of the loch between the humps of trees until they reached Glengarry Forest.

Lewis led the party down from the main road and along the rough track that led into the first car park.

"That *was* fun!" Jenny, dismounting from her bike, was all smiles and all italics. "And I'm *starving*! Good! Egg and cress sandwiches! My *favourite*."

"You made them, remember?" Even Ham, who had always lived with Jenny was surprised at her new-found enthusiasm.

"Still my *favourite*!" Jenny spoke with her mouth full and flourished her half-eaten sandwich ecstatically. She turned to Peter, "Would it be all right if we played in the river after lunch? It looks lovely and *cool*! Please! Pretty please!"

She was almost bouncing up and down with excitement like a ten year old child.

"We'll go and have a look," he replied cagily, adding, in an attempt to prolong this more malleable joie-de-vivre, "I'm sure we'll find a suitable spot. We've got just over an hour before Prue is due to collect us."

The river that wound through the forest with a confusing sense of direction, expressed its own adolescent mood-swings: now slow and sullen; now a fury of whiteness;

now posturing picturesquely with mini- waterfalls; now flirting round small stones to fill shallow pools. They chose one of the latter stretches. Peter, lying back on his elbows on the bank, watched indulgently through half-closed eyes their paddling, splashing each other and racing improvised boats and, suffering a short-term memory loss, decided that parenting was a piece of cake. He could afford to be more relaxed, he decided; could give them a bit of free rein; develop their initiative.

Jenny came out of the river with water cupped in her hands and poured it over his face. "To keep you cool," she said sweetly. "Aren't you coming in? We all want you!"

"Jenny," he sat up and addressed her as a colleague, "you know how Prue is coming to give us a lift back to the junction with the road to Kinlochhourn?"

"Aye, aye, Captain!" There was a hint of amusement in her voice but her smile was friendly.

"I'd really like to cycle all the way back. Do you think that you three could do the minor road on your own and look after each other? It's very quiet."

"Fine," she chirped. "Just fine! But only on condition that you come in now and get at least your big toe wet."

She held out her hand invitingly to pull him up.

How was he to know that Ham had made a water-bomb out of the cling-film wrapped around his sandwiches? Gasping with the shock of cold water while they all shrieked like banshees, he told himself firmly that he must laugh with them; that this was definitely initiation rather than dislike.

Out aloud he said, "Now I *will* have to ride back all the way to get myself dry."

Collapsed on the bank and weak with laughter, Jenny gasped, "If only I'd brought my camera."

He thought, just thought, of pushing her in.

"Sure you feel up to riding back, Ham?" Prue hesitated before helping him to unload his bike at the junction of the road to Tomdoun and the main road to Skye "If you like I could drop you off at Inchlaggan and you could do the last bit?"

He felt tempted.

"After all you're quite a bit younger than the others and you've done very well."

"Yes, go on, Ham. You go in the car," urged Jenny.

That settled it.

"I'll cycle," he said firmly. "Thanks…" he flung after Prue as she climbed back into the driving seat.

Ham mounted his bike and pedalled vigourously ahead, determined to show the stuff of which he was made. The other two appeared to be dropping further and further behind. He eased off his effort and still they lagged. He passed under the beeches and freewheeled lazily down past the long white house at Ardachy, past the old shearing shed to the slip road, just a short track, leading down to the loch and an improvised landing stage, There he skipped flat pebbles across the flat surface of the water until the swans swam across his range. They had cygnets, he noticed, grey and fluffy with untidily arranged feathers, and one of the adult swans was holding its wings out sideways into smooth round arches as though it was elbowing its way through the water.

The wheels of the other two bikes skidded on the gravel as they braked.

"Why did you wait?" Jenny sounded cross.

He ignored the question. "Wish there was a boat here," he said to Lewis.

"You can't even row!" snorted Jenny.

"Can so!" he retorted. "Learned at cubs."

Lewis removed himself from the bickering and walked out onto the landing stage. Jenny followed him with her eyes.

"Look!" Suddenly it was the kind sister voice speaking low, too low for Lewis to hear. "Look, Ham, you're so much faster that we are. You're a much better cyclist. You ride on to Tomdoun and wait for us there. I've got a couple of pounds. You could buy a coke at the *Rod and Reel* hotel and sit on the verandah and wait for us. We could have a rest here and then come on slowly to join you."

Ham looked towards Lewis but he was staring out towards the loch, shading his eyes to concentrate exclusively on the view.

"O.K.," he said and the money changed hands.

Better cyclist or not, by the time he had reached Inchlaggan, he was feeling the effects of his earlier efforts.

"Now pace yourself," Peter had said to him earlier. "Don't push it!" He liked Peter even if Jenny thought he was a pain and Lewis would probably like Peter too if he didn't think he had to agree with Jenny all the time. He rounded the bend into the coolness of the little birch wood and stopped in one of the passing places for a few sips of water. "Keeping hydrated is important," Peter had said. He was beginning to wish he hadn't listened to Jenny and water-bombed Peter. Peter had laughed, but still …

The little wooden gate leading off the passing-place had lettering on it. He spelled it out: *Garry Gualach.* He thought he had heard the name before. On an impulse he chained his bike to the fence, pushed open the gate and scampered down the steep path, leaping over the odd trailing fern, sure-footed and light, until he reached the shore of the loch. There was no house there; not even a shed; just a small improvised landing-stage and a rowing boat pulled up out of the water with the oars shipped inside. He grinned to himself, switched off his conscience, pushed the boat out until it floated and scrambled aboard. It was difficult rowing: more difficult than it had been at cubs on the rowing pond. It must be because of the current.

He seemed to be able to pull more strongly with his right arm than his left, which meant that the boat jerked forward in a series of semi circular movements. It was hot too. The steep river banks intercepted any breeze and the heat seemed to beat down from the sky and reflect back up from the water. But gradually he seemed to be picking up speed. "Got the knack of it now …" he panted to himself. "Just have a wee row … and then… put the boat back …No harm done …" and having spoken the hull of the boat bumped against something invisible and stuck fast, He strained on the oars without being able to move either forwards or backwards. Hanging over the edge of the boat to peer through the dark peaty water, he could still see no obstruction.

"Help!" he wailed, but his voice, dry and rusty in his throat, was sucked up by the heat around him.

He called again and again, but the only reply was the echo of his own voice and the scornful laugh of the gulls he disturbed.

After Ham's departure, Lewis continued to stand on the landing-stage and stare out over the loch 'for all the world,' thought Jenny, 'as though he doesn't realise that his golden opportunity has arrived.' Jenny, her expectations honed both by the *Dangerous Situations* section of the parent-approved sex education course at school and by the confidences of her more experienced class-mates, felt that her friend had definitely missed his cue.

"He's away," she called cheerfully when Ham was well out of earshot.

Lewis appeared to be intrigued by the gaps between the planks on the landing-stage. He knelt down to examine them minutely.

Jenny, knowing that he had demolished all his lunch, examined the remains of her own leftovers for a potential lure. The chocolate had melted into the sticky, inedible gunge her mother had predicted, but she still had a packet of crisps, a slice of fruit-cake and a can of coke with which to work.

"Time to picnic," she called in the organising, motherly sort of voice to which she could expect an instinctive reaction from him. He straightened up and joined her. She did not appear to be hungry so he finished her crisps and demolished the fruitcake and lay back replete with his eyes closed and his hands folded across his stomach.

"We'll have the coke sip and sip about," she suggested.

She took first sip, moistening her lips to make them wet and sweet and lay back beside him so that her arm just touched the hairs on his. She was encouraged to feel his arm quiver slightly in response, so much so that she became inventive.

"Oh, no!"

"What?" He half opened his eyes.

"I've got something in my eye. A bit of grass, I think. Could you take a look?"

He sat up. She remained lying down with one hand shielding the affected eye, but she lifted her chin helpfully up towards him.

"I'm not very good ..." he started.

"There's no-one else and I can't see," she wailed helplessly.

He bent over her obediently and removed her hand gently from her eye. "Try to open it."

If she could only just manage to flutter her eyelids. She could. And opened her mouth slightly so that he could see her soft, pink tongue lolling about between her coke-sweet lips. His hand was shaking slightly as he pulled down her lower lid, disclosing a rim of uncluttered but unattractive pink, like raw flesh. He would concentrate on that.

"It's just that you don't want to kiss me, isn't it?" Her voice shook with genuine humiliation.

"Course I do," he re-assured, "It's just that ..."He didn't finish because he could hardly say, "because I don't know how." He took a deep breath and brushed his lips experimentally against hers, but her soft pink tongue was an electric shock as it thrust hard, sudden and unexpected to meet his, a shock that somehow galvanised his right hand into pushing up her T-shirt and feeling for the bud of a nipple, any nipple, and then generated an urgency in his groin that was agony. He rolled over, away from her to hide the rapid swelling in his cycling shorts.

"Need a pee," he muttered gruffly and made off towards the whin.

Hot with sudden shame, Jenny pulled down her T-shirt, sat up, drained the last of her coke and burped aggressively. Then she flung the empty can viciously towards the loch.

"Non-bio-de-gra-dable," warned a sing-song teachery voice in her head.

"You *slag!*" went another, a school-girlish one this time, pure and scornful.

"And you've sent your little brother off on his own," reproached a third motherly one.

"Got what I deserved!" It was her own voice out loud. "But all I wanted was one bloody kiss. No big deal!"

She went and picked up the can before calling out in the direction in which Lewis had vanished, "I'm away. You can catch me up!" and left without awaiting his reply.

"Gross!" Jenny panted to herself as she rounded the bend into Inchlaggan, still with its cottages and its gardens and slowed down in case the collie moved from its recumbent position. "Got acne on the back of his neck! And he's so boring!"

A quick glance over her shoulder re-assured her that Lewis was not busting a gut to catch up with her. "Much he cares about me! I could be abducted …raped for all he knows!"

The collie raised its head obviously disturbed by this possibility, shook it in a "What is the world coming to?" gesture, yawned and settled its chin on its paws.

It was when she rounded the bend into the wood that she heard a bleating wail threading up from the river beneath and slowed down to listen. She saw Ham's bike abandoned in the passing-place at the same time as the second whimper reached her ears and was through the little wooden gate before her bike had fallen flat to the ground.

"I'm stuck!" he screamed when he saw the gleam of her yellow cycling hat through the riverside growth.

"I'm stuck!" he shrieked again when Jenny emerged on the shore.

From the shore, three-quarters of the way across the river and about seventy metres downstream, he looked tiny.

"The boat's stuck!" yet again with his voice breaking on a sob.

"It's all right, darling. I'm coming!" she called in the tone she usually reserved for Jelly.

She tore off her hat, kicked off her shoes and started wading through the river. The iciness of the water was hard, cold metal shackling her legs, colder and harder as it got deeper. She took a deep, shuddering breath for a parallel dive across the surface and started swimming hard. Her legs were so numb that she could not feel the resistance of the water as she kicked and her lungs seemed to be shrinking so that she had to gasp rapidly for air. She started counting her arm-strokes, reaching as far forward across the water as she could to pull her incredibly heavy body forward. She started to lose count and the cold wasn't blue it was black and it blotted out everything except Ham's annoying yelping, disturbing her peace. "Jenny! Jenny, are you all right?"

"Of course I'm all right, silly," she muttered.

Her legs had been pulled down under her, pushed up behind her, she was floating on her back. Then the river suddenly stopped carrying her, released her and her feet touched ground, still about six metres upstream from Ham. She could stand now, rocking slightly at first. With the water below her waist, the sun a warm shawl across her shoulders and the current behind her, she could wade, swinging her hips because of the stiffness of her legs. Ham, silent in the boat, wasn't just her brother. He had become pitiable; a small, frightened animal, whimpering, with tears on its cheeks.

"It's all right, darling," she said again very tenderly between breaths. "You're just stuck on a sand-bank. I'll push you out and then climb in."

Getting Ham afloat was the only easy part. Lifting the dead weight of her legs to clamber into the boat sapped all her strength, even with Ham pulling, and the boat tipped alarmingly. At last, she was slumped against the warmth of his body on the rowing-bench and feeling was returning to her lower limbs, spreading like pain down her legs. They took an oar each and zigzagged across, moving downstream between each pull until they reached the shallow water of the other side.

"But I found it up there!" Ham pointed dismally upstream to the landing-stage.

"O.K., we'll get out and tow it back up," Jenny decided. "It'll be easier that way."

Then as she bent over for the rope, she felt a sudden cramping pain in her stomach and threw up.

"Yuck!" remarked Ham, instantly forgetting his debt. "And you've been eating crisps and ..." he started accusingly.

"Shut up!" she retorted, wiping her mouth on the back of her hand. "Just shut up and pull, will you. I'm not doing all the work!"

Peter pounded his resentment onto his pedals as he rode up the eastern edge of the loch. How wise of John and Jane to parcel their brats off onto him while they enjoyed a stress-free stroll along the southern shore. As far as he was concerned the cycling trip was a never to be repeated failure.

The first part, cycling just with Ham along the quiet road, had admittedly been enjoyable. It wasn't the whole activity that rankled: it was Jenny's unpleasantness, her determination to resent authority which in this instance he had been unfortunate enough to represent. Lewis didn't appear to have a mind of his own. That was what he would say at feed-back time. John, self-opinionated clot, had actually time-tabled the evening: dinner from seven until half-past eight at the hotel; feed back-time over coffee, again at the hotel from half-past eight to nine; forward planning from nine to nine-thirty. During 'feed-back time' he would make it clear, speaking objectively and calmly, but stressing firmly the most pertinent words, that in his opinion loch-netting could *only* be enjoyed either *solo* or in *congenia*l company. Furthermore, if it was necessary for safety's sake to have a group leader, any member of the group refusing co-operation should be suspended from at least two future activities. Good! Except that he had a sneaking suspicion that Jenny might actually enjoy suspension. Pity his grandmother wasn't around with the leather belt with which she'd punished his minor, anticipated or imagined infringements. That would wipe the smirk off her face.

Jenny balked at his commands, made fun of him and belittled him in order to promote herself as leader. A dose of her own treatment might prove effective. His dirtiest weapon, the one most likely to inflict the maximum hurt was sarcasm. He recalled with a smile her discomfort when he'd quipped that yellow suited her: so some casually dropped personal criticism might further embarrass her. And then of course, he could always ignore her. All these tactics could humiliate …

Then again what would he gain by hurting Jenny? Nothing but self-disrespect. To-night he would simply admit that he found Jenny difficult to handle and leave it to her organising father to make sure she would become some-one else's responsibility next time round.

"Now enjoy your ride!" he commanded himself.

He turned off into a lay-by for a drink, removed his hat and let the wind lift the hair matted with sweat against his scalp. The lay-by was well placed scenically and he sat with his back against a forestry commission escapee pine, sniffing the warm resin of it and gazing out across the loch.

It came out of nowhere, without sound, the bird skimming the water and then ascending high above it, holding its position in the sky almost kestrel-like before stooping with a flash of white. The legs swung forward for a clean lift. He held his breath as it swooped low over the water, dipping almost to the surface with the weight of the fish gleaming wet, curling between its talons and then as it flew away with smooth unhurried flight to disappear amongst the pines on the far shore, he felt inexplicably as though his anger and resentment had been plucked from him and were being disembowelled somewhere amongst those distant pines.

"The bird visits to bring peace and enlightenment."

True! But he had learned that first the hard way. His grandmother had cherished a pastel print of a plump, meaty-looking dove, suspended in an impossibly vertical position, wings outstretched and holding a green sprig in its beak. In the background, behind the aura of "light" that haloed it as thickly and palpably as spilled egg yolk, there was nothing but water – black, black water – so that the poor bird had nowhere to land.

"That's the whole point," his grandmother had snapped impatiently when he had pointed out the lack of roosting facility.

"That's silly!" He had commented with unintentional irreverence.

"That bird," she had enunciated hard and cold, gripping him by the shoulders so that her horny fingers drove in just above his collar bones and shaking him as she spat out each word with short, hard jerks that made his head throb "is a *holy* bird. It is the symbol of peace. OF PEACE AND ENLIGHTENMENT!"

With the repetition of the last two words she had released his shoulders to deliver hard but rhythmically slaps across the side of his aching head and the whole episode had been painful enough for the ineradicable etching of this little childhood vignette upon his memory. After that he had always imagined that bird to be eyeing him with peculiar disfavour, as though he were a singularly inedible worm and when, some years later, one of his cousins smashed the picture with a football - and with impunity- only its lingering association with pain had prevented him from applauding.

Ham splashed along the river's edge, tugging the boat behind him, feeling it moving like a living thing, turning its nose to resist the current. He didn't know what Jenny was making such a fuss about: it was easy towing in the shallows when the current was sluggish and the water refreshingly cool around his ankles. She must be uncomfortable sitting on the sharp stones of the shore and there was a patch of nettles right behind her. He wondered if he should warn her and decided against it. If Chris were here they would both laugh their heads off when she shot into the air with a nettle-stung bum. It would be a good story to relate to Chris next month – about how he'd dared "borrow" the boat and row it almost right across the river through a strong current. He'd leave out the bit about the sandbank because that didn't really matter. He'd just say how he'd had to wait for the others to catch up and, to fill in the time, had taken himself for a row. He smiled in anticipation of Chris' reaction.

There was a tall figure on the landing-stage, standing hands on hips and staring straight towards him.

"Jenny!" he yelled for support, freezing momentarily in his tracks so that the prow of the boat caught him sharply behind the thighs. Then he saw it was only Peter and waved cheerfully but "only Peter" was bearing down upon him looking far from friendly.

"What the hell do you think you're doing with that boat?"

"I ... I went for a row." There was no time to think up any other explanation.

"You ..." Peter seemed to find it difficult to express himself and his voice sounded hoarse as though he'd done a lot of yelling on Sports Day. "You actually took a boat, some-one else's boat without their permission. You had the stupidity, the crass stupidity, to go out on the river with no life-jacket ... nothing?" His eyes flashed across to the crumpled heap that was Jenny. "Did she go with you?"

"N-not exactly," Ham muttered.

"But she let you do it?"

"N-not really ..." Ham was beginning to realise that solo heroism could entail solo blame, "but she did join me later."

Peter longed to seize the boy's shoulders and shake the story out of him, stop him from protecting his sister. "I'll tie the boat up. No!" He raised his hand to check any opposition.

"It needs to be done properly. Go and get … your sister." He could not bring himself to name her.

Ham trotted off obediently and stood over Jenny.

"Peter wants you," he relayed and added a warning to "watch the nettles" because he felt the necessity to get her on side.

She looked up and he saw that she was crying. Jenny crying?

"Stop gawping at me!" she snapped. "Go and tell his lordship I'll be along when I'm good and ready."

'Typical' thought Peter when Ham had repeated her words verbatim and had been pleased to see from the way Peter's eyes flashed in Jenny's direction that he had a comrade in disgrace.

With the boat secured and the oars checked, Peter addressed Ham tersely, "Stay here and don't move! Perhaps you can be trusted to do that."

He strode off towards Jenny and Ham heard him shouting angrily at her when he had covered only half the distance between them, but he couldn't make out the words. Jenny heard him clearly but remained immobile.

"Jenny, I'm up to here with your behaviour. You're out the box! Of all the teenagers I have ever known, you are quite definitely …" She was soaking wet. The thin folded arms in which her face was hidden were covered in goose-bumps. Her shoulders were shaking, either with laughter or weeping: probably the former, knowing Jenny.

"Just come on!" he finished impatiently. "In half-an-hour I've got to fetch the walkers."

Putting one hand behind her to push herself up, she encountered the nettles and with the shock of the sting, forgot to hide her face, ashen and streaked grey-brown from where she'd wiped at her eyes and her nose with muddy fingers. Peter knelt beside her, an arm hovering tentatively around her shoulders without actually making contact as though she were some kind of human cactus.

"Jenny," he coaxed gently, "Jenny, what on earth happened?"

She just shook her head, unable to speak at first and then blurted out almost incoherently between sobs, "I thought Ham was going to drown...I hate him ... I thought ..."

"You can tell me later," he interrupted. "Let's get you home. Ham," he stood up and shouted, "get over here!"

"Thought you said I wasn't to move," muttered Ham peevishly as he joined them.

"Leave out the cheek! Now, you and I are going to have to help Jenny back up to the road. O.K., Jenny?"

She nodded, submissive for once.

"Put your arms around our shoulders and we'll support you as much as possible."

Grateful for the help despite herself, Jenny found her strength returning as she moved and by the time they reached the narrow path up to the passing place, she could cope on her own with Peter beside her in case she needed support and Ham ahead, ostentatiously clearing odd bits of shrubbery out of their way.

"We'll not risk you on your bike," Peter said.

"I can manage." But she eyed the bike doubtfully as she spoke.

"No," he said firmly, "we'll hide it down the path and I'll collect it later. You can travel on my cross-bar – strictly illegal of course and uncomfortable, but the safest option. You'll need to put your hat on."

As she hitched herself onto the cross-bar, it did occur to Jenny that had Peter been younger and therefore fanciable, she would probably enjoy the lift. Peter was unfortunately a generation apart, but he had been very kind to her, despite the fact that she'd played him up.

"I'm sorry," she said indistinctly as they set off.

"What?"

"I'm sorry I was difficult and all that." Perhaps she should offer an excuse. "I'm going through a sort of phase," she tried lamely.

"That's all right," said Peter from somewhere above her hat. "We all have our phases."

April had spent a different day: a day in which she felt totally dispensable and didn't know whether she enjoyed it or not. Throughout her adult life she had been deferred to: at work by the entire factory staff; at home, which was more onerous, by May. Now May had departed on an expedition which Prue thought would develop her self-sufficiency and Prue and William, her companions for the day, were an independent unit, absorbed with each other. She was free to amuse herself but any ploy she *had* developed almost relied on interruption to sustain her interest and she had spent the day restlessly turning from one occupation to another with only herself to blame for their imperfect completion of anything.

She was pleased, therefore, when Lewis emerged from the shadows at the bottom of the drive: unexpectedly pleased, having dismissed him on their first meeting as a nondescript young man the sort she would be unlikely to employ as he had insufficient initiative for management and would prove a social misfit amongst the conveyor belt staff. He had not proceeded up the drive. He appeared to be inspecting the tyres on his bike. Then he described a few circles, testing his brakes so that the gravel spattered. He must be shy about being the first one home and she could do with having some-one to take under her wing. She went to the top of the drive and hailed him in a cheerful, hospitable voice. He cycled slowly up to her and stopped without dismounting as though ready to take off if necessary.

"Stiff and sore?" she enquired briskly.

"Sort of ...thanks." He was non-committal as though unsure of the correct response.

"Where are the others?"

"Peter decided to cycle all the way," he responded readily and then spun a pedal round looking down at it. "Ham ... the others ... have gone down to look at the river ...I think ... bikes in passing place next to the gate." He went on quickly, "I'd better go and change."

April felt herself dismissed. Prue was standing at the kitchen door with William on her hip as she re-entered the house.

"Reckon he's been up to something?" she grinned

"I don't think ... I don't know ..." April allowed herself the luxury of indecision. "Do you think William would like another walk?"

It was over an hour before the other three arrived home. Lewis had retreated to his tent where he lay on top of his sleeping-bag, shivering in his sweat because going to the house for a shower would only expose himself to a possible suggestion that he might like to cycle back and check on his companions. He told himself firmly that he was indifferent to their fate and could not be criticised for having ridden past the bikes without investigating. It was odd though that Ham's bike had been neatly propped against a tree and chained while Jenny's had just been flung down as though suddenly abandoned. That was Jenny all over. Impetuous! His mother was probably right about girls.

He heard his name called and Prue's legs in their blue jeans appeared at his tent opening. He crawled forward on his stomach and peered up at her.

"I'm taking the car up the road to check for the others," she said. "You come with me and show me where you found the bikes."

She left him no choice. By the time he'd reached the car, William had been strapped into his seat and was voicing his disapproval but before Prue could start the engine, Peter appeared at the foot of the drive with Jenny on his cross-bar and Ham trailing sulkily a metre or two behind. Lewis made it back to the tent, diving through the opening as the cycling party crested the drive. From his place of relative safety he listened in.

"O.K.?" he heard Prue's enquiry from close beside his tent. "Sh-sh," she soothed the still moaning William.

"Not altogether," Peter's voice held the hint of a smile in it, "but it's something to improve on."

"You mean you'll come again!" Jenny sounded surprised but pleased.

After all she'd said to him earlier about Peter! His mother had been spot on about girls being two-faced.

"Some-one's got to lick you into shape! Make a team of you!" Then he spoke quietly and Lewis guessed from the direction of his voice that he was addressing Prue. "Now Jenny could do with a hot, sweet drink, a warm bath and plenty of T.L.C..She stinks like pondweed and she's had one hell of a time."

"Of course," Prue replied and William's vehement protests probably meant that he was having to share his mother's attention with Jenny.

"You," Peter's voice was hard, must be speaking to Ham, "had better spend some time working out what to say to your parents if you want to escape their wrath. I shall be telling them the whole story. And you, Lewis," his voice shafted straight through the tent-flap, "will be explaining to me why you didn't stop when you saw the bikes, even if you and Jenny had had a tiff."

So that's what she'd told him. Lewis sighed with relief. He'd just stick to the same story and spare himself the details.

If Peter, analysing the cycling expedition as he escaped in the car to fetch some of the walkers, suspected that he could claim only limited success, John, slumped on a conveniently flat stone at the water's edge to loosen the laces of his walking boots, knew certain discontent. Unlike the cycling group, the walkers had suffered no lack of esprit de corps; if anything, there had been a surfeit of share and care. He could have done without Jane's repeated, "Are you all right, dear?" which gave the others the wrong impression. The twin disappointments had been the absence of most of the loch and, it must be faced, his own lack of physical fitness.

On the plus side, he had established his role of leader firmly, he felt, *and* without being at all overbearing right from the time they all edged their ruck-sacked bodies out of the cars into the car park in Glengarry Forest and waved Peter and April good-bye. "Gather round! Gather round!" he had invited, recognising in his own voice the comradely timbre he reserved for the sixth year elite in their last term and furthermore, he had good-humouredly ignored May's whispered prattling, partly to herself, partly to June, as he attempted to instruct. Feeling that Harry might recognise the fact that his instructions were lifted straight from Bellingham's *Guide to Rambling for Schools*, he had been careful to intersperse merry quips, at which they had tittered. Solely in order to avoid embarrassing the female contingent, he had chosen to omit the instructions re *the disposal of human waste when the bowels are activated by exercise*. In any case, he had left the shovel at home and suspected that the plastic teaspoon in his packed lunch would be inadequate. He had, after all, warned them all not to eat fruit at breakfast nor to include it in their packed lunches. He had ended his instruction on a gallant note. "It is important that we all keep together, walking at the pace of the slowest walkers. So, ladies, if you would like to proceed …" And with a mock bow, he had motioned them forward.

He would have conceded that Jane's fitness probably matched his own or even, seeing she had become the chief dog-walker, that she had the slight edge over him. June was obviously sturdy and durable. May, he felt, he could rely on to be the least athletic member of the group. There he had made his mistake. Her regular attendance at the gym where she laboured assiduously as much out of deference to her father's memory – for it was he who had arranged membership for all factory staff – as to validate her painfully undefined staff status, had built up remarkable stamina for her years and that, coupled with her exuberant nervous energy, sent her scampering forward at an unforeseen turn of speed.

"Slow down!" he panted to her after the first mile. "You have to pace yourself, you know!"

"I think you're going a bit fast for him," Jane translated, adding quickly as she saw May flinch at the hint of potential criticism, "You're doing awfully well!"

May had frowned fleetingly in failure to comprehend how, by simply walking, she could merit such praise, how she could be "doing awfully well", then interpreted it merely as an overture to friendship and remained clamped to Jane's side for the rest of the walk, twittering happily and harmlessly – Jane told herself repeatedly that it was harmless – about the lustre of Jelly' coat, the blueness of the sky, the intermittent visibility of the loch and the delicious tastiness of her sandwiches. Jane had kept on smiling indulgently and when May asked her where she should put her lunch wrapping, restricted herself to indicating May's rucksack.

For most of the way, the track was wide enough for the party to walk in pairs. Jane and May led with Jelly, followed by June on her own and then Harry and John who gradually seemed to fall some distance behind. May, happy enough to defer to her new friend for her needs, did not attempt to engage June in conversation and Jane, after a few opening gambits had been greeted merely with a smile and a nod, concluded that June had hearing problems and made no further efforts. June was indeed experiencing hearing problems. In the absence of her headphones, for she had reluctantly decided that it would be anti-social to plug herself in, she found herself involuntarily playing the *Hebridean Overture* in her head.

Watching her square frame press on doggedly ahead with even-paced, rhythmic strides, Harry recalled an article he had scanned during an over-long stretch in the dentist's waiting-room about how it was possible to read walkers' personalities from the way they moved. Fit though June undoubtedly was, there was a tension in the hunching of her shoulders and her motionless arms with their defensively jutting elbows which suggested to him that she saw the walk as an extension of duty rather than a source of pleasure. He found himself wondering vaguely if she had a life beyond duty. John, beside him, was labouring somewhat. He had become silent, saving his breath for the effort of the walk. He had already made several stops, ostensibly to record entries in the note-book he carried and now he made yet another, mopping his face with his handkerchief before taking out his note-book.

"The others should be looking round more instead of racing on ahead." His voice was unnaturally high, almost whining. "*We* are having to make observations for the *entire* party."

Harry peered short-sightedly over his shoulder. "Did you make a note of the crossbills?" he asked.

"N-no, not yet. Well I mean I saw them of course but I didn't think them sufficiently loch-side, if you know what I mean …"

Harry was not sure that he did. He pursed his lips and suggested gently, "Maybe, as this walk isn't strictly loch-side, we should include anything of note that we see."

"Of note, yes," John conceded, trying to remember whether Jane had ever mentioned crossbills when listing the common garden birds she fed. "Of *note*!"

Harry went on persuasively, "After all this is the track others will follow once your idea catches on."

"Right!" agreed John and wrote down "cross-bill" with a hyphen.

Harry observed that he had not put it under the forest section, but decided it would be wise to suggest the adjustment later on, given that the others were now out of sight.

They had caught up with the others at yet another forestry commission gate and cattle grid which gave not onto more forest but onto rough pasture where a small stream ran along the side of the road and sheep, eyed hungrily by Jelly, were dotted around rough pasture. Jane had removed her socks and walking boots and was sitting by the stream with her feet in the ice-cold water. She had looked up at John and smiled, "Sometimes I think you can drink through your feet," she said. "Come and try it."

Too weary even to unlace his boots, he had sunk down onto a convenient boulder inconveniently placed in the sunlight, surreptitiously wiping the sweat off his face with the back of his shirt sleeve while all the rest who had joined Jane, made a neat row sitting alongside the stream I t was like picking teams when he was at school with nobody ever wanting to be in his team. They were sitting with their backs to him so that he had been unable to catch or join in with their threads of conversation.

The fact that the others had had to put on their socks and boots again gave him a head start and he was at last able to lead his small party down past a farmyard with tractors, past a farmhouse where a friendly looking farmer's wife came out to hush her barking collies until rounding a bend and crossing a bridge they were walking alongside him with their backs at last to Ben Tee which meant, surely, that they were on the homeward strait. Temptation had appeared in the guise of a farm truck which passed them, slowed down just ahead of them and waited.

"Anyone want a lift?"

John had not known just how he had found the strength to refuse. He had insisted on another three stops "for everybody's sake" before they reached the pick-up point and growling at the back of his mind had been the certainty that they all knew that he was the one who needed them most. When he finally slumped down on his last rock to wait for April and Peter tears were stinging in his eyes and he turned his back on his party and gazed out over the loch.

Jane was standing with her hand lightly on his shoulder, saying nothing.

"It's no good," he said dully. "I've left it too late. I'm too old for all this lochnetting carry-on. I wish I'd never started it."

"That's where you're wrong," she said very definitely. "It will never be as difficult as it was today. You'll get stronger as we do more. One day you'll think of this walk as being just a short stroll. You've been wonderful the way you've kept going," she added patting his shoulder. "I really thought you were going to jump onto that truck."

"So did I!" he laughed and laid his hand on top of hers on his shoulder.

Behind the barn, well out of view of the kitchen door, Ham sat by the stream that ran a straight purposeful course down its stony path towards the river below with the icy water on his feet as his only comfort. Jenny had been swept into the house to be mothered by Prue. Lewis, in their tent was apparently asleep, not speaking anyway. Peter was not only furious with him himself, he was even going to grass him up. Fancy telling him to think up excuses! There were none. Peter knew that.

He heard the cars crunch across the loose stones on the drive and the doors open onto voices. That silly May was laughing and Jelly was barking.

"Ham!" That was his father's voice. Of course his mother would have rushed inside to make sure that darling-little-horrible Jenny was all right. Peter must have told on him in the car when he collected them. He could have waited until his parents were less tired and grumpy.

"Ham! Over here now!"

What? Was he going to tell him off in front of everyone? Typical!

"Ham! Ham! If I have to come and look for you, you'll be sorry!"

Wouldn't make any difference.

"Ha-am!" That was his mother. Two against one. "Ha-am! Sorry, Lewis, I thought he might be in the tent. Ha-am!"

Then it was all over with Jelly's excited yelps as she rounded the back of the barn and buried her cold nose between his elbow and his side in welcome. Three against one! Standing over him the parent-force was big. Seeing there was no-one else there, he started to cry but they were merciless. His father still found him "thoughtless, senseless, disobedient and untrustworthy". His mother still accused him of "helping himself to what did *not* belong to him". Did he know the word for that? Well, did he? He howled more pitifully. Still unmoved and in unison they declared themselves shocked and ashamed. "Totally shocked and ashamed!" Did he realise he could have caused his sister's death?

No, he hadn't. In horror at the thought he stopped crying.

There were a few moments of silence except for the trickling of the burn and the rasp of Jelly's tongue as she washed herself, obviously unwilling to take sides. Then the inevitable sentencing. He would not be eating at the hotel. They would park the car where they could keep an eye on him while they enjoyed their dinner and he could please himself as to whether he would make sandwiches out of scraps left over from lunch or go hungry.

"Just for tonight?"

"Tonight and tomorrow night," spelled out his father clearly with cruel emphasis, "and if we are extremely lucky that might teach you to think before you act."

With that they departed. Jelly went with them without a backward glance. Presumably she was going to get her dinner now. How would they feel if he were to make himself dogmeal sandwiches? Sorry? He doubted it!

With the light drawing up slowly, almost imperceptibly from earth to sky, Harry and Peter lingered on the verandah of the hotel after the others had left by car enjoying the softening of definition, the water-colour blur of the landscape before them. The exuberant bulk of the birches on the boundary of the field below welled up into a greyish-green cluster of earthbound cumulus nimbus The tiny dark shapes that moved on the hill sides opposite were red deer grazing and browsing as they wound their way around the folds of the slopes: those that remained stationary were presumably rocks or logs.

"Mind if I smoke?"

The question was rhetorical. Harry had already stuffed his pipe and Peter merely smiled absently as the glow of the match lit up the soft pink pouches of flesh on the inside of Harry's leathery hand as he shielded the flame against the intermittent evening breeze that flapped the Virginia creeper lightly against the walls. He drew slowly and exhaled.

"Good meal."

"Excellent!" agreed Peter. "And I must say I was ready for it. Poor old Ham with his baked bean sandwiches."

"He deserved them!" Harry was merciless. "What he did could have ended in tragedy."

"And it would have been partly my fault because …"

"Rot!" Harry took the pipe out of his mouth and swivelled his head round on his scraggy neck to face Peter belligerently. "Bloody rot! How on earth do you work that one out? My dear boy, we all know you're God's gift to the legal profession but as far as I know sixth sense has still eluded you."

Peter, reddening at the sharpness of his tone, started to explain, "You see I reckon I should have stayed with them. *I* sent them off on their own. And I did it mainly because I wanted rid of Jenny."

"Why you did it is irrelevant. They would have been completely safe if they'd followed instructions."

He tugged at his pipe and screwed up his eyes at the possible red deer before continuing. "You know if you're going to assume responsibility for everything – whether it's your fault or not – you're going to lead a dog's life."

"Well if it's a life like Jelly's, I really wouldn't mind," grinned Peter, hoping to introduce a lighter note.

Harry, stung by the suspicion that one of his very rare attempts at fatherly advice was being dismissed too lightly, was determined to hammer the point home.

"I mean it, Peter. You seem to think you have to subject everything you've done that hasn't been quite perfect to a rigorous post-mortem when really what is required is a decent burial." He tapped the bowl of his pipe on the table intermittently to emphasise his words, dislodging a scattering of ash. "You've got to relax. Got to … I don't know… not mind making mistakes, being in the wrong, being human. Just lower your standards will you and *leave the ash alone*, damn it. In the scale of things, ash simply does not matter. Peter, you're a man, not an anally retentive robot."

"Robots," pronounced Peter in a cold, tight voice, "do not I think, have anuses. Or would it be 'ani'?"

Harry didn't reply. There was a silence between them. And a great distance. They were as far apart as Scotland and Italy; as widely separated as the loneliness of a stifled childhood from the loneliness of incipient old age. A bat flitted across the sky line, looping and scooping in indirect passage, calling inaudibly to find its way forward.

"I'm really sorry, mate," Harry said at last, speaking very quietly. "I've gone and shot my mouth off. It's just that … you've made me proud and I want you to be happy." There he'd managed it. He turned his head again to face Peter, "Can we just bury all this and have another whisky together?"

Peter smiled, dismissed as being of secondary importance his theory about alcohol and dehydration after exercise and said, "Yes, but let me get them. You sit still and fix your pipe. You're looking tired."

He disappeared through the door and Harry suddenly realised that he was not only tired but cold as well. He knocked out his empty pipe and followed Peter into the warmth and brightness of the bar.

Chapter Ten

The First Expedition

Loch Poulary

Waking early because his stiff body was uncomfortably cramped within the confines of his sleeping bag, John woke Jane to seek her opinion on his programme for the day ahead.

"Oh, just go with the flow!" He thought he could detect a note of impatience in her voice and his suspicions were confirmed as she went on briskly, sitting upright and looking fiercely down at him, "For heaven's sake, John, this is supposed to be a leisure pursuit. Your – our - findings on Loch Garry, Loch Poulary or any other bloody loch don't have to be exhaustive or conclusive. I thought the point was to start something which could be continually updated. No?"

"There's no need to shout," he hissed.

She had not been shouting but the walls of their tent were not even canvas: they were that new-fangled, lightweight stuff and he felt it would be inappropriate and unsettling – unsettling was the better choice of word – for the others to hear that he, their leader, was himself under instruction.

He pulled on his jeans painfully, walked stiff-legged through an incipient drizzle up the rise behind the barn and peed long and hard against the trunk of a diminutive pine. A battery of midges rose up in protest from the long grass around the base of the tree and he zipped up hurriedly.

"Just go with the flow," he muttered to himself. "Does she want me to abdicate all responsibility?"

Over breakfast there did not seem to be any flow to go with. Jenny's absence (she had been granted breakfast in bed as a concession to her having suffered at the hands of her brother the day before) leant a certain blandness to the tone of the conversation. They ate, slouching in their chairs or leaning heavily forward on their elbows and were apparently incurious about the day's events. Frustrated, John gathered up the shreds of his authority and directed them towards Ham.

"Steady on!" he ordered. "Five rounds of toast are more than enough!"

"Yes, if you've been able to guts yourself the night before," retorted Ham, answering back cheekily as though he had forgotten that his rations had been limited as a well-deserved punishment. He stretched across for yet another slice.

"Leave the table!" commanded John. A bit hard but how could he expect others to have any faith in him when his own son showed him such disrespect.

Ham put down his toast and left behind him a silence even more awkward than before.

"Everybody's exhausted," salvaged Jane, "including Ham. He's hardly ever cheeky. John, what about giving us the morning to do our own thing and we could perhaps do something together this afternoon?"

That's what she meant by "going with the flow": a euphemism for a take-over bid. He opened his mouth to say, "but we are supposed to be doing Poulary, looking at Loch Quoich", noticed in time the relief on every face and emended it just in time to, "Just what I was about to suggest!"

John had allotted to himself non-specific chores or, as he put it to the others, "I'll fill in." This, he had thought would give him the opportunity to act in a tactfully non-supervisory capacity. May could have told him that he would end up by being a dog's body but May was not into analysing her own situation and he was not into seeking an opinion on his decisions from anyone, let alone May. This morning it was Jenny's turn to help wash up but Jenny was taking full advantage of her status of semi-invalid thereby creating a vacancy which he seemed to be expected to fill. He sighed, picked up the tartan dish-cloth which April handed to him without looking at him and gazed gloomily out the window at one of the column of electricity pylons that strode across the hill behind the cottage.

"What man does to nature," he remarked didactically, "is immoral."

The mention of immorality galvanized April into shaking her marigolds relatively free of soapsuds and gazing at him questioningly. Her own moral code, inculcated during childhood, embraced the humanitarian version of the Ten Commandments, the rights of the worker and the responsibility of management but did not relate to the realm of nature.

"Those pylons," he elucidated, rubbing the window clear of steam for a sharper glower.

April knew a sudden irrational resentment.

"They're not the prettiest things in the world maybe," she conceded. "You may find them distasteful. But have you stopped to think what it was like for the people living here – the real people rather than casual droppers in – before we had electricity. It might be ever so romantic doing everything by candlelight but I can assure you that in winter when warmth and hot food are necessities for life, there's not all that much space for romantic illusions."

John felt snubbed and retaliated, "Sorry, you'll have to do this fork again. Not up to standard."

She took the fork, ignoring the comment, and scrubbed at it vigourously with a long-handled brush.

"People and their romantic notions about unspoiled countryside have a lot to answer for," she continued remorselessly. "Take the dams for example. There are two near here – one at Loch Quoich and one at Loch Loyne. What a hue and cry some folk – mainly those who didn't live here - made! Well the dams brought us cheaper energy and much needed employment ..."

"*Us?*" he queried with a crooked grin, working his dishcloth so firmly around the rim of a glass that it squeaked, "You consider yourself a local then?"

April had never thought to categorise her status. She couldn't claim to be a local but neither was she a tourist.

"I feel I belong," she said eventually.

They finished the washing up in silence, April enjoying a sudden surge of contentment and John even more convinced than earlier that things were not turning out as he had envisaged. April's points of view coming from a true, weather-beaten, local venerable with a lilt to his voice and eyes trained to focus beyond the horizon, would have been welcome and valued. Coming from the Edinburgh next-door -neighbour and a subordinate team member at that, hardly even a team member, more of a camp follower, they were definitely out of place.

After the last dish John did not wish to linger in the kitchen.

"Must go and make some arrangements," he offered vaguely by way of an excuse to April.

Outside the drizzle had matured into a heavy downpour falling almost silently, just the sky seeping into the earth. It completely obscured the heads of the pylons so that the strings between them swooped intermittently from nowhere to nowhere. Despite the wet, just outside the kitchen door Ham was playing keepie-up with his football, rather unsuccessfully because his view of the ball was impeded by the hood he had pulled over his head against the rain. He looked up as the door opened and held the muddy ball to his chest with both grimy hands.

"Dad," he whispered and John, realizing that the child had been waiting for him, swallowed the criticism of his filthy state.

"Dad, I'm sorry I was cheeky."

John hugged him, filthy ball and all, and together they crossed the squelching grass to the barn.

Nobody looked at him as they entered. Harry had a leaflet spread out before him on the table and was busily scribbling notes in what John recognised as a school jotter; Lewis and Peter were absorbed in a game of chess; Jane and May were engaged in building a tower of brightly coloured bricks for William and Prue was trying to persuade him not to knock it down before it was completed. He sat down gingerly on a vacant chair and pretended to be absorbed in the *Atlas of Scotland*.

Harry looked up, leaving a forefinger midway down his leaflet to keep his place.

"Picked this up from the hotel last night," he said as though aware that John was not fully absorbed in the *Atlas of Scotland* and would welcome distraction.

"Uh-huh?" John kept his eyes on his book.

"Apparently Ham exposed himself to greater danger than we realised. Listen to this: '...legend has it that at least one water kelpie was reputed to live in the River Garry and, over the years, was responsible for the deaths of several children. In one instance a child saw a horse feeding on the rich grass at the edge of the river and tried to catch it by throwing his arms around its neck. The creature immediately flung up its head, neighed and made for the river. When he tried to let go, the child found he was stuck fast to the horse's neck and cried for help. His sister, trying to prise him off, stuck hard to him and so in turn did the children, seven in all, who came to help. The piteous cries of the children were heard while the hoofs churned up the shallow waters and then the waters closed over all the heads and there was a deathly hush.'"

"There were some horses – ponies actually – on the far side of the river ..." Ham started thoughtfully.

"And if only you'd grabbed one of them!"

Jenny stood in the doorway. She didn't look as though she'd just got up thought John. She could have done the washing up instead of arranging her hair.

"Any more interesting bits?" asked Jane.

"Oh, aye! Amongst other pieces of info, the road we walked yesterday round the North side of Loch Garry is called the *Coffin Road* because it was the route which the crofters on the other side of the loch used to take when they needed to carry a body to the graveyard at Invergarry There are also bits and pieces about fishing – Loch Loyne is mainly pike, Loch Poulary is ..."

"Don't need to tell *me* about fishing," John broke in. "Dad fished all these lochs."

He looked round to see what impression he had made on his listeners, but when Harry had stopped speaking, they had reverted to their occupations.

"I rather thought," he said slowly and pointedly, "that we would be gaining our information from the locals rather than using ready printed bumf available to every Tom, Dick and Harry."

"And is there any reason why we shouldn't do both?" Jane's tone was sharp and he could feel her glare boring into the back of his neck. After all their years of marriage did she not know him well enough not to suspect him of anything as petty as jealousy?

"Where d'you think we'll find the locals then?" mocked Jenny. "You can count me out if you're planning on a door-to-door do." Her argument gathered momentum. "It's not safe. One of the locals could be a murderer or a rapist or a child molester, or ..." she ran out of inspiration.

"Or a drug-dealer or a mugger," supplied Ham, looking enthusiastic about the project.

"Don't be so silly, Ham," snapped John. "I'd planned on sending people round in pairs of course."

"Just like Jehovah's Witnesses," Jenny explained soothingly to her indignant brother, "except, Ham, I have to say you look more like ..."

"If you think about it, we might see quite a few locals at the hotel this evening," Jane interrupted, "and we could look for more leaflets there as well."

She looked up to smile from John to Harry as she spoke.

"Diplomat extraordinaire!" muttered John sarcastically to himself.

It was painfully obvious that William had no intention of tiring of his demolition game. Jane felt her broodiness palling and her indulgent smile stiffening into an enforced rictus. Furthermore her left leg was numb from the cramped position she had assumed on the hard floor.

"Pins and needles!" she remarked briskly, struggling to her feet and flexing her leg.

May looked up, simultaneously smiling her sympathy and frowning at her own helplessness at suggesting an appropriate remedy. Ham and Prue continued slavishly with their building and shrieking "Whoopsadaisy!" .

"I think you did too much yesterday," John remarked. "You're not used to that much exercise."

She had no option but to stifle the retort, which lodged suffocatingly in the hollow of her throat between her collarbones, and walked towards the door. The rain had eased back into a sullen drizzle. Intermittent drips from the guttering forged a vertical, semi-permeable barrier round the barn and splashed into little hollows worn into the earth by year after year of intermittent dripping.

June, in waterproof jacket and trousers appeared at the open kitchen door of the cottage, speaking over her shoulder to some-one, presumably April in the kitchen behind her. On seeing Jane she froze as though caught in some subversive activity, and then nodded.

"Need to stretch my legs," she said tersely as though she felt an excuse was required.

Jane interpreted this correctly as, "Need to escape from this enforced camaraderie including you," and nodded back her understanding.

"Good idea," she said and watched June push her ear plugs into position and escape down the drive before she turned back to the company in the barn behind her.

"Rain or no rain, I'm going for a walk," she asserted and added casually, "Anybody coming?"

John took off his reading glasses and screwed up his eyes to regard her as though she were an obscure, even alien, species yet to be identified.

"And I thought we agreed to go with the flow," he observed, raising an eyebrow.

"Yes, well I'm creating flow for anyone who wants to go with it ," snapped Jane, "and Jelly's capable of creating quite a lot of flow if she's not walked very soon."

"Well," drawled John, replacing his glasses and turning his attention back to the notebook in which he had scribbled his findings of the day before, "certainly those who want to must feel free to accompany you. Unfortunately, I have too much paperwork."

"There you see," Jane could not curb her reaction to his pomposity, "you all have permission. I'm going to get waterproofed."

Struggling into her waterproof trousers in the cramped space inside her tent she addressed Jelly who had followed her and was loyally shaking her wet fur onto John's sleeping-bag,

"Jelly, if I ever retake my marriage vows remind me to leave out the 'for worse' part."

Ten minutes later she shut the door on John's well-meant advice to walk Indian file on the side of the oncoming traffic if they were to follow the road and set off accompanied by Ham, Jelly, Lewis and Peter. Ham scooped up his football from a muddy puddle next to the barn and stuffed it up his sweatshirt.

"So Dad doesn't see it and say, 'Ham, it's not safe to kick balls on the road,'" Jane heard him confide to Lewis in a cruelly perfect imitation of John at his teachery worst.

"Well, wait until we're on a straight stretch of road and you can see ahead," she compromised. "Shall we go towards … Kinlochhourn?" hesitating before Kinlochhourn because Poulary was actually the next stop on the road to Kinlochhourn, but to say "Let's go towards Poulary," would be carrying insurrection a step too far.

Lewis and Ham raced ahead in search of the straight stretch leaving Peter and Jane to lag behind. They fell even further behind because Jelly, on the lead, protested at her restriction by peeing onto every cowpat, sheep dropping or rabbit dropping at lead's length. Still, it gave Jane the chance she had been waiting for.

"I'm sorry about yesterday," she said. "That nasty incident with Ham and the boat must have spoiled your cycling trip."

Peter opened his mouth for a polite denial, closed it and tried to analyse how he did feel in retrospect. If he were to be honest – and Jane invited honesty – he felt guilt.

"It was mostly my own fault actually," he said. "I should have been the one sentenced to baked bean sandwiches. I shouldn't have left the three of them alone together just because I wanted to cycle all the way."

Unexpectedly she laughed a dry little snort of laughter before replying, "You probably needed your solo cycle ride," she said. "You must have had quite enough of Jenny by then. Terrible mother that I probably am, I was delighted that she hadn't opted for the walk and ..." she broke off and pointed to a cluster of purple in a hollow by the roadside, "just look at those marsh orchids. Masses of them."

"M-m-m-m." Shocked by Jane's admission, Peter's appreciation of the orchids was muted. He really liked Jane and was trying desperately to reconcile her surprisingly lax attitude to motherhood with his own exacting standards, with the blackness and whiteness of the bleak moral code he set for himself and others. From his cousins' jibes when out of adult earshot, his uncles' and aunts' indiscreet observations and his grandmother's pointed silences he had been aware from earliest childhood that his own personal family life deviated in every possible way from the perfect norm as upheld by St.Paul-as-interpreted-by- St. Grandmother and that somehow original sin appeared to have originated with him. He would have hoped that Jane Maitland, her sexuality blissfully enshrined in matrimony, and her children dutifully conceived in wedlock, would at least be making some pretence at embracing the ideals of motherhood.

In the confines of the enclosed space they were inhabiting, the bubble of air locked between the low cloud overhead, the loch mist rising to one side and the hill fog descending from the other, his thoughts must have transmitted themselves clearly to Jane.

"We love Jenny very, very much," she explained gently, "but she's going through an adolescent phase just at the moment which is quite exasperating."

Beyond the bend in the road, in another world, he could hear the football throbbing on the road.

"Yes," and he smiled down at her, "she told me she was

going through a phase when she apologised."

"Apologised?" They had rounded the bend onto the straight stretch. Jane bent to release Jelly and she bounded off to join the boys and the football. "Well if she apologised you've achieved more than we ever have. You'll have to teach us the secret of your success."

"I think she felt really guilty." He frowned as he tried to recollect the scene with the limp, unnaturally subdued Jenny on his crossbar leaning against him for support. "I *do* like Jenny," he added truthfully, "even though I definitely did not like her earlier that day and I think I *can* understand how you love her and yet want to escape from her."

"She's sweet, horrible, charming, rude, loving us, hating us …"Jane left the catalogue incomplete. "I expect I was the same at her age. How about you?"

Peter thought hard. After a few more metres of navigating the puddles draining from the varying camber of the road he said, "I don't think I did adolescence really. I suppose growing up is wanting to please other people, then wanting to please yourself and then trying to do both. I think I had to miss the middle bit out."

He looked down at Jane, needing some sort of endorsement of his theory, but her head was down as she negotiated her own passage through the puddles.

"Well, you've made Harry a proud man," she said eventually and he had to be content with that because they had reached the rough Forestry Commission road leading down from the main road to Loch Poulary and the boys and Jelly were awaiting direction.

"Would you like to go down?"

Peter hesitated. Jane would like it if they 'did the loch.' John would not like it. Harry would say, "Please yourself."

The rain had drawn up into bulbous white cloud and the small loch at his feet reflected that ceiling and lay smooth and heavy, a pool of mercury trapped between the soft slopes of pastureland on one side and the sharp serrations of pine on the other. Irregular columns of thin cloud, waif-like in their flimsiness, drifted across the metallic surface from the south west, rising instinctively as they neared the banks of fir to claw their way uphill, threading over and around the points of pine.

"Let's do it," he said.

"If we just did the eastern side, perhaps," said Jane. "We haven't time to go all the way round before lunch and that does leave the forestry side for the others."

Even though the distance was not far, the edges of the loch were frayed, unravelling along the grass verge, and with the ground unbelievably soggy underfoot, their progress was laboured. As they had to walk in single file along the narrow path, more of a sheep track really, conversation was limited to hazard warnings such as, "Look out! Deep puddle! or "Slippery stones here!" Jelly, in no mood to race ahead, skulked reproachfully at Jane's heels and Lewis' alternate grunts and sighs communicated his dissatisfaction non-verbally.

"That was some walk!" remarked Ham as they started up the gentle slope across firmer ground to rejoin the road.

"The more difficult a thing is, the more credit to you for having done it," puffed Jane morally. "You can feel really pleased with yourself."

"All I feel is really hungry," said Ham. "All right for you lot scoffing your guts out again tonight." Having reached the road he pushed his football down out of his sweatshirt. "Look! I'm having a baby!" he declared. "Come on, Lewis!"

"I'm tired," responded Lewis and it was Peter who kicked with him along the homeward journey leaving Jane to attempt to initiate conversation with Lewis, a futile task which she abandoned after the first hundred metres.

If Peter had difficulty with his moral code, needing to

adjust it from time to time, giving it increasing elasticity of tolerance as he warmed towards aberrants like Jane whose concept of the ideal – in her case the obligations of motherhood – seemed to be shaped by life rather than to shape her life, May experienced no such difficulty. Her moral code was purely and simply to do what was expected of her and never to remain idle and it never occurred to her to sit in judgment on those whose expectations she was expected to fulfil. Her instructions for the day from April had been to 'help Prue entertain the guests' with the form the entertainment was to take left alarmingly unspecified. John's disapproving scowl on Jane's proposed departure had been sufficient to prevent her from accompanying the outing to Poulary; John and Harry, their heads bent over John's notebook which they were attempting to decipher, were non-reactive to the hospitable smiles she flashed nervously across at them; Jenny, her long legs slung gracefully over the arm of a chair was paging through a magazine , smiling to herself at secret thoughts which May felt instinctively she could never have shared and Prue was concentrating all her entertainment skills on William. Any attempt on her part to address William would certainly be met with blank silence: William still didn't have a name for her; didn't recognise her role in his world of family. If she were to attempt a dialogue with Prue, he would doubtless scream his indignation at the interference to his monopoly of his mother. She could therefore regard her entertainment task as covered and it was time to report for further duty.

After calling April's name several times and gaining no response, she eventually cornered her in the little sitting-room, sitting upright in an upright chair in front of a coal fire, deep in a slim paperback volume entitled *A Guide to Satisfaction at Work for Employer and Employee* by Caroline Parry. She looked up with a frown as May entered, sighed and managed a tight, little smile.

"Everyone happy?" she asked despairingly, hoping against hope that a negative answer could engender further employment for May.

May nodded.

April returned to her book, searching with an index finger for her place on the page she was reading.

"I could dust in here," May suggested brightly. "Keep you company."

"Good idea!" April looked up as she spoke but her finger remained firmly on the page, "But don't mind if I don't talk. I have to concentrate on this. I need to digest it properly before we return."

May began her dusting routine with a strained attempt at perfect silence that was more distracting than William at his noisiest, tiptoeing on the balls of her feet so that apart from the odd giveaway squeak of a floorboard, April could never be quite sure where in the room she was, moving the heavy furniture gingerly across the thick pile of the carpet, scratching the surface of April's concentration. April found herself pricking up her ears for the breathy sighs, the gentle clicks as china ornaments were replaced or the muted tap of a picture frame against the wall that would indicate May's position in the room, as though she were awaiting a fly she wanted to swat. The crash of the picture when it fell brought the same relief to the mounting silence as thunder when humidity builds up to an intolerable level.

"Oh!" May shrieked, the need for silence forgotten. "Mother's picture!"

The oil painting of the cottage, the work of their mother, had fallen onto the coal scuttle. The heavy frame was still intact but when they lifted it, it was to find that the black knob on the lid of the brass coal scuttle had penetrated the canvas and in lifting it, they ripped it further.

"I'm sure we can have it mended, May," soothed April,

her arm round the shaking shoulders of her sobbing sister. "Mother would understand. It wasn't your fault. The string has worn. Look, it's all frayed. Don't cry so."

It was her genuine distress for her sister that put the idea in her head although at the time it was nothing more than an attempt to drag May's attention away from the damaged painting.

"It really is time you took up your painting, May," she said firmly. "You really should start sketching again.: Mother used to love your drawings. It's a talent you got from her."

May blew her nose loudly and looked to her sister for further instruction.

"What … what should I sketch?"

"Those flowers over there. Those bluebells you picked yesterday." April indicated the vase on the window-sill. "I've plenty of typing paper. It'll do to start with."

May was still sketching the bluebells when the Poulary walk returned and dimly, through the sitting-room window, she overheard the hissing of the altercation in the front garden behind the redcurrant bushes where John and Jane were giving vent to their annoyance with each other, believing themselves to be out of earshot. But she just smiled. They were in their world and she was in hers. When she finished the flowers, she would, she thought, tackle her own sketch of the cottage. After all it had stopped raining and she could tuck her trousers into her socks against the post-rain midges and April had not issued her with any other orders apart from the one to draw.

After lunch the official visit to Loch Poulary took place in watery sunshine, officially led by John accompanied by sundry others. When, having finished his sandwiches John enunciated "Poulary now?" omitting its title of Loch as one whose intimacy and expertise with lochs earns him the right to familiarity, there was initially no response until Ham, late for lunch after the unofficial Poulary visit disposed of most of his mouthful of sandwich and plugged the silence with a thick response, "I'll come."

"Good boy!"

His father nodded approvingly and added on a sudden generous impulse, "And I've decided that you may eat with us in the hotel tonight, Ham." He caught Jane's eye. "That is if you promise never to touch a boat again without permission."

"Promise," obliged Ham lightly and easily. "Thanks, Dad."

Having in the meantime thought of an excuse, he rationalized his reprieve to Harry afterwards as they walked together. April, Prue, William in his buggy, Ham and Jelly were well ahead but Harry had adjusted to John's slower pace and the two of them had fallen behind.

"I like to be firm but fair," he said. "Ham had no right to take the boat and he had to know that but with all the exercise he's taking, he needs his calories."

"Quite," responded Harry agreeably.

"I'm sure he's learned his lesson?" John far from sure could not keep the question out of his voice. "We never hit our children. Well, not really. I suppose they've both had the odd smack when they were smaller, but we do try to make the punishment fit the crime." He was not himself convinced of the connection between going hungry and taking a boat but in theory it sounded good. "Good, fair discipline is essential don't you think?"

"I'm sure it must be," Harry concurred readily, "but then I've no experience of disciplining a child – at home that is. School, of course is different."

"What about Peter?" John stopped in his tracks and gazed at his friend in astonishment. "You must have had rules for Peter."

"More like he has rules for me," chuckled Harry. "Yes,

I probably did initially but he would never have broken them."

John looked at him suspiciously. It was out of character for Harry to try to score over anybody. Proud though he was of Peter, he would have thought he was unlikely to boast superior parenting skills.

"Loch Poulary already!" Harry pointed ahead. "It really is just on our doorstep."

With the change of light, the brightness of the morning had disappeared from Loch Poulary's surface. It lay under a comparatively cloudless sky like a great purple bruise, absorbing the darkness of the forest beside it, reflecting nothing. William's buggy moved slowly and gingerly over the loose stones of the track that led down to the loch, over the bridge and up into the hills beyond and it was easy for John and Harry to catch up with the advance party. The roots of the pine trees were a stabilizing influence so that the forest bank of the loch was much smoother and more solid than the fragmented bank on the opposite side. Even so there was no way that the damp earth would allow easy progress with a buggy.

"I'll take William home," said April firmly.

William who had been rocked asleep by the jolting of the buggy over the stones made no demur. Prue opened her mouth to object but April continued in her most managerial tone, "He won't miss you. He's fast asleep and good for another hour. I've got some reading to catch up on and you look as though you could do with some fresh air."

Having spoken, she prised Prue's hands off the buggy handle and started back off up the track.

"Thank-you," called Prue after her, anxiously sweeping the hair off her forehead, and received a backward wave in acknowledgment as April scurried away before Prue could change her mind.

The walk along the loch presented no hazards which

called for attention. Moreover the continuous stretch of forest to the left and the unbroken plane of dark water to the right from which the slope, now full-blown bracken, now incipient heather faded into the hills, leant a changelessness to the scenery, a focusless blandness which formed a perfect backdrop against which Prue could play the rancid thoughts that had been lurking at the bottom of the laundry basket of her mind and now whirled around, spinning by centrifugal force like soiled clothes brought to life in a washing machine, grotesquely writhing and posturing with uncanny motion. There was little conversation to distract her from them: John was conserving his breath; Harry was remaining silent out of consideration for him and Ham was racing ahead impatiently, disregarding his father breathless urges to, "Pace yourself, my lad." By the standards of *Every Woman's Guide to Complete Motherhood* – kindly bought for her by June in Fort William – she was not only a complete failure but had also provided William with a very shaky foundation for success and happiness in life.

"Bird!" shrieked Ham. "Golden eagle!"

He was racing back towards them, waving both arms in a haphazard, windmill direction. The bird, when they managed to locate it was soaring very high above them, blissfully out of earshot of Ham's shrieking, but even so they could make out with the naked eye the eagle-like wing projections.

"It's a very large bird." Harry took his field-glasses out of his case and focused. "I don't think it's a golden eagle. I think ... yes it is ... it's a white-tailed eagle."

"A what?" shouted Ham.

"A white-tailed eagle. They released some on Rhum some years back and they've spread inland. Have a look through the glasses and you'll see the sort of white fan on the end of its tail."

"Oh ....yes," Ham murmured as he focused on the bird.

"The sun's shining through its tail."

Prue and John had a turn at studying the bird as it obligingly circled lower to give them a closer view of its attributes.

"Well, it's as big as a golden eagle," said Ham, justifying his recognition skills.

"Bigger, in fact," said Harry. "They can lift fairly large prey, these guys."

"He'll not take Jelly." Ham laid a protective hand on her collar.

"Never heard of one lifting a dog." Harry replaced his field-glasses in their case. "Lucky to see that one. Well done, Ham. Shall we push on or is this the end of the loch."

Although the loch had petered into a multi-islanded section with the water running swiftly between small islands, flat and green as water-lily pads, according to the map the river was marked as starting further upstream.

"This is definitely river," panted John in a tone that brooked no argument and closing the map quickly as he spoke. "I'm disappointed. Would like to have gone further but we'll have to go back. Rules is rules."

And he started retracing his steps, leaving the rest to catch him up which they managed with no difficulty.

Ham walked with Prue on the way back and she found his constant chatter disrupted her thoughts most delightfully "No, Ham, I wasn't allowed to go to football matches in Aberdeen. I was brought up by a very strict aunt who only just allowed me to play tennis on the rare occasions when the sun shone – as long as I wore a tennis dress a good four inches longer than any of my mates and two pairs of enormous white cotton knickers."

'And I survived,' she thought. "So will William."

Chapter Eleven

The First Expedition

Loch Loyne

"And to-day," Peter, lying flat on his back in the tent he shared with Harry, aimed at mimicking a German accent, "we find out vot mein Fuhrer has in store for us *ven* he lead us to ze *won*derbaar Loch Loyne."

And he raised his arm in a mock Nazi salute.

Harry leaned on one elbow and studied the aquiline profile of his son. "You don't like him much."

Peter lowered his arm slowly. "To be honest I don't know him to like or dislike but I don't like his leadership style. You're going to have to reform him."

"Me?" snorted Harry.

"Well," Peter ticked the members of the team off on his fingers, "who else is there? Jane probably swore to obey him at the altar; Jenny has the cheek to do it but not the necessary tact; Ham only thinks of his football and his stomach; April wouldn't consider it part of her job remit; May would rather die; June is only half with us – voluntarily - and Prue also just on the periphery – but involuntarily; me – no way Jose. That leaves you."

"Thanks a bunch," said Harry. "I have to work with him and," he added smitten by a sense of loyalty, "I really do like him. It's easier once you realise that a lot of his guff covers his consciousness of his inadequacies."

"Trust you to be charitable," sighed Peter.

"Come on, Pete. This is a learning process for all of us

and John has to learn how to lead, or, more probably, how to allow others to lead."

"What do you think I have to learn?" Peter turned towards him smiling but Harry didn't answer.

Over breakfast, John seemed intent on proving Peter right.

"Now let the marmalade represent Loch Loyne," he plonked it down centrally on the table where they could all see it, "and the butter here ..."

"Butter substitute, actually," put in Jenny, automatically attempting to debunk him, "low-fat, cholesterol-free ..."

" ... represent the church at Tomdoun," he finished, raising his tone to override her. "Progressing at a sensible, steady pace because the outward journey is largely uphill and it is a hot day, we will start here and he dug the butter knife into the butter substitute and ..."

"Dad," Jenny was flushed with embarrassment, "for heaven's sake there is a clear track, in fact the remains of an old main road, running all the way like this," and she delved into a cereal packet and trailed a fistful of corn flakes from the butter to the marmalade, " and nobody needs directions. Now, may I have the marmalade for my toast, please?"

Harry saw Peter frown and smiled to himself, suspecting that his son was torn between applauding John's put-down and deploring Jenny's lack of filial respect."

"You're absolutely right," he said smoothly to the ruffled John. "It *is* a lovely day. Surprising after yesterday?"

And he wondered as he spoke how many times social awkwardnesses had used the vagaries of the Scottish weather to act as distraction techniques.

'This lochnetting'll make us or break us,' thought Harry

as he slid carefully into the back seat of his own car and felt May shudder slightly as his thigh brushed against hers. The Maitlands seemed intent on waging some kind of internal war and he was no nearer in getting to know the Reynolds sisters: the April-May-and June complex had remained an obscure code, like a sort of Cretan Linear C, or perhaps like some three-headed classical monster: even as he had gallantly insisted that one of them – and the other two had predictably ushered April forward – should take the front seat next to Peter, he had known that they would definitely have preferred to remain as a body united in the back. Prue, standing now outside the house with the sun gleaming off her beautiful hair and William chewing toast on her hip, were creatures apart.

"How come," he said, leaning forward to address April, the spokesperson, "you three are all months of the year and Prudence is 'Prudence?'"

It took April so long to answer that he saw May anxiously turn her head towards June, the deputy spokesperson.

"Well, Prudence was born in October," April obliged eventually, "and, besides, Mother named her. Father named the rest of us."

Small talk exhausted, the remainder of the journey was completed in silence - apart from June once hissing at May, "You're squashing me," as May shrank increasingly from Harry's male presence.

The Maitland car doors opened almost before the car stopped and the family imploded.

"In the car," John was busy alienating the one member of his family with whom he was currently not feuding. "*Ham,* I told you to leave your football in the car. I am not walking along listening to its bloody bouncing all the way."

Although John's "largely uphill" translated itself into a very gentle slope, his predictions about the heat were spot on.

The road, mainly forested on either side was sheltered and only the soft brush of the very tops of the firs stirred with the faint promise of a cooling breeze. The road, however, was wide enough for them to walk three or four abreast easily without the need to choose or avoid companionship. John, saving his breath for any emergencies, did not attempt to organise them and the tensions of the day before and of the morning actually eased into the fellowship of a common pursuit.

'Maybe it will make us rather than break us,' thought Harry optimistically to himself as they all laughed at Jelly's attempts to catch up with a roebuck which had broken cover. She was left barking ignominiously at the unfairness of life as it cleared a small fence easily and was soon only a provocative flash of marzipan rump as it played a taunting slalom between the dark trunks. Streams could be heard running along deep , moss-covered channels which they had worn beneath and through the roots of trees and where the streams spilled out along the road life too spilled out in the shape of tiny dark frogs, prehistoric looking dragonflies, other cling-film insects, the ubiquitous midge and wagtails flicking and darting. They stopped for Jane to administer first aid to Lewis, moaning in agony after having been bitten by a cleg on his cheek.

"Let me do it for him." Affected by this sudden general surge of goodwill, Jenny took the cotton wool swab out of her mother's hand and dabbed very gently at Lewis'cheek. Lewis, although obviously initially ill at ease at the take-over bid, manfully submitted to her attentions and almost grew to enjoy the sensation.

Harry took advantage of the first-aid break for a long swig from his water-bottle

"Not thirsty, John?" he enquired of his beetroot-faced friend.

"Not I," replied John rather too emphatically. "Getting fitter!" And he patted his stomach to claim a reduction in his girth.

As they progressed the trees retreated and they could see the 'new' road to Skye, winding around a far hillside with the metallic bluebottles of vehicles buzzing out of earshot along it. Their track now described almost a complete semicircle around heath and scrubland. The air was fresher and as they walked, plucking bog-myrtle leaves and crushing them in their hands to release the sweet herby scent, they set up a merlin and watched it fly low over a small lochan nearby.

The sudden exposure of Loch Loyne was a shock.

"Well, I know it's been dry up here but I didn't expect this!" John took off his cap and ran a hand through his hair, so that the sweat trickled down into his eyes, stinging them and blurring his vision.

They stood in silence staring into the empty socket of the loch below. Long since dammed to flood the valley including the old road, the loch had dried up to the extent that it had dwindled into the odd stagnant pool or sluggishly flowing stream between stretches of sand and dark, treacherously deep mud patches.

"Never seen it this low," muttered June, standing apart from the others, hand on hip.

"It's a dead place," whispered Ham and Harry knew what he meant because to him too it was indeed the ghost of a loch.

The heat lay heavy on them as they walked down the short stretch of road towards the boulders, large as tombstones, haphazardly marking the periphery of the dry loch. Although partially eroded, the spine of old road projected visibly out of the loch bed like the dorsal skeleton of a huge monster and they followed it, crossing a small stone bridge, its tar surface now creased and wrinkled like a sloughing snakeskin, over one of the streams and passed a small island of green trees to the far side.

"Like Moses taking the Israelites across the Dead Sea," said Ham and nobody said, "Red Sea not Dead Sea" because "Dead Sea" in this context seemed more accurate.

They were very quiet on the road back, but it was the companionable silence of those who had shared a loss, the united silence of mourners going from the funeral to the wake.

"Hadn't realised that water was such a living thing," confided Peter to Harry when they reached one of the streams across the road that buzzed with small life and Harry nodded.

John was lagging so far behind that no-one noticed that he had slumped to the ground until Jenny, turning round to look for Jelly, saw the dog sniffing tentatively at his crumpled form and licking his face.

"Dad!" she shrieked. "Mum! Dad's dead!"

John, the leader, heavy and inert, opened his eyes and through a haze inexplicably part very dark, part blindingly bright, saw the blurred faces of his followers above him and heard Jenny's second shriek as she proclaimed him alive.

"Jus' give me my cap," he murmured through cracked lips and groped on the ground with his hand in search for it, found it and pulled it over his eyes so that they could not see his shame.

Jane, kneeling beside him, took his hand. "What is it darling?"

"Dunno," he replied. "Be all right in a bit. It's so hot."

She tried to open her water bottle but her hands were shaking and before she managed to unscrew it, Peter had produced his. She removed his cap, splashed the water over his face and gently replaced the cap.

"Some-one, please help me move him into some shade, somewhere. Under that tree over there, perhaps."

Peter bore most of the weight, assisted by Harry, Jane and Ham. Jenny gave the orders.

"Gently, now! Lift him gently! Don't drag his feet.

Ham, keep Jelly out of the way can't you?"

"My guess is," June surveyed him critically from a distance, "that he simply hasn't taken in enough fluid." She took a swig from her own water bottle and added as she twisted to replace it in her belt, "That is quite honestly the most elementary mistake anyone can make."

"Shut up!" said Ham and burst into tears.

Jenny ignored her and Ham and knelt beside her father, " Daddy," she spoke slowly and loudly, far too loudly and clearly for his liking, "did you forget to bring your water-bottle this morning?"

He closed his eyes and tried to drift back into unconsciousness.

"Did you?" she cooed and changed her tone to address Ham sharply, "Stop bubbling and look in his knapsack."

Sniffing juicily Ham burrowed in the discarded knapsack for the water-bottle that would exonerate his father and shame the unfeeling June, but without success. Jane raised his head gently and gave him a drink from her own bottle. The water trickled into a delightfully cool well at his throat.

"I'll go get our car to fetch him," offered June suddenly. "The 4x4'll be better on this rough road." She turned after a few metres and shouted, "Best wet a cloth and put it at the back of his neck."

By the time she returned with the car, John was sitting up with his back against the trunk of the tree, Ham's T-shirt soaking round his neck and Jenny fanning him with a leafy branch – "to keep the midges off." She turned as June drew up and caught John in the eye with one of the leaves.

"Perhaps," suggested Harry to Jane, "it would be best if you and Peter went with him to the hotel and the rest of us could join you there? Everybody else all right?"

Everybody else nodded. John, with one hand shielding his injured eye was heaved up into the front passenger seat and the others watched the cloud of dust behind June's car billow and subside flatly on the windless road before setting off in its wake. Forty minutes later they arrived at the hotel to find John looking perfectly healthy but reclining on a comfortably cushioned sofa with a large glass of cold water and Jane, Peter and the hotel proprietor hovering round him. Jenny, fully satisfied that her father was out of all danger, switched her attention to the hotel dogs and cooed soothingly over a small and endearing puppy that had followed them into the sitting-room. Ham, feeling his semi-naked state, remained outside on the hotel verandah swinging his legs to set up a breeze and trying to pacify Jelly who did not share Jenny's attitude towards the hotel's dogs and was venting her disapproval vocally. No-one came to help him shush her. He was always just left out of everything. June, the ex-friend, who had insulted his ex-dying dad brought out a glass of orange juice and laid it on the table in front of him. He tried not to look at it but when he did he saw that the ice inside it was fidgeting coaxingly and beads of cool condensation were forming on the outside of the glass.

"Thanks," he said, fingering it, just to feel its coolness, without looking at her.

"I'm sorry," she said awkwardly. "I always shoot my mouth off."

He took a sip of the orange juice and grinned at her.

From where Harry was sitting at the table set in the large bay window in the hotel dining-room, he could gaze out across the glen to where Ben Tee glowed sharp and clear in the mellow, forgiving light of evening that detailed only what was good and perfect. The mist circling the lower slopes was faintly iridescent, a confusion of millions of imperfectly formed prisms.

"You could never catch that on camera," he said to April, seated beside him.

"No," she agreed politely. "Isn't the sea bass delicious?"

The sea bass was indeed most delicious but he felt a degree of exasperation at the predictability of her reply. Having been seated next to April on all three evenings he had quickly learned that her conversation seemed to be confined to three safe subjects – food, the weather and gardening. To veer off those was to unsettle her. She would quickly revert to the tried and tested. These sisters were creatures of habit. Or were they? Unexpectedly, May leaned across her sister towards him.

"You could paint it though," she said firmly.

Perhaps, then, 'habit' was too strong a word; perhaps 'creatures of custom?' But then weren't they all? After supper Peter would probably expect to have to join him out on the verandah where he could smoke his pipe and they could both sip a whisky. Well, perhaps he would forgo his pipe and suggest that they all break habit and stay on in the bar for a drink and an informal chat.

His idea met with general approval but John and Jane looked at each other when he made his suggestion.

"Actually, we were thinking of taking a run to Loch Quoich," explained Jane hesitantly.

"We've left it out," put in John.

"But we quite fancied going just together, just the two of us," Jane admitted sheepishly. "We were going to sneak out once the children were in bed." She hesitated. "I don't want to burden you all but if we could leave them with you just now ...We'll be less than an hour ...Probably have time for a late drink..."

The road to Loch Quoich was deserted except for the deer: a cluster of hinds, some with calves, eying them curiously from among a group of trees below Kingie and further on the stags, just distinguishable in the evening light against the tawny hillside, twisting their antlers towards them and pausing on the brink of flight to view them before vanishing soundlessly.

"We're, that is I'm, not ready for this one," said John to Jane when they parked the car on a promontory overlooking Loch Quoich.

Loch Quoich below them was jasper and sardine-stone and mother of pearl set in a rough hewn band of jagged white platinum and separated from the jasper, sardine-stone and mother of pearl sky at its far end by the merest dark hint of dam wall threading across its surface, more like a line of fusion than of separation. They left the car, shutting the door very quietly and walked hand in hand down the old white road that trickled down the slope, slipped under the water and would surely surface invisibly, a slim white resurrection, on the far side somewhere between the folds of the hills beyond. Beside them a rough white stone bleated complainingly, metamorphosed into a sheep and led its lamb to a safer spot further along the hillside, looking reproachfully over its shoulder at them as it went. They didn't talk because there was no need, even though the earlier plan had been to talk things through.

"And it was man-made, that dam part," murmured Jane against his shoulder in the car on the way back. "That part was where they submerged the village in the name of progress and people lost their homes. Perhaps some of them lost their identities even."

"Still," he started but he could not finish. He wanted to say something like ..., something to sort of explain that it was not possible that something like that could be entirely man-made because it was too beautiful, but he lacked the right words. Words were not always necessary. Sometimes they clouded communication. So, instead of speaking, he stopped the car by a small stone bridge over a stream with an unidentifiable tree beside it and an unidentifiable signpost pointing out some unidentifiable path and kissed her.

Chapter Twelve

The Second Expedition

Adjustments

The expedition for Loch Ness and Loch Oich had been scheduled for the 12th –18th August but, since the lochnetters, with the exception of Harry, were to be out of Edinburgh for the rest of July and the start of August, the pre-expedition meeting could only take place on the 9th, three days before departure.

"Not ideal," John had commented in a flat voice when phoning to inform Harry shortly after their return from Tomdoun, "but then what is?"

Harry suspected that John's sombre mood had something to do with the background of a high-pitched battle of words over which he was trying to speak. The Maitlands' French holiday had been booked six months prior to Jelly's arrival and, with the evaporation of Moira's assurances that she could help look after Jelly "from time to time", the only solution, that of booking Jelly into kennels, was meeting opposition.

"You can't take her there!" Jenny's wail was clearly audible though nasally distorted by the phone. "It's cruel! Look at her eyes! She thinks she's going back to the dogs' home. I can stay behind and look after her. I don't want to go to bloody …"

"You can't!" snapped Jane. "Don't be silly! You know you can't."

"For heaven's sake, sh! I'm on the phone!"

"June would look after her," Ham, eagerly with

undiminished volume.

"Excuse me a moment, Harry. June can't look after her. The Reynolds sisters aren't back until the end of next week. They've decided to spend an extra fortnight at their cottage."

."Don't you two think for a moment that we haven't explored all possibilities?" Jane was now managing to make herself heard. "Your dad and I don't like it any more than you do but we've got to be sensible."

"Well I'm not going!" Jenny's decibel level made it impossible for John to hear what Harry was saying.

"Sorry, Harry?"

"Nor am I!"

"Jelly won't want YOU!"

"Sorry old man, would you repeat that. The kids are kicking up about Jelly going into kennels."

"I said, 'I'll take her,'" said Harry. "She'll be company while Peter's away."

So with Jelly for company, Harry pottered his way through the period between lochnetting trips, making a start on all the chores he had deferred until the long summer break and abandoning all of them unfinished. Peter had taken himself off with a group of friends to explore part of Norway he hadn't previously visited. Harry always thought it strange that with Peter's Latin blood and upbringing he seemed drawn to the Scandinavian countries and this time his post-cards revealing the most picturesque aspects of his whereabouts were as enthusiastic as ever. Did Harry know, the first one asked, where in Edinburgh he might learn to speak Norwegian? A later one enquired whether it would be all right if he invited some Norwegians, number and sex unspecified, to stay. Then the phone-call to ask meticulously after Harry's health and to clarify his request: there would only be one Norwegian visitor this time and she was a girl. To warn Peter off holiday romances, given that Peter himself was a product of one of Harry's school trips, would hardly be subtle but Harry could recognise his own qualms in the over-hearty enthusiasm in which he replied, "Yes, of course, Peter!" He then tried to forget his misgivings by completing one of his chores, namely the clearing out of the spare bedroom, by the deadline he had originally given himself – the end of July.

April Reynolds had indeed made an unprecedented and unilateral decision that they would abandon the firm to the capable hands of Archie, the foreman, and remain at Tomdoun for a further fortnight after the end of the Trades Fortnight. Her sisters had been too astounded to find voice to disagree even though June and Prue had both independently felt rather miffed at the lack of consultation. So the sisters arrived home on the 29th July to be reproached by a shaggily hedged garden full of weeds, a bedaisied lawn and a hall floor ankle deep in post.

"If we go away for a whole month again," pronounced June, "we'll need to get a temporary gardener to keep the place in shape."

April sniffed, feeling criticism somewhere, and said nothing.

A gardener might be nice anyway," Prue agreed, adding mischievously, "we could do with seeing muscly arms and a hairy chest – maybe even a builder's bum – in amongst the cabbages."

"Speak for yourself!" laughed June.

"Anyway," persisted Prue, " it would give us time to do other things at week-ends besides the garden."

"What things?" puzzled May. "What else …"

"Will…i…am, you mustn't tear letters. It's naughty!"

Prue rescued a mauled envelope from his clutches.

"Or if you must chew them, chew the brown ones," June instructed. "They're just bills!"

She picked them out and took them upstairs to the tray in her bedroom marked *Immediate Attention*. The room smelled faintly musty and, as she pushed open the window, a strand of cobweb stretched to its elastic limit, snapped and hung, dangling indecisively. Leaning out so far that the window-sill pressed uncomfortably into her rib-cage, she could see further into the garden of No 10 than she had realised before. She saw Ham's muddy football lying abandoned on the overgrown grass and smiled.

When, on the 6th of August, leaning out of her window again, this time to clear her head of the jostling accounts figures refusing to be harmonized into order by *The Marriage of Figaro*, she saw the Maitland washing hanging on the line and heard Jane telling Ham very sharply that if his muddy football went anywhere near her laundry she would not be answerable for her actions, June gauged accurately that the Maitlands were back and that their French holiday had met with only limited success.

"Actually it was pants!" confided Ham to her later when he had obediently kicked his football away from the washing so that it landed in amongst the Reynolds' recently weeded cabbages. He enlarged: the rainfall in the Loire had been unseasonably heavy; Mum had done nothing except go on about all the wild flowers; Dad and Jenny had kept having rows because she wouldn't speak French and laughed at his accent when he did and yes he, Ham, had learned some French which he repeated proudly, *"Defense de toucher!* It's what they say to you when you go round chateaux."

By the evening of the 9th however, the Maitland

household not only appeared to have recovered their good humour as they welcomed the loch-netters, all of whom congregated on the doorstep at the same time in one congenial admix, they had all obviously spent considerable time and effort over their preparations. John had erected a flip-chart, re-arranged the seating so that every-one could have an uninterrupted view of it and had placed on the table by the door a pile of folders each containing the official Loch Garry report, Ham's blog, a map of the Great Glen and spare paper for note-taking. Jane had prepared another gourmet meal with help from Ham while Jenny, having enlivened the tedium of her Continental holiday by reliving Peter's rescue of her and elevating him to hero status, had devoted most of the day to a beauty preparation calculated to make him forget the generation gap between them.

As John picked up his marker pen and smiled his brittle introductory smile, Jane, perched on the window-seat beside Jenny, automatically hunched her shoulders in nervous sympathy.

"Relax!" she instructed him and herself silently.

"Everyone here?"

"Why don't you take the register?" Jenny muttered just audibly beside her and Jane pursed her lips in a breathless "Sh!"

"Lewis won't be with us this time round ..."

"This time or any other time," Jenny announced loudly, looking straight at Peter, thereby subtly intimating her availability.

"Jane's "Sh!" was loud and clear this time and accompanied by a reproving tap on Jenny's tightly jeaned leg.

"As I was saying," continued John smoothly, "we don't have Lewis but we do have April taking an active part and Prue and William too, though this meeting is past William's bed-time. And I believe Peter is bringing a friend. Right, Peter?"

Peter nodded.

"Jane's cousin's family have called off for unspecified reasons …"

"There's nothing unspecified about chicken-pox!" Jane, hot in defence of her cousin, forgot her supportive role. "Their youngest simply has chicken-pox and she's *very* unwell with it."

"Jane's cousin's family has called off with or without unspecified reasons," conceded John in a tone of mild amusement and he bowed with self-conscious dramatisation in Jane's direction. "That means we have one extra boat up for grabs. The non-refundable deposit on it's already paid so whoever were to take it would only have to pay the balance."

There appeared to be no takers.

"Well if anyone knows anyone who feels like taking it …" John shrugged and dismissed it. "Anyway we've lost Jane's cousin's family – with the exception of their son, Chris, who I believe will be tagging along with us. Now be warned! Chris is an enfant terrible!"

"What's an *enfant* whatever?" asked Ham suspiciously from the floor at John's feet and added loyally, twisting round to face the listeners, "Chris is really cool – even if he does support Man U."

"O.K., O.K.," laughed John. "He's just insufficiently disciplined. Only too common these days, lack of discipline. But those kids! Their parents have no common-sense and the children really do exactly as they please and …

` "You'll excuse me, won't you?" Jane of the ill-disciplined, nonsensical extended family smiled graciously round at everyone except John. She no longer cared if they all leaped to their feet and booed him. In fact she might just lead the protest. "I've got to finish off our supper."

"Shall I help you?" Ham at least was bored already.

"No, no, you stay and listen to Dad," she encouraged,

closed the door behind her and added, "and interrupt just as often as you like."

She did not return until she heard the drawing-room door open on a babble of conversation and Ham put his head round the kitchen door, swung on the door-handle in the disapproved fashion and announced, "Dad says we're ready. I'm starving."

Leaving the lochnetters to heap their plates, she went into the drawing-room to collect glasses and was able to glean the outcome of the meeting from the flip-chart displaying John's block capital chalk-board hand.

Accommodation

Reynolds – Tomdoun Cottage
Pete & A.N. Other – camping
Harry – B&B in Drumnadrochit
Maitlands- Boat & Cottage at Laggan

Loch Ness 12th – 15th
Boat 1 – Maitlands
Boat 2 - ?
Cycling – Pete & A.N. Other
Places of Interest – Harry & ?Reynolds

Loch Oich 15th-18th
15th Dinner for all at restaurant/hotel/whatever
16th Walk/cycle round loch
17^{rh} (Watersports on Loch Oich & Visits to Loch Tarf and Loch Ruthven

Result- 5 lochs done!

"He'll start notching lochs on our bed-posts," she remarked acidly to Jelly who had tailed her in.

"All all right?" she enquired sweetly, putting her head round the dining-room door on her way through to the kitchen with the tray of glasses. "I'm just coming to join you."

After the door had closed on Harry and Peter who were the last to leave, she did not even wait for Jenny and Ham to retire before turning on John and hissing, "Don't ever speak about my family in public like that again."

John, elated by the enthusiasm of his group, by the fact that this trip would cover five lochs this time and by the brandy liqueur in which he and Harry had indulged, frowned as he struggled to recall what on earth he could have said to provoke such an over-reaction.

"You must be tired," he finally excused her generously. "It was a lovely …"

"Yes, it was and yes, I am," she snapped. "I'm tired of a lot of things. In fact I'm so tired that I am going to bed. Clear up properly and don't wake me by banging around when you come up. There's to be nothing left for me to do in the morning."

"Wow!" she heard Ham say as she passed the landing. There was no mistaking the admiration in his voice and she didn't know whether to laugh or cry.

She slept late the next morning, arriving downstairs to find that the only evidence of the loch-netting meeting was the flip-chart still in the drawing-room and the fact that Jenny and Ham in the kitchen were breakfasting on smoked salmon quiche and sherry trifle respectively. As she entered the room, Ham engaged her support.

"Mum, Jenny says that if you and Dad get divorced, she'll go with you and I'll go with Dad and I suppose that's O.K., but she says that you lot'll get Jelly and that's not fair."

"Rubbish!" Jane poured herself a coffee. "Dad can have

both of you. Jelly and I will keep each other company. Won't we, Jel?"

Jelly wagged her tail with limited enthusiasm because her eye was on Jenny's quiche.

"Where is Dad?"

"In the garden, chasing rabbits," said Jenny with her mouth full. "Are you going to …"

But Jane was already outside in the sunshine, cradling a cup of coffee and watching John down in the vegetable garden wedging spiky branches of berberis into the hole in the hedge at the bottom of the garden through which the rabbit had presumably vanished and pausing every now and again to examine his ungloved hands ruefully. She put her coffee down and fetched a pair of thick gardening gloves from the greenhouse.

"That's the trouble," she confided to Jelly who had joined her. "I always want to protect him from life, from people, from what might hurt him, but he doesn't see the need to protect me. That's what happened last night when my family were fair game." She smiled ruefully. "He thinks I'm tough. Perhaps if I started playing feminine and weak like her next door and fluttering my eyelashes whenever he …"

Right on cue rose a high-pitched scream from behind the wall they shared with the Patersons. It brought Jenny and Ham to the kitchen door.

"Thought Dad might have stabbed you," said Jenny cheerfully licking her fingers.

"Don't be silly!" John had dropped the berberis and come up to their level for a possible view of the source. "Your mother doesn't scream like that!"

Moira's scream had subsided into a less piercing, keening vibrato.

"She's at the fish-pond," whispered John.

"Maybe Patrick's drowned."

"Shut up Ham!" Jane approached the wall and offered a tentative, "Are you all right, Moira?"

"I've just had an awful shock," wailed Moira, "and Patrick's golfing. I can't tell you over the wall. I'll come round."

Having staggered as far as the Maitland sofa, Moira clasped a mug of coffee to her bosom so that it neatly divided her breasts, and indicated that she was fighting to frame a sentence by alternately drawing shuddering breaths and shaking her head as she released them. Jane stole a look at John to see how this display of helplessness and vulnerability was affecting him, but he was standing with his back to the light and his expression was in darkness.

"In the fish-pond," Moira whispered so quietly that Jane saw the door handle turn and the door edge open an inch or two to allow Jenny and Ham audience.

"Yes?" encouraged Jane. "In the fish-pond?"

"There was ... I can't say it. It's too awful. I'm so ashamed. But I'm sure it wasn't ours. It must have come from the neighbours ..."

"That's us!" clarified John tersely.

"The other side, put in Moira hastily. "They're in trade you know, and ..."

"And what was it?" Jane already half-suspected.

"A rat, whispered Moira, "and it was dead!"

"Well, it's a shame but ..."

"I'm sure John will scoop it out for you," suggested Jane hastily.

"Would you?" Moira's eyes were dry but her lips were moist and trembling. "Oh John dear, would you?"

"Of course!" John leaped to his feet and made for the door, nearly falling over his eavesdropping son on the way out. "Want to come with me, Ham?"

Jenny sidled through the door and fixed Moira with a quasi-sympathetic gaze.

"You mustn't feel badly, Moira," she said kindly. "I read somewhere that we're never less than ten feet away from a rat. It's just that one of your ten-footers got into your fish-pond."

"Fetch Moira more coffee, please Jenny," said Jane firmly.

"I couldn't possibly," giggled Moira. "I've got the tiniest bladder, you know" And she patted the area of her abdomen which she imagined to house her bladder. "O-oh!" she squealed, forgetting her bladder and gesticulating towards the flip-chart, "What is that?"

Jane explained the headings.

"O-oh! What fun!" enthused Moira. "Though I don't know about the Reynolds. Still they're not boating, are they? And we'd love to take the spare boat. That's if Patrick doesn't have any golf arranged. We could come with you and, what's more, we could help you with the water sports too. We went on a water-sport holiday quite recently, you know, and …"

"We saw the DVD," said Jane dully, "and actually, I'm not sure if the boat's still free. I'd have to ask John."

"They say Loch Ness stinks in summer," remarked Jenny brightly.

"I've never heard that," said Moira severely. "The things children come up with! What with Loch Ness smelling and rats ten feet away!"

"And your rat's disposed of," said John cheerfully from the door.

"And we buried it so that you wouldn't find it in your bin," put in Ham in honeyed tones. "We made it a nice little grave next to the lady statue with funny hair and no arms"

"Not next to Aphrodite!" pleaded Moira. "Tell me you didn't put it next to Aphrodite?"

They didn't tell her so she changed the subject.

"Well, anyway, thank-you. It's a great relief and do you know if you still have a free boat, John?"

She indicated the clip-board and John, reeling from the transition from the rat beneath 'Aphrodite' to the boat, replied without thought, "Yes, of course we do."

When Helga flew into Edinburgh Airport early on the morning of the 10th, Harry, who at Peter's insistence had accompanied him to meet her, was able to pick her out as she came through *Arrivals* before Peter's breathy, "There she is!" 'Snow Queen,' thought Harry. 'Seen her before!' as his mind played back to the illustration of the Snow Queen on his childhood Hans Andersen with her face luminously pale against the black dust cover of the book. But this Snow Queen's smile was wide and her hand warm in his.

"I have just to get my suitcase off the carousel?" The statement rose at the end like a question needing approval. They both nodded. "I hoped not to be long. It's so good of you to fetch me."

"Not at all," assured Peter.

"Good flight?" enquired Harry simultaneously as they both stooped to reach for her hand luggage and bumped heads in the process.

In the two days prior to their loch-netting departure, they continued to fall over each other in their efforts to ensure Helga's comfort. Peter was torn between needing Harry's support and wanting to do everything for her himself. Harry felt himself miscast both as father and as host and struggled to find a suitable role. For the first time in their relationship friction threatened and Harry actually found himself hungrily anticipating the peace which the little B&B in Drumnadrochit surely promised?

Chapter Thirteen

The Second Expedition

To Loch Ness On The Glorious Twelfth – without a grouse?

Peter had decided that they would set out early on the morning of the 12th to allow Helga to do some sight-seeing. He had provided her with a list of 'places of interest' in alphabetical order and invited her to prioritise. Harry, effacing himself behind his paper, heard Peter rhapsodising over the merits of each and every site to Helga's bewilderment and his own chagrin as he recalled the politely detached attitude of the unresponsive teenager he had escorted to these self-same 'places of interest' in an attempt to engender some awareness of his Scottish heritage via his newly acquired father. Her final choice had included the Hermitage of Braan, the crannog on Loch Tay, the Queen's View, the Soldier's Leap, the Osprey Centre at Loch Garten and the battle-field at Culloden and this meant an even earlier departure than Peter had originally envisaged.

As it turned out the frequent stopping to view brought relief to Harry who remembered too late that he was prone to travel-sickness when in the back seat of a car. Nonetheless when they barely had time for a sandwich at the look-out point at the Queen's View before being ushered out the car, he found himself pleading, "Peter, for heaven's sake, leave some for next time!"

"If you're tired, Dad, stay in the car."

Peter's voice was only just audible from behind the camera with which he was attempting to capture Helga against the infinity of Loch Tummel, but the note of impatience was so unmistakable that Harry had to bite his tongue to stop himself from retorting, "It's not *the* car. It's *my* car."

Despite Peter's attempt to keep to his schedule, they were too late to pay a proper visit to Culloden, although he insisted on turning off the A9 and driving to where the Jacobite flags, riding high on an up-current, marked out the rough, sun-bleached heather of the battlefield. When he switched off the engine the silence was broken only by a single thread of sound, the thin lament of a skylark.

It's a sad place, I can see," Helga whispered. "I think there are ghosts here."

Harry, about to launch into an historical account of the Jacobite dream and the bitter finality that was Culloden, saw Peter's hand slide off the handbrake to reach for hers and held his whisht.

Although it was almost eight o'clock before they passed through Inverness and turned off along the road to Drumnadrochit, Peter still insisted on drawing up in a layby so that he could capture Helga against their first glimpse together of the dark waters of Loch Ness. Harry, feeling tired, hungry and definitely *de trop,* regarded Loch Ness with a jaundiced eye, reminding himself that it represented nothing more than a flaw, an unpardonable geological fault, forcing a rift between the mountains that must have sat side by side so companionably before being wrenched asunder by earth movements deep, deep below the surface. When they eventually reached Drumnadrochit, he insisted that he register at his B&B before they even thought of food. Finding the house was easy, even though it had been freshly painted since its picture had been posted on the internet. It was now very white instead of pink, with the front garden 'landscaped' into a sterile admix of pebbles and paving stones and vegetation restricted to green tomatoes in a glass house. A paradoxical sign read *Welcome* and *No Vacancies.* Peter opened the boot and offered to help Harry in with his case, but Harry waved his offer aside and bent to unclasp the gate.

"No vacancies, I'm afraid."

A tartan-aproned woman with a tired foreign-sounding voice stood in the open doorway gesticulating towards the notice-board.

"I'm booked in. I'm Harry ..." Harry smiled, advancing confidently towards her.

"Sorry!" She didn't look sorry, just fed up as though she was having to explain the simplest rules of a well-known game to a particularly obtuse beginner. "Same here as elsewhere. If you're not here by six and haven't phoned, the room is re-let. We're full!"

Harry stared at her in disbelief.

"Try up the road." Her gesture was more dismissive than informative. "You might be lucky."

Peter met him at the gate.

"Too late," said Harry, aware that he was fixing Peter with a baleful gaze. "We've wasted too much time on the way up."

Peter, he was glad to see, looked suitably reproached.

"I suppose I'll just have to share your tent," he relented and smiled. "Just see you don't snore."

As Harry depressed the button to replace his case in the boot, Peter plucked at his sleeve.

"I've only brought one tent," he whispered hoarsely.

"What?"

A blotchy red stain crept across Peter's cheeks towards his ears. They still stuck out a bit thought Harry but not as obviously as when he was a hollow cheeked fifteen year old.

"Oh, don't worry! It was just a joke!" They both knew it

wasn't. "Let's get something to eat."

It was a toss-up between "eating fish and chips while Nessie-spotting" as per Peter's plan or a sit-down meal somewhere.

"It's your choice, Dad." Departure from his plan must mean that Peter was really feeling guilt-ridden. "Your choice and I'm paying."

"Well unless somebody's remembered to bring the anti-midge stuff, I'd rather eat indoors." And Harry swatted at his left ear-lobe to prove his point.

No-one had brought it. Another flaw in Peter's provision and Harry was happy to expose it.

"I'll drive."

Peter handed over the keys and relinquished leadership. Harry drove in silence to a small hotel they had noticed on the way in to Drumnadrochit from Inverness. Helga had laughed as she read its name, *Nessie's Nest*. Peter and Harry had shared scepticism.

"*Nessie's Net* more like," Peter had jeered. "Nothing like a monster to suck in the gullible tourist."

"Is this a good idea?" Peter queried as Harry turned into the car park of *Nessie's Nest Under New Management.*

Harry did not bother to reply.

The new management was obviously very new and very eager. They had only opened at the start of the week. The meal was absolutely no problem. Chef would be delighted. Yes, they could most certainly give Harry a room. Overlooking the loch would be overlooking the road, but the road was very quiet at night. Hope they liked the décor. Her cousin was an interior designer – not quite Laurence Llewellyn Bowen, but you never know … Harry was not to carry his case upstairs. No! Absolutely not! Iain would be glad to bring it up. Would Harry like to see his room and freshen up before the meal?

Harry was led upstairs by Christine, pledging herself at

every step to gratify his every whim. Peter stood with Helga in the vestibule with its cream walls stencilled with thistles and bluebells and the odd, extremely odd, capercaillie and waited for him to pass out of earshot.

"Perhaps," he said to Helga, "we should spend the night here too? Keep the old man company? Save his coming out again to-night to drive us to our camping spot?"

"Oh Peter, you are so kind to your old father!"

Helga was quite literally and very invitingly open-mouthed with admiration.

Coming downstairs again, Harry saw Peter and Helga leaning shoulder to shoulder over the reception desk, heard Christine's clear voice asking, "Twin-bedded or double?" and wheeled round swiftly into the bar where a log fire cocked a snook at the Highland summer and any conversation from reception was rendered inaudible by a merciless clanging coming presumably from the kitchen,

"And yon's our chef on a good day," grinned Iain cheerfully ass he poured Harry a double Drambuie.

If Harry, scanning the loch from his bedroom window in the half-light of the moonlit August evening, had been able to see through the trees and just around the bend to Urquhart Bay on Loch Ness, he might just have been able to make out the white slipper-shaped curve of the *Lass of the Loch* nosing gently against its mooring rope. If he had been able to communicate with John who was sitting on his own on the rear deck masked in a midge-net while the rest of the family – plus Chris of course- adapted monopoly to Jenny's rules, he would have discovered that John had had his fair share of discomfort that day too.

Like Peter, John had aimed for an early start – not

because he planned to do any sight-seeing on the way up, but because he wanted to pick up his boat from the boatyard at Fort Augustus, undergo the obligatory instruction and sail away before Patrick could arrive and start showing him the ropes. Not that he had much evidence that Patrick knew any more about boats than he did but Patrick had the smell of natural leader, something which he suspected he himself lacked.

"Visiting friends on the way up," he lied glibly to Patrick the previous evening when the latter, strolling past his gate, newspaper under arm, saw him loading the car for an early start and raised a quizzical eyebrow.

"What friends," Ham enquired before Patrick had passed out of earshot and John noticed Patrick's shoulders give the little shudder that could only mean he was laughing.

"Aunty Jean," he bellowed loudly enough for the next-door-neighbour-but-one to hear. "You remember Aunty Jean!"

Fortunately, at that moment Jane arrived from the station with Chris and in his excitement at seeing his cousin Ham forgot about Aunty Jean and any other aunt, real or imaginary.

This episode was closely followed by his show-down with Jenny at supper. Entirely the girl's fault. Jenny had been building up towards it during the course of the afternoon. Firstly for reasons which totally escaped John, she expresses a prudish disgust on learning from him that Peter's companion was female, expressing her view that the terms *slut* and *slag* were too good for her. Her mood was further exacerbated by the arrival of Chris and she informed everyone, including the unperturbed Chris, that she detested him. After this an ear-splitting argument with her mother, who had dared to suggest that as it would probably be chilly on the loch, it might be necessary to cover up with much heavier clothing than that worn by the nubile youth draped across the decks of the boats in the boatyard's brochure, ensured that she drew her chair up to the supper table with a thump which expressed her blackest of black moods.

"There is absolutely no way," she announced with deliberate finality, flashing her eyes in her father's direction, "*absolutely* no way that I am leaving here at the crack of dawn. It's ridiculous!"

"Eight o'clock is hardly the crack of dawn," John retorted sharply because he was tired after loading the car. "It actually cracks long before. Not that I expect you to be an authority on the subject."

Jenny smoothed the butter fastidiously over her bread, carefully judged the angle at which she laid down her knife and finally raised her eyes to his while biting savage and unblinking into the slice.

"I'm not leaving until eleven at the very earliest so you can put that in your pipe and smoke it."

Chris gave a little gasp and remained open-mouthed at such insolence, his expression indicating clearly that such open insouciance never occurred in his household.

John lost his temper.

"Go to your room at once!" he bellowed at Jenny and glared at Chris.

To his horror Jenny burst into tears and as usual it was Jane who resolved the issue, controlling everything the way she always felt she had to in that irritatingly calm authoritative way.

"Actually I've been thinking," she said gently, "that it might be better to take two cars; better for several reasons. It would mean that you could go up with the boys and the bikes, get the boat, learn how to handle it, etc. and Jenny and I could shop before we come up, walk Jelly on the way up and join your later with the shopping and the dog. That would save time. What do you think?"

Later on he had magnanimously put his arm round

Jenny's thin shoulders and whispered, "Sorry I bellowed."

She just shrugged his arm off and glared at him balefully, but at least there had been no-one else to witness *that* rejection. Not like later when he and Jane and Jenny were composing picnic lunches in the kitchen and they heard Chris's clear treble floating in from the garden. "I'd rather go with your mum, Ham. Your dad's kinda scary." In fact all the Reynolds sisters probably heard him too – and the Patersons. Ham's reply was lost amidst Jenny's sniggering.

"Congratulations!" Jane nudged him encouragingly. "Not much scares that young man!"

Still he felt rejected and the sourness lingered in his mind overnight so that when he rose early the following morning the day had already curdled.

For all that, the trip proved surprisingly peaceful. Ham and Chris who had spent most of the previous night catching up on each other's misdemeanours, slept most of the way slumped against each other on the back seat and John negotiated the A9 smoothly to the *Hebridean Overture* with no-one to object to his choice of music. They arrived at the boat at half-past eleven and the welcome they received was watered down with reproach.

"Ye're early!"

Jim Mac Donald ran a hard weathered hand over the crisp stubble on his cheek as though to imply that had they arrived at noon, as his brochure recommended as the earliest time of arrival, they would have found him clean-shaven.

"That's because we forgot to go and see Aunty Jean," Ham supplied conversationally.

The paperwork completed, Jim led them along the canal-side towards the loch.

"Thae two at the end's yourn." Jim yawned as he spoke and folded his arms across his chest in a gesture to absolve himself from any guidance in choosing. "You take first pick."

"I think we should leave the larger one for our friends, don't you boys?" John suddenly found that his confidence was ebbing. "Greedy to take the bigger."

"It's the one nearest to us though," Ham seemed disappointed. "You can always take the biggest if it's nearest to you."

"Yon," Jim indicated the bigger, "has got bow-thrust."

That settled it. John was not having anything to do with "bow-thrust" whatever that was. It seemed to him an unnecessary and aggressive sounding complication.

"We'll just take the *Lass* and leave the *Lady* for the Patersons.

Jim pursed his lips in a thin straight line as though repressing comment and raised his eyebrows expressively. Then he placed two fingers in his mouth and let out a strident whistle. A boy in blue overalls looked up from his task and jogged towards them, wiping his hands on the seat of his overalls as he came. Still a couple of inches shorter than Jim and minus the stubble but with the same facial features and square stocky frame, he could only have been Jim's son.

"Donald here'll show you what's what." Although apparently addressing John, Jim's eyes were following a yacht appreciatively as it powered upstream towards the lochs. "Then it's up to you."

With his apprehension mounting, John heard himself becoming bossy. "All aboard boys! OK, Chris?"

His concern proved misplaced. Chris and Ham skipped lightly aboard but he himself had to accept a helping hand from Donald to heave himself over the edge onto the unsteady buoyancy of *The Lass*.

"You'll soon get used to it," Donald had grinned.

Close up Donald looked no older than Jenny. The singsong intonation of his voice betrayed a well-rehearsed recitation as he launched unselfconsciously into instructions.

John managed quite successfully, he thought, to contrive the polite smile of one already in the know. Ham and Chris appeared spellbound. Having finished the verbal instructions, Donald in one swift boomerang-like action, jumped ashore, untied the boat and jumped back in with the rope which he proceeded to fold with arms that seemed disproportionately long in one so stockily built. For all his youth, Donald was a good and patient teacher and by the time Jane, Jenny and Jelly had arrived, John felt sufficiently proficient to be able to show off his skills and give commands.

That brief period of slightly unrealistic euphoria was the high point of his day, he reflected now, sitting on his own on the rear-deck and a degree of innate honesty compelled him to recognise that he himself had provoked the deterioration, had asked for the petty mutinies that ensued through his dogged determination to keep ahead of Patrick. Of course there would have been time for Jenny to browse the little shops of Fort Augustus, for the boys to watch the boats ascending the locks "for just a little while", for them all, in fact, to watch the boats while enjoying a picnic lunch in the sunshine. Of course Ham and Chris could have taken a turn at the wheel. On the open loch anybody could have taken a turn at the wheel if he hadn't forbidden it, afraid of losing time.

"This isn't a race, you know," Jane had remarked acidly, handing him a sandwich as he navigated - egg mayonnaise, his least favourite. She hadn't even bothered to ask him first what sort he wanted.

The evening was really drawing in around him now. He could feel it creeping over the flesh of his bare, midge-bitten arms. From behind the shadowy folds of the midge net only the very bright was clearly discernible, the white hulls with their reflections shivering faintly on the moon-frosted loch and a blur of swans on the far bank, shaking a flurry of watery tail feathers before waddling , cumbersome on invisible legs towards a nesting place. He was tired after his early morning start and the stress of keeping ahead of Patrick. Bed would be good but the galley table which was to convert into a bed for himself and Jane was seemingly public property, used just now to support monopoly. "I'll leave domestic arrangements to you," he had announced to Jane from behind the wheel and without taking his eyes off their course. They had tied up in Urquhart Bay before he had discovered that she had put the two boys in the forward cabin, the only purpose built sleeping quarters, so that she could "keep tabs on them day and night."

"Well you should have taken the bigger boat. I don't know what you were thinking of!" she had snapped when he complained about the galley table.

"If you really want to know what I was thinking of," he had retorted savagely, "watch Patrick trying to park *The Lady*."

"Can't be worse than you," Jenny had scoffed.

"Can't it?" He had felt smugly confident. "Wait and see!"

Unfortunately they had all taken his advice. They had all waited to see and they had all watched Patrick swing the boat skillfully into position alongside the quay at Urquhart Bay,

"Well done, Patrick!" he had heard Jane over loud and overgenerous with praise as he had locked himself in the lavatory.

"Bow-thrust!" Patrick's voice had boomed back. "Makes all the difference you know."

They, Patrick and Moira, had been smiling as they had walked up to Drumnadrochit for a meal, holding hands at their age.

The door slid open and Jane was silhouetted against the yellow light.

"Games over!" She drew the cardigan more closely

around her shoulders. "It's lovely out here but it's pretty chilly. Come on in! I'm making hot drinks. You look as though you could do with one."

He wanted to say, "No thanks! It's OK. I like it out here," just so that she would not have the double satisfaction of predicting his need and satisfying it. But it was cold so he followed her inside.

Later, on the window side of the galley table bed Jane listened to the family settling around her and cherished this intimacy at a time when they seemed to be pulling apart, coming unspliced like a fraying rope. The thudding from the boys' cabin, the thumping of pillows, giggling and whispering grew less frequent. Jenny up the steps was snoring inelegantly and by this time Jelly would be curled up at her feet. John beside her was stiff and rigid as he was when conducting one of his private post mortems of the day. She tried hard to keep both sympathy and encouragement out of her voice.

"Tomorrow will be good," she murmured vaguely. "The weather forecast is brilliant."

"Yes," he agreed carefully matching his level of enthusiasm to hers. Then he sat up. "What's that?"

John's hearing had always been more acute than her own. And then she heard it too: a dull throbbing like a rapid heart beat, shuddering through the water, almost from the depths as though the loch itself had suddenly come to life. As it grew stronger, the waters lifted, tilting and lowering the boat on a rhythmic wash. She pulled the little curtain back from the window. Light silhouetted the black, rocky outline of the bank below Urquhart Castle and then she had to shield her eyes against the pair of enormous, unblinking searchlights that rounded the corner.

"Helicopter," she whispered. "Let's go and see."

They watched from the deck, sharing the warmth of a thick blanket hastily snatched form their bed as the lights swept remorselessly across the foreshore. The water flattened under the downdraught from the blades so that the *Lass* rocked violently in the wash. As the lights played cursorily across the little harbour they were engulfed in noise emanating and ricocheting in a cataclysmic dialogue. In the wild strobe lighting, Jelly at their feet could be seen intermittently, rigid from nose to tail and barking inaudibly. Jenny was beside them, long-legged in a skimpy night-shirt, trailing a blanket.

"What is it?" she yelled, clutching at John's arm.

"Air-sea rescue," he replied.

"Has there been an accident?"

She was nervously chewing on the corner of her blanket as she used to do ten odd years before.

"Don't know." He added comfortingly. "Could just be an exercise. Don't worry."

The lights were slim shafts probing further out on the loch, the noise subsiding, the movement of the boat more sluggish. Jelly was growling and wagging her tail, simultaneously congratulating herself on having barked away the brute and daring it to return. John patted her.

"Well done, Jelly. You put that beast in its place."

Jenny laughed spontaneously and squeezed his arm.

Strangely united by their experience, they returned to their beds and fell asleep with the natural rhythm of the loch restored and playing on the hull.

Harry was asleep by the time the helicopter arrived but Peter, lying hot and indignant on top of his bed, was irritated by its feverish pulsing as it scanned the loch. Although he drew back his curtains to watch the methodical probing of the light, he could feel only mild curiosity. Harry, the innocent source of his frustration and therefore the focus of his rage, had in all fairness made it quite clear that he and Helga should feel free to do their own thing. They could have done. Even now they could be somewhere like the Lake District, close and free as they had been in Norway. "Heavy summer rainfall in the Lake District!" he had informed Helga when she had suggested that they go there. Was it only the uncertainty of dry weather that had warned him off? It had rained in Norway and his tent had leaked in the middle of the night. He had crawled into Helga's tent, just because it was the third nearest, and then into her sleeping-bag and had continued to bed down there day after night after day, long after the others had assured him that his own tent had quite dried out in the long days of sunshine that followed. Was it some warped form of filial duty or some anachronistic grateful obligation that was responsible for forcing him to honour his commitment to his father's loch-netting trip and was equally responsible for his having turned down Helga's innocent suggestion that he should join her in the spare-room at home. He had been unable able to find words to explain to her that their bedded togetherness would be an embarrassment to him in his father's house. He had tried to compensate her by planning a sight-seeing trip on the way up which had only left his father exhausted, her still needy and himself guilt-ridden on both counts. At the reception desk of the hotel he had been on the verge of booking a double room for them to share when he had sensed his father descending the staircase behind him and altered the booking to two rooms without looking at Helga. At dinner Helga, sitting opposite him with her soft fair hair falling round her face, brushing her neck and then her shoulders and with her lips soft and warm against her wine glass, had directed all her own conversation towards his father, had been totally absorbed by all his worn-out anecdotes. She had kissed his father lightly on the cheek as she left them early for bed and thanked *him* for "a wonderful day."

Peter had received merely a vague smile and been warned off with a platonic "See you in the morning." OK! Suited him!

The drone of the helicopter was louder now, more insistent. He wondered if it had wakened her, if she too was leaning her elbows on the window-sill, if the searchlights were flashing teasingly on and off her nakedness. He could perhaps find out? In the teeth of anticipated rejection he ran barefoot, soft and fast down the corridor. He opened the door quietly, closed it, leaned back against it and kept the urgency out of his voice.

"I thought you might be frightened of the helicopter," he whispered so as not to wake her if she were asleep.

"Yes, Peter, I am very frightened." He could hear the smile in her voice. "You have come to comfort me?"

As he bent over her, she locked her arms around him and drew him down so that he would be able to make up for the rejection of the spare-room, the arduousness of the sight-seeing, the booking of two bedrooms and so on and so forth until it all ceased to matter. At about half-past three when he felt her stir against him, he did murmur a reluctant caution. "Darling, you have to ride a bike tomorrow" and felt her laughter against his own lips as she whispered, "I'll ride side-saddle on your cross-bar." With that minor problem resolved, he pressed on with renewed energy.

Chapter Fourteen

The Second Expedition

The Loch Ness Monster

At Jenny's suggestion the captain and crew of *The Lass of the Loch* ate their breakfast at one of the little picnic tables alongside the water's edge. There were only four seats but John was happy to stand a little apart from the rest of the family bacon roll in one hand, mug of coffee in the other and gaze out over Loch Ness through half-shut eyes. The harbour itself was still in early morning shadow but the sun illuminated both the open loch and the shore opposite with the glaring intensity of stage lighting. The stage floor was matt with the peat-dark waters of the loch which absorbed the sunlight rather than reflected it but the backdrop of the hillside on the far shore glistened with an uneven texture as though it had been painted in oils and blurred its greens into its browns with the odd shock of yellow. They were still in the wings, John and the excitedly chattering breakfast group, waiting for their cue to sail out in front of the footlights and play their part in the drama of the day.

The curtains of *The Lady* were still drawn close, but when John nudged against her as he eased *The Lass* out of the harbour, Patrick surfaced onto the deck with a towel clutched around his waist. He waved with a show of unconcern, but as they drew further out Jenny reported, "He's peering over the rail to see if you've damaged him, Dad. He's trying to grab the rail and hold onto the towel. Oops! He ..."

"Jenny, you could just stop the running commentary and come and steer once we're past these red and green buoy things," John cut her off good-humouredly.

"I asked first," Ham protested, "and Chris was next."

"And you'll get your turn so stop whining. We need you two to keep a look-out at the moment. One to port and one to starboard and first to spot what might be Nessie gets the prize."

"What's the prize? Which is port and which is starboard? What does Nessie look like? Where are the glasses?"

Knowing the answer to none of these questions, John concentrated on handing the wheel over to Jenny.

"The trick is to move it as little as possible," he explained. "The current and the wind change her direction so you have to keep making minor adjustments but just move the wheel a little."

He stood behind her staring fixedly ahead.

"Got something!" Ham, whose turn it was to have the glasses was triumphant. "Dad, I've got something!"

"Jolly good!" commented John without turning his head.

"What have you got, Ham?" Jane emerged onto the deck dragging a deckchair and attempted to swing its parts into a stable, meaningful arrangement.

"Could be ... Hang on! I've lost it! No, there it is ... I think... No, I don't think it's Nessie. No, it looks like somebody snorkelling."

"Snorkelling! In the middle of Loch Ness! Don't be so silly, Ham. Doh! You snorkel in clear water where you can see the bottom."

"Never mind Ham, Jenny! Just you concentrate on your steering," warned John.

"It is a snorkeller. No, hang on! He hasn't got a snorkel mask. I can't see that thing that sticks up. You know. The breathing tube."

"Very nice!" Jane settled herself gingerly on the deck chair, relaxed and stretched her legs out luxuriously.

"Hi there!" Ham bawled at the snorkeller. "Are ...

you… looking … for … Nessie? He doesn't seem able to hear me?"

"Lucky him," murmured his sister.

"And he's not wearing a wet suit even. He's got on a sort of blue shirt and ..."

"John, stop the boat!" Jane had joined Ham. "Give me the glasses, Ham! Don't argue!"

The engine died down and there was nothing but the water slapping against the hull. Jane took the glasses off to adjust the focus. She knelt on the deck, resting her elbows on the lower rail and looked again.

"John," she called huskily, "come here and take a look. I think this could be a swimmer in trouble."

John looked.

"O.K.," he said slowly, "we'll circle him and take a closer look."

On closer inspection, Jane's first thought was that the object in the water was some sort of morbid prank, just a dummy, shirt and trousers stuffed with foam rubber or some other porous material which allowed it to float, moving unresistingly up and down in the undulating water.. The "dummy" appeared to be floating face downwards in the water, with just its torso clearly visible and the limbs, if they existed, tailing off somewhere below the surface. As they edged nearer, the arms showed dimly, sepia brown beneath the peaty water. Then she saw the hair floating out on the water, spreading out reddish purple, the colour of some exotic seaweed or alternatively some trendy hair dye, the shade that Jenny might hanker after.

"It's just a girl!" she cried out, stuttering over the words because her teeth were chattering.

Through a drumming in her ears as though she herself were under water she heard the blur of John's voice.

"Jenny! Boys! I want you in the galley now and stay

there till I say you can come out. And shut the door!"

Then he was kneeling beside her with his arms around her.

"I'm sorry. I'd send you below too but you're going to have to help me."

He reached for the boat hook.

"Don't hurt her, John."

At the first prod, Jane gasped, fearing that he would sink the body, but it appeared unexpectedly buoyant, the humped back bobbing up and down as though it was shaking with laughter. Then he managed to hook the waistband of the trousers and drag the sodden creature up against the boat.

"Hang on to me tightly, Jane," he said. "I'll lean over as far as I can."

He had rope looped in his hands and she understood what he was trying to do. She clasped him tightly around the knees as he leaned over burying her face against his blue-jeaned calves so that she could see nothing. She felt him straining and stretching and tried not to visualise what he was doing but he must have succeeded in looping the rope around the neck and using it to lever the body until he could heave it over the rail because he collapsed onto his back with the effort and lay there with the sodden corpse on top of him, the eyes in the grey spongy face gazing sightlessly, hopelessly up to the sky where a sudden blaze of seagulls, excited by the catch, burst into irreverent laughter as they wheeled hungrily.

Crouching on the deck, Jane hid her face in her hands and felt the rocking of the boat as John extricated himself. Then his hand was wet on her shoulder.

"Stay there," he said, "while I fetch something to cover her."

With Jane having joined the rest of the family and only the blanketed hump for company, John restarted the engine. Impossibly the brief journey to Urquhart Bay seemed uphill with the boat juddering against the friction of the water, its histrionic shuddering replacing the normal cacophony of family background. Jenny must have switched off her radio and there was no sound of voices from the galley. John had gone down briefly to ask Jane to alert the emergency services. She had already done so. The others had shrunk back from him staring in morbid fascination as though at a memento mori, taking in the slimy wetness down the front of his shirt and jeans from where the sodden body had sprawled across him. He had kept his dialogue as brief as possible and relieved them of his presence.

As he turned in towards the bay, Jane came up through the galley half-door, her eyes on the mug of tea she was trying not to spill. Under the other arm she had a bundle of clothes he recognised as his own.

"I could hold the wheel while you change," she said placing the mug on the sill beside him and added with the ghost of a smile, "I'll try not to run aground."

The wet shirt was sticking to his chest as he peeled it off and he longed for a fierce jet of water to sluice down his body – something more akin to a fire-hose than a shower. However, at least the dry clothes would allow him access to his family.

He took the wheel back from Jane. She bundled the wet clothes into a bag and stood beside him, close without actually touching him. As they lined up for entry into the harbour he could see blue lights flashing through the trees; the creamy bulk of an ambulance drawn up alongside the harbour and small figures in green and dark blue clustering and separating, growing larger until the faces had distinguishable features. One of the blue ones detached itself and motioned him to the far side of the harbour. He swung the boat round and reversed into position with an ease of which at any other time he would have been proud.

"You hold the wheel a minute," he said to Jane, unsure of where he had left the rope and wanting to spare her proximity to the blanketed mound, "and I'll tie her up."

But he didn't have to. One of the policemen had jumped aboard and thrown the rope to a colleague. Then he ushered Jane and John inside the galley and followed them, hesitating as he did for just a moment on the threshold. John was convinced that before he had even introduced himself, his swift gaze had comprehended the full extent of their fear and misery. In the gaps between his body and the door frame they could glimpse brief, green fragments of paramedic bearing down purposefully towards the body. Then the sergeant stepped inside, closing and shuttering the door behind him so that the voices outside became muffled and the necessary investigations were reduced to intermittent rocking and vibrations.

"You've got children on board," he observed.

"Three," answered Jane, "and a dog."

"Right," he nodded. "Best then that we get you all off the boat while we do what we have to. We can ask our questions somewhere more comfortable. Say ten minutes to get bits and pieces together for the rest of today? I'll send a WPC to help you. OK? Please keep everyone inside till we fetch you out."

He opened the door just wide enough to allow his exit.

With the help of a brisk, round-faced young police woman whose smile and demeanour reminded John of a courier on a tour bus, they were ready in time for their evacuation. Ham held John's hand tightly as they hurried across the deck, averting their eyes from the screen which had been erected around the body and from the liquid oozing out from under the screen and darkening the deck.

"Your cars are up on the road."

WPC Brown ushered them through the quayside bustle

towards the steps. On the way along the water's edge they could see *The Lady* still berthed where she had been earlier. Moira, hanging over the rail in a bright red headscarf, had field glasses trained on *The Lass*. Patrick by her side waved and beckoned them across. In reply John shrugged and pointed to the police cars.

"Just the neighbours," he remarked casually to WPC Brown. It was odd how easily Moira and Patrick had dwindled into perspective. "But I suppose we ought to tell them where we're going."

"I'll let them know for you." Her tone implied 'and put them in their place' and John wondered if Moira had already made her presence felt among the police. "They can join you later if you're sure that's what you want."

"Whatever."

John shrugged again. He was becoming very comfortable about surrendering any responsibility to the inexorable dictates of the law. The sun was warming his back now as they mounted the steps. Halfway up they stood aside to allow the downward passage of two men in noiseless rubber boots and crisp white overalls that rasped and rustled with their descent.

"Those overalls are absolutely no good for bird-watching," commented Ham severely. He had been studying intermittently and largely unproductively for his Scouts' ornithology badge for quite a few months now and went on to expand. "They're no good because one, they show up and two, they're noisy."

"Perhaps they're not going bird-watching," observed John drily. "Perhaps they've got another hobby. In you get, Ham."

Jane and Jenny with Chris between them were already ensconced in the first of the police cars. John, Ham and Jelly climbed into the second.

"This is cool!" Ham was enthusing although his hand was still tightly in his father's. "Are we locked in so that we can't escape. Can't we have the lights on? Can't we ..."

John leaned back in the police car, closed his eyes and allowed them to take him wherever.

Chapter Fifteen

The Second Expedition

Loch Ness - Reshuffling the Pack

Harry, the victim of prickly heat, was sitting in his car in the Fort Augustus public car park, alongside the Fort Augustus public toilets. Although both front windows were rolled down to their maximum, there was no breeze to provide a through-draught. The Reynolds sisters were not due for another fifteen minutes – probably ten he optimistically told himself. Being sticklers for punctuality, they would be sure to err on the side of earliness. Helga and Peter had politely suggested that he accompany them for a stroll up the locks, but he had unselfishly refused, saying that he needed to wait for the Reynolds sisters and thereby sentenced himself to this uncomfortable vigil in the car.

He took his *Places of Interest on Loch Ness* jotter out of the glove compartment and dated the first page. A group of German tourists of indistinguishable gender, all long-shorted and peak-capped had gathered round the front of the car, chattering and laughing. One, drawn a little apart, was inscribing idly in the dust with the toe of his/her trainer; another hitched a haunch onto the bonnet of Harry's car, felt the heat of it through the thick cotton of his/her shorts and rubbed his/her haunches ruefully. His/her companions laughed and Harry laughed with them, feeling more empathy with this group of unknowns of whose language he had only the most rudimentary comprehension than he had had with his own son and his son's girlfriend since Helga's arrival.

After Helga had gone to bed early the night before, he

and Peter had sat in uncomfortable silence with Peter flicking noisily through his booklet, *Cycling Round Loch Ness*, more Harry felt to irritate his father and provoke him into early retirement than because he needed information. Eventually Harry had obliged, had agreed that they would meet for a 7.45 breakfast to allow for an early start and had retreated to his bedroom and a soothing view of the moonlit loch. The following morning Peter had been profusely apologetic when he arrived at the breakfast table at nine o'clock, followed shortly by Helga who had not after all been party to the 7.45 agreement but had quite unnecessarily felt the need to be apologetic too. In fact they had almost been apologetic in unison, re-enforcing Harry's irritation at being forced to play the role of gooseberry. After the apology, Peter had lapsed so quickly into monosyllables as to become almost uncommunicative.

"Bad night?" Harry had enquired solicitously.

"No!" Peter had been quite definite.

"You look quite tired," Harry had persisted, sipping his third cup of coffee, just to keep them company.

"Helicopter," Peter had gulped with his head bent low over his cereal bowl.

"You heard the helicopter too, Harry?" Helga asked. "I hardly slept after it had gone."

He hadn't heard it. Peter and Helga were together in having heard it. He hadn't.

"See you at the car,"he had excused himself. Pausing on the way to pick up a paper he had heard them laughing together, laughing in a liberated way as though some stricture had been removed. It had really annoyed him.

As the young Germans wandered off, one of them, the one who had propped him/herself temporarily against the car waved to him. It was a young man, he saw now, unshaven, grinning at him because he had shared their laughter. Harry waved back and watched them moving between cars, talking over car roofs, laughing, over-reacting by jumping back in exaggerated alarm when the driver of a red Corsa cautioned them with a braying hoot. Harry recognised the red Corsa. The driver was sitting very upright, her head poking forward over the steering wheel and swivelling from side to side in her search for a parking place like a tortoise peering stiff-necked around the rim of its shell. It was Miss April Reynolds.

Harry would have been surprised – probably aghast – if he had had any perception of how fervently Miss April Reynolds was looking forward to his company and the chance to leave her errant family behind. They never realised, she had thought the day before in her bitterness at the coup which had placed her beside May on today's adventure, that organising family life was her way of caring for them, of loving them even, if that wasn't over-sentimentalising the issue. It had been her father's way of loving. Now it was hers.

She was not sure whether it was Prue's arrival or the commitment to loch-netting which had triggered the reluctance for her sisters to follow her orders: the two events had followed so closely, one after the other. Prue had convinced her that the loch-netting would boost May's confidence, set her along the road to greater independence, yet it was June, solid, dependable, confident June who seemed to be undergoing transformation, not necessarily for the better too. In the past she had always thought that she and June enjoyed a perfect working relationship, sharing commitment rather than intimacy. June had never been one for confidences and it had never worried her. Her father, she knew, despite his pride in his mathematical daughter's academic achievements, had been concerned about June during her university days and had once, only once, admitted his concern to April adding the advice,

"Keep her busy. Keep the nonsense out of her head and she'll be fine." April had never known the precise nature of his concern but then she had been no closer to her father than she was to June now.

It was after the first loch-netting expedition, after they had returned from Tomdoun, that the first major confrontation had taken place. She and June had arrived home from work, later than usual because there had been a lot of catching up to do, to the sight of May dithering in the front garden. Her purpose had been, it transpired, to distance herself from the heresy being committed in the kitchen where Prue was making raspberry jam, singing a song April had heard on other people's car radios and beating her wooden spoon rythmically against the side of a brand new jam pan.

"Not jam!" April had said on entering the kitchen. "Please, Prue, do not tell me that you are making jam!"

"All right," Prue had giggled, "if you want me to lie, I'm making raspberry soup. Probably will be anyway. It's taking ages to set."

"Prue, our family makes jam! We can have any sort of the finest quality jam at any time, free, gratis and for nothing."

Prue had grinned at her. "Home-made jam's so much nicer."

April had chosen to ignore the remark, allowing silence to voice her intense disapproval.

"Jam's nisher," echoed William, sabotaging the silence. "Jam's nisher, Aunty Ape."

"Yes, jam's nisher," June said, smiling and scooping him up, "and if you're a very good boy, Mummy will give you a great big dollop."

Follow that? April had retreated to the garden, tight-lipped, but deep down choking back tears. For how long had jam not been her business, her pride, her raison d'etre? June, who had worked with her daily, knew that she often checked the fruit herself, put herself in charge of quality control, regarded any customer complaints, rare though they were, as more hurtful than personal criticism. May had skirted the house and appeared at the edge of the row of radishes, standing stiff and awkward like an overdressed scarecrow. To hide her emotion, April had reached for the hoe that some-one had carelessly left lying and had hoed furiously, uprooting incipient lettuce in the process and May had continued to hover wordlessly, her eyes wide at the uncharacteristic destruction. When they had returned indoors without a word having been exchanged between them, June and Prue had already completed the bottling together, cleared away the mess and were playing with William and his toy cars. They had not even looked up when she came in.

That was another thing: June adored William. June who up to this point had shown no interest in small children, had repeatedly scoffed at the idea of ever marrying and having her own – even in childhood role play she had stubbornly refused ever to play mother – was a complete pushover where William was concerned. That had led to the second and more serious confrontation. From time to time, April had observed, William could be very naughty. It was, she had been at pains to point out to Prue, just normal childhood naughtiness, but she felt constrained to add that he was being inadequately checked for it. June had made a moue at Prue, but neither of them argued at the time. Then on a wet Sunday afternoon when gardening had been rained off, she had found herself alone with William in the back sitting-room. William had been in the mood for exploration. By climbing on a chair and leaning over the arm he could run his fingers along the top of the low bookcase holding austere leather-bound volumes of the classics until they came in contact with the smooth surface of a valuable but unattractive vase. It was German in origin, April had understood from her father who had inherited it from his mother. It was overpopulated by overweight nymphs sporting round a gushing spring and doing ancient Greek pole dances around cracked Corinthian columns which were obviously suffering from subsidence.

"Mummy!" William had pointed at a nymph with improbably scarlet nipples.

"No, not Mummy, and don't touch please, William."

In response William had given her a challenging smile and patted the vase again to see what reaction he could provoke.

"Don't touch, William!" Her voice had been louder, sterner.

William had been delighted. He balled his fist and punched the vase. It rocked before falling and for a moment appeared to be balancing sideways before thumping to the floor with a dull thud and breaking into two pieces.

William, shocked, had begun to howl so loudly that both Prue and June had come rushing into the room. Prue had picked him up and hushed him. June had turned on April accusingly.

"What on earth did you do to him?"

April, outraged, actually raised her voice. "*I* did nothing. *He* broke Father's vase after having been told twice not to touch it. He's a spoiled, disobedient child!"

"Did you smack him?" June pursued her interrogation.

"Of course not! But a good hard smack would do that child absolutely no harm at all!"

Prue had distracted him from his evil aunt by giving him a pair of cloisonne birds, presumably so that he could bang them together. April had calmed down and attempted to explain the situation to June but had not succeeded in getting her on side.

"It's only an ugly old vase," June had said. "Looks as though it should house somebody's ashes."

Prue had laughed. May, a shadow behind the door, had

remained silent throughout but later made a very neat job of gluing the two halves together. April had made a point of thanking her. May's support was better than no support.

The rift had begun to affect the smoothness of her working relationship with June too. Although just in little ways, June had appeared to be less committed to the family business, questioning some of April's decisions, decisions which had nothing to do with the financial side of things and were therefore not part of June's remit. Then out of the blue she had said to April, "I hope you are not thinking of pushing William into the family business."

"Of course not!" April had been really stung. "What do you think I am?"

After all this time did June have absolutely no idea that she, April, did what she did from a sense of duty instilled by their father and that, although her pride in the family business was deeply rooted, she had had to make personal sacrifices along the way, sacrifices which she chose not to dwell on even in her most private moments, never mind confide to anyone else. She would certainly not be demanding them of William or anyone else in the next generation.

June had apologised quickly and had actually nipped out to buy April a sheaf of stiff, long-stemmed yellow roses and presented them awkwardly with a repeated, "Sorry about what I said." April had allowed May to arrange them and they had all united temporarily in their admiration of the flowers and the arrangement but the froideur had remained.

This time as soon as they had arrived in Tomdoun, June had suggested that they should convert the summer-house into a playroom for William. They had all three agreed- May too, but it had been Prue and June who had sat together on the two-seater sofa, planning its furnishings and equipment as a surprise for William. To May's obvious delight they had consulted her about colours, shown enthusiasm about her tentative suggestions. April had been left to carry on with the day-to-day running of the business and the running of the house – nothing more. Then had come yesterday the decision by June that she should be the one to accompany May to Loch Ness. So she wasn't even really useful: she was dispensable. If it were at all possible that June might have made this decision considering that *her,* April's, confidence needed boosting, or *her* world widening, she might have been grateful, but as that was impossibly the case, she felt side-lined.

She locked the car, checked the doorhandles herself, although May had already done so and walked towards Harry, hand outstretched, with the welcoming smile she usually reserved for the Health and Safety Inspectors at the factory.

"Just to clarify things, make it easier," Peter said, not without pride in his organisational skills. He pushed the piece of paper headed *Cycling Schedule* across the wooden table to Helga as he spoke, being careful to circumnavigate the little puddle of orange juice where she had spilled her drink on sitting down. "Of course we don't have to stick to it. Feel free to make whatever changes you like. If we do stick to it we should make Loch Dochfour before dark."

In reply, Helga removed the straw from her mouth and leaned across the table towards him so that the warm cleft between her breasts deepened and darkened.

"Kiss me," she murmured, her lips moist with orange juice.

"Here? Now?"

"Kiss me if you want me to follow your schedule."

It was broad daylight, bright sunlight. This was not Norway. He glanced surreptitiously over his shoulder. Turning back he caught her in the act of posting his carefully prepared schedule through a slit between the table slats.

"Hey! YOU!"

She laughed and swung her long legs over the bench. "Come on! Let's get going!"

Apparently she had changed her mind about the kiss. He retrieved his schedule, blew the dust off it and strode after her. Catching up with her, he took her hand and held it in the full knowledge that this would confirm them in the eyes of others as a unit. "I, Peter," he was declaring silently to all witnessing tourists, thronging the banks of the locks without giving him or Helga a second glance, "am taking this woman as my … My what?"

The man in the cycle shop had remarked when Helga was trying out her bike, "Your girlfriend looks fine on that one." He had felt himself blush at the assumption. But she was his girlfriend wasn't she? After Norway, after last night what else could she be? Between adults like themselves a tacit understanding surely sufficed. "Will you be my girlfriend?" was something for young Jenny and that callow youth, whatever his name was … Lewis.

They had reached the place where they had propped up their bikes and chained them together.

"You will go first, Peter," she decided, tucking her hair deftly into her helmet. "You remember my sense of direction?"

"There's only one cycle path. You can't go wrong unless you go backwards. You will lead and I shall follow to protect you. No arguing!"

"Protect me in case the monster comes out? But I think he stay in the water>"

"One dark night he/she is reputed to have crossed the road in front of a car," Peter replied. "But don't worry. It was a long time ago. Before the drink-driving laws. Anyway monsters find argumentative Norwegians indigestible."

His schedule had not allowed for her phenonmenal

274

energy. After a comparatively sleepless night she could still pedal so strongly and effortlessly that they were well on their way to Drumnadrochit by the time he had scheduled them to be coming down to Invermorriston. Somewhere down to the right the dark peaty waters of the loch, concealing their monstrous secret invited inspection, but he could not take his eyes off Helga and the way stray strands of her hair escaped from her helmet and blew behind her. "If this is loch-netting,"he muttered to himself, "it's the best sport ever. Thanks, John, wherever you are."

Chapter Sixteen

The Second Expedition

Loch Ness and Tourism

John, on the crazy golf course at *Nessie's Nest*, was squinting through the trees at what looked uncannily like Harry and April walking arm in arm towards the entrance to the hotel. After the events of the morning anything and everything were possible. The police cars had transported them to the nearest hotel named, to Ham's delight, *Nessie's Nest*, where the new owners, having been circumspectly briefed by the police had foreseen and supplied their every need. They had been interviewed shortly after their arrival. Sipping hot coffee and lolling in low, deep chairs, upholstered in clan tartans that clashed and warred with one another with historical accuracy, the retrieval of the sodden body had seemed so remote to John that it was as though it had been performed by some-one else and he had merely been an impassive onlooker, struggling to remember the details. Ham, on the other hand, had been able to recall the details perfectly: exactly where he had first seen the body and what it had looked like. "I thought it was a snorkeller," he admitted, hunching his shoulders with embarrassment, "and my sister thought I was mad. Didn't you, Jen?"

"Well it was an easy mistake," cooed Jenny who had fallen temporarily into the protective big sister role.

The upshot had been that they would be able to return to their boat at about three o'clock and police cars would be sent to fetch them. Christine, co-owner of the hotel with her husband, Iain, had suggested that they fill in the time before lunch by trying out the newly constructed crazy golf course.

"It will help you work up an appetite," she had beamed, "and the crazy golf course is absolutely unique."

"Can't qualify unique," went the schoolmaster in John's head but, after having seen it, he had instantly forgiven the erroneous semantics. It was monster-dominated. Nessies contorted into all possible positions but always retaining the same toothy grin, formed the obstacles. At the last hole the player was required to drive the ball with such force through the gaping mouth that it shot out of the equally wide anus into the hole.

"You could even do it backwards," Ham observed admiringly. "Shove it up its arse and watch it come out her mouth."

"Don't say 'arse' please, Ham," reproved Jane mildly.

"What should I say instead?"

Jane feigned deafness and addressed John, "Chris and Ham will play with me and you can play with Jenny. O.K?"

"Fine," said John.

John enjoyed the game with Jenny, hearing her laugh at her mistakes and his. She was remarkably adept at steering the ball round impossible corners and they reached the Urquhart Castle hole where the player was expected to circumnavigate the castle before sending the ball through one of the tunnels provided between the humps on the back of the supine Nessie and he was still stuck behind the castle when Jelly started barking and wagging her tail furiously, He looked up to see the clones of April and Harry, arm in arm, their heads bent close together.

"That is just like ... "he started to remark when another clone appeared, scurrying after them clutching two handbags.

"I think I've locked the car," the clone of May Reynolds called uncertainly after the pair.

"The Harry clone stopped and turned round.

"I'll see to it, May. I'll just get April up to my bedroom first," he called back.

Jenny was giggling and whispering at John's shoulder, "Do you smell romance? Shall we finish the game or shall we go inside and have a sniff round?"

"We'll finish this hole," he decided. "Then perhaps we should go in. We could finish the game after lunch."

As after seven attempts, he still could not get his ball between Nessie's humps, he conceded the hole to Jenny. The other three were still at the third hole, mainly because Chris and Ham had entertained themselves by having sword fights with their putters when Jane was trying to concentrate on her shot, successfully diverting her attention. Her dissuasion was becoming steadily more aggressive.

"But they're not even sharp," Ham was protesting. "You can't even draw blood with them."

"I'm not telling you again," Jane started and broke off when she saw John and Jenny approaching so that Ham and Chris never learned their intended fate if they were to disobey. "Have you two finished already?"

"Harry and party have just arrived," explained John. "We're going to check they're OK. Anyway it's lunch-time."

"Good, I'm starving," said Ham. "Do we have to finish the game first?"

"Absolutely not!" said Jane. "Or, if we do play after lunch, you two will play separately."

It was definitely Harry's car in the car park. And it was definitely Harry descending the stairs, smiling down at their enquiring faces, as they arrived in the foyer.

"Had a bit of a hiccough," he said, "but I think everything's under control. How about you lot? Decided to become landlubbers for a while?"

John sat at the bar with Harry, sipping lager and filling

him in with the events of the morning out of earshot of Jane and the children who were seated round a table, examining the lunch menu and enjoying Christine's home-made elderflower cordial. "Just brought out for our very special guests," she had assured them.

Iain, behind the bar, had heard it all before when, at Christine's suggestion, he had eavesdropped on the police interview, but he listened again, leaning forward on his elbows on the counter and shaking his head from time to time to express his regret at the unfortunate turn of events. He found Harry's mishap of the morning anticlimactic by comparison, excused himself and went to calm down the chef who could be heard warming up vigorously in the kitchen.

On his way in to Fort Augustus with Peter and Helga, Harry had noted advertisements for *An Historical Appreciation of the Legend of the Loch Ness Monster*, to be held in a local village hall and the quaintness of the title had attracted his attention. April had fallen in with his suggestion that they should make it their starting point and May, of course, had concurred. *The Appreciation* had consisted of a slide-show held at *half-the-hour on the hour every hour w*ith the slides elucidated by Matthew, a stocky middle-aged man whose face was ringed with hot, red fuzz, alternately hair and beard. His wife, Maisie, a diminutive, dark-haired woman with swift, bright eyes and swift, neat movements served tea/coffee/fruit juice and digestive biscuits labelled 'organic' from a table covered in red-checked plastic at the back. They had joined the end of the queue for the half-past eleven showing, filed into a hall from which the half-past-tenners had sucked out most of the fresh air, leaving behind a fetid stench of sweat, mildew and cheese and onion crisps and eventually occupied three of the last four chairs.

The exposition was nothing if not dramatic. "Nessie lives!" proclaimed the red-haired evangelist. The silence following this announcement was broken only by furtive and inadequate attempts at translation by the tourists, most of whom appeared to be non-English speaking. "Oh aye, and how she lives!" he re-asserted, rubbing his hands together in a way which suggested that Nessie's lifestyle would paint Loch Ness red. "I do not expect you to believe me without proof in this scientific age, so proof is what you are about to get!"

Despite his natural born cynicism, Harry felt himself drawn into a suspension of disbelief. Some of the older material he had already seen: photographic reproductions of alleged sightings of Nessie taken on early cameras could only display indistinct outlines on the screen and provide unsubstantial evidence. It was the later slides he found fascinating: fragments of bone washed up on the shore of the loch after a storm were shown alongside "authenticated" reproductions of correlating skeletal parts of prehistoric reptiles and cross-sections of fossilised excreta containing largely vegetable matter. These were exciting his attention when April Reynolds suddenly seemed to snuggle up to him, her head against his shoulder. This was a development he had not envisaged. Consequently, the next two slides, comparing the vegetable matter in the excreta to the vegetable matter in the loch and a comparison of the spraint, as it was termed, to the projected circumference of a Nessie rectum attracted only his perfunctory attention. Then he felt her sliding down against him and realised with a mixture of apprehension and relief that she had fainted.

"It was just the heat," April murmured apologetically while lying flat on her back on the wooden floor of the hall with a rucksack under her feet to raise them above the level of her head. Matthew, now armed with a pointer with which he was attempting to delineate the finer details of Nessie's digestive tract, appeared completely unabashed despite the fact that those of his audience, about sixty per cent, whose command of English was obviously less well honed were obviously far more interested in April.

"Does she do this often?" Harry had enquired of May. "Faint, I mean."

"Oh no!" May had appeared horrified at the mere thought of April succumbing regularly to weakness. "No, no, no!"

Eventually April had recovered sufficiently to sit on a chair with a glass of water and acknowledge self-consciously the concerns about her expressed in several different languages as the tourists filed past her, their attention unfortunately diverted from the collection plate for donations on the opposite side of the aisle. She then reluctantly agreed to Harry's insistence that she lie down for an hour before any decision be made about the programme for the rest of the afternoon and allowed him to drive them to his hotel.

Foreseeably, April spurned the decadence of a tray upstairs and joined the rest of the party for lunch, dismissing their solicitude with a firm, "Thank-you. Just the heat!" which did little to reassure May who sat at the table with her head permanently cocked towards her sister while concentrating on the business of eating: scratching pate onto melba toast with quick twitches of her knife; supping soup with eyes rolling warily over the rim of the soup spoon as she bent forward with each sup. Eventually she settled into a staccato rhythm, a sort of morse code eating; nod, nod, nod, into the spoon, apologetic dab with the napkin at lips drawn thin, sip of water, nibble of toast, nod, nod, nod, dab, sip nibble, Da Capo. But April appeared completely normal, expressed her polite concern at the unhappy experience of the boaters and suggested that after coffee, Harry might drive her to collect her car after which they could then proceed as planned to Urquhart Castle.

Having offloaded the companions to whom he privately referred as the "Victorian Preserves" to collect their car, Harry delayed his journey to Urquhart Castle to buy an afternoon paper and scan it, hoping that there would not be any reference to the gruesome incident in which his fellow netters had found themselves enmeshed in the morning. There was no mention of it but he decided that stress must be either infectious or contagious because he definitely felt he had had enough for the day and was sorely tempted to drive past Urquhart Castle and head for a quiet snooze on his bed in *Nessie's Nest*. That, of course, was out of the question but, having parked as directed, he took his time emerging from his car and crossing the road. The traffic was helpfully heavy. Between intermittent cars, buses, coaches, caravans, lorries and fleets of bikes he could see his "Victorian Preserves" seated on a bench just inside the entrance to a mobile stall offering miscellaneous refreshments and mementos in an attempt to please all. As he watched, a pair of Japanese tourists, hand in hand, detached themselves from what looked like a coach party and stood behind May, looking at a white rectangular block she was balancing on her knee. By the time he could no longer justify not crossing, the Japanese man had initiated conversation with her, was waxing ever more insistent in what little English he had and increasing his volume in an attempt to attain clarity. He handed his multiple cameras across to his wife for safe-keeping so that he could aid his communication with expansive gestures.

"You give!" he sang out pointing at May. "We pay."

That was clear. A woman buying Edinburgh rock at the stall scuttled away without her change, glancing over her shoulder in alarm.

"A present from Scotland! Buy a present from Scotland!" warbled the stall vendor, cheerfully pocketing the change.

A lone piper started up his drone a few metres away.

In the face of all this competition the Japanese man had to make a supreme effort.

"You give now!" he screamed, bowing to show that he meant no aggression. "We pay now!"

"Me give now what?" squeaked May. "April!" she appealed.

But April had divorced herself from the scene by producing a small pair of opera glasses and was employed in analysing Loch Ness, drop by peaty drop.

"Is good! Is very good!" the man yodelled patiently, gesturing at the white rectangle which Harry now recognised as a sketch block. "Is castle! Is very good! I buy!"

"No, no! You no buy. I no sell. You want? I give!"

She tore out the page and held it out to him. It fluttered between them like a flag of truce.

"No! No! Must pay!"

"April!" beseeched May of her stone-deaf sister. The coach had started up and was throbbing impatiently. The Japanese wife was tugging at her husband's arm with a conjugal violence that threatened their photographic records. May gazed wildly around in desperation. She did not see Harry. She did spot the boxes of Edinburgh rock on the stall.

"A present from Scotland!" she quoted, thrusting the paper at him.

He responded instantly to the international language of

tourism, relaxed, smiled, pocketed his wallet and took the sketch.

"Thousand thanks!" he murmured and bowed. His wife bowed, clanking the cameras, and as they exited bowing they bumped into Harry, modulated into a higher pitch of surprise and modified to "Thousand sorries!"

"You've made a friend," observed Harry. "I didn't know you were an artist!"

May hid her confusion by carefully wrapping her sketch block in polythene, tucking the corners in clockwise and replacing it in her shopping bag.

"April said I should start again," she apologised. "She brought me the drawing stuff. I can't waste it!"

"Come on!" April cut the conversation short. "Let's do the castle then!"

Chapter Seventeen

The Second Expedition

Loch Ness - The End of the Second Day

As three o'clock approached, the mood of the boating party sobered.

"Do we have to go back?"

"Of course, Ham! Don't be silly!" Jane regretted the harshness of her tone immediately. The child was only expressing what they were all feeling. "You see," she went on gently, "it's a bit like falling off a horse. Jenny will tell you that when you fall off you have to get straight back on. That way you get rid of your fear. You conquer it. Right, Jenny?"

"Right," obliged Jenny, adding unnecessarily. "That's why there are more women riders than men. Women have the guts to get back on!" She looked round challengingly. "It's a scientifically proven fact!"

Fact or not, Jenny was the last to climb into the police car, delayed merely by the need to untie and retie the laces of her trainers.

As they approached the steps leading down to the harbour, Jane - in the police car with Jenny and Chris - could see the twisted yellow ribbon of a police cordon drawn taut from the railings on either side and a tight cluster of people crouching beside it with bunches of bright yellow flowers that exactly matched the cordon. They seemed to be composing a wayside shrine. A red and white Aberdeen supporter's scarf hung limply above the flowers like an article of clothing, carelessly dropped by a dog-walker and knotted onto the fence by a helpful passer-by. Below it cellophane wrappings shone with metallic brightness, obscuring the flowers they protected. Only a small girl with skinny brown legs and a new-looking pink and purple jacket noticed the cars drawing up a few metres short of the shrine and stared at Jane curiously, clinging to a woman's hand for balance as she shifted backwards and forwards on her heelies – the same sort that Ham used to have. The police driver turned to address Jane.

"We'll go down the private road to the harbour," he said. "We don't want to disturb that lot. I'll just go and tell your friend to follow us."

As he walked towards Harry's car bearing John, Ham and Jelly, Jelly made it clear that she had had quite enough of the police for one day by barking loudly and aggressively thereby attracting the attention of the small girl with the heelies who shrilled something unintelligible above Jelly's barking and waved the hand clutching her bunch of yellow, open-eyed daisies in the direction of the police car. A youth with unnaturally black hair scraped into a pony tail, who had been crouching to make adjustments to the shrine, straightened up, glanced at the police car and shambled up to it, kicking idly at a stone. He bent down at Jane's open window, elbows out sideways, fists in pockets. His breath was hot with some unrecognisable alcoholic spirit and Jane could see that some of the ruddiness of his face was due to incipient acne.

"Thanks for pulling Michelle, my girlfriend, at least the girl who was my girlfriend, out and ..." He tailed off and looked down at his feet for the missing words.

"It was a pleasure murmured Jane automatically and then cringed at her response. "I'm sorry," she added. "We are all very sorry."

She knew that her voice was cold. She knew that she was unfair to resent the way he had intruded into her carefully crafted dismissal of the soggy mess of flesh as impersonal detritus, something to be bundled off to the appropriate authorities and forgotten. She did not want to hear that the spongy upturned face with the colourless, concave eyes had belonged to warm-blooded Michelle who could arouse love and grief. As they passed slowly down the slip road to the harbour she felt Jenny beside her shaking with sobs. Chris was staring out of the far window, his head turned from her.

"Come on!" she said briskly, leaning forward to pat Chris' hand then put an arm around Jenny's shoulders. "Life goes on!"

The Lass and *The Lady* were the only boats in sight, rocking in synchronised rhythm at opposite ends of the harbour. Moira, in white sweater and white trousers with a navy-blue scarf knotted jauntily around her neck, was perched on a picnic table, her head flung back and her back arched with the dual purpose, Jane decided, of minimising her double chin and maximising any residual tilt of her breasts. Two men, one short, one tall, both bald and one woman with a camera on a tripod were engrossed in whatever she was telling them.

"Hanging from her lips," muttered John to Jane as he, Ham and Jelly joined them.

"Yuck! Who'd want to?" sneered Jenny, uncomfortably aware that she was still red-eyed. "And you can see her nipples through that sweater. She's too old for nipples!"

"Nipples," sniggered Ham, nudging Chris.

"Don't be catty," reproved Jane half-heartedly.

The deck of *The Lass* had been scoured clean and smelled of a mixture of carbolic and disinfectant. Jelly sniffed at it suspiciously and snorted disapprovingly.

"She prefers it a little bit dirty," explained Ham to the sergeant who had greeted them on their arrival. "It's more like home when it's a little bit dirty."

"I'm sure you'll manage to mess it up a bit," he smiled and turned to John and Jane. "Jim MacDonald's sending his son. Donald, over. Should be here any minute. Thought you might prefer to have someone take the boat on to the next jetty. Give you all a break. You deserve it."

"There's chocolate and stuff on the galley table," shouted up Ham who with Chris was giving Harry a guided tour of *The Lass* with a special demonstration of how you could shower while sitting on the loo.

"Just a few bits and pieces for you." The sergeant leaped ashore and gave Harry a helping hand to follow him. "We'll stick around until you push off. We've got odds and ends to see to anyway."

"With the inside of *The Lass* just as they had first seen it and all evidence of the day's activities removed, Jane almost believed that she could dismiss the body as a weird nightmare. She could perhaps go back in time to the moment when she had sunk into the deckchair to relax. She retrieved it from the locker and erected it – more easily this time.

"*There* you are. I've been looking for you *all* day!" The press must have had enough. "You poor, poor dears. Now tell me all about it."

Moira panted a she spoke with the effort of heaving herself over the stern, seated herself on a locker and, with hands pressed between her knees, gave a little schoolgirlish wiggle of expectation. "I want to hear *all* the details."

"Was that the press?" Jane countered to divert her.

"And how it was! I'm ex*hausted.* And television too. Just local news I think but still they wanted to hear *all* about it. I didn't let on that I wasn't actually on the boat with you. After all a body's a body's a body and I wanted to spare you the trauma of an interview. Speaking of trauma, Patrick is worried about you having to return to the boat, thinks perhaps some of you could spend the night on *The Lady* - if you're actually traumatised that is, but I said ..."

"Oh yes!" exclaimed Jenny, emerging onto the deck.

"That's such a kind idea, Moira. Ham and Chris are so traumatised you wouldn't believe! I really think you should take them ..."

"Fuck off!" It was unmistakable, even through a mouthful of chocolate.

"Ham!" Jane soared into control. "Ham, go to your room, I mean your cabin, at once and stay there until I say you can come out! Not you, Chris!" as Chris attempted to follow him. "He's in solitary confinement and on reduced rations."

"Maybe we could keelhaul him," gloated Jenny.

With the sudden arrival of Donald, Ham, sulking and chocolateless on his bunk, was forgotten. Moira was jettisoned. Jenny took the wheel and simpered about how nervous she felt so that Donald obligingly stood so close behind her that his nose was almost in her hair and his vision surely obscured. But The Lass took to the loch without mishap. Jane watched with half-closed eyes and an inner satisfaction as John made a dog's dinner out of opening a deck chair and erecting it next to hers.

"You," she remarked tenderly, "have been really wonderful today."

"What! Come again! Did I hear you?"

I said, "What would you like for supper?"

He smiled, leaned over and kissed her.

"You are tired, Peter?"

Standing on her pedals, Helga circled him before coming to an abrupt halt. Then she stood on one leg, leaning forward on her handlebars and flipped idly at a pedal, spinning it in circles. Drawing alongside her he followed her gaze. To their left the steep upward slope of the loch-side terrain had become gentler, softer and greener, allowing pasture for some reddish-brown and white cattle. Beyond this field was a camping site, the upper slope of which, provided stations for incomplete, gap-toothed rows of caravans and mobile home and was separated from the lower slopes on which a few tents were randomly scattered by a belt of rowan and sycamore and a low flat-roofed building with opaque windows and black drainpipes which could only be an ablutions block. At the gate leading into the site was a wooden shed very like the ones displayed at garden centres and a gaudy ice-cream van. He frowned: they were still a few miles from Loch Dochfour for one thing and for another, he had not envisaged spending the night with Helga at a public camping site, possibly surrounded by other tents.

Glancing sideways at him, she noted his expression and slumped further over the handle-bars, her shoulders hunched pitifully. His reaction was swift and chivalrous.

"If you want to stop here for the night, Helga, that's absolutely fine."

As they wove their way around the potholes with which the little lane leading to the site was pitted a short, stocky man heaved himself out of a striped deck-chair next to the shed, pulled his T-shirt down over his sagging belly and waddled the short distance to transfer his weight to the ice-cream van by leaning his elbows on the sill. While they were just out of earshot he muttered something into the shadow behind the sill at which there was a guffaw of wheezy laughter. Embarrassed and angry, Peter glanced quickly at Helga but she gave no sign of discomfort. The man turned to face them, wiping his hand wetly across his mouth as though to indicate that the joke was over and it was time to do business and opened the shabby leather wallet hanging from his shoulder.

"Two tents or one?"

It seemed to Peter a totally unnecessary and loaded question and he responded by raising his index finger silently to deny the occupant of the ice-cream van the benefit of his reply.

"That is one tent," clarified the man loudly.

Peter paid the pitching fee and the deposit on the key for the ablutions block in silence.

"You can leave your bikes inside the hut if you like," carried on the attendant as though unaware of having caused any offence. "We don't normally allow it but you are the only two on bikes. The others are all doing it the easy way."

To Peter, his tone implied that the easy way was also the most sensible way.

"Thank-you," said Helga warmly. "You are very kind" She gave him a bright, friendly smile. "I bring my bike when we have unloaded."

Most of the tents appeared to be clustered round the ablutions block. Lower down on the slope random clusters of bushes provided a measure of screening.

"Quieter down there," agreed the man solicitously, apparently reading Peter's thoughts and he winked at Peter. "More private like."

Peter misdirected his irritation. "Come on!" he snapped at Helga who had removed her helmet and was shaking her hair free. "We don't want to waste time."

"Well I wouldn't if I were you," chuckled the attendant, looking at Helga's hair appreciatively.

"We need to do our research," snapped Peter coldly, again barking at Helga and cycled off in the direction of the furthest gorse bush. Helga followed him in silence, unpacked her bike and cycled back to the shed. He had the tent up before he saw her emerge and run lightly towards him, turning to smile and wave to the attendant. As she approached him the smile faded from her face.

"Peter, you are mad?" she hissed joining him. "That man is kind and you are rude to him and rude to me."

"I'm sorry if I was rude," he said with no remorse, "but if you think he's kind you're being naive. He's ..."

"And I do no research," she interrupted. "You want to do research, you go and do it and leave me in peace."

She disappeared, crawling through the mouth of their tent with an ungainly wiggle of her rump. He bent stiffly to offer some attempt at reconciliation, only to have the tent flap dropped in his face. After a few moments spent jingling the change in his pocket against the key of the ablutions block, he decided to ease his aching calves by taking a stroll and, not wishing to enter into any dialogue with either the gate-man or his ice-cream chum, turned up in the direction of the cattle field. Past the ablutions block and a dull, repetitive throbbing drew his attention. A boy of about Ham's age was engaging lethargically at swing-ball, his face sullen, his racket hanging limply. Behind him a middle-aged couple were seated under a bottle-green awning attached to a caravan, the woman watching the boy, the man apparently absorbed in his newspaper.

"Why won't you play with me, Gran?"

"Andrew," the man folded his paper, "leave your grandmother in peace. She's worn out with running after you."

He caught sight of Peter, smiled tersely, muttered a greeting and returned to his paper. The boy, alerted to the presence of an audience, began to play energetically, swiping at the ball with aggression, leaping and darting before each hit.

"Good stuff,"Peter murmured encouragingly and proceeded towards the cattle field and a scene of mid-afternoon torpor. Most of the cows were lying down with spaced-out eyes and lolling jaws from which green saliva trickled. The few who were standing grazed idly, fuzzily bright in the sun, surrounded by a halo of glassy-winged insects against which they slowly swished tails. Even the bull, for bull he was, complete with a ring in his nose and heavy, low-slung testicles, appeared inert, sluggish, rubbing an itchy rump against a gate-post and casting a jaundiced eye at the plethora of opportunity.

"No fun when it's your job?" Peter addressed him. "In any case take it from me, sex is only ..."

A small missile whizzed close by the bull's head causing him to twitch an ear. Another hit him on the flank. He turned a large bemused head and licked the spot absently at which a delighted chuckle came from behind one of the vacated mobile homes. Acting swiftly, Peter was just in time to prevent the launch of the third missile by grabbing the wrist of the boy who had been playing swing-ball.

"What the hell do you think you're doing?"

The boy grinned up at him, delighted to be the object of attention.

"You are coming with me."

Although he still held Andrew by the wrist, the child offered no resistance and trotted along cheerfully by his side.

"What's he been up to this time?" The grandfather looked resigned, the grandmother apprehensive.

"Throwing stones at cattle. He hit one too." Peter wished the grandfather would at least simulate horror. "He hit it on the side! Hit it hard!"

"All lies!" The child grinned challengingly at Peter.

"Thank-you," the man addressed Peter. "We'll try to prevent it happening again."

He stood up, grabbed the child and pushed him into the caravan.

"Thank-you," echoed the grandmother and scuttled up the steps in their wake.

Out of the corner of his eye Peter saw Helga's bright yellow T-shirt outside the ablutions block and his fingers closed triumphantly around the key in his pocket.

"But it's my favourite programme," the child was wailing from inside the caravan. "I hate you and I'll tell Mum and ..."

Peter moved out of earshot back up towards the cattle-field and leaned on the fence, happy in the knowledge that Helga would have to trail up after him if she wanted the key.

Chapter Eighteen

The Second Expedition

Loch Ness – Sticky Situations

"Honey," was Peter's half-waking thought. "I'm embalmed in honey. Is that good?" He analysed it and knew a moment's ambivalence: sweet honey, golden honey, sticky honey, entangled in a spider's web of sticky honey. No! He stretched an arm out of his sleeping-bag to free himself. The early morning sun through the taut, honey-coloured canvas was pouring syrupy light thickly over everything he could see; over him, over Helga lying beside him, her sleeping-bag zipped tightly against him after yesterday's unresolved friction.

"Helga!" he whispered.

She blinked and half sat up so that her sleeping-bag slipped down over one breast. She pulled it up to her chin.

"I was snoring?"

"Yes," he lied, "but it doesn't matter." He gave her a sad, self-sacrificial smile.

"I'm sorry." As she scratched her head sleepily the sleeping bag slipped down again. This time she left it.

"Helga, I'm sorry I hurt your feelings yesterday."

"Oh, Peter."

The bottom shelf of his book-case at home was dedicated to manuals which he kept carefully arranged in alphabetical order. *Sex and You*, placed between *Self-confidence Building* and *Television Repairs*, had only enlivened his previously arid existence by engendering erotic fantasies that were sufficiently vivid to give him a lively sense of what he was missing. He recalled it briefly now as he rolled over and decided that it had outlived its usefulness. When he returned home he would donate it to Oxfam as a charitable act towards the sexually unskilled. The chapter on *Sensory Enhancement During Intercourse* he now realised was oboslete with its hackneyed insistence on subtle lighting, schmalzy music, satin sheets and musky perfumes *to arouse and prolong sexual appetite*. Not a mention was made of the arousal possible on hearing the slow glissando of the admitting zip on a sleeping bag; of the sight of warm honey light on creamy nakedness; of the scent of anti-midge lingering in the soft fold of a neck; of the sides of a tent pulsing faster and faster with his movement, with her movement with both their movement; of the blissful affirmation of his skill when her long drawn out sigh of complete satisfaction went on and on incompletely. He was sure he could still hear her sighing although one ear was pressed snugly between her breasts. And still on it went, more like hissing now, like a puncture or …He wheeled round on his knees and stuck his head out of the tent flap, holding the opening shut below his chin. A small figure was crouching by the flat back wheel of his bike.

"You!"

The boy jerked up and without a backward glance ran up the slope towards the caravans, vanishing behind the ablutions block.

"Just you wait! I'm coming!"

"That is good!" he heard a muffled giggle behind him.

"I'll wring his scrawny little neck!" His righteous exasperation was wriggling desperately to vent itself, to free itself like a fly from her sticky flypaper of temptation, a flypaper that was sticky and sweet and golden.

"Peter, you know you have the cutest dimples just above …"

"The little bugger's let my back tyre down."

"We just blow it up later."

"Need to sort it out now!" He reached for his boxers.

"Later please, Peter. Please!" He knew that her voice was indistinct because she had turned on her side away from him. "I think you prefer the boy to me."

It was too early in the day for him to work out a novel, non-physical way of re-assuring her, but on the plus side, when an hour and a half later, he did embark on revenge, Helga went with him. As they passed though the tree belt he could see from the way the ball was swinging slowly, nudging against the pole that it had only recently been abandoned.

The grandmother stood helplessly in a cooking haze just inside the doorway of the caravan, shielding her eyes as she gazed towards the vacated swing-ball although the caravan was still in shadow.

"He was there a moment ago." She sounded lost and defensive. "He really was. I really have been trying to keep an eye on him."

"Saw us coming," Peter observed.

Helga smiled at her. "You are having a difficult time, I think."

"Difficult!" She glanced behind her, stepped out of the door and lowered her voice. "School holidays, you see, and his mother's spending them in the Bahamas with the new boy-friend and he's *de trop*." Her lips pursed sourly around the 'trop'. "Andrew's spoiled, you see. Always had his mother." Her husband emerged towelling his head vigorously. "He's been at it again, Mike. He's let down this gentleman's tyres. And he's disappeared. Excuse me! Bacon's burning."

'Mike' took over. His voice was flat. "Look, I can only say that I'm sorry. I'll bring him down to apologise and make him pump up your tyre as soon as he re-appears."

"Fair enough," said Peter feeling magnanimous.

"It's not really fair," said Helga on the way down. "It's his mother who should be pumping the tyre up."

"She's entitled to some fun," protested Peter.

"And go off for the school holidays and leave him with his grandparents? My mother would never have done that. Would yours?"

"Yes!" thought Peter but he said nothing and she continued.

"They do not play with him. Grandparents should be like best friends, I think."

"In a perfect world," Peter conceded.

"In a *normal* world."

It was less than ten minutes before grandfather and grandson appeared. As usual Mike's pale, oval face with its colourless eyes and washed-out hair was expressionless, bland as a wooden porridge spoon. Andrew, red with rage and indignation, was squirming in his grip.

"What do you say?" Mike droned, releasing him long enough to prod him sharply in the back.

"Ow! I haven't had any breakfast yet," whined the child.

"Andrew, if I have to tell …"

"Sorry!" It was aggressively loud and aimed in the direction of the ice-cream van which had just arrived.

"I beg your pardon?" Another sharp prod.

I am very sorry that I let your tyre down." It was enunciated with slow deliberate insolence, to no-one in particular.

"Why did you do it?" Helga asked gently.

He shrugged.

"You were bored?" He nodded and looked at her solemnly.

"If you pump up the tyre properly, I will come and beat you at swing-ball."

He grinned and set to work pumping with a zeal he was unable to maintain and had to slacken off and alternate between pumping and resting. His grandfather stood silently behind him idly watching the traffic on the road below. After the fourth go Andrew asked, "Is that enough now?" Peter agreed that the tyre was indeed hard.

"Are you really going to play with me or were you just saying it to make me do the tyre?" he addressed Helga.

"You don't have to." Mike sounded weary. "Reckon the only thing owing to him is the sound smacking I'm not allowed to give him." He flexed his right hand graphically as he spoke and cast a baleful, pale eye at his grandson.

Helga ignored him and put a hand on Andrew's shoulder. "Come down for me as soon as you've finished your breakfast."

"I'll be watching you," the child replied, shaking an old-fashioned finger, "to make sure that you don't cycle off in the meantime."

"See what I mean?" said Helga triumphantly to Peter as they watched Andrew run up the slope ahead of his grandfather.

Helga won the first round of swing-ball, mainly because Andrew was playing with a bacon roll in one hand, snatching bites from it between shots. Spurred on by his loss, he came into his own after that, crowing delightedly as he wrapped the ball around the pole. Peter tried to think clearly. The capacity for motherhood was a facet of Helga he had never seen and surely that, coupled with the physical attraction that they shared, could mean that he was watching his potential life partner down there, carelessly swinging a racket and laughing. He strolled up to the fence to commune with the bull and to think rationally without her slim-limbed distraction to influence him. She was a bit like his honey dream; sweet and golden and yet so sticky that he became entangled, confused in her. The slow movement of the ruminating, bovine jaws proved conducive to clear thought and by the time she had joined him, slipping her arm around his waist under his shirt to confuse him totally, he had reached a decision and made a plan

The same newly risen sun that had filtered honey through the walls of Peter's tents and sent him warm and willing into Helga's sleeping-bag, prised through the rectangular panes of June's sash window at the croft-house at Tomdoun and, re-enforced by the sturdy ringing of her alarm clock, urged her to rise, to don her overalls and to run the gauntlet of the early morning midges en route to the summer-house they were converting into a playroom for William. She had been looking forward to making a start on this painting job and had found it difficult to hide her disappointment at the change of plan but April had indeed looked pale, although she was adamant that her faint was nothing, and Harry, who had tailed her car back to Tomdoun, had been obviously concerned. Prue, of course, had William and she herself was the only possible substitute companion for May. She had decided that by rising a few hours early she would be able at least to apply the undercoat – or most of it- before setting off with May to meet Harry.

Harry was standing in the Fort Augustus car-park when they arrived, leaning against his car, arms folded as he watched swifts wheeling and screaming overhead.

"Hi there!" he hailed them, rubbing his hands together, shoulders hunched almost as though he was apprehensive. "Time for a coffee while we firm up on our plans? Yes, of course," he answered his own invitation. "I know just the place."

He led them past the swing bridge to the start of the canal where tourists were milling and darting like the swifts and boats were lined up waiting for the signal to move forward into the locks.

Over coffee he took his rolled up jotter out of his pocket, turned to a clean page and dated it.

"Plans!" he said. Now, if I were my son, Peter, I would

have drawn up a proper hour by hour schedule, but as I'm not, I'd like to keep things fairly elastic and informal."

"Fine!" agreed June flatly. She found this schoolmaster mode irritating. Obviously ill at ease, he was taking refuge in his profession. Well, she wasn't going to help him by playing school-girl.

"Yes, fine," echoed May in the docile tone of a first former.

"We could wander along to the Abbey. Yes? Lovely old building and May, if she wanted to, could do a sketch of the Abbey. Then perhaps we could carry on to Foyers where we could have lunch and toddle along to the waterfall which, if you believe the guide books, is spectacular."

If she didn't respond he might dry up. May was listening attentively, stirring her coffee with that three clockwise, three anti-clockwise, three…

"We could also take a look, from a distance, if we dare, at Aleister Crowley's house. You know who he was?"

"Yes," June responded untruthfully because she was no longer listening.

May shook her head.

"Time to fill you in later. May might even like …"

June had stopped listening because of the woman she had been idly watching through the window; the woman in the kind of limp, pink dress with sagging hemline that she associated with the environmentally aware. The woman had lifted her carrier bags into the boot of a silver Volkswagen Polo, heaving them with a peculiarly familiar sideways shift of her shoulder and as she did so June had felt her stomach muscles involuntarily contract with an instinctive urge to lift them for her, even though the slight frame had thickened with maturity and stiffened from much heaving over the years. The woman shut the boot, noiselessly, her shoulders still slightly stooped from the effort of carrying. She would be tired, might have one of her headaches even …

"Would you like me to drive?"

June did not realise that she had spoken out aloud and frowned as May, still stirring her bloody coffee, intruded into her dream with an inane, "Are you all right, June?" But, as she looked back out the window, the dream had not shattered . It continued with unusual smoothness. Mattie was sitting in the driver's seat. She was brushing her hair back from her forehead, hunching her shoulders. June craned forward. Mattie was drawing her knees up, swinging her legs in, keeping them tightly together as usual and her shoes still looked too big and heavy for her feet. The door closed noiselessly, she realised, because Mattie really was outside and there was a tangible, thick pane of glass and a distance of at least twenty metres between them.

"June, are you all right?"

Harry this time and his voice was loud. But Mattie was still there, starting up the engine soundlessly, her soft, fair head darker now – mousy almost – bent forward as though listening for a response when she turned the key.

June stood up. Her exit, a narrow passage between the tables, was blocked by a stout woman enjoying a crude, over the shoulder laugh with a man of the same height and the same girth. They were wearing matching dark-blue sweatshirts embroidered with thistles. By the time she reached the door, she could just see Mattie's car turning the corner at the swing-bridge, just see the roof of it glistening over the parapet. She leaned back against the pebble-dash wall, pressing painfully hard against it, her fingers itching at its stuccoed pimples, and closed her eyes.

When she opened them, Harry was standing in front of her with two mugs of coffee. May hovered behind him with a third.

"Too hot in there." It was a statement he didn't ask her

to confirm. "We'll sit at one of these tables outside. As he spoke he pulled out a chair for her, took a handkerchief out of his pocket and dusted it. He was giving her time, she knew. May, who was still staring at her from the other side of Harry, began stirring her coffee yet again, this time at a frantic pace.

"See, May," she laughed harshly, "you've knocked up two sisters in two days. Just what did you put in my coffee?"

May looked at Harry and laughed because he did.

Bulbous, adherent wads of grey cloud lumbering their way across the sky made it difficult for Ham to know exactly where the sun was by the time he steered *The Lass* in the direction of the next mooring point. The loch seemed to him a sort of no-colour, flickering dark and bright at the same time like the lines of black and white dots on the television screen when the picture vanished. Dad had appointed him to the wheel this morning although Jenny had angled for another turn and Chris had wanted to steer and technically, if you thought about it, Chris was the guest and should have had first go. He reckoned Dad was trying to make up for the unjust way he had been punished the day before for swearing when Jenny had provoked him. As the sun rose higher, the North Easterly that had been sniffing suspiciously around the prow of the boat was beginning to show signs of aggression, whipping white crests from the waves which thudded spasmodically against the sides of the boat so that it stuttered jerkily forward.

"Just as well we're heading for Loch Dochfour," remarked John who was standing beside him. "Loch Ness can be very tricky in a strong North Easterly. We'll tie up at one of the pontoons on Dochfour and you can do some exploring."

He took the wheel as they neared the lighthouse at the entry to the smaller loch and Ham went to sit next to Jane on the sheltered rear deck and sip a mug of hot tomato soup. As neither Chris nor Jenny were within earshot he confided, "I'm glad we're leaving Loch Ness. It's scary. With all that Monster stuff I mean," he added because he didn't want her thinking that he could possibly be afraid of just bodies.

"Do you know," said his mother in the voice in which she used to tell him stories when he was little, but he didn't mind it today, "that it's somewhere around here that the Loch Ness monster rose up out of the loch and St. Columba sent him firmly back into the deep water and blessed the loch?"

"Who was St. Columba?" He wanted his mother to go on speaking like that.

"His name was Colm and he was an Irish prince. The story goes that he was involved in a killing in Ireland and fled, putting to sea in a coracle which was a rather flimsy boat. He said that he would build an abbey where he landed and he was washed up on Iona. After building his abbey there, he travelled across Scotland, spreading Christianity and doing good work – like banishing monsters and other evils. He was much loved."

Ham sipped his soup and listened. Half shutting his eyes so that the real shoreline became a blur, he could imagine St. Columba standing just below the lighthouse, barefoot on the pebbles, shifting his feet because of the discomfort of the stoniness. He was tall, thin and brown with the wind catching his long hair and he was holding up his arm. The blessing was coming from his hand like a sort of Star Wars laser beam, piercing the loch, with circles spreading out from it across the whole surface. Much, much further out there were bubbles as the monster submerged itself, snarling resentfully, but the circle of ripples smoothed out the bubbles and spread out over the shore in little waves. As the others weren't there, he leaned his head against his mother's shoulder and she put her arm around him and pulled him close.

Harry, backing hastily as the roadside dust spurted from June's dynamic take-off, felt both relief and resentment. Being lumbered with those two Reynolds sisters was definitely drawing the short straw and something which he would eliminate from all futue lochnetting expeditions. The trouble was, he had to face it, that he didn't really belong anywhere this time. There had been no walking party in which he could be included. There would not have been room for him on a boat and he was certainly not wanted on Peter and Helga's cycling trip. A father without a partner, he decided gloomily, was a social misfit. He walked down to the shore of the loch and gazed out across it, across the dark water that flooded a fault, a deep flaw on the surface of the earth, a flaw which ran deeper than the North Sea itself. No amount of water could ever compensate for a schism of that magnitude. He felt the icy coldness blowing up from the depths which no warmth could ever penetrate and shivered. He could understand why Aleister Crowley, who had boasted that he was the most evil man on earth and who had allegedly conjured up wicked spirits and entertained them to the extent that none of the locals would venture past Boleskine House at night either alone or in company, had chosen this place to commit his atrocities. He could understand too why the loch aroused fear; fear of a monster spawned deep within its flaw. You could never quite cover up a flaw, something which happened long ago in your past. It would haunt you with guilt and insecurity. He reckoned it was the same for the loch.

He turned briskly towards *The Hiker's Arms* at which he was to meet Peter. There would be time, perhaps for a coffee? No, he would wait for Peter and they could have one together. Good of the boy to phone him and suggest they meet. Especially with the Snow Queen around!

Standing on his pedals, although the road surface was practically level, Peter pedalled slowly with laborious swinging movements of his hips towards his meeting with Harry. Yesterday evening's phone call to his father to arrange this meeting had been prompted by a sudden longing for the sheer normality, banality of his father's company and conversation. Helga had been barely speaking to him and he had been at a loss to know how to put things right without losing face. Since then, he felt, his relationship with Helga had moved up several notches to a point at which a mutual future was definitely conceivable and the purpose of this meeting had changed accordingly. He now had a request to make and it was difficult to know how to put it without upsetting the old man. The inn arrived before he had perfected his speech so he propped his bike against a wall in the car park and wandered idly towards the loch, slowly unbuckling his hat.

> "*Oh what can ail thee knight-at-arms*
> *Alone and palely loitering?*

Have you fallen prey to a fairy's child? Has the Snow Queen bewitched you?"

He had not heard his father coming up behind him. He smiled stiffly and wished that he could think up a reply which indicated coldly, but without rancour, that his private life was not up for discussion. Except that it was. That was the purpose of this meeting.

"Come on in and have a drink." Harry patted his shoulder. "I know we're both got to take to the road but one drink should be O.K. You just don't know how glad I am to have some sane company."

The dimness of the foyer was only partly dispelled by electric plastic candles shaded in sepia cardboard. The walls were hung with the masks of stags and cases of enormous stuffed fish with buck teeth. Harry motioned Peter across the bar to a corner in which two brown leather chairs with sagging seats and deeply inset with brass buttons like boss-headed drawing pins were drawn up to a low table displaying a cardboard *No Smoking* sign pocked with brown cigarette burns.

"What have you been up to, Dad?" Better not to launch straight in with his request and it was a non-offensive question: his father's experiences with the Reynolds sisters were unlikely to be on a par with his and Helga's.

While Harry outlined the tedium of the day's passage, Peter worked out what he was going to say and perfected his mental script as Harry concluded with "… and that brings me up to the present."

"Sounds as though you enjoyed yourself," Peter commented inappropriately and before Harry had time to expostulate went on with, "Dad, there's something I really do need to talk to you about."

The waiter delivering the whiskies interrupted both his speech and his train of thought. Obviously short of customers, he took his time arranging the coasters meticulously over the two most noticeable glass rings on the table and centring the glasses on them with painstaking care. Harry started systematically patting his pockets for his wallet in the usual irritating way, even absentmindedly patting the pockets of the sports jacket he wasn't wearing and …

"I'll pay!" snapped Peter. And he paid and overtipped the waiter with a dismissive, "There you are!"

"Well spit it out then!" Harry actually seemed to have realised that this was a meeting of importance. Peter found his place and took a breath.

"Dad, Helga and I are not just casual friends. I think we're on the brink of something permanent."

"Congratulations, my son. Is it to be Norway or Scotland?"

It was a step too far and the interruption was unhelpful.

"I don't know yet," Peter replied testily. "We haven't discussed it. Scotland I hope but I need to speak to you before I discuss the future with Helga."

"Isn't that rather putting the cart before the horse. Not that I'm comparing the lovely Helga facially to …"

"Dad! Please just listen!" Peter took a sip of his whisky but it didn't relieve the dryness of his mouth. "Helga and I … if we set up together … both need to know what I've got in my genes."

"I rather thought you both knew that," Harry remarked dryly. "Oh! Sorry! You mean genes as in G-E-N-E-S, the hereditary ones rather than the Levis?"

"Yes, of course I do. The fact is, Dad, to put it bluntly, can you be absolutely sure you're my father?"

"*What?*"

Peter knew it wasn't necessary to repeat the question. He remained silent. His watch was ticking so loudly that he couldn't think straight. He kept his eyes on the table and watched Harry's hand shake as he replaced the glass on the coaster. The brown liquid slopped out of it and formed three droplets on the surface of the table: two biggish ones and one very small, barely visible, like two parents and a child. Despite the fact that he had reasoned his request to himself, had decided that the question was imperative, scientifically justifiable and his only honourable course of action, Peter felt hot tears in his eyes.

"I'm so sorry," he murmured.

Eventually Harry said wearily, "Surely they told you about me … your mother or your grandmother?"

My mother," said Peter quietly, "never told me anything. My grandmother told everybody else – and me - that my mother had caught me off a lavatory seat. You know. Like an STD. I never heard my mother contradict her. But she wouldn't dare. You can't blame her. My grandmother was something else. As I grew older my mother went out more and more often, with more and more men. Stayed out all night with them." He looked up at Harry. "Honestly, Dad, when I came to live with you I couldn't believe my luck. Kept thinking it wouldn't last and I'd have to go back."

He wiped his hand across his eyes and felt Harry's hand squeeze his other arm affectionately as he tried to lighten the tension with "Well I've been called many things. " There was a smile in his voice and he picked up his glass again with an almost steady hand. "But never, absolutely *never*, a lavatory seat."

Peter smiled back, grateful.

"The thing is, Dad, we could find out whether you were my biological father by a simple blood test."

"And if I'm not?"

"I suppose I'll have to try and find out who is. I owe it to Helga and our unborn children … if we have them." He paused and took a sip of his drink. "Will you like being a grandfather?"

"Seems I may not even be a father."

"Come what may from the blood test," Peter stated firmly, "I shall always think of you as my father."

Cycling back to the camping spot he and Helga had chosen together, Peter did not feel the relief he had promised himself once the request was off his chest. He had hugged his father as he left, something he had not done for some time and was amazed at how insubstantial his old man had seemed; like holding a bird and knowing the fragility of the bones beneath the feathers. He felt guilty and cruel. He felt like a bully. He felt like crying.

Helga was sprawled on her stomach inside the tent with his map spread out before her and a red ball point pen in her hand. He stretched down beside her and noticed the little red crosses she had made, four near Drumnadrochit and two where they had camped the night before.

"You," he said with mock severity, smacking her bottom lightly, "are a vandal. Look what you've done to my map!"

"I always do this," she replied.

"Drumnadrochit was four star accommodation and last night was two star. That right?"

She spluttered laughter. "No, Peter! You are so stupid. At Drumnadrochit we make love four times. This morning only twice. And to-night will be? Who knows. Maybe if we start early we break the record."

"What did you mean when you said you always do this?"

"Well' obviously, not always! Sometimes. Last year I go to France with Pierre. I take my father's map. When I come back he wants to know what all the red crosses are. I say we sight rare birds there. France, I tell him, is full of rare birds. Quick thinking!"

"Where is Pierre now?" He tried to sound casual.

"Pierre," she replied pulling his shirt over his head just when he needed to be able to see her face, "is history."

"Died of exhaustion," he muttered.

June offloaded May and, instead of going into the house, made straight for the summer-house ostensibly to see if her under-coat had dried but really because she needed to spend some time alone. The undercoat had dried nicely and evenly and, with many hours of daylight still stretching ahead, she should be able to get the first coat on. She slipped quietly through the back door and on up to her bedroom to put on her overalls and old trainers. She could hear May's voice droning on, recounting the events of the day to April and Prue who were listening with a patience she almost despised. How could they expect May to improve when they indulged her eccentricities, actively encouraged her to bore them to death?

"Make it snappy, May," they should be saying instead of their intermittent "Did you really?" and "How interesting!"

Bright sunshine yellow for the inside walls Prue and May had decided. She herself would have preferred blue, but "Yellow is a stimulating colour!" Prue had said firmly. All right then! Yellow it had to be!. "William must be stimulated at all costs," she said to the invisible Mattie standing behind her in the summer-house.

Mattie laughed the way she always laughed when June wanted her to. She was wearing the limp pink dress with the endearingly sagging hemline. Her face was a bit blurry because June wasn't sure what it would be like yet, not feature by feature. She let her put her head on one side so that the limp, mousey hair fell over the blur of her face.

"It's a lovely colour," she said in the old high-pitched childish voice, "even though, like you, I would have preferred blue. You do paint beautifully, June."

And the thought slithered coldly into June's mind that Mattie sounded a bit like May, nervous and trying to please.

"Rubbish!" she said out aloud and Mattie vanished, frightened away.

Try as she might, June was unable to reincarnate her, not without the May-like persona. So she gave up and finished the first coat alone.

The following morning John eased *The Lass* smoothly away from the pontoon. He had been afraid that their return across Loch Ness to Fort Augustus might be prevented if the North Easterly were to blow any more strongly but the heavy, grey skies of the afternoon before had dispersed windlessly and the only disturbance on the dark water was his own wake as he moved towards the centre of the loch.

"Funny!" he remarked to Jane who was standing alongside him as they passed the lighthouse at the entrance to Loch Ness. "The loch seems convex, swollen in the middle and sloping towards the shores."

"Mmm," she agreed as was her habit when she was thinking of something else.

John bumped into Helga and Peter at the shop at Foyers when he went to buy milk and stretch his own legs and Jelly's and had jokingly offered them a lift to Fort Augustus, expecting a firm refusal – from Peter anyway.

"Oh yes please," Helga had replied brightly. "That will be wonderful. I think you have come down from heaven."

"But, Helga, we're supposed to…" Peter had started frowning.

"Stick to the schedule," she had finished for him pulling a face. "But, Peter, we have to go up the hill right away from the loch and I think it is a very high hill."

When about an hour later they came aboard complete with bikes and baggage, Jane was shocked by Peter's appearance.

"You look as though you haven't slept for a week." Peter nodded wryly. "What about you, Helga? Actually you don't look too bad."

"I'm used to it," she smiled with a dismissive wave of her hand.

Peter muttered inaudibly, declined both coffee and bacon roll and gratefully accepted the offer of Ham's bunk for the morning. And Peter was still sleeping when together they lined up to the Abbey clock tower for the approach to the Caledonian Canal. Jenny pulled on a sweater and joined her parents at the wheel.

"Look!" she shouted triumphantly. "Donald is waiting for us. He said he would."

The chunky blue-overalled figure ran alongside the boat to the mooring point and caught the ropes Jenny threw to him. Then he stood, grinning, hands in pockets, shifting from foot to foot with an occasional sideways glance at his father who was strolling down towards them carrying on a sideways conversation with a man on the opposite side. Father and son came on board together.

"You've had a tough time." A nuance of sympathy was just detectable and Jim McDonald stroked his stubble in embarrassment at having revealed his softer side. "We … the boy here (with a jerk of his thumb) and I … are sorry."

He held out his hand as though offering formal condolences and bowed slightly first at Jane and then at John as they shook hands. Donald looked on, beaming happily.

"You're going on to Loch Oich, you said?"

"That's the plan," agreed John, "once we get unloaded."

"*The Lass* is due to collect our next lot at Loch Oich to-morrow and Donald here," another jerk of his thumb as he half turned towards his son and sniffed loudly, "Donald here …What in heaven's name have you put on yourself, lad? You stink worse that that *Autumn Breeze* stuff your mother will squirt in the toilet when visitors come!" He turned back. "As I was saying, Donald here thought that if he took her up through the canal this afternoon, you might like to go for the ride." He shrugged in a take-it or leave-it gesture. "Kids might like to go through the locks."

"Yes please," said Jenny demurely, "I'd love to go." She smiled at Donald who obligingly turned a deeper shade of red and then scowled as Helga announced, "That sounds wonderful. I think I come too."

"Unfortunately, Jane and I will have to drive the cars round," John said, "but if Donald is happy to take the others that would be very kind. Thank-you very much."

"'S O.K." said Jim. "Lad should be finished his chores and ready to start about two."

They completed the unloading of their luggage to the cars without waking Peter, despite the fact that there was a moderate amount of thumping in the cabin from Ham and Chris as they cleared their bags out. He was still sleeping when *The Lass* was being towed through the locks at Fort Augustus. Donald entrusted the wheel to Jenny, quite safely as the engine was switched off, and left her nominally in charge while he and John towed the boat from lock to lock. At the top of the ladder John and Jane waved them off along the canal.

"Sorry you couldn't go," said John.

"I didn't really want to," Jane smiled at him. "When did we last spend an afternoon alone together, have 'time for ourselves' I think the expression is? Let's walk Jelly along the tow-path a bit"

She slipped her hand into his. Jelly, liberated from her lead and feeling firm earth under her paws, frisked and barked to the consternation of a mallard family, who took to the water in the wake of *The Lass*.

By the evening of the 15th when he drove towards Invergarry where he was to enjoy a meal with his fellow loch-netters, Harry had regained his cheerfulness and become a man with a mission. Having reflected on his unfulfilling role as escort to the Reynolds sister, he had decided that he needed to define his own contribution to this loch-netting business. While he was prepared to co-operate, he was not prepared to be a spare part – too much like his remit in school at the moment – as though he had a permanent *Please Take* sticker on his back. It would, in future, be his role to research and compile the myths and folklore surrounding the lochs: for it seemed that these great peaty pools were not only surrounded by irrefutable historical facts that stood out clear as visible landmarks, misshapen through time like the stunted, wind-twisted trees, but facts too that told of humble lives sucked beneath the rich green of the encroaching marshes and of secret acts as treacherous as the slopes of the land-slipping mountains. There were also the elusive, unsubstantiated threads of folk-lore that swirled, ephemeral as mist over the surface of the lochs. It was these mists he wanted to chase.

His relationship with his son, biological or non-biological – like soap-powder he thought – caused him pain rather than surprise when he thought about it. He had always felt that there was something which prevented Peter from committing fully to family membership. His polite detached interest in Harry's relatives and past was reasonable. He could understand that now, understand too the boy's anxiety to please, to be the best, to cause no trouble at all, could see how it stemmed from a fear of being sent back like shop-soiled goods. After last night he felt strangely closer to Peter than ever before and he was looking forward to their meeting to-night.

He was not the first to arrive. The Victorian Preserves were already sipping variously coloured soft drinks in the drawing-room. Looking at them, he wondered how he could ever have grouped them together into a homogeneous unit. They didn't even look alike, not really. Prue was standing at the window, the dark green of her dress almost black against the evening light falling through the sash window onto her copper hair with William on her hip. Incongruously, from nowhere came a sudden sadness that he had never seen Lucia dandle Peter on her hip, swinging him gently, soothingly.

"You should teach him to say 'duck', Prue, not 'quack-quack.'" June the only one still wearing trousers, her concession to evening -wear being a long sleeved jet-black top embedded with black sequins, overlapping scale-like to form a protective armour. 'Like an Amazon' thought Harry. Perhaps he could venture, 'One breast or two?' He decided not.

Prue turned laughing and saw him. "Hello, Harry," she said. "What do you think? 'Duck' or 'quack-quack?'"

"Quack-quack!" William nodded firmly.

"Other people will laugh at him," June protested, "if he doesn't learn to speak properly."

"He'll learn," Prue assured her, hugging William as she joined the party. "He'll learn only too soon."

The arrival of Helga and Peter interrupted the conversation. To make more seating available the Victorian Preserves reduced and congealed into a row on the sofa, squashed in so tightly that they could hardly raise their glasses to their lips. Prue managed to extricate herself and perched on the arm of the sofa.

"Oh! So sweet!" Helga dropped onto her knees before William who immediately grabbed a fistful of her hair.

"Will –i – am!" chorused the couch.

"It's all right," Helga laughed. "See William, you can have this instead. See it opens like so and shuts like so."

She gave him her key-ring to play with. It was the first time Peter had really noticed it. It was a model of a French baguette which hinged open to show a tiny collage of the popular sights in Paris. A gift from Pierre? He grimaced. With luck William would break it and he would buy her a little model Nessie to replace it.

The Maitland family staggered their entry. Ham and Chris first, elbowing each other came zig-zagging in their direction only to deflect towards the chrome bar stools.

"Hello!" they shouted across in unison, having seated themselves on the same chair, shoulders hunched, skinny brown legs trailing.

"Ahoy there, landlubbers!" John's greeting had all the awkwardness of a premeditated address as he followed Jane into the room and he swiftly covered up his embarrassment by offering a round of drinks. He had just mastered his order when

Jenny arrived with Donald, almost unrecognizably scrubbed up and after making the introductions, he forgot the order and had to take it again only to be interrupted again by Jane with, "Hang on, John! Here come Moira and Patrick!"

Moira, in soft clinging purple, paused in the doorway to scan the room before picking her way on tiptoe across the carpet with Patrick's hand propelling her from the small of her back.

"I'm the little new girl," she introduced herself. "You'll all have to tell me what to do."

It seemed she had forgotten to include Patrick. Jane, perched on the arm of John's chair, was suddenly struck by the frequency with which Moira used the word 'little': she used it with 'lovely' as in 'lovely little' with 'nice' as in 'nice little' ; she used it as an intensive Jane decided grammatically ; but then, on the other hand, she used it most often to apply to herself and her possessions as in "Silly little me!" or "one of my little ways", making herself diminutive, pettable. Next time she used it, Jane vowed, she would say, "Not little at all, Moira. Don't worry! You're quite big really. Hefty, actually. Especially round the thighs!"

"…and then after the meal," John was explaining to her, "we'll be having a meeting to swap experiences and firm up on the next few steps."

Jane decided to switch the attention from Moira.

"It's nice that you could all come," she addressed the couch. "Will William be all right?"

"I'm staying the night," Prue explained. "So when he gets tired I can just pop him up to bed."

"You too?" Moira picked up on the conversation. "Patrick and I are staying here until the eighteenth. He's actually left his golf would you believe?" She paused to take a sip, her eyes moving round the company over the rim of the glass. "But then we're ever so keen on water sports."

"That is good," Helga encouraged innocently. "I too like them, particularly the water-skiing. I used to do much water ski-ing. Particularly in Italy."

Peter tried hard not to visualise an Italian holiday for Helga and, and ... Pietro perhaps ... with red crosses fringing Lake Garda.

"Peter I think has not done much water sports. I teach you that, Peter. This holiday," she explained to Moira who looked very much as though her Bloody Mary had turned to pure lemon juice, "Peter teach me all about Scotland and I teach him some things too."

Peter hoped she would not itemise, but before she could they were summoned to dinner.

John lingered outside the dining-room door, ushering the others ahead and waiting for his chance to seize Ham and Chris and, as he had promised Jane, "scare the daylights out of them."

"Don't be too hard," she had warned. "Ham is more sensitive than we give him credit for. He was really upset about the drowning."

"O.K.," he had laughed, "I'll leave out the bit about pulling their nails and drawing their teeth."

"Hang on a minute, lads," he started fairly mildly. "I just want to tell you that I expect no silly behaviour to-night, no being cheeky to Moira directly or indirectly."

"Do we get something for behaving?" asked Ham.

He frowned. There was a thin line he decided between positive re-enforcement as advocated in the most progressive educational establishments and bribery. Ham was in danger of crossing it.

"At home we always get something for behaving," remarked Chris, "like sweets or extra spending money."

"I don't bribe my children," he squashed loftily, "but be good and I'll re-consider whether I let you go white water

319

rafting."

"Yes, Dad," said Ham submissively. Chris said nothing. He was looking puzzled. "Couldn't understand how being good can bring its own reward," John commented later when he relayed the conversation to Jane.

He was to wish with hindsight that he had uttered some sort of warning to Jenny, not that it would have made much difference, even though since the drowning episode he seemed to have gained more respect from all his family including his rebellious daughter. At the insistence of the other netters, he took the head of the table and Jane the foot - "like Mummy and Daddy," Moira commented sweetly – so that Jenny, seated halfway down was not all that visible and just out of earshot of both of them unless they raised their voices. She took full advantage, helping herself to red wine liberally, although she knew that her limit was supposed to be one glass watered down. She prodded her salmon diffidently and breathed goodwill all around the table indiscriminately, even at Helga. Having a man of her own now, she could afford to be generous so "Are you and Helga having a good time?" she sang out to Peter. Then she frowned, dimly aware that she sounded like a maiden aunt at a children's party, her lips moving as she struggled to rephrase,

"What I meant to say …" she started, but the appropriate wording eluded her and she giggled self-consciously.

"What did I mean?" she asked Donald.

But Donald was absorbed by his steak. Even Jenny could not compete with an Aberdeen Angus sirloin.

"Peter, what I meant …" she was overcome by giggling again.

Peter kept his eyes on his plate.

"It's all right, Jenny," Helga smiled serenely. "It's kind of you to ask and we have been enjoying hugely the lovely scenery around Loch Ness, but we are disappointed that we see no monster."

May laughed – it came out as a nervous cackle – but it was a laugh. John was thinking that he had never heard her laugh before. She drew Jenny's attention too and she kept her eyes on May while she refilled her glass and gulped noisily.

"Have you enjoyed it, May?" she hiccoughed loudly and benevolently. "We all felt sorry for you the day you had to play goo- gooseberry to Harry and April." Without adjusting her volume she explained to Donald, "We were playing crazy go-golf. And we saw ..." she shook with laughter ... "saw Harry taking April ..." more spluttering laughter, "up to his be- bedroom. And poor May had ..."

"Jenny!" Jane intervened. "Jenny! I want you to go to the car now please and check that Jelly's all right."

"Why can't Ham go?" she whined querulously.

"Go now!" John ordered adding, as Jenny piloted her glass unsteadily to a precarious landing on the table narrowly missing a candle and knocking over a salt cellar. "I'll come with you."

"See you in a bit." She swayed tenderly over Donald. "You be all right without me?" She glared round the table. "You all go-got to look after Donald."

John grabbed her arm and escorted her from the room.

Jane broke the silence. "Look everyone. I'm terribly sorry. Jenny isn't used to alcohol. She'll be very ashamed in the morning and ..."

"Don't worry, Jane," interrupted Harry. "I can assure you we've all been there!"

It sounded comforting but, although he could recall several drunken indiscretions on his own part, he could not remember any on Peter's. And the Victorian Preserves?

"At least I have," he amended.

"So have I," said Prue. "Forget it, Jane."

Moira looked pointedly at Patrick and raised an eyebrow, but he shook his head at her.

The meeting after dinner was not fully attended and gradually petered out. Jane had taken Jenny home and Ham and Chris went with her voluntarily. William settled uneasily in a strange cot and Prue took her coffee up to the bedroom. Harry's interest in researching folk-lore was approved by all. May developed hiccoughs. Peter yawned repeatedly despite his lengthy sleep and Helga dragged him off solicitously "for an early night." As soon as they were clear about the arrangements for the exploration of Loch Oich, the Reynolds sisters trooped upstairs in a body to bid Prue good-night and Harry gave John a lift back. At John's cottage they both got out of the car and leaned against it. The wind had got up, blowing away the midges and ruffling the surface of Loch Oich. An oddly shaped moon was slowly dominating the darkening sky, gleaming on the hulls of three boats as they rocked and nudged at the jetty at the Well of the Seven Heads. One of them would be *The Lass* but John was not sure which one. They could just make out the tawny dome of Peter's tent on the little beached spit of land beside the jetty. The light of an odd car or two wove between the trees that bordered the lochside road to Invergarry.

"This was our favourite loch," John said quietly, "my Dad's and mine. Our favourite."

Jane came out and walked towards the car. "Coffee, Harry?"

"No, no thanks. Thanks, but must get back. Could be a tiring day tomorrow. 'Night all."

Chapter Nineteen

The Second Expedition

Loch Oich

The rest of the world always awoke before Loch Oich. John remembered that from his childhood: how it lay slightly curved, relaxed as a sleeper with the sunlight draining slowly down the steep-sided hills, rippling unevenly over the heads of the pines, while the traffic from the wide-awake places busied itself along the road from Laggan to Invergarry.

"This was my favourite loch," he said as he put his arm around Jane who had joined him at the window. "My Dad's and mine. I think this one is going to be the best so far."

Jenny, coming reluctantly to a consciousness punctuated by inconclusive dreams and uncertainty about her whereabouts, didn't share his optimism, She didn't have a headache, nor could she recognise any of the other hangover symptoms vividly described by those at school who lived exciting lives. Perhaps it was because she had had been so sick last night. "A good thing!" her mother had remarked grimly, holding her hair out of the way while she retched onto the roadside verge with Ham and Chris inside the car, commenting over-loudly about the quantity she was spewing forth. Perhaps it was because of the glassesful of water her mother had thrust at her and forced her to drink. Then again, and she smiled to herself, perhaps it was because she could hold her drink. Her triumph was swiftly quenched by another surge of consciousness bringing with it the certainty that she had indeed been out of control and that her attempts at humour could have been interpreted by some as offensive. Her father had left her with that impression when he had dragged her from the table. The reality was that she had been offensive to April, May and Harry; had caused embarrassment to Peter, Helga and Donald; had been an object of ridicule to Ham and Chris and her parents would certainly not be speaking to her. Well, she would not speak to them either. When they scowled at her over breakfast, she would scowl back. She could outscowl anybody. She would just... There was a tap on her door.

"Cup of tea, Jenny dear?" asked her mother.

Across the loch on the small strip of beach below the Well of the Seven Heads, a thin wisp of smoke was gradually burgeoning with a flickering orange that disappeared and re-appeared as Helga crouched down to blow her fire into life.

"It's coming," she called to Peter who was searching for more twigs in the shrubbery behind her and setting up drifts of midges as he disturbed the long grass and green lushness. "We will soon have breakfast, I think."

A pair of swans with three grey-grubby cygnets, patrolling just off-shore were eyeing the fire speculatively, obviously sharing her optimism about breakfast.

"You should see all the midges!" he called back. "It's incredible."

"You will be all right though," she replied smugly. "I have covered you well."

She had indeed sprayed him all over with anti-midge spray, and insisted on rubbing it in, even attending to parts which no self-respecting midge would ever intrude into and ignoring the printed instructions about avoiding sensitive areas with the result that he had experienced some pleasant and unpleasant tingling sensations.

"And you've done the fire very well." He bent over her and kissed the top of her head. "I'll away up to the shops for sausages and rolls. I see the door is open."

She smiled up at him and as he smiled back he felt the shadowy forms of Pierre, Pietro, Pedro, Petrus and any other red cross holiday manifestations reconcile themselves to a watery death in the loch – temporarily.

June had slept badly, woken early and completed painting the woodwork in William's playroom by the time April and May were ready to set out on the Loch Oich expedition. She hoped Prue would be pleasantly surprised and that there would be time perhaps before the eventual return to Edinburgh, for the two of them to explore Fort William and Inverness for suitable floor coverings: something durable and bright. Prue would, of course, suggest that they should consult May about the colour. Hopefully, May would not be invited to accompany them on the shopping spree.

May tapped nervously on the door as June forced the lid back on the paint tin with her foot and poked her head only just inside.

"It looks lovely," she ventured.

"Don't touch *any*thing, May!"

"April says," May started before remembering that April had actually said, "Go and tell June to hurry up," and frowned at the impossibility of this communication, "we're ready," she concluded lamely.

"Tell April I'm not ready and I'll come as soon as I've cleaned my brushes and changed," retorted June, tipping white spirit into a bucket and leaving May in a quandary as to how to translate that message into wording appropriate for April's ears.

Harry parked outside the Maitland cottage and, before he had time to admire the morning beauty of the loch, was effusively greeted by Jelly who flung herself at him, dripping water down his trouser legs.

"She's just had her morning swim." Jenny emerged form the lochside path, swinging a lead. "The labrador part of her loves the water. I'm sorry she's wet you."

"That's all right!" Harry ruffled the shaggy, black fur on Jelly's back. "What's a little water between friends?"

"And," Jenny was near enough now to be able to lower her voice, "I'm very sorry about last night." She traced a line on the ground with the toe of her trainer and blushed. "Sorry about what I said about you and April. It was very cheeky and I'd had too much wine and I know it's not true."

"Are you sure?"

Jenny looked up. His face was serious but his eyes might be laughing at her from behind his glasses.

"I…"

"Forget it, Jenny. It is really nice of you to apologise, but it really was no big deal."

"I only hope April feels the same way," murmured Jenny as Jane appeared with a towel for Jelly, calling backwards over her shoulder, "And do it properly, boys," before smiling at Harry. "Hello, Harry. Jenny, don't bring Jelly in until she's dry. Come in, Harry."

"Hello, Jane! Multi-tasking as usual?"

"Multi-bossing," muttered Jenny. "Come on, Jelly. I suppose *I* have the honour of drying you."

By eleven o'clock on his watch, John was in despair. The routes for the cyclists and the walkers had been decided with the cyclists setting off along the cycle track to the west of the loch and returning along the footpath to the east while the walkers were to take the footpath and return the same way, but the debate about where or when the cyclists and the walkers should meet, or even if they should meet, seemed interminable with participants failing to respond to the suggestions of others before putting forward their own novel solutions.

"What comes of not having a proper meeting the night before," he confided to Harry. "Women do have to be pinned down."

"Never thought you were one for sado-masochism," muttered Harry out of the side of his mouth before adding more loudly, "and anyway I rather think that the whole ethos of loch-netting should be fluid."

"Uh-huh," John rather liked that phrase. He would commit it to memory and preserve it for a radio interview.

By eleven- thirty it had been decided that it would be better if they did not have a planned meeting-point but that at half-past two, Peter would phone John for a check up on the situations of both parties.

"That's men for you," whispered June into William's ear, "present company excepted of course but you're hardly a man. They take half an hour to decide anything."

She had wrested William from Prue, insisting that Prue was to hire a bike from the *School of Activity* and leave her to have "quality time with my nephew." *Quality time* was a phrase that Prue had never expected to hear on June's lips and she had been stunned into handing over her child with the minimum of caveats.

Almost noon and the hands of John's watch had almost joined in wry congratulation by the time they were variously organised and almost ready to go. Rucksacks were finally checked. Peter had completed his check on the other bikes in his party and was concentrating on the one Prue had just wheeled up.

"Sorry to join you at the last minute," she said breathlessly, "but June insists that I go with you. I hope I won't hold you back. Can somebody show me how this bloody cycle helmet fastens."

Her fingers were shaking, partly with excitement, partly with nervousness.

"I do it for you," and Helga leaned her bike against the obligatory rowan by the door of the cottage. "It's quite easy really. I will teach you."

"Thank-you," breathed Prue gratefully. "I do hope I'm not going to hold everyone up. I haven't cycled in years."

"Don't worry," reassured Helga. "We go slow here. Not like the time I go up the Alps in Switzerland with my friend, Pierre. He hold the *maillot jaune* for two etapes of the Tour de France."

Prue did not look greatly re-assured. Neither did Peter.

As John watched Ham wheeling his bike forward he had a sudden urge to call him back, to take him with him along the path by the loch which he had so often trodden with *his* father and show him *his* favourite places. Jane laid a hand on his arm

"Take him later," she whispered. "You don't really want to do it when everyone else is around."

Sometimes he wondered if Jane was psychic.

It was noon.

The walkers had finished tying their walking boots and were tucking their trousers into their woollen socks to dissuade any lurking ticks from ascending to places warm and soft. April and May were flourishing bright new walking poles because as May confided to Harry, "April says you never know *who* you're going to meet." She looked worried as she said it.

"I'm sure that was a joke," responded Harry. "You've got us all to protect you and the poles are a jolly good idea on the uneven ground."

Jelly, ball in mouth, was ready to accompany anyone anywhere, provided she didn't have to wait any longer and it was unanimously agreed not to wait for Moira and Patrick who had not turned up and had sent no message.

"Still bonking, I expect," Chris had sniggered to Ham.

"No, they've got a water-bed. Remember? Moira was boasting last night that they had a water-bed."

"You can still do it on a water-bed. You just have to take precautions."

"Well maybe they didn't take them. Maybe they've drowned."

The rest of the party had not even speculated. Moira and Patrick were after all, comparatively speaking, outsiders.

They went their separate ways at seven minutes past twelve.

"Timing is important," John said.

The cycling party arrived at the swing-bridge at North Laggan just as the warning lights began to flash and the barricades came down. They watched as the road before them swung slowly to one side to allow the passage of three small motor cruisers and a yacht powering in their wake with its masts bare of sails.

"Wish we could have got through the barricade onto the bridge," shouted Ham to Chris above the snorting and revving of the motorbikes behind them,

"Well, to-morrow …" Chris began to bellow.

"Don't even think it," yelled Peter. "In any case the man wouldn't open the bridge with you on it."

Prue, gazing back over her shoulder towards the cottage as though she expected to see William toddling after her, barely heard the exchange. She frowned to herself as she tried to remember whether she had reminded June that William liked his banana mashed.

"You are worried, I think?" Helga's voice was warm and kind.

"I've never left William before," Prue confessed half-laughing, "Not with anyone."

"It is good for him I think," pronounced Helga sagely. "In Norway I work for a private nursery owned by my mother. He will not cry for long after you leave him."

Prue smiled at her gratefully.

"I had no real knowledge of children before I had

William," she admitted. "I am learning as I go along."

"I will help you while I am here," re-assured Helga so confidently that a smattering of irritation began to curdle in Prue's gratitude.

Arrival at the start of the cycle-path brought rebellion.

"Peter!" Helga was aghast. "This path goes very much uphill. We are better, I think, to stay on the road. It is an easier ride and much nearer to the loch."

Peter hesitated.

"Everybody vote with me!" incited Helga.

Ham waved his arm in the air with a flourish in support of her. After a second Chris followed his example.

"The thing is," Peter began slowly, "I'm not taking the younger ones along the road. The traffic is fast and dangerous. I couldn't live with myself if something happened."

"We've been on a main road before," Jenny, though more inclined to side with Peter, had a suspicion that she might be included in the "younger ones" classification. "Remember, Peter, when we did Loch Garry we …"

"Yes, I know, Jenny, and you all did very well, but this road is narrower and faster and carries very heavy traffic. No, Helga," Peter steeled himself. "Sorry! Not on!"

"We could divide up, I think," Helga persisted. "You go up onto the cycle path with the children and Prue and I stay on the road. Poor Prue! She is not used to cycling."

"I'd rather go on the cycle-path if it's quieter." Thoughts of a motherless William and a resentment of the phrase "poor Prue" combining to give Prue's voice a very definite edge, "and if I'm slow, no-one need wait for me." She could not resist adding, "You should be O.K. on a steep path,

Helga. You went over the Alps. Remember?"

"As if I could forget," sighed Helga. "It was wonderful."

"Helga, I can't stop you from going on the road if you want to," Peter snapped. "I'd rather you went with us …"

"You are so sweet to worry, Peter, but I be very careful and I wait for you in the car-park for the old bridge at the other end of the loch. Now give me a kiss."

He obliged, blushing, while Chris stuck a finger down his throat and Ham sniggered.

"See you later, " she waved. "Be careful, Peter. There are wolves in the forest, I think."

William had not taken his mother's tender parting admonition, "Be good for Aunty Jew-Jew," too much to heart. With an eighteen-month old's conservatism, he was opposed to change. There had been too much scene-changing recently for his liking and he was not averse to expressing his feelings loudly and clearly when his repeated pathetic bleats of "Mummy, Mummy" failed to bring her running to his side.

"Duck!" shouted June, pointing to the swans and trying to make herself heard over his wailing. "Quack-quack!" she bawled, desperate enough to forget her scruples about baby-talk. "O-o-oh! *Big* quack-quack!"

William was still inconsolable. Jane had given June the freedom of the cottage and before Prue could hear his screams and come wheeling back, she carried him inside, closing the inner and outer porch doors behind her to muffle his output.

"William like a drink? Lovely fruit juice?"

Outrage.

"For heaven's sake, William, I'm not Lucretia Borgia. I'm your Aunty Jew-Jew."

She carried him to the window in search of distraction. Through the trees she could make out the bright clothing of the cyclists as they moved slowly onto the cycle path.

"There's Mummy!"

The crying stopped so suddenly that the silence rang in her ears. She was able to collect her wits and think deviously.

"Aunty Jew-Jew is going to put William in his buggy and take him to watch Mummy. We'll just wash your face so that Mummy doesn't think I've been battering you."

Still gulping back sobs, he submitted to having his face flannelled, being buckled into his buggy and given his brown plush tortoise to hold.

"See Mummy?" he whispered hoarsely, twisting round to face her, his limited experience of adults having taught him that they needed constant prompting and reminding.

"Yes," she re-assured him and herself, qualms that he might just jalouse that the faces and forms of cyclists that she would point out to him along the road were not Mummy beginning to assail her, "We are. We are going to watch Mummy. Now show Tortoise the ducks."

William obligingly held his tortoise up in the vague direction of the loch with its face pointing towards himself.

"Yook, Torty! Quack-quack!"

It was progression and as the wheels of the buggy rumbled over the little path to the quayside, June continued to distract him. In fact they engaged in a mini-competition to see who could point out the most landmarks to the unresponsive Torty and it was William who with "Yook , Torty! Lady!" pointed out Mattie.

    The footpath along the east side of Loch Oich followed the contours of the loch, dipping down in places almost to the surface of the loch, and was so narrow at first that it was necessary to walk in single file. Jelly threaded her way between the walkers, taking refreshing dips at whim and shaking her wet fur liberally over each and every one of them.

    "What I love about this loch," John called back from his position as leader, "is the fact that you can get so close to it."

    Harry, bringing up the rear, smiled indulgently. "What I love about this loch," had this morning almost become John's catch-phrase as he enthused over various features. He wondered idly to himself if there were any myths or folk-lore that he would be able to unearth about Loch Oich. Of facts there were plenty: the grim story of the Well of the Seven Heads was well substantiated historical fact; geographically, Loch Oich was the highest point in the Caledonian Canal link, the mid point and possibly the busiest of the three lochs. Fishing trawlers, dark and rust-stained from their battles against the capriciousness of the North Sea, the Irish Sea and the Atlantic, ploughed their way apparently on automatic pilot between the red and green buoys, as deserted as though the crew were all below, grabbing the opportunity for rest and respite. Large pleasure cruisers strung with bunting coasted cheerfully through with passengers waving from the decks to anybody prepared to reciprocate their greetings and small cruisers like *The Lass* and *The Lady*, nosed exploratively into jettied inlets or processed purposefully in a line towards the swing-bridge which would allow them access through the Laggan Lock to Loch Lochy. He could understand why John as a boy had so loved this loch above all. In some places promontories of stunted oak overhung the water, providing dark secret watery places guaranteed to liberate childish imaginations, in others slim crescents, new moons of white sand, almost hidden from the path by vegetation, offered opportunities for the stealthy landings of pirating marauders as they slipped canoes silently in and out of the waters. The loch-side path seemed suddenly to be blocked and they followed a well-worn track up onto the disused railway line, long since dismantled and partially obstructed by the same land-slip that, having quarried the hill-side above, had descended to destroy the loch-side path. The railway path was considerably wider and the party reformed self-consciously into groups. John walked ahead with May and Harry, noticing the speed with which April scurried to catch up with them, wondered with a degree of amusement whether she was determined to scotch any suspicions that Jenny's indiscretion of the night before might have hatched. He fell into step beside Jane and as they walked together, felt a sudden unpremeditated urge to confide in her. It was something about the way in which they adapted to each other's rhythm of walking perhaps, or something about the way in which they could share unembarrassed silences. He wanted to talk to her about Peter; tell her about the forthcoming blood-test and about how after the result the future was so unclear; tell her how he had misread, misunderstood the boy on his arrival in Scotland to live with him; tell her how vulnerable Peter really was, so vulnerable that he was surely no match for the experienced Helga. He wanted to hear what she would say. But already John was leading them back down onto the single file path through the loch fringed woodland, across wooden bridges spanning the clear, cold streams that could be heard above, but not seen, as they plunged in waterfalls over rock faces.

"Mattie!"

It was just a dry whisper and the woman, slumped in a faded, striped canvas deck-chair, with her arms hanging limply down so that her knuckles brushed the grass, her legs stretched wide apart under the thin, light-blue skirt that clung to her damply from elasticated waist to pearly white mid-calf, never opened her eyes.

"Yook, Torty! Lady no shoes!"

William was right and the bare feet were the same as June had always known them, perhaps slightly thicker around the ankle, but still with the same tiny pink toes that looked like sea-shells. She had said that to Mattie once and Mattie had laughed, pleased by the comparison and coquettishly hidden her feet under the purple throw they had chosen because of its rich colour. But the cheap Indian cotton had lost its vibrancy after the first wash, had faded to a greyish lavender. The feet were definitely the same even though the gathers from the skirt's waistband now opened unflatteringly around the girth of the hip-line and the clinging material could not disguise the hefty thighs.

"Mattie!"

She was standing beside the deck-chair now, having left William and Torty on the path. The eyes fluttered open. She remembered that too. Whereas other people were capable of instant wakefulness, Mattie had always hovered in a state between sleep and waking. She could see the face on the pillow beside her, the short fair eyelashes beating up and down slowly like a butterfly fanning damp morning wings in early sunshine. Then she would pass the tip of her tongue over her dry lips as though tasting the day that had dawned. Sure enough, the tip of the tongue protruded. June relaxed. She was on familiar ground.

"Mattie! It's me, June!"

Mattie sat up, darted a swift glance over her shoulder towards the house and struggled out of her deck-chair, grunting slightly with the effort. She looked at June in amazement.

"Oh, Mattie!"

Mattie stood up and the world burst into the most glorious operatic aria as June flung her arms around her. The cheek against hers was as soft as she remembered it. The body felt different. Mattie's breasts, the soft "little molehills" of before had grown into formidably fortified structures that obstructed close contact and the shoulder-blades, the spine, previously so pathetically palpable were not discernible under their fleshy padding. Further more, June felt the body stiffening, bracing itself into a determined unresponsiveness. She drew back.

"June," said the long-lost Mattie holding out a hand, "lovely to see you."

She glanced again over her shoulder towards the door. June took it as the prelude to an invitation.

"Oh, I'm sorry. I can't come in just now ..." she started and stopped because her attention had been arrested by the man walking round the side of the house, bouncing a tennis ball on an old tennis racket from which a couple of snapped strings were hanging down. He was of average height but very thin with a hairiness that gave him a vaguely pre-historic appearance. His dark hair hung to his chin and from there a beard, the sort that June associated with religious fanaticism took over. Most striking were his eyebrows- thick, black, irregular and as mobile as independent life forms. He took a stand so close to Mattie that June retreated a few more steps.

"We have a visitor?" he asked, his voice very deep, very smooth.

The 'we' was unbearably painful. June registered the pain behind her knees; felt them give slightly.

"Just an old university friend."

Just?

"Actually," June started and stiffened herself against the pleading in Mattie's eyes, "Mattie and I were flatmates for well over a year."

"Really?" One of the eyebrows moved upwards without bending. It just levitated towards his hairline. "Well, you *will* have to come to supper then. I'd love to hear just what Tilda got up to before I took her in hand. Was she a naughty little thing? Will we have to put her on the naughty step?"

The smile that was in his voice was lost in his beard. He put his arm around Mattie. June could not look at either of them. Right on cue William, bless him, started girning.

"I'll have to go. I'm sorry!"

"Not before we make a date," he called. "Tomorrow evening?"

He was following her down onto the path. Mattie remained where she was. June couldn't think straight.

"Seven o'clock?"

"O.K.. Thanks." She was breathless. She had to get away.

William was girning because Torty had taken a nose-dive onto the path. June picked up Torty and restored him to the arms of his owner.

"My name's Oliver by the way." He was still there. "And," he lowered his voice, "we don't call Tilda 'Mattie' any more. She says 'Mattie' reminds her of a time when she was rather a doormat to a much stronger person. Felt herself bullied." His voice sank even lower. "Reckon some bloke was taking a bit of a loan."

"Yook, Torty. Yook!"

William was fascinated by the beard and the way it twitched when Oliver spoke, but the word 'beard' was not yet in his vocabulary.

"Yook, Torty! Man! *Funny* man!"

June reminded him of his quest for Mummy and hurried him away.

"You go first, Jenny, and go steady. Don't leave us all behind. Chris and Ham follow Jenny and Prue and I will bring up the rear. O.K. everyone?" Let's not waste any more time."

He smiled round but the smile was little more than a straightening and thinning of the lips and Prue guessed that Peter wanted to move swiftly on to brook any discussion on Helga's defection.

Jenny, biddable and compliant as never before, was careful not to set too punishing a pace, glancing over her shoulder from time to time to assess the progress of those following her. The uphill climb was steep and Prue's calves soon ached with the strain of pedalling, but with her heart beating fast from the exercise, she felt exhilarated. They seemed to be riding along a bright strip of sunlight with the pine plantations high and dark on either side of them, shutting off the rest of the world so that the possibilities of William waxing hysterical at the absence of his mother or Helga coming to a sticky end under road haulage were problems of another existence. The silence that surrounded them was not as much the complete absence of noise as the fact that the curtain of pine reduced sound to a sympathetic level: even the noise of the traffic below modulated to a swell and surge, regular and rhythmic as the surf on shingle.

As they freewheeled lazily down towards Invergarry, Prue felt triumph.

"You did well then, Jen!" Peter patted Jenny's shoulder as she unwrapped her sandwiches. "Your pace was just right."

Jenny smiled and blushed and knew confusion. Perhaps she did fancy Peter after all? Perhaps Donald? Maybe she could run them concurrently as possibilities to be on the safe side. After last night she could not be sure of Donald. On the other hand, Peter was old and he had Helga. Except that Helga had been a right cow this morning. She nibbled at her salad sandwich, gazed into the distance and said with sweet concern, "Wonder how Helga's getting on?"

Peter turned away from her without replying and busied himself with something in his saddle-bag.

"Ham and I think she's hitched a lift from a lorry-driver and is sunbathing somewhere," Chris put in brightly. "Sunbathing with the lorry-driver on the banks of Loch Oich. Sharing sandwiches and…"

"Look at that bird," broke in Prue. "I'm sure it's a golden eagle."

It was enough to arrest Chris' speculation.

"I'm not sure," said Ham. "It could be a buzzard."

"No," Prue shook her head, "It's too big and look at its wing-tips. You can see the long finger things clearly."

Peter took glasses out of his saddle-bag.

"I think you're right, Prue. Anybody want a peek?"

While Peter was gazing skyward, Jenny pulled Chris aside, yanking him by the front of his shirt and whispered savagely, "You don't make remarks about people's girl or boy-friends." She shook him slightly. "What you said about Helga was not funny."

"Ow!" He tried to shake himself free. "You started it. Let GO!"

"Something wrong?" Peter turned round from helping Ham to focus on the bird.

"Nothing at all," beamed Jenny. "I was just smartening Chris up a bit."She tweaked violently at his shirt collar and released him.

May made a decision.

She made it while the rest of the walking party were packing up their picnic lunch and preparing to walk on.

She thought it through clearly even while April was reminding her to screw the top tightly onto her thermos flask.

She said loudly and clearly, "The rest of you please go

on. I want to stay here and sketch."

"Sketch what?" April frowned, too shocked to
remember that she was supposed to be encouraging May to
"take initiatives." "Small steps forward," Norman Paterson had
been irritating enough to clarify when he had interrupted her
board meeting to discuss May's progress and mistaken her
natural reluctance to adapt suddenly from the world of
marketing for an inability to understand the simple English of
"Encourage her to take small steps forward on her own."
Choosing colour schemes for Prue or arranging flowers was
surely what he would mean; not demanding to be abandoned in
the middle of nowhere to the mercy of every passing sex-
starved male. If it had been June, fine. But May?

May was waving her hand towards a little ruined croft-
house, roofless but still very white.

"That would make a lovely sketch," she said looking
not at April but at the house, "against all those bushes and
things. And I could put in a few sheep."

Just as she finished speaking, a shaggy-coated ewe
appeared co-operatively in the wall cavity that had once been a
doorway, bleated peremptorily for its lamb, eyed the picnickers
half warily, half accusingly as though they might be guilty of
abduction, flicked an ear and trotted off still bleating.

John looked at the stretch of loch they would be
exploring on the next leg of their walk, where it narrowed,
became island-strewn with an indecisive border of water and
grass and long-stemmed reeds, hazardous for boats that
departed off course, richly safe for water birds and aquatic
mammals, and sighed inaudibly.

"I know this path very well," he said. "I've been along
it often before - even though it was a very long time ago. You
others go along as planned and get the bus back. I'll wait until

May has finished her sketch and walk back with her." He was suddenly aware that he was speaking of May in the third person, directing his suggestion to April and turned apologetically to May. "That O.K?"

"Fine," May smiled. "Thank-you."

April fixed May with a stern gaze and spoke sharply, "Do you think that's fair on John?"

For the first time May wavered. She looked from April to John and back to the croft-house.

"Thing is," said John, "I'd really like a sketch of this place if May doesn't mind. My father and I used to camp right here and the house was ruined even then."

Without wasting a minute May settled herself on one of the white stones which must have been dislodged from the house with sufficient force to send it rolling down the slope towards the loch and took out her sketch pad.

"Yook, Torty! Flower!"

Ten seconds later, "Yook, Torty! Gwass!"

William was making every effort to engage her interest, to get the game going again.

"Look, Torty..." June attempted but nothing presented itself.

She did not feel as though she was experiencing disappointment or sorrow, just a deep sense of absence, of nothingness.

"This must be what hell is," she said to herself out aloud, "a nothingness, a vacancy."

William twisted round uncertainly, thinking that the communication was meant for him and failing to understand it."

"Look, Torty! Boat!"

They'd had 'boat' before but William seemed perfectly happy for it to be repeated and it left her free to follow her thoughts. Remembrance of another such time of nothingness came to her like a sudden sour regurgitation. It was a time she had experienced years ago as a child that first Christmas after her mother died. Her mother had been dead two months and she and April had long since been disabused about Father Christmas by their father who believed that children should never under any circumstances be lied to. Yet, in the full knowledge that her mother was dead and Father Christmas was a non-person, she had still hung up her stocking, modified to just a sock actually, a small grey school sock, but she had made sure it was clean, and never thought to doubt the magical potential of that time. She had woken early on Christmas morning and shivering in the dark and cold, felt eagerly along the bed for the re-assurance of the bulk she would be allowed to explore later when the others were awake. Her first thought when she could only feel the flimsiness of the empty sock was that she was too early. Then she heard the clock on the landing and counted the chimes up to seven. There were presents later on, thoughtful presents, useful presents, but the loss of that secret magical time when she could feel the bumps and bulges in the dark and guess at their potential, left her not only with a sense of shame at her own naivety but also with an overwhelming sense of loss, a vacancy.

"Mattie," she whispered, "you're nothing but an empty sock."

She looked down at William's fluffy head.

"Look, Torty! Bicycle! Mummy on bicycle!"

No response. William was asleep. Just as well as the sturdy figure coasting along the road bore so little resemblance to Prue that even William might have rumbled her deceit. He could only just have fallen asleep because he was still vigorously sucking his thumb and Torty was in danger of falling out of his relaxed grasp. She rescued Torty, stuffed him into her pocket and wheeled William back to the cottage. He hadn't had his lunch yet but it would be better, she judged, for him and for herself to let him finish his sleep first. She wheeled the buggy carefully into the cottage and sank down on a chair, gazing sightlessly out on the smooth waters of the loch.

To the disappointment of Ham and Chris, Helga beat them to the car-park for the old bridge and when they arrived, was standing studying a sheaf of post-cards fanned out in her hand with her bike leaning up against a tree. Peter had to struggle not to let his relief at seeing her temper the coldness with which he meant to convey his displeasure at her defection. "There is," he had planned to say to her, "such a thing as team-spirit."

She pocketed her cards and approached him hesitantly swinging her hat diffidently and said, "I am sorry, Peter. I should not have done that, I think."

"'s O.K.," he responded gruffly, realising his remark about team-spirit was now superfluous and that he had nothing else left to say except, "I'm glad you're safe."

"Did you get a lift?" Chris asked eagerly.

"Clever you," she smiled. "Yes, actually I did. I cheat."

"I'm getting the second sight," announced Chris triumphantly, holding his fists to his eyes in the style of binoculars, "I'm like that chap at Dochfour, the Something Seer, the one who your mum said …"

"Was it with a lorry-driver?" butted in Ham.

"No," Helga smiled, "actually it was with Moira and Patrick."

"Some second sight!" scoffed Ham.

Over the yelps and grunts of the boys who were settling their differences with an impromptu skirmish, Helga explained that she had diverted off the main road through the grounds of Glengarry Castle Hotel.

"They were so beautiful," she said. "The grounds go right down to the loch where there is a little jetty and there was a boat there and there is, too, a lovely old ruined castle with a very sad story. I go into the hotel because I am thirsty and I think too how nice would be a sandwich. I finish my sandwich and I buy some postcards to send and I hear behind me Moira and Patrick. They say I should have some coffee with them and they will run me to this car park." She looked at Peter self-consciously and made a moue. "And I am in a weak moment and I agree."

"What shall we do with her?" Peter avoided a personal response by turning to the others with his hands held out in mock exasperation.

"Throw her into the loch!" Jenny's eyes were gleaming. "Where are Moira and Patrick now?"

"They say they go to Inverness to shop and they see us bright and early to-morrow for the water-sports."

"That's all we need," groaned Jenny.

"Time for the off," said Peter. "Helga, you slot in behind Jenny, our leader, and the rest of us will stay as before."

As they waited in pairs at the swing-bridge, Prue turned to Peter to suggest that he might like her to change places with Helga, noticed the expression on his face as he watched Helga laughing about something with Chris and Ham and decided against it.

April walked, Harry decided, like a woman driven: she seldom glanced either to left or right and fixed her eyes resolutely on the vanishing point of the path, be it at merely a few yards before it curled out of sight behind high bracken or at a far point at which a barely discernible thread of path dwindled into obscurity. From her repeated glances at her watch, he judged that her goal was to accomplish the task within an acceptable time limit. Enjoyment and entertainment were non-essential by-products of the exercise.

Outwardly purposeful and self-possessed though she may have seemed, April was actually experiencing an uncomfortable sensation of guilt which led in turn to a disconcerting absence of self-recognition. First of all she had made a wrong decision: she should not be walking with Jane and Harry. She should instead have remained with May and insisted that John went forward with Harry and Jane. Then, and even more disagreeably, came the realisation that she hadn't made the decision at all: she had actually allowed herself to succumb to decision-making by others. It had happened so suddenly, she excused herself. May had been uncharacteristically firm; John had just as surprisingly abdicated leadership and Harry had picked up her rucksack and helped her on with it as though taking her company for granted. She had just fallen in, given way and this was not her customary modus operandi. She had acquired a stone in her shoe which was digging into the sole of her foot but, she decided, she would not stop to remove it she would suffer it as self-inflicted punishment for her stupidity.

On the other hand, perhaps she had been flexible rather than merely weak. She didn't really know flexibility. She, in her position of responsibility, could hardly be expected to know it, but at the end of June she had arranged an afternoon session on *Flexibility At Work* for her factory workers when, after two unexpected resignations and one unfortunate sacking, she had realised that it would be profitable if the remaining staff agreed to multi-task. She had even attended the session herself. It had been conducted by Caroline Somebody or Other who had come highly recommended by a business associate in the strawberry retail business and whose glossy brochure had arrived in a satisfactorily thick cream envelope. Caroline, just "Caroline" she wished to be addressed as, had, judging from her ignorance about the hierarchical structure within a factory, never worked in one and therefore had exuded exotic, alien appeal for the workers who had subsequently scrawled glowing tributes in their assessment forms – at least half of them suggesting that these sessions should be held regularly. That of course would be unthinkable in the interests of the company meeting its projected productivity. It was too early to tell whether the session had produced its desired effect. April had never thought of flexibility as being something which should be expected of management: not of her role nor of June's although of course May's remit was nothing if not flexible. On the other hand, this loch-netting business was not the factory; she was not the leader here; leader of a sub-section perhaps but that was all and perhaps in that capacity her flexibility as a team member to the extent of allowing her role to be dictated by others, would be appropriate. She would perhaps, as Caroline had suggested to the workers, have to play her part in recognising if and when her role needed to be changed. It would follow then that her role now was to be a good companion to Jane and Harry.

But how?

She had a vegetable garden interest in common with Jane. She could at least ask if she too had root-fly in her carrots. Or perhaps she could begin by asking them kindly to wait while she removed the stone from her shoe.

June was spooning mashed banana into William when Mattie rang the door-bell. It rang piercingly sharply like a dentist's drill in slow motion and she opened the door, frowning as much at the noise as at the ill-timing of the interruption. Mattie, quivering slightly, was standing a good two metres from the front step as though poised for retreat and June thought that the nervousness which had made her seem so fragile and appealing as a girl had matured into something absurd, ill-befitting a matron. Her voice when she spoke was unnaturally high and her speech fragmented.

"June, I was wondering … if you're not busy … I'm afraid I tracked you back here … I'm sorry if I disturbed your baby … if I could have a word … in private?"

"Well. I'm afraid William will have to listen in," responded June dryly, "but there's no-one else here at the moment. Come in. If you go straight ahead and sit down," she indicated the sitting-room with her spare hand, "I'll just collect William's banana from the kitchen and join you."

Mattie hunched her shoulders as she tiptoed through the

hall as though she was frightened of taking up too much room and waited for June and William to join her before perching nervously on the edge of a chair. June deliberately concentrated on giving William the rest of his mashed banana, leaving Mattie to struggle unassisted with her opening gambit.

"Lovely baby!" she ventured at last, hands on knees and rocking slightly. "Do you have any other children?"

"No."

"We have three," Mattie confided in a tone which would have been appropriate for confessing an indulgence in too much cream cake. Over the top of William's plate of banana, June could see Mattie's feet, could watch the tiny pink toes squirming nervously in the clumsy open-toed sandals. "We have three dear little girls. My mother is with us. She's taken them out for the day to give us, you know, time for ourselves."

"That's cosy."

Mattie sighed, presumably to indicate that she had given up on the preamble. June smiled at William and returned his spoon to the plate for a refill.

"June, about tomorrow evening?"

June kept her face expressionless, but the spoon in her hand began to shake irritatingly.

"Tomorrow evening when you come to supper? Please don't let on about us, about you and me, about our friendship when we shared the flat. Oliver would be upset if …"

"If he knew you were a lesbian? If he knew that you and I had had a deep, caring, loving relationship? Well, he won't find out over the supper table because I don't eat with disloyal friends, even less with disloyal partners."

"I'm not disloyal!" Mattie's lip was quivering and the loose flesh beneath her small pointed chin shook in sympathy. "And I am NOT a lesbian. You were … were a phase I was going through."

"Well you're through it now," said June. "Good-bye."

Mattie turned at the door and hesitated, fingering the door handle. Then she spoke in a normal voice as though nothing much had taken place, "What excuse would you like me to give Oliver? For your not coming to supper tomorrow, I mean? He is going to wonder."

"Don't worry," June kept her tone level, "I have got manners even if I am still a lesbian and I will be dropping him a line to explain truthfully just why it is I am unable to dine with you."

"But …"

"And now please go!"

Mattie went.

Cycling easily back along the lochside route taken earlier by the walkers, Jenny could understand why it was that her father loved this loch.

"It would be nice to take a picture," Helga said to her, "but the trouble is that a photograph would not give the … the depth. That is not, I think, the right word."

"I think it is exactly right," said Jenny thinking that if it weren't for Peter and for the fact that Helga was competition, she might actually like her.

A photo would be useless. It would be flat. It couldn't give the sense of the varying depths of the loch or the drift of the clouds or the hills that billowed out towards the water, their stiff, pine-forested skirts frill-hemmed with a froth of lighter green deciduous woodland at the water's edge. It wouldn't give you the interplay between dark and light, the light in unexpected places like the silvery backs of leaves disturbed by the wind or the shining of falling water in shady places. It would paralyse all movement, losing the shifting surface patterns of the waters mid-loch and the sudden bubble-rings of fish in the dark satin water near the shore. It would reduce all this to three layered strips of sky, hill and loch.

A sudden scream of two low-flying jets surrounded them, ricocheting off the hill sides and thundering between them just as they caught up with May, John and Jelly. The dog cowered low to the ground, shaking with fear. John picked her up and she burrowed into his chest, holding her head under his jacket.

"Poor, poor Jelly," said Helga. "Perhaps she can have one of my sandwiches from my packed lunch that I did not eat."

She opened a rucksack and produced a sandwich. Jelly withdrew her head from John's jacket and looked at it sadly, indicating that she could not be consoled by mere food.

"I'll have it," said Ham.

"You're disgusting! Next you'll be eating out of the dog's dish." Jenny turned to Peter. "O.K. if I walk back with Dad. I think Jelly needs me."

"Of course," said Peter.

"I'll stay with Jenny just in case ..." Helga broke off indecisively.

Prue next to Peter heard him mutter, "Case of what? Case I murder you when we get home. Case …" She lost the rest and a little further on, she too fell out when they met June and William walking along the path to meet them.

"Mummy?" said William uncertainly.

She took off her hat.

"Mummy!"

June wheeled her bike and she carried William, hugging him.

"Have you had a good day?" she asked June. "Has William behaved?"

June concentrated on the second part of the question.

"He missed you at first, but he soon settled down and behaved beautifully."

"Helga was right," said Prue.

As far as Peter was concerned, Helga was all wrong.

Apparently she was disposed to linger at the Maitland's cottage. First of all she availed herself of Jane's offer of a bath, lingering in the relaxing warmth of it while Peter who had already showered before her arrival, waited impatiently. Then she found it necessary to follow the bath by giving Jane a lengthy account of her meeting with Moira and Patrick.

"They come tomorrow," she promised as Peter ushered her towards the door. "Moira say she is writing you a note to say sorry about today."

"Well, we're not sorry," said Jenny. "Can't wait to read the excuse though."

Eventually Helga was walking back to the tent by his

side. They walked because they had chained their bikes to the tree outside the cottage for safety. Peter felt Helga's hand tentatively slipping into his and he didn't actually reject it. He just didn't respond by closing his fingers around hers. Nor would he allow himself to be tricked into conversation by responding to any of her observations and she eventually withdrew her hand and lapsed into silence until they reached the comparative privacy of their tent-site, screened from the next tent by a couple of stunted sycamores. Then she turned and faced him.

"Peter," she said with irritating patience in her voice, "I say to you already that I m sorry. I am sorry then. Now I am not sorry because you sulk."

"Fine," he said and disappeared into the tent, leaving her outside. In the comparative darkness, he lay on his back with his hands locked behind his head and stared at the roof of the tent. Her abandoning them had hurt because she had defied his leadership in front of everybody. She had hurt his pride then, only his pride. What really irked him was the spectral figure of Pierre that lurked between them; Pierre of the raging testosterone with his red cross scorings defacing the map of France like graffiti in a public loo; Pierre with his bilious maillot jaune for *two whole etapes* of the Tour de France. He could almost smell Pierre's B.O. as he sweated up the Alps. "All B.O. and garlic," he muttered. "Who'd want to share a tent with that?" The thought made him feel better. Helga was very quiet outside. He sat up noiselessly and peeped out of the tent flap. She was sitting on a log of wood, coolly writing her post-cards, her hair still wet from her bath falling forward in thick damp hanks over her face. He felt a rush of protective tenderness threatening to overwhelm him and fought it down with "Writing post-cards? Don't forget to find a really pretty one for Pierre." He crawled out, stood up and stretched. "Send him one of Invergarry Castle. You'll be able to say you went there all alone."

"Peter!"

He could hear from her voice that she was looking directly at him. He preferred to look at the loch. "Peter! You are jealous of Pierre?"

"Not jealous," he shrugged and swilled the phrase around his mouth exploratively, "hardly jealous, I would say. Just fucking annoyed at being used."

"Don't swear at me."

"Do you honestly think that I don't realise now that you've just been using me as a Pierre substitute? Eh? Go on! Deny it! Tell me that you didn't try to imagine it was Pierre bonking you, Pierre you were pawing and clawing in the dark, Pierre …"

"Please, Peter! Please! Please stop!"

She was crying. He wanted to cry too. He had a right to cry.

"Well, tell me it wasn't true."

There was silence. A speed boat towing a water skier swept past. Watching the figure into the distance allowed him to blink away his tears. The wake hit the shore in pulses. When they had dwindled almost to nothingness she replied.

"It is true when we were in Norway at first, Peter. When you kiss me sometimes at the beginning I shut my eyes and pretend you are Pierre. I am sorry for that. But it last only a very short time – less than a week, and all the time since, Peter, I give myself to you, not to Pierre."

He frowned but he spoke gently," If it is me, Helga, then why do you speak so often of Pierre."

"I think I speak of him because I love him very much at one time and for a long time I am missing him."

"Are you still missing him?"

"Of course. I will always miss him."

"Well fucking well go back to him then."

For a long time she did not reply. Probably considering his suggestion as worthwhile, thinking about booking her flight. Fine! He'd run her to the airport with pleasure.

"But, Peter, he is dead. He is killed in an air crash last summer."

"You never said."

"No, this is the first time I say, 'Pierre is dead.'"

She had stopped crying but her face was pale and wet as she looked out over the loch. Peter knelt at her feet and picked up the fallen post-cards. He took a long time arranging them in a neat pack before he slipped them into her pocket. Then he took one of her hands in his and kissed the palm of it.

"Helga, I am terribly, terribly sorry."

She half smiled. "Fucking sorry?" she asked.

"Fucking, fucking sorry! I was jealous but," he kissed her cheek, "I wouldn't have been so jealous if I didn't love you so much."

It didn't matter that she didn't reciprocate, that she didn't say she loved him too. That might take time. He would understand. He would wait. In the meantime as she leaned against him, he kissed the top of her head.

"You smell of shampoo instead of anti-midge," he said.

Chapter Twenty

The Second Expedition

Taking Risks

On day two of Loch Oich April learned early on that, even as leader of her subsection, her role demanded that she practise flexibility in her dealings with that sub-section. It wasn't that the sisterhood were challenging her authority as much as they were ignoring it – and her. She didn't seem to be included in anyone's plans. June had persuaded Prue to join the water-sports group, insisting that the separation would do both Prue and William good and that she herself would enjoy spending more time with William. She would, however, prefer to remain at Tomdoun where William had plenty of toys and felt more at home.

May had decided to do more sketching. Her sketch of the little ruined croft had been greatly admired and she had shown it to John who had assured her that when she had finished it off to her satisfaction, it would hang, framed, in a place of prominence. Her self-confidence had been boosted to such an extent that she had turned down her portion of the bakewell tart which April had made for supper as peremptorily as if she had been June.

"Sorry, April," she had smiled, "but I don't like bakewell tart. I never have really. I'll just have an apple."

She had also refused to be pinned down by April as to what and where she would be sketching, replying airily, "I'll just start with the Well of the Seven Heads monument and move on to whatever I fancy."

So April was in fact beginning to wonder if in the scheme of things, in what Caroline had termed *the big picture*, she had a role apart from organisation of others. When they didn't require her organisation it left her in a limbo which was unpleasant. She put on her apron defensively, tying it on firmly behind her back. At least she could look the part.

When Peter and Helga arrived at the Maitland's cottage, Jenny was still controlling her sunrise. She did this most mornings. The technique was to withdraw her head in slow stages from under her duvet, allowing her to filter the crude sounds of morning and to let the light break through gradually. She had barely past first light when she heard Helga laughing dimly and frowned because she had not yet perfected her strategy for the day; her plan for the further demotion of Helga in Peter's favour and the substitution of herself. Helga's laughter suddenly grew unbearably loud. Some insensitive person had opened her door – probably her brother for whom the skill of knocking was far too advanced.

"Jenny," said her mother sharply, "come and have your breakfast *now*, please. Everybody is here now that Peter and Helga have finally arrived."

"Coming," Jenny yawned.

Jane translated this correctly into, "Go away and leave me alone," and responded with, "I mean it, Jenny. Our party is leaving in half-an hour and you'll have to look after the water-sports people. Make them coffee, etc." She turned in the doorway. "Out of bed, now!"

On principle Jenny gave herself an extra five minutes or so … perhaps longer … before uncurling. After the previous day's cycling, the straightening out process hurt. Showering and dressing were even more painful – a fact which her insensitive mother chose not to take into account when she welcomed her into the coffee-smelling rabble of loch-netters with an evil look and a sighed, "At last!"

Helga was sitting very close to Peter, almost leaning against him. They smiled at her at exactly the same time. She gave them a disinterested half-smile back.

"Afternoon, Jenny," said her father – his idea of a joke. *Dad, you just don't know how much you sound like a 1930's edition of Boys' Own.*

"*I* don't see *either* Ham *or* Chris," she retorted pointedly.

"They've had breakfast and are walking Jelly."

Answer for everything haven't you, Mum, and please don't be afraid to put me down in front of everyone.

"Never mind, Jenny," smiled Helga. "I think we girls need our beauty sleep more than the boys realise."

Oh, what the little diplomat you are, Helga. I'm sure you've impressed everyone. Particularly Peter.

Out aloud she said with great dignity, "Mind if I take my coffee through to my room? I've a few things to do."

"We'd all be delighted," replied her father, waving her through expansively and she distinctly heard him muttering sneakily something about "got out of the wrong side of her bed this morning,"

On her stiff progress through the hall she spotted a white envelope on the doormat and bent to scoop it up with painful alacrity. The address was scrawled. She could only just make out *To Jane.*

"Moira's excuse," she said to herself. "I'm having first read."

Any qualms she might have had about opening some-one else's letter were counterbalanced by the fact that she was still smarting under the humiliating, belittling treatment meted out by her parents. She put her coffee mug down firmly on her bedside table, perched gingerly on the edge of her bed and ripped open the envelope. If anything, the scrawl within was even more illegible than the writing on the envelope. She read aloud to herself haltingly, following the script with her index finger.

My dear Jane, I don't know how to ask this of you. I am writing to you in … disappear? … *no despair.. .* Sounds just like Moira. Probably laddered her tights… *You know the truth. I did love you…* What on earth? … *I am unable to deny it. I still do, but you must see that there is no future in our relationship. My children are my future now. You must feel the same about your little boy* … What about me? Why always Ham? … *Please don't break up my family. Please, please dearest Jane, keep our affair as a precious secret known only to ourselves. …*Oh, Mum, Mum, what have you done?… *If you don't I shall have to take my own life. Believe me, I will always love you, Mattie .* Oh, Mum … Who is this Mattie? Oh, Mum …

Jenny did not even notice the pain in her legs as she dropped to her knees beside the lavatory and retched.

The road that curled round one side of Loch Tarf offered a sufficiency of passing-places and a dearth of parking.

"I suppose," remarked Peter who had driven the four of them in Harry's car, "as it's a source of drinking water, they don't want too many people parking beside it."

"Need to preserve its freshness," murmured Harry getting out and stretching.

The little loch cradled on the lip of a hill had the sweet, fresh smell of rainwater that he associated with lochs high on hills. The plateau surrounding it belied the steepness of the gradient leading up to it from Fort Augustus and there would still be half a mile of unrelenting climb to the shoulder over which the road disappeared. But for the moment this was a place of rest and refreshment; a watering hole for the spirit.

Although the loch was compact enough to be circumvented in a morning's walk, it was fenced round to prevent pollution seeping to its waters and it was impossible to tell whether or not they would be able to circle it completely. Faint paths that could be footpaths overgrown by summer herbage or possibly sheep-tracks joined the roadside at either access point.

"How about splitting up?" suggested Jane. Two of us start at one side and the other two on the other and, even if we don't meet up, we'll probably cover most of it."

Accordingly, Peter left Jane, John and Jelly at the eastern end where a passing place broadened to allow both parking and the erection of weather-beaten prohibitions and drove himself and Harry back to the western end where a faint rough track advanced towards the loch a few metres before suddenly aborting.

Harry had often privately thought of his and Peter's lives as being akin to a Venn diagram – two overlapping circles with only the intersection in common and the rest of the circles as dark and remote to each other as the wrong side of the moon to the star-gazer. He had never trespassed into the privacy of Peter's circle, sensing that there were within it things which the boy preferred to leave in the past and assuming that nothing in his own past could be of any interest to Peter. So, when Peter following close behind him along a faint trail of suppressed grass between budding heathers suddenly demanded, "Tell me about you and my mother," he felt as though some tacit code had been violated and could only gasp, "Why?" followed after an interval of silence by, "It was such a long time ago, Peter. I could have the details wrong ..."

"But was it important to you?"

"Of course it was!" He frowned at the implication. "I

wasn't into casual affairs."

"But after that holiday you never tried to contact each other again …"

"And who, may I ask, told you that?" Harry snapped.

The relaxing walk with Peter to which he had been looking forward seemed to be, as far as Peter was concerned, an opportunity for interrogation and his catechism had an accusing edge to it.

"I just assumed …"

"Well, you just assumed incorrectly. And why, may I ask, has it taken you a dozen or so years to develop this curiosity and …"

"Dad, look! No, it's too late. It's dived. Watch beside that little island. I'll get out the glasses. Hang on! There's another one …"

"Black throated divers," murmured Harry.

Both birds surfaced together, sleek and shining wet, and were moving apparently effortlessly towards them, holding their soft grey heads proudly on the stiff black and white striped necks.

"So clean-cut," breathed Peter, "immaculate …crisp …"

The birds dived simultaneously and he took the glasses down from his eyes, holding them against his chest. He spoke without turning his head, his eyes riveted to the place where the birds had last dived.

"I wasn't meaning to pry, Dad. It's just that … well … with Helga going back to Norway next week … I'd like to think that things … There they go again. They've moved further out into the loch … That things between us are not going to fall apart." He hesitated and raised the binoculars to his eyes so that his face was partly obscured. "I am sorry if …"

"No, don't be sorry," Harry responded gently, grateful for the fact that the faintness of the trail forced him to keep his eyes trained to the ground. "I'm not proud of the fact that your mother was a single parent, you know. But I did write to her … wrote several times after I returned to Scotland. She never replied and so I never found out about you… The one nearest us is the male I think. Wonder if I can get a good shot on my camera from here … She never replied and I reckoned she wanted to call it a day."

"Probably never got your letters," said Peter. "Probably intercepted by my grandmother …"

"What! The one who called me a lavatory seat?"

The tension between them ebbed as they both grinned. Then Harry screwed up his eyes, pointed his camera at the birds and zoomed in towards them.

"Think that'll be O.K." He lowered his camera. "I really want things to turn out for the best for you … and for Helga," he said.

He bent over his rucksack to replace his camera and, as he buckled it safely in, he was able to avoid looking directly at Peter and to ask the question that had been burning in his mind since Helga's arrival.

"Reckon she loves you?"

"I'm not sure," shrugged Peter.

This was a problem, thought Prue grim-faced as she yanked Jenny back to the cottage, that she would solve for herself without input from Helga, however much she felt the need for back-up. Helga, child-expert, could dish out advice apropos the rearing of William; Helga, ex-lover and cycling companion of one who had worn the maillot jaune – temporarily - could radiate her cycling expertise; Helga, veteran on waterskis, could stoop to help and support the novitiate. If she asked, Helga would probably not hesitate to crawl into the teenage jungle and sort Jenny out. But she, Prue, was not going to ask. Before she left for Loch Tarf Jane, concerned over her daughter's pallor and chilly reassurances that she was "Quite O.K. thank-you, Mum," had after all asked her, Prue, to keep an eye on Jenny and call her if necessary and this Prue would do without referring to Helga's undoubted omniscience.

When it had been time for the water sports people to leave the Maitland's cottage, Prue had knocked on Jenny's door, called her name and eventually been admitted. Jenny's face had been a lurid, damp, pulpy mess – the result of weeping evident even under an overlay of heavy make-up.

"Are you all right, Jenny?"

"Fine," Jenny had spat out nasally. "I've just got hayfever."

"Indoor hayfever?"

Jenny had shrugged on a cardigan without replying and plugged herself into her MP player on the way to the School of Water Sports, presumably to avoid being drawn into conversation with any of them.

"Boy-friend trouble!" Helga had diagnosed expertly in Prue's ear.

Prue had not thought of that. Jenny had certainly stuffed something that looked like an envelope under her pillow when Prue had followed her into her bedroom. That boy from the boat, Donald, could just have given her the brush-off, dropped a *Dear John* off at the cottage. Why had she herself not thought of that?

Out aloud she had said airily, "Who knows?"

The water-ski instructors for the morning had been a pair of Australians who, despite the fact that one was dark and one was fair, could have been brothers: both were tall, broad-shouldered; both with lean brown faces that made their eyes bluer and their smiles whiter. Furthermore both were equipped with a complement of muscles that only wet suits could set off to perfection.

"We have died and gone to heaven, I think," moaned Helga rolling her eyes at Prue as they put on their wet suits.

"You're supposed to be taken," Prue had reminded her rather too sharply.

Jenny had appeared uncharacteristically immune to their charms.

Helga, to her obvious delight, was to go first on her own and she had shown even more pleasure when it was suggested that she might like to do "a double act" with one of the instructors later.

"I am liking the sound of that," she had agreed.

Jenny and Prue would have a beginner's lesson after her and finally Chris and Ham would have their session. As the four learners were sitting on the jetty, idly swinging their legs in the water, Jenny had suddenly broken her sullen silence and turned to Prue.

"What did they say their names were?"

Prue, waving to Helga as she flashed past had had to think for a moment.

"As far as I can remember, the dark one is Simon. The fair one is definitely Matt because I remember thinking …"

"Matt?" Jenny's voice had been sharp. "Are you sure it was Matt?"

"Yes," Prue had smiled at her, holding her legs out of the water as Helga's wash threatened to swamp her. "You know, Matt short for Matthew. Don't you like the name?"

"No," Jenny had replied coldly, "actually I hate it."

During their instruction session, Jenny had alternated between sullen unresponsiveness and overt impertinence. With her natural athletic ability she had mastered the basics with an ease which her instructor, the ill-named Matt, was ready to praise, but she turned down his compliments as ungraciously as possible.

"Well, you Ozzies are not the only ones to be good at sport even though you like to act as though you are," she had sneered.

"Never for one moment thought we were," Matt had grinned good-humouredly.

"Didn't realise that you could think. Thought you were all brawn and no brain."

Prue, squatting uncomfortably over the water on her skis, had muttered uneasily to herself, "Young lady, wait till I get you ashore!"

She had, however been unable to contain herself until then. Jenny had continued to snap and jeer so that in the boat on the way back she had acted in loco parentis.

"Jenny, that is quite enough. When your mother hears how you've been behaving, she'll be furious."

"My mother," Jenny had screamed above the engine noise and deliberately facing away from Prue to give Matt and Simon the benefit of her response, "has no right to criticise my behaviour. She is a slag!" She had paused only to add like one inspired, "We think she's HIV positive and *that* is catching!"

She had then burst into tears, sobbing violently and allowed Prue to march her back to the cottage.

"We'll bring the wet suits back later," Prue had called over her shoulder to the two Australians, standing side by side on the jetty, standing close to give each other moral support.

"Fine," they had breathed in unison.

May had completed her sketch of the Well of the Seven Heads to her satisfaction and glowing pinkly packed away her sketching material – not entirely from exposure to the August sun. It had been a thoroughly agreeable session. Many of the constant stream of visitors to the shop at the Well of the Seven Heads had stopped to peer curiously over her shoulder and had expressed their admiration in English, in broken English and indeed in unfamiliar tongues but it had been easy to gauge from the tone of the remarks that appreciation was intended. She had already decided where she would go next. In fact she had made up her mind the day before, as soon as she had seen Helga's postcards of the old Invergarry Castle, but had thought it prudent not to reveal the plan to April to avoid provoking an alarming catalogue of mishaps likely to befall her.

As she made her way under the shade of the oaks that lined the road to Invergarry, she experienced a delicious thrill of guilt. It was a long time since she had stepped out of line. There was the time in that truncated childhood of hers when June had persuaded her to hide with her behind the old horse-hair sofa and share out the bag of jewel coloured boiled sweets which Aunt Margaret had brought them as a sort of exchange when she finally shunted the baby Prudence up to Aberdeen. In a strange way she had felt then that she and June were justified. June had eaten most of the sweets while she had enjoyed unwrapping them and holding them brilliant, bright and translucent up towards the light. And all the time a thrill of guilty fear had enhanced the glowing colours and sharpened the sensation of sweetness. Her father's lecture on theft had been long and boring and the consequent deduction of pocket money predictable - as her father always reckoned that loss of income must be the severest of punishments - but this wonderful act of disobedience had shone brightly in her memory through the ensuing years during which she seemed to be expected to shuffle off all her childhood pursuits and peccadilloes and aim at assuming a serviceable sense of responsibility.

Through the trees now she could make out the landslip on the far side of the loch, a ghastly weal excised into the face of the hillside where great rocks, dislodged at last by the steady swelling of water deep within the hill, had thundered down, carrying all before, splintering great trees, blocking the lochside path and partially dissolving in the loch itself to form over time a soft green peninsula. Caught up in the drama of what the landslip had been, she missed the gentle hooting of the small white van that had drawn into a parking place just ahead of her. The driver thrust his head out of the cab window as she passed, an impossibly shaggy head of unkempt red curls.

"Like a lift, hen?"

The elbow resting on the open window was rough and hard but the area from elbow to T-shirt sleeve bore the tattoo of a dragon in blue ink, reminding her of one of the blue stencilled patterns her mother used to iron onto tablecloths and then embroider. She looked up at the face, hesitantly. It was ruddy and rough like the surface of a brick.

"I'm only going to Invergarry Castle," she said. "Thank-you just the same."

"I can drop ye aff there nae probs.," he said. "Hop in!"

April would be horrified but April was safely in Tomdoun. She hopped in. Inside the cab she sniffed the exotic pungency of tobacco, sweat and stale beer. On the shelf below the glove compartment two empty beer cans rattled against each other and dribbled amber liquid as he swung back onto the road. The glove compartment was partly open; a whitish rag streaked with black oil was hanging out and she could see the gleam of tools inside. He was saying something to her but she couldn't make out what over the throbbing of the music that vibrated round the cab so that even the windows shook. He turned the music down and tried again.

"Ye're stayin' at the hotel then?"

"No," she shook her head, "I'm just going there to sketch."

"Sketch? Ye're an artist then?"

It was a title she would never have thought to give herself. She hesitated before repeating lamely, "I'm just going there to sketch. Oh!" as he slowed down and indicated right, "You don't need to turn into the hotel. I can just get out here."

"Haud yer whisht as they say in these Highland parts. I ken how tae treat a lady."

As they drove slowly up the drive towards the hotel, they passed the old castle on the way. There was scaffolding around it May noticed. When she sketched it she would ignore the scaffolding. Or perhaps not.

"That's what I want to sketch," she pointed out, "the old castle."

"Wantin' me tae put ye aff here then?"

"I'd better go up to the hotel first. I thought I could have a bite of lunch and ask permission to sketch. I thought I should, you know. Ask permission, I mean."

"Quite right. I'm always askin' permission." He was smiling to himself and she didn't understand the joke. "Reckon it's wrong jus' tae help yersel'.'"

"That's what I thought."

In the hotel car park she thanked him and slipped out her seat with a sense of achievement. Her sisters would never believe what she had just done – accepted a lift from a strange man in a white van. But then here she was no longer just May, the second sister, without portfolio, Jill of all trades and mistress of none. Here she would be an artist and for the sake of her art, she would do what *she* thought best and the sooner they accepted that the better for them. Shocked by her own wayward thinking she crunched over the gravel into the hotel.

Jane, leaning back comfortably on the back seat of Harry's car, was having difficulty in staying awake. Jelly, with her head on Jane's lap was already snoring gently and twitching in her sleep. The morning's exertions had been followed by a delicious plateful of steaming macaroni cheese at a small inn. They hadn't managed to circle Loch Tarf completely, but John had been contented with what they had achieved. John was generally more contented these days she thought; leaner, fitter and happier about life.

The road to Loch Ruthven, stretching thin and straight over the hills, appeared to be sparsely populated. They passed through only a couple of tiny hamlets with immaculate gardens and no visible inhabitants. Apparently unconnected with anything as secular as civilisation, little churches surrounded by open countryside were scattered as randomly as molehills along the roadside.

"No shortage of faith," Harry was observing. "What's the difference between the Free Church of Scotland and the Reformed Free Church?"

Apparently nobody knew and the question hung unanswered until it was interrupted by "Steady on!" as Peter turned the lock sharply to avoid missing the turn off to Loch Ruthven.

Loch Ruthven lay below a curiously conical outcrop - 'like rocks on a beach where the sand has subsided beneath them' thought Jane - and was an R.S.P.B. conservation site.

"That means Jelly has to stay in the car," said John. "Poor Jelly! First no loch-bathing because it's a reservoir; then no loch-bathing because it's a bird sanctuary.

"I'll take her for a wee dander along the road and then catch you up," yawned Jane. "I could do with stretching my legs. It'll wake me up."

"Sure? I'll gladly go with you."

"I'll be fine."

She wanted a few moments privacy anyway; the chance to phone Prue. Jenny had assured her mother when Jane had phoned her from the inn that she was fine, but she had sounded uncharacteristically meek and Jane was still worried. Jenny didn't do meek. She and Jelly set off down the hill. Even though it was hot, early afternoon when most respectable birds take siestas, she could hear the chipping of a stone-chat on the hillside behind her and the twittering of tiny gold-crests as they fossicked through the little fir plantation on her right. She took out her phone and pressed Prue's number.

But Jenny did do meek. When faced with white-hot, blue-star fury, she most definitely did meek. When knowing herself to be justly deserving of the fury, she did cringing meek.

"Oh, Prue, I'm so, so sorry," she whispered.

The letter was shaking in Prue's hand. Near tears herself, she had no compassion for Jenny.

She had marched the little minx sobbing, heartbroken, making a complete exhibition of herself, back to the cottage and demanded an explanation for her behaviour. It was easier than she had anticipated: Jenny, unable to be the sole bearer of the knowledge of her mother's infidelity, adultery and general slaggishness, had beckoned Prue into her bedroom and, producing the letter from under her pillow, had handed it over to her.

"Please don't tell anyone," she had hiccoughed piteously.

"That depends," Prue had responded tersely and frowned, mystified as she tried to decipher the scrawled contents. Then suddenly, "...*please dearest **June**... not please dearest **Jane** ...* she had said loudly, stabbing at the phrase with her index finger. And, Jenny, if you had only looked carefully it starts, *My dear June.* Give me the envelope. There you are! See! It says *To June* you stupid, interfering little ..."

"Oh!" Jenny's smile was radiant. "That's wonderful. That means ..."

"That means, you unutterably selfish, spoiled, self-centred little brat, that you have had the cheek to open and read a very private letter to my sister. Your excuse? You thought it was for your mother!"

She was screaming with rage and Jenny stepped back from her, arms outstretched to ward her off.

"It's all I can do not to take my hand across your silly, arrogant, smug, little face!"

"Oh, Prue, I'm so, so sorry."

"Get changed!

Prue slammed out of the room to change out of her own wet suit and to retreat out onto the patio, letter in hand to try to think. She could not understand the letter; the reference to June's little boy didn't make sense. It was highly unlikely that Mattie was the water-ski-ing Matthew and, anyway, she was sure she would have known if June had been involved in an affair. But the letter must be June's. Who else? And it had been opened and June would know it had been read. She could spare June that. She would buy an envelope on the way home, re-seal it and copy the 'To June' as accurately as possible. And she would silence Jenny by fair means or consummately foul. She might enjoy the latter.

But Jenny proved co-operative about the silencing. She stood white-faced in the open doorway with a mug in her hand.

"I've made you some tea," she said, waving the mug tentatively in Prue's direction so that she slopped tea onto the patio tiles.

Prue thawed sufficiently to give her the faintest glimmer of a smile.

"Thank-you, Jenny. Go and get a mug yourself. We've got stuff to sort out before Helga and the boys get back."

Jenny returned, mug in hand, but remained standing until Prue said, "Sit down," and motioned her towards a bench.

"Jenny, you must understand that if this is for June – and it may very well not be – it contains very personal stuff meant only for her eyes."

Jenny nodded.

"And whoever it is, you have no right to the knowledge of its contents and must never repeat what is in the letter …"

"I won't, Prue. I swear it on …"

"Never mind the swearing dramatics. Just keep that mouth of yours firmly shut."

"I will," said Jenny eagerly, "I truly will." She added lamely, "This is the only time I've ever opened some-one else's letter. I'll never do it again. I thought it was just from Moira and …"

"Discussion closed!" Prue held up her hand. "Do you have an envelope that would fit the letter?"

"Oh yes!" Jenny sprang up with alacrity. "In my writing-case. I'll get it now!"

May, acclimatized now to people peering over her shoulder as she sketched, never even looked round at the person who had drawn up alongside until, instead of the obligatory, deferential murmur of appreciation delivered sotto voce, presumably not to disturb her concentration, she heard a confrontational, "Afternoon ma'am." Although the police constable – ginger-haired, freckled and snub-nosed – had addressed her in the deep base of a much older man, May decided that he was only about twenty- two – twenty-four perhaps – maybe twenty-six?

"Good afternoon," she smiled with a slight inclination of her head in his direction and returned to the difficult bit of the old castle where the wall appeared to bulge slightly, or maybe the scaffolding pole wasn't quite straight, giving the wall the illusion of bulging.

P.C. Stewart cleared his throat to indicate that he

needed to prolong the dialogue.

"Ma'am," he pursued, "mind if I ask you how long you've been here?"

May knew that one had to very accurate with the police.

"I think that I've been here for about half-an-hour – perhaps a little longer because I had to move my stool to get it into the right position – so that I could see around this corner here on my left. Perhaps I've been here about forty minutes," she ventured hesitantly and then brightened. "The lady in reception would be able to tell you. She was so kind…"

"Half-an-hour is fine," he reassured hastily. "And during that time did you notice a white van passing you?"

"No!" She could be very definite this time. "Only Moira and Patrick passed. But they didn't recognise me. They must have had had lunch here too, but I don't think they're staying here. They booked into a hotel in …"

"Thank-you for your help ma'am. We're looking for a white van, registration number ST 53 B; driver red-haired, thick set. If you see a vehicle of that description d'you think you could notify the police station at Fort William on this number?" He scribbled on a page in his notebook, tore it out and handed it to her. "I wouldn't try approaching the chap yourself though. You never know with these blokes!"

She folded the piece of paper neatly in four and put it in her bag.

"I'll not be accepting a lift from *him* then," she said brightly.

"I'd certainly not advise it, ma'am," he laughed, replaced his cap and strode up the drive. May picked up her pencil and frowned once more at the bit of wall that bulged.

John's first thought, when stretching out his stiffness in the car-park at Loch Ruthven , was, "Why the hell would any

self-respecting duck park itself here? It's a real back-of -
beyond pool in the wilderness!"

He kept his opinion to himself, however, in sudden
awareness that his ornithological ignorance was asserting itself
visibly to anyone who looked in his direction. "Ecce homo
ignoramus!" screamed his brilliant white T-shirt raucously to
the muted moss-and-lovat clad birders swapping birding
experiences around him, all of whom appeared to be tastefully
strung with telescopes, binoculars and cameras, leaving their
hands free for tripods, bird reference books and knobbly,
rough-hewn walking-sticks. There was a behaviour code to be
mastered too: apparently you walked in single file, even where
the path was wide enough to permit the passage of two abreast,
with your eyes slightly narrowed and fixed on a distant point,
presumably because you could see what others could not hope
to and when you met likeminded you boomed out very loudly
– to prove that birds were not afraid of your voice _ "NICE
DAY! SEEN ANYTHING INTERESTING?" The trick then
was not to wait for a reply before launching into a catalogue of
your own enviable finds.

He fell in behind Harry and Peter and tried to remain as
inconspicuous as the white T-shirt would allow.

The path led down towards a boat-house and a small
inlet in which a rowing-boat rocked gently, passed a
diminutive sandy beach on which bucket moulded sand-castles
must only recently have been abandoned and rose up, narrow
and rocky through low woodland with wryly twisted branches
and the perpetual rustling of birds. To John's relief the hide
was empty and they were free to spread themselves along the
benches and open the windows that gave out onto the loch.
Immediately below the hide a thick reed-bed offered screening
to the birds and frustration to their watchers and to their right a
broad plane of loch stretched to the far bank.

"Trouble is," John confided, having consulted the wall-chart on the back of the hide and found nothing to match its illustrations on the loch, "I'm really bad on birds anyway. And water-birds are impossible. They're forever ducking their heads under or diving. Half the time their heads and shoulders are submerged and their hulls are always submerged. And they go skulking in and out of reed-beds. Suspicious habits if you ask me."

"You'll learn," chuckled Harry, "when you've done enough lochs. See! There's a red-throated diver near the far shore. Look just to the left of the silver birch. You can spot them no problem. Apart from their red necks, they cruise along with their beaks in the air. And hang on! Look! A Slavonian grebe! Two of them!"

John lowered his own glasses to work out the direction in which Harry was training his.

"There, John! Follow a line straight down from the tallest fir on the far bank!"

"The one with the gold on its head, Dad?"

"Aye! Is she not a beauty?"

They remained uninterrupted in their viewing, the only sounds, the scratching of Harry's pen as he jotted down findings and the coarse quacking of mallards as they shared a dirty joke or two. John, looking at his watch realised that half-an-hour had passed without Jane's having joined them.

"I'll need to go back for her." He sounded and felt reluctant. "When you two have finished, perhaps you could start along that path past the hide. Hopefully it'll take you to the crannog."

"The crannog," Peter was interested although he kept his binoculars to his eyes, "is, I take it, like the one at Loch Tay?"

"I very much doubt whether it has been restored," said Harry, "but it'll be worth taking a look at. "O.K., John, we'll make a start in a few minutes."

John retraced his steps to find Jane still in the car-park, seated on a smooth rock like an over-dressed, stranded mermaid. Jelly tugged on her lead and whined a greeting.

"It's really too hot to put her in the car," Jane explained. "See anything?"

"It was magic!" returned John. "I'll keep Jelly. You take the glasses and have a bit of time in the hide."

As it was, Jane met Peter and Harry just past the little sandy beach.

"We couldn't go on." Peter sounded disappointed as the three of them rejoined John and Jelly, "There's a notice asking people not to go along the path in case they disturb nesting birds."

"So that's it!" John frowned.

"That's it for now *only*," replied Harry. " We can never do a loch finally and completely. They're always changing, thank heaven."

Jenny, by the time Prue restored her to her parents, had almost returned to normal, having worked off her guilt by slavishly applying herself to the preparation of lunch, performing any outstanding housework as ostentatiously as possible and offering an obsequious apology to the Australian duo that left them more ill at ease than her impertinence had done. The first sign of the return to normality came after she had washed and dried the lunch dishes with, "Ham, I am not touching your manky apple core. Come and bin it yourself.!"

"It's biodegradable," the very freshly green Ham countered patiently. "It goes on the compost heap."

"And just where, nutcase, is the compost heap here?"

Ham compromised by chucking it amongst the bushes down by the loch where the ground was relatively soggy and decomposition would be, he judged, a matter of seconds. He then returned to trail mud across the carpet Jenny had meticulously vacuumed.

"It's just a little bit of mud I think, Jenny," soothed Helga who was reclining full length on the sofa. "I vacuum it for you later when it has dried."

'Dear, sweet Helga!' thought Jenny viciously and exchanged looks with Prue that almost restored complete amity between them.

Helga, however, forgot the carpet and went for an extra hour of water ski-ing. Jenny remembered herself, reverted to meekness and cleared up the carpet before accompanying Prue and the boys to an archery session, walking just behind them as befitting one who knows her place. She would have retrieved all Prue's arrows for her too if Prue had not whispered savagely, "Penance over, Jenny. For heaven's sake get back to normal."

So Jenny relaxed and snapped back to normal without much difficulty and, when her parents returned, greeted them with appropriate coolness, reserving her warm welcome for Jelly.

Prue set off for home immediately after their return, the letter resealed and safely stowed in her rucksack, and rehearsed its handing over to June all the way back to Tomdoun.

It wouldn't be the first thing she'd do, wouldn't let June think that she considered the letter important. She would pick William up, cuddle him, ask what sort of a day he'd had, they'd all had before reaching casually for her rucksack and saying, "Oh, by the way, Sis, this arrived at the cottage." Then she'd shrug off-handedly and add, "Don't know whether it's for you or some other June."

She remembered only just in time to divert into the grounds of Glengarry Castle to fetch May. "Good sketching, May?"

May rambled on.

Then, perhaps she could ask June to help her bath William and that would provide opportunity to watch June without June feeling watched. Later, a stroll up to the hotel for a drink or a drive down towards Kinlochhourn to watch the red deer might be an idea.

There was a road block at Invergarry and a young constable tried to stick his head through the car window and remove his cap at the same time.

"We meet again, ma'am," he said to May. "No sightings at the old castle?"

"N-no, no thank-you," replied May flustered.

"What's all that about?" Prue asked more out of courtesy than curiosity as they drove off.

"Oh … they're looking for a van," replied May vaguely and jabbered on.

Perhaps looking for red deer in the glen would be better than a drink at the hotel. That way June could talk to her without being looked at. You had to keep your eyes on that narrow little road to Kinlochhourn.

Loch Garry shone as never before without Prue noticing it. Ben Tee was sharp and brittle. The kelpies galloped invisibly in and out of the River Garry, spooked by the disgorge from the Kingie Power Station. The cattle grid rippled as noiselessly as the snow fell on Gairich. She only knew that she was home and that the letter was burning a hole in her rucksack.

As it was, William unearthed the letter from her rucksack while she was in the loo and was happily chewing the corner of the envelope when she emerged, having re-rehearsed mentally while washing her hands.

"No, William!" She shouted and smacked his hand, leaving him rigid with shock for a good half-minute before he started to sob.

"Prue!" June was stunned into taking the letter without noticing it.

"Read it!" Prue screamed silently. "Read it and re-act so that I know what to do." To William she said sharply, "Don't make such a fuss!" but she picked him up and hugged him.

June disappeared upstairs with the letter. Prue heard her shut her bedroom door, heard the muffled thud of her feet as she crossed the floor, heard her own heartbeat.

April intruded into the silence insensitively with, "Let's see your sketches, May." and May rustled the bag as she produced them, one at a time, prolonging the rustling and the observations. Prue carried William upstairs and paused outside June's door. "Want to help me bath William?" she called in an extremely normal voice.

"Be with you in a minute," was the muffled reply and she heard June blow her nose.

By the time June joined her Prue was blowing bubbles for William and she resisted the temptation to look round. June knelt beside her and held out her hand for the soap so that she too could blow bubbles.

"I had an affair," she said. "It's over now. That's what the letter was about."

The soap had slipped out of Prue's hand and she had to burrow under a protesting William to find it.

"Oh," she said eventually, "I'm sorry! Men are brutes."

June laughed a dry mocking laugh; a laugh that said, "You, my younger sister, have led far too sheltered a life to know anything."

"I have had the odd affair myself, you know," responded Prue indignantly.

June just shook her head as though the intricacies involved were far beyond Prue's comprehension. "Let's just say it's over!"

Subject obviously closed.

"Come on, poppet. Let's dry you." Prue swung William up in a towel and left June in the bathroom to swirl the water around thoughtfully for a moment before she pulled the plug out with finality and scoured the bath vigorously.

"Among other things, walking in Glen Nevis, looking for otters at a certain place on Loch Linnhe, taking the steam train to Mallaig," Harry replied, the pipe in the corner of his mouth nodding up and down as he spoke. He withdrew the pipe and gesticulated with it to emphasise the salient point of his communication. "And don't, my dear boy, think for one moment that I 'm doing this to leave you and Helga alone together. My motives are purely selfish. I want to do these things and I want to do them alone. When I return I shall be much more sociable and I will chum you along cheerfully to a medic of your choice for the blood-letting you so desire."

"Where are you going to stay?"

"At *The Salmon's Leap* in Fort William where I shall be exceedingly comfortable. I shall not need the car. It's all yours but if pressure of work permits, you can meet me at the station on my return."

"I'm not due back at work until Helga's gone."

"I'm not coming home until after Helga's gone. She goes in four days?"

"Yes."

Peter and Harry were standing alone on a jetty just below the cottage where Helga was finishing the last of her post-cards. Peter walked to the end of the jetty and sprung on it experimentally. It vibrated beneath him clumsily, swaying from side to side at the same time so that he nearly lost his balance.

"I'm not sure about the blood-test," Harry just caught.

"In fact I'm not sure about a lot of things," He raised his voice, "You know, you can't see your reflection in this water and you can't see down to the bottom either. Suppose it's the peat."

"Makes good whisky," said Harry relighting his pipe.

"Why?" said Ham querulously. "I want to play monopoly with Chris."

"That," John was getting angry, "is something you can do at home when you've left this loch far behind."

"I'll come with you." The offer from Jenny was unexpected and unwelcome. The walk along Loch Oich was to have been a father and son thing. "O.K., I get the message. It's not me you want."

"Of course it is," he lied. "I just never expected you to offer."

Despite John's misgivings, Jenny proved a remarkably good companion, sensitive to her surroundings, knowing instinctively when to keep silence and when to share an observation. An evening breeze was blowing strong and fresh, carrying the scent of water on it. They walked as far as the ruined croft where the white, white stones were creamy warm in the evening light and the sheep huddled together against the chill in the wind. Car lights along the road flickered like candles through the shivering leaves of the roadside trees and laughter strung across the water from a boat moored somewhere.

Jenny picked up a smooth, grey stone from the shore, roughly heart-shaped with a white thread like a solidified snail trail running through it.

"We'll take it home and put it in the garden," she said slipping it into her pocket.

Chapter Twenty-one

Going Public

Lochnetting Moves Forward

School re-opened after the summer break exactly a week after the lochnetters returned from Loch Oich. On the evening of the last day of the holidays, John finished his summary of the second expedition more or less to his satisfaction, took off his glasses and gazed idly out of his study window. Through the longish grass on the lawn he could just make out the heart-shaped stone that Jenny had transported carefully from Loch Oich. She had used scarlet nail varnish to daub *Oich, July 2008* on it and placed it on a spot under the larger apple tree where, she had judged, it would be relatively safe from Ham's footballing.

"Think I'll bring back stones from all the lochs in future," she had remarked, thereby indicating that despite being completely unable to express any enthusiasm for the loch-netting project, she would feel aggrieved if left out of future expeditions, "and build a sort of cairn."

He smiled, sighed, walked over to the calendar, ringed both the September holiday week-end for the next loch-netting expedition and the Saturday evening preceding it as the date of the pre-expedition meeting and regretfully reconciled himself to the fact that he would soon be so fully submerged in school-life that loch-netting would have to dwindle to secondary importance.

But the ideas cuckoo chick knew better. Despite the fact that the breeding season was over, that the shadows lay longer and pointed it to migration, it had work to complete before the long flight south; missionary work that would ensure the safety of its breeding ground when it returned in spring. It preened itself to oil its wings against the dampness of the increasingly heavy dews, shook its ruffled feathers into order and urged itself to work with a braying squeak of "Carpe diem!".

The first day of term was an in-service day for staff only, allowing John to leave for school as early as he liked, secure in the knowledge that Jenny and the state of her hair were still safely – and silently - in bed. As he opened his gates, April, unusually alone in her car, was backing out of her drive and he wondered briefly if all was well with the other two, now clearly identifiable as June and May, who usually accompanied her, but she waved back cheerfully enough to dismiss any anxiety on their behalf. There were only three other cars in the school car park when he arrived, parked in the three spaces nearest to the school entrance where he himself would have preferred to park this time last year. But today he parked in the furthest corner from the school underneath a rowan tree in which a blackbird was foraging early berries and its indignant squawks followed him as he strode briskly across the car park. The morning sun on the white school building bleached his sight and lingered as a dark blue blur across his retina as he entered the front door, but once through the door he was on automatic pilot and could have made his way to the staffroom blindfolded. He was early enough to spend the first half-hour back at school comfortably seated in the staff-room with a cup of coffee and the contents of his bulging pigeon-hole which he could expect to be predictable, and hold nothing of interest. A note from the head congratulating him warmly on his excellent exam results would have brought a glow of pride had he not noticed similar notes in the pigeon-holes of most of the other heads of departments. As it was, it irritated him because he knew from having scanned the school's exam results on his return from France that his results were indeed far superior to most. She probably thought that she was being democratic, non-divisive and all the other anti-competitive epithets she could be relied upon to spray around with the efficiency of an over-endowed tomcat. The programme for today's in-service followed the same sequence of events which always launched the start of the school year and was a waste of paper. Then, as anticipated, there were from the usual parents, the usual letters ranging in tone from obsequious through politely censorious to blatantly threatening, all demanding that he appeal for their sons/daughters to be upgraded. All were expecting the impossible and he paper-clipped them together to give to the departmental secretary with the usual instruction to issue them with the standard "absolutely no way letter".

The last envelope he opened was small, white and hand-addressed and it released a brief whiff of jasmine which was soon smothered by the heavy pungency of staffroom coffee. Although he recognised neither the home address nor the handwriting, a sixth sense seemed to be informing him that this was a letter from a friend. It was signed simply *Katie* and he frowned in his attempt to recollect a "Katie" as he started to read.

Dear John,

I have been wanting to contact you but the only J. Maitland in the phone book turned out to be a woman and I didn't think you were having a sex-change. I phoned the school but they refused to give me your home phone number and said I had to write, so here goes although I'm nervous about writing to an English teacher.

I wanted to thank you for your encouragement at the in-service . I have managed to enrol for a midwifery course which starts in September and I am really looking forward to it. Dad was very understanding and has managed to replace me so I'm all set.

Also, I wondered if you had started your loch thing and if I could join in some time? Hope you don't mind me asking.

Mark tried to come back to me when the flirty florist finished with him. The cheek! I half want him still and walking round lochs in my spare time might help. By the way I have started riding lessons and am coming on really well! Cantered last Saturday! So maybe I could ride round some lochs with your daughter as you said, though I think you could have been joking.

If you are willing to let me in on the loch thing, please phone me on my mobile – 0776895555. I don't know if I mentioned before that I've done my Duke of Edinburgh and so I have a little experience of expeditions. Sounds as if I'm applying for a job!

Love,

Katie xx

He smiled as he tucked the letter into his pocket to take home with him. Of course, Katie from the in-service last spring. Across the staffroom he could see a nautically clad bulk that was Ted Warburton advancing towards the coffee table. At his approach, the little crowd that had collected around it dispersed in an indecent haste which meant some of them went milkless and others sugarless. Coffee in hand, Ted looked round and spotted John and John, subsequently forced into experiencing second-hand a cruise of the Carribean – in a top deck cabin suite which was apparently the envy of all on board – found to his own amazement that his pity overcame his irritation.

Harry walked to school with a spring in his step. This time he could revel in the fact that it was the last time he would walk to school on the first day of the school year. He anticipated that his retiral would bring Mandy Attwell as much relief as it would give him. She had warned them all last term in one of her lengthy Head Teacher addresses that the falling school roll would necessitate staff cuts, the "saving grace" apparently lying in the fact that some members of staff would be lost through "natural wastage" and with the words "natural wastage" her eye had alighted on him.

"Horrible terminology!" he had laughed to Peter at home later. "Made me feel like a turd on its way to the sewage plant."

Peter had not laughed.

On his return to Edinburgh at the end of last week, Peter had not only met him at the station but also taken the remainder of the afternoon off so that he could prepare a special welcome home supper that even Harry with his fastidious palate had found completely delicious. The only trace of Helga had been a tub of scented talcum powder left in the bathroom, with the lid carelessly lying to the side. Peter had not mentioned her and to the enquiry as to whether or not he had had a good time in Harry's absence the guardedness of his responding "Yes" had warned Harry that he had been unsubtle. The subject of the forthcoming blood test had been left to Harry to broach, and for Harry to arrange the appointment and Harry had been unable to fathom whether this stemmed from Peter's consideration for his father's feelings or from his own reluctance to discover the result.

"It won't change anything," Harry had assured him, "unless you want it to."

"Unless *you* want it to," Peter had countered abruptly and excused himself under pressure of paperwork.

The appointment was for 4.30 on Wednesday. Harry had entered it in his diary and ringed the date on the calendar under the phone for Peter's benefit but he thought it unlikely that either of them would need a memory prompt.

Arriving at school, he avoided the staffroom where everyone else would be obsessed with exam results and took himself to his own classroom. The walls were bare. During the holidays somebody – possibly the cleaner – had removed his posters, torn down the Acropolis in Athens, the Colisseum in Rome and the aerial map of Delphi, leaving the drawing pins *in situ* surrounded by small, tattered ruffs of paper. The posters themselves lay carelessly folded across his desk. Forcing himself to think rationally, Harry decided that his anger was out of place.

"Must move on," he said to himself firmly. "Must go forward."

He folded each of the posters carefully and was putting them in his brief-case as Mandy Attwell opened his door and then knocked.

"Just looking in to say hello," she smiled her encouraging first day of term smile before contorting her face into an unconvincing semblance of complete astonishment. "Oh! You've taken your posters down."

So she *had been* in on it.

"Yes!" It was his move now. "I've just pulled them all down. I thought some really exciting ones about how to manage pocket money would do instead? Or perhaps some diagrammatic, abstract illustrations about how to have sex while avoiding both AIDS and pregnancy? And for that dark corner I've got a really tasteful Pirelli ..."

"Oh Harry!" Mission accomplished she was on her way out without listening as usual. "What I like about you is that you're *so* adaptable and ..." She shut the door on the rest.

Without having visited his pigeon-hole in the staffroom, he was without the benefit of the in-service programme for the first day. On a whim he dismissed it as irrelevant to his needs: he had no exam results to be assessed; no department to run; absolutely no need to be instructed on registration procedures. On the other hand he did have a need to escape to the library and do some theoretical loch-netting. Following his whim he found that he had the library to himself. Sheena, of course, would be "mingling" – "cross-referencing" she would probably call it. He smiled to himself as he traced the route they had followed around Loch Garry. "If I just had my pipe," he murmured, "life would be perfect."

When John joined him in the library during the lunch-break, he still had the map spread out in front of him although by this time he was deep in an article about the whereabouts of water kelpies.

"Skiving,eh?"

"Didn't miss much did I?"

"No, nothing really." John just stopped himself from adding, "Nothing relevant to your needs." On a high after the excellence of his exam results had at last been singled out for special comment, he felt both pity and a sudden generosity swamping his common sense. "Harry," he began hesitantly not because of any difficulty in expressing himself but rather because he feared he could be making an impulsive, over-generous gesture he might well later regret, "I would be grateful if you could be in charge of planning the next few expeditions, you know, grouping lochs together, etc.."He had no option but to respond to Harry's expression of amazement. "Well, you know how you're much better at the Outdoor Ed. thing than I am." He had to modify that. "At least at present you are. I might improve."

He leaned low over the map to avoid looking Harry in the eye.

"Thanks." Harry's voice was gruff. "Thanks ... I'll enjoy that ... and you'll soon get the hang of the ..."

His sentence remained unfinished and after a few seconds it was unnecessary to finish it.

May was actually late! Late for her Monday morning appointment. It was exactly seven minutes past eleven when she arrived and Norman Paterson had already reconciled himself to the dismal progress of the test-match and was attempting to suspend his cynicism about the sports columnist's predictions of a golden future for Martin Webb, the latest and youngest British tennis star who, having survived to the third round at Wimbledon last June, could apparently expected to be seeded before long.

"Unbelievable!" he murmured on three counts as Gillian, averting her eyes from him and almost unrecognisable in a blouse buttoned to her chin ushered the unpunctual May through the door and murmured with chilly reproach which seemed directed as much to him as to May, "I'll have to make fresh coffee."

"I'm sorry I'm late!" May shouldered all the guilt and blurted through her apology. "We – that is June and Prue and I – and William of course but he's only a baby so you can't blame him – only came down from the North this morning. We really did think we'd left in plenty of time only ..."

Under his level stare she found her thought processes crumbling. And she had felt so much better about coming this time, so much stronger, felt as though he was sure to approve of what she had achieved. She had gone walking in a crowd, with other people, not just with the sisters and she had done her sketching ... and that. And she had – with hindsight – appeared to have had a lift from a well-known drug-trafficker – actually gone in his van. "Scary stuff!" Prue had said when May had recognised his photograph the next day in the *Highland Voice*. But Prue had also said how well she must have coped, kept so calm and ... The trouble seemed to be that when she came into this room it seemed as though she had to behave in just the same way that she always behaved here. He, Mr. Paterson, seemed to expect it.

"And what have you been up to?" He was smiling at her now, remaining professional as always, despite the fact that he was still trying to remember what he had actually said to Gillian last night when she had asked his professional advice, in his capacity as a medical man, about the advisability of having silicon tits. He could remember what he had done to re-assure her, just not what he had advised. Whatever it was, it seemed to have had the wrong effect.

May frowned at him. That was the way Jane spoke to Ham. Only Ham was just a child. *Up to*? She had been going to show him her sketches. She had some with her. But that didn't fit, now. The May he expected to see was cack-handed and incapable. When her hand trembled as she carried her coffee-cup to her mouth how could he be expected to believe that she could wield a pencil. She almost didn't believe it herself. It was being in that room. As long as she was being distracted by the distinctive ticking of his clock and the rustling of his newspaper under his desk, as long as she was semi-nauseated by the rich smell of coffee overlaid by the sickliness of the air-freshener spray he used to disguise his cigarette smoke, she could not move away from the May who belonged in that room and would never have dared to complain.

She left her coffee half-finished and stood up.

"I'm sorry," she said humbly because she really did feel guilty and apologetic. "I'm terribly sorry but I'm afraid I have to go."

He stood up so quickly that the paper slipped to the floor in a confusion of broadsheets that would need sorting later. "Go where? Go how?"

She frowned, fidgeted with the clasp of her handbag, shook her head as she abandoned an attempt to explain what she herself did not fully understand and had reached the door before she was suddenly inspired.

"A date," she whispered.

John Maitland may have thought that he had seen April Reynolds setting off for *work* without June or May, although in fact May only accompanied them on a Monday if she had to fill in a vacancy, but at the bottom of Damhope Road April turned left instead of right, aiming for the city centre rather than following the road which gradually narrowed before branching off into an industrial estate where it ramified into a carefully planned grid system on which by far the most prestigious building was the one that housed *Reynolds Fine Preserves and Marmalades.* Moving slowly in the column of city-bound traffic, she smiled to herself at the thought that none of the three sisters had any idea that she too was abandoning her station at the family business – though just temporarily – just for the morning.

June and Prue had remained at Tomdoun to finish equipping the barn as a playroom for William, June having thrown herself into the task with a purposeful zeal as though to blot everything else from her mind. May, had chosen to remain with them and would be vacillating happily between offering increasingly confident advice on colour schemes and disappearing for hours on end with her sketch-book. No-one had asked for April's help and all three expected her to return to the factory on the due date, now well overdue for both June and May.

She had returned home feeling resentful and discontented, both alien sensations, and, furthermore, she had found it inexplicably difficult to settle comfortably back into her executive bedroom. She found it suddenly oppressive – constraining even. Never before had she even noticed the sharpness of the corners of the rigid, dark Victorian mahogany or the dullness of the rusty-red curtains, their dried blood colour streaked faintly with mustard yellow where the pile of the velvet had rubbed; never felt the embarrassment of the double bed, worn down on the side where she had always slept alone and with an overbearingly intricate headboard carved with overblown peonies and overfed cherubs with sagging buttocks who gazed down at her with superior expressions as she lay between the sheets, smirking no doubt about her unrelieved virginity. And then the tragedy of the looking-glass! On the day after her return, armed with step-ladder, nail and claw-hammer she had attempted to move it down to a level at which she could more easily study her reflection. Perhaps it was because of its heaviness, perhaps because her hands were sweaty, clammy with nervousness, but anyway it slipped through her grasp, fell to the floor and shattered, cracking from a central point so that she had to pick up lethally sharp, pointed shards of glass.

"I'm sorry," she had whispered repeatedly to whoever. To the ghost of a father who would no doubt dock her pocket-money for years? For life? Then, catching herself in the act of the ludicrous apology, she felt a completely new emotion, an anger at the injustice of her situation.

The trip into town this Monday morning was for the sole purpose of refurnishing her bedroom to her own personal taste without consulting any of her sisters. She would, however, return to the factory at lunch-time in plenty of time for her meeting with Caroline Parry arranged for two o'clock when Caroline was calling for an "update" whatever that might mean. But in the meantime the day was hers.

"Carpe diem!" she urged herself aloud and then remembered that that was one of her father's favourite maxims, though never used in relation to unnecessary, purely cosmetic interior design, and wished that she could cease to speak his language. "Break the mould," she muttered. But then that phrase too she had inherited from him.

Jock stood in front of Jane on the doormat dusting his

feet. As one who had been accustomed from childhood to being told off for having muddy boots, the dusting had now become a ritual of courtesy and the more he felt he had to butter up his host, the longer he dusted. Today he dusted very thoroughly.

"Hi!" he said. "Mind if I have a few words."

Just in time Jane recognised him as Ham's Scout Leader and smiled.

"Of course," she smiled. "Come in! Coffee?"

"I'm afraid Ham's gone into town with his sister," she added as he followed her into the kitchen to make coffee. "They've gone to buy new trainers for P.E – trainers on a strictly limited budget."

He laughed, looking up from where he was kneeling beside Jelly in front of the Aga, tickling her tummy as she lay on her back with her paws in the air and her tongue lolling out of her grinning mouth and said, "This is a lovely kitchen! So warm and bright!"

"My favourite room in the whole house," agreed Jane. "I loved it as soon as I saw it. Would you like to stay in here for your coffee then?"

He was dunking his second ginger-nut before he started to explain his mission and even then he spoke hesitantly as though not quite sure how it would be received.

"It's two things really," he said slowly, "and perhaps it's really your husband I should be speaking to ... But, anyway, here goes. Firstly a television company has approached me – doing a documentary about scouting. Probably it's because the producer is a friend of my cousin's. Seems they've decided to focus on two Scout groups – one English, one Scottish. Ours is the Scottish, obviously."

'Obviously,' thought Jane. Aloud, because there was something about him that evoked motherliness, probably the hole in the elbow of his sweater, she said, "Your coffee's getting cold."

"Obviously," he picked up, "we want our kids to be doing something sort of Scottish and just before the holidays when I didn't know about all this television stuff I mentioned to your husband that we might perhaps do a loch or two with him. He didn't exactly say 'No'; gave me the impression it might be possible, can't be sure that he was all that keen ..."

"I'd have to ask him," pronounced Jane non-committally.

"And the other thing," he dunked the same biscuit three times so that a saturated fragment fell off and floated on the surface of his undrunk coffee, "is that I mentioned this lochnetting just casually, just in passing you understand, to Mark – that's the producer guy." He took a slurp from his coffee at last, eyeing Jane over the rim of his mug as though expecting her to remonstrate but she merely topped up her own mug and smiled encouragingly, so he licked away the crumb of sodden biscuit adhering forlornly to his upper lip and continued. "Mark thought he might like to do a separate thing on loch-netting, thought it a wonderful idea. Anyway he said to sound John out. John is your husband's name? " He put his mug down and relaxed back in his chair. "That's why I'm here."

"And I'll tell John everything you've said," promised Jane. "And now, for heaven's sake let me get rid of that disgusting mess and fix you a fresh mug."

The bright, strong primary colours they had used to transform the barn into a playroom for William had dominated June's mind with their intensity. After the recent wretched scenes with Mattie, the old, imagined relationship with the same but different Mattie lurked in the back of her mind like an old photograph in blurred sepia – not quite real, definitely belonging to a place and time which was no longer relevant to the here and now. But even while she measured and laid the brilliant yellow and white squared vinyl flooring – soft enough to fall on, definitely not slippery and positively spill-proof – and slapped a red paint-brush across a diminutive table and two tiny three-legged stools, the realisation of the shapelessness of her own future would sneak into her mind: the knowledge that there would be the bright times - like the one she was enjoying at the moment with Prue and William and the colour and the laughter – and the busy times when she concentrated on the finances of *Reynolds Fine Preserves and Marmalades*, but what would she dream of when she plugged herself into her music and to whom would she be singing on her solitary Sunday car-outings?

There was not much time for pondering the future on arriving back at No.11. After running an agitated May – agitated because punctuality seemed to be her religion and she knew she was late - to her appointment with Norman Paterson, there was only time for a brief unpacking and an even briefer lunch before driving out to the factory where she had promised April she would join her for a meeting with the formidable Caroline. Without wanting to know why, she felt guilty about April and her sense of guilt increased when she arrived in April's office to find Caroline already seated with a cup of coffee in her hand and a propitiatory basket of *Reynolds Very Finest Preserves and Marmalades* balanced very precisely on her knee.

"Hello *June!*" The inflected June expressed Caroline's gracious ease, that of the self-appointed co-host. "*Lovely* to see you again."

"Am I late?" June's guilt escalated to semi-paranoia.

From the wall behind April her father, gilt-framed and uncompromisingly blotched in thick oils, pressed his thin lips into a determined smile and assessed her objectively, all-seeing, all-knowing.

"Not at all," Caroline took it upon herself to reassure her. "I came early. Rotten thing to do to busy people."

She smacked her own wrist gently so as not to upset her coffee.

"Coffee, June?" April's voice held a brittle edge. "I *thought* you would probably prefer to lunch at home with the others."

"We were late getting back." June, recognising in her own voice a sullen, teenage like resentment at having to explain herself, shrugged nonchalantly.

"I was hearing about your loch-netting," purred Caroline with the conscious smugness of the peacemaker. "I think it's *wonderful*."

"Gets us out of a rut," June conceded.

"In fact," Caroline prepared herself for making an important announcement by setting her coffee cup on the table and laying the basket on the floor beside her left foot with exaggerated carefulness, "I think it could be just what we're looking for."

Her eyes moved from April to June, from June to April, her eyebrows slightly quirked in expectation of their immediately grasping just what it was she was alluding to and agreeing rapturously.

"I don't quite follow you." It was April who admitted defeat.

"Initiative building?" Caroline held out the clue gingerly as though offering a petit four to a pair of rabid rottweilers.

Neither sister responded.

"Togetherness?" she prompted with just a hint of exasperation in her voice, leaning forward towards them and massaging her right calf with a gesture that drew attention to its shapeliness

"I'm afraid," said June wearily, "you'll have to spell it

out in simple English."

"Many of the firms I have handled," Caroline picked up her coffee cup and leaned back in her chair, settling herself comfortably for what might have to be a lengthy explanation, "find that by organising activities that encourage initiative and a sense of togetherness they can inspire team spirit like never before."

"Are you actually suggesting that we march the workers round a couple of lochs?" asked June impatiently.

"Are you suggesting that we either intrude into their free time or sacrifice a couple of days' productivity?" April was scandalised.

"It's not what you do for heaven's sake: it's *how* you do it!" Caroline snapped. She was human after all, human and vulnerable. June warmed to her. "The way April described loch-netting to me didn't seem much like 'being marched round a couple of lochs'. The activities she described were varied -offering choice – and ... and the chance to engage in pursuits which they might not otherwise ..." She interrupted herself. "Why do you think that what appealed to you wouldn't appeal to your staff? You 're all members of the human race you know."

"Of course," murmured April diplomatically if uncertainly.

"And if *you* don't like the idea," the challenge was aimed directly at June, "*you* will have to come up with something else and do it soon because on a scale of 1-10 your factory scores a pretty poor 4 on staff motivation and stimulation."

"On whose scale may I ask?" countered June aggressively.

"Mine!" spat Caroline prodding the basket of *Reynolds Very Finest etc.* irreverently with a toe. Her eyes blazed and her ear-lobes, the only areas free of make-up, glowed red with anger. June suddenly urged to seize her by her skinny, shakeable shoulders and kiss the lips pursed into a small, red rosette of anger and to do it right there in April's, in her father's office. But instead she smiled at the pert, angry little face.

"I'm sorry," she said. "Actually I think it's a brilliant idea." And she continued to smile blandly while Caroline stared at her for a full twenty seconds before crossing and re-crossing her legs and signalling re-adoption of her official persona by taking a pen and a large pseudo-leatherbound diary from her brief-case.

"Well, may I suggest," she said with her official smile re-emerging, "that you produce a plan in outline and we meet to discuss it next week. Can we fix a time?"

After she had departed, bearing the basket of *Reynolds Very Finest* deferentially in both hands, thereby reminding June of one of the magi in a Nativity play she had been allowed to witness before her mother died, followed by Ted from *Labelling* with her brief-case in one hand, her lap-top in the other and his eyes firmly fixed on her tailored behind, April exploded, hissing through her teeth so that neither of the secretaries could overhear.

"June! What on earth possessed you? Have you thought what John will say?"

"The situation will require diplomacy." June took refuge in Caroline-speak. "I will, of course, be supporting your application to him."

John closed the front door of No.10 behind him and hesitated. An unseemly brawl appeared to be taking place in the kitchen. His instinct urged him to sneak through to his study, shut the door, become absorbed in a newspaper/book/computer game/whatever until the row subsided and he could emerge to ratify any decision Jane had made, authorise any sentence she had pronounced. His conscience prompted him to wade into the thick of it and help Jane out. He opted dishonourably for the retreat to the study and was half-way across the hall when Jelly suddenly rumbled him and rushed to greet him vocally, announcing his shameful presence to the rest of the family.

"Traitor," he murmured tickling her affectionately behind the ears, set his brief-case down in the middle of the hall and opened the kitchen door.

Jenny, seated at the table, swinging on a tilted chair, alternately taking bites out of a large pancake and licking jam off her splayed fingers, was deliberating exuding an air of provocative nonchalance.

"He really is a spoilt brat," she was observing to Jane who was standing beside Ham with a restraining arm around his shoulders. "You need to discipline him."

"It's not fair! I hate you!" Ham, frustrated by his comparative inarticulacy, tears of humiliation on his lashes, could only repeat himself. "I hate you. I hate you! Let me go!"

He paused to sniff and wipe his grubby hand across his eyes and John took advantage of the moment of silence.

"Jane, what on earth...?"

"Mountain out of a molehill," opined Jenny, "he …

"Jenny, I prefer to hear the story from your mother."

"Suit yourself," she shrugged, calmly helping herself to another pancake.

"You're getting fat!" screamed Ham. "Fat! Fat! Big, fat bum!"

"Ham, be quiet," said Jane. "Both be quiet," she amended feeling through his shoulder an electric quiver of indignation at having been yet again singled out for criticism. "Sit down and have a pancake, John, while they're some left. There's tea in the pot. Uh-uh!" She held up a warning finger as both children started to speak. "My turn. As you know, John, it's Jenny's birthday in October and she wants to have a party."

John pulled a wry face but said nothing.

"I said it would probably be possible – with the usual reservations – not more than twelve, no alcohol and we would be present. Then she said she would like to hold it in the cellar and ..."

"The cellar's mine!" screamed Ham. "You gave it to me when we moved in. She got riding lessons and first choice of bedroom. You said I could have the cellar. It's my secret, private place!"

"Yes, I know," soothed Jane. "That's all true. But I can't help thinking that a party in the cellar wouldn't half save the rest of the house. What do you think, John?"

John pointed to his mouth to indicate that it was full of pancake, but, in reality, he needed the time to think coherently. Eventually he took a sip of tea, swallowed and spoke.

"After Jenny's fourteenth which I would rather forget than remember, I think a party in the house is a non-starter. The cellar *is* Ham's. If Jenny wants to borrow it for a party she has to negotiate terms with *him*."

"So you're leaving it all to me?"Jenny brought her chair down with a thud and glared at him. "You're actually trying to say that it's Ham's decision."

"Got it in one," smiled John, "and if you want your party you'll have to use your well-honed, persuasive skills to butter him up or bribe him."

"Don't know what well-honed means," Jenny pushed her chair back and stood up. "I can't bear to look at you," she hissed at her father and made for the doorway where she turned with her hand on the door-handle. "I, for one, do not believe in bribery!"

They heard her bedroom door slam

"What do you think she's going to do to butter me up?"

said Ham apprehensively as he reached for a pancake.

"Heaven knows," smiled Jane, "but please wash your hands before you start on those. Oh, by the way, John, I had a visit this morning from somebody who very definitely wants to butter *you* up."

"I think it's a ghastly idea!" Prue spoke vehemently. "William, I don't think you ought to have Aunty May's sketch-book. No, William! William, Mummy said "NO!""

"Don't take it out on him," June remonstrated mildly, removing the sketch-book and putting it out of reach on top of the upright piano. "Why so opposed?"

His attention diverted from the sketch-book, William prised open the lid of the piano and banged his sticky palm down on the keyboard, screamed with delight and continued with the alternate banging and screaming while his mother and aunt continued their debate.

"Because it's taking advantage," Prue frowned her effort to justify herself. "Loch-netting was John's private idea, his dream and we, well we sort of intruded into it because we thought it would help May. And it *did* help May, "she asserted, "but I don't think we can expect him to take on the factory. Not yet anyway. He's still just feeling his way. Has nobody ever thought to get that piano tuned?"

"No, not really," said June, adding reasonably, "None of us can play. Well, what's the harm in telling him about Caroline's idea and seeing if he can fit the factory in at a later date ... if he wants to ..."

"O.K.," Prue shrugged, "but this time I'm not doing the asking."

"Fine!" retorted June hotly. "April's anti; you're anti and May ... well! Who needs support with sisters like you three? I'll go ask myself!"

However, when June crossed the threshold of No 10 at exactly a quarter-to-nine, a time she had judged to be propitious, she was not alone but accompanied by May, following close at heel and clutching the perfected sketch of the ruined cottage at Loch Oich.

"I could come with you and give John the sketch he wanted," she had observed brightly when June had announced her intention of calling next-door. Then, misinterpreting the cold silence of the remaining two sisters had added defensively, "He *said* he wanted it. He *asked* me to do it. But if you think ..."

"I'm sure he'll love it," Prue had reassured and April had attempted something similar.

The door was opened to them by a radiantly happy Jenny.

"Guess what?" she had started breathlessly, omitting any sort of appropriate salutation. "We're going to be on television. You too! All of us! The lochnetters!"

Jane appeared behind her in time to arrest May's headlong flight.

"Don't worry," she laughed. "Nothing's been decided yet. Come in and sit down. May, that's beautiful!"The admiration in her voice was unmistakably genuine and May flushed with pleasure. "John will be thrilled. Go and call Dad, Jenny. He's in the garden."

It was Peter who answered the phone at the back of ten and Harry missed neither the look of eager anticipation as he picked it up nor the note of disappointment in the "It's for you," as he handed it over, with his face turned away.

"Are you sitting down?" John's tone was so flat that Harry was unable to gauge whether the potentially shocking news was wonderful or disastrous. "Harry, in one single day our little band of loch-netters seems to have stretched to include a troop of boy scouts – plus a leader or two, a factory load of workers and a television crew; oh – and I nearly forgot – a lass I met on in-service who wrote to me and whom I phoned back this evening. She has pledged herself enthusiastically to join us in September. Harry? Harry, are you still there?"

"Yes," said Harrry, "just."

"It might just make a tad of difference to the way you plan our next expedition?"

"Yes," said Harry, "quite."

"It's too late to be trying to make any sense out of it all now." John sounded weary. "How about you come to supper on Wednesday – day after tomorrow – and we'll have a bash at sorting it out?"Harry hesitated. "Peter, too, of course if he's free and willing. We're going to need all the help we can get!"

"I'm not quite sure about Wednesday." Harry's tone was guarded. The blood-test was at 4.30. How would Peter, how would they both be feeling afterwards? "We'd love to come but we've something on earlier which might make it a bit tricky. Could I have a word with Peter and tell you first thing to-morrow?"

"Fine," said John.

"In the meantime try not to dream about drowning them all," chuckled Harry as he hung up.

Chapter Twenty-two

Going Public

Being Propelled Forward

As it was, the supper with John and Jane promised to be a welcome distraction. Harry broached the invitation as he thought sensitively, making it clear that he would support any reluctance on Peter's part.

"Why on earth not?" Peter's tone was almost brutally matter-of-fact and he spoke without looking round the edge of his newspaper. "Neither of us has anything on to my knowledge – other than that blood-thing at 4.30. Not unless you've suddenly acquired a hot date."

Harry, feeling the sarcastic edge as yet another rebuff, remained silent, picked up his empty coffee mug and made for the kitchen.

"By the way," Peter went on in the same casual drawl, "the blood-test is on me."

Harry wheeled round in disbelief. "What?"

"It's not free, you know." Peter was flipping casually through a magazine as he spoke, his head bowed so that Harry could not read his expression. "You can't prove your paternity - or lack of it – on the National Health. Just as well! In our state of moral decline we'd bankrupt the Health Service in a matter of weeks if every Tom, Dick or ..." He broke off in time. "Did you know," he picked up on a subject he obviously considered more interesting than that of his paternity, "that a horse is unable to vomit?"

Harry continued on into the kitchen, placed his mug in

the dishwasher and went straight to bed without bidding Peter good-night The next morning he left early for school to avoid chatting over the breakfast table and used part of a free period to book himself into his favourite French restaurant for Tuesday night, leaving a note for Peter to that effect, only just refraining from adding "on a hot date." On returning home at half-past ten, after an unusually mediocre meal, he found his own note still folded and apparently unread and lying beside it one from Peter announcing his intention of going "out" and advising Harry not to wait up.

"Prioritise!" Jane commanded herself firmly, tying herself into a multi-task apron. "Get on top!"

Jelly, lolling in front of the Aga, eyed her uncertainly. Jane's tone was dimly reminiscent of the training days of her puppyhood.

"It's all right, Jelly." Jane shook off her shoes and drew out a chair to stand on so that she could reach her *Surpassing Suppers* cookery book and choose something that she could manage and Harry would appreciate. "But with the rest of the family high as kites over their television debut, I've got to get on with things and keep my feet on the ground. Like this!" And she jumped off her chair.

By mid-day, she had cause to feel satisfied with her efforts and allowed herself to take a belated mug of coffee into the garden, but even there she could not shut her eyes to what needed to be done.

"Tomorrow, we'll tie up the dahlias," she said aloud to Jelly, "and the Brussels sprouts could do with a good watering. And if we dead-head the roses..."

"Coo-ee, that you Jane?"

I f she didn't reply and just scooted back inside, Moira might just think she hadn't heard. She turned to slink in just as Moira's head appeared over the wall.

"Damnit," only Jelly heard, "she's got the steps."

"Got a minute?"

"Not really," replied Jane truthfully. "I'm doing a supper-party tonight."

"It will only take a teensy little minute," Moira wobbled precariously on the garden steps and clutched the top of the wall with two marigold clad hands.

"I've got something to show you," she whispered as Jane and Jelly appeared round the side of her house and then raised her voice, "Oh, you've brought *her* too!"

"Well, I'm not coming in" replied Jane reasonably, smiling at the thought that Jelly was an excellent insurance policy against being coaxed into Moira's unsullied house. "What do you want to show me.?"

"My new little person," Moira resumed whispering. "He's just so sweet. Come on down. And I wanted *you* to see him especially because we got him when we went loch-netting with you."

"You don't mean you dragged him out of a loch?" Jane stared in disbelief at the plastic whiteness of the three foot high statue of a boy clasping a rose to his chest with one hand and scratching his bottom with the other.

"Of course not, silly!" snapped Moira. "While you lot were doing your thing on Loch Oich, Patrick and I did a little retail therapy. It was such a wonderful opportunity to do something really meaningful together and Patrick felt he had to spoil me a little after my disappointment at Loch Ness."

"Disappointment?"

"You remember! Those newspaper people virtually promised to print my picture in the paper. In the end they didn't even mention me. Just used all I told them about my terrible experience with the drowned body and then left me out completely. I said to Patrick,' That's the last time I ever do anything for the media!' Anyway, this is the result."

"I see," said Jane and struggled, "It's ...It's ..."

"I know," agreed Moira, "leaves you speechless. Don't let her sniff him." Jane grabbed Jelly's collar. "Patrick and I wanted a statue for that corner. At least I did and Patrick agreed. So we started off at a monumental mason's just outside Kilbennochy, but there was nothing suitable. You couldn't really put a Virgin or an angel beside Aphrodite."

"Conflict of interests?" smiled Jane.

"Too many clothes," said Moira. "There's nothing as beautiful as the naked human body. This part of my garden is, after all, a celebration of the beauty of the human body. Well, after the mason's we went to a garden centre and as soon as I saw little Paddy here, I fell in love with him."

"Paddy?"

"I've got this photograph of Patrick, aged nine, completely naked on the beach and believe it or not, this little man is the spit image of him, right down to the way his little willy curls so sweetly."

"I must remember that," said Jane.

"The only trouble is," Moira tilted her head on one side, "he's so white he makes the others look quite grubby so I've been having a good scrub at them." She flexed her marigolds. "You wouldn't believe what I've prised out of their crevices, bless them. It nearly turned my stomach."

"And talking of stomachs," picked up Jane skilfully, "If I don't get back to the kitchen now, my guests will have to have fish and chips from the carry-out. Thanks for introducing me to Paddy, Moira. I'll send the others round some time to see if they recognise Patrick. Must go! Jelly, come!"

Alderson McTavish was more than a solid, well-respected firm of Edinburgh solicitors. Over the years the successors of the late Mr. Alderson and the very late Mr.

McTavish had narrowed and redefined their recruitment procedures so that those who filled the hand-made leather shoes of their predecessors would fit them with Cinderella-like precision – except, of course that the recruits were no Cinderellas in other respects: for one thing, they were never female, although for obvious reasons this was not made explicit in the precisely worded vacancy advertisements appearing on the retiral or untimely death of a partner in the right, the far right, newspapers; and for another, theirs was no rags to riches story, applicants having been drawn only from those schools whose fees were calculated to suit the purses of the upper middle classes and of those moneyed individuals who could afford to ape the upper middle classes. Given this refined atmosphere, Peter had assumed that he could write *4.00: Medical for P. Aitchison* in the firm diary without anybody thinking to enquire as to the nature of his ailment, but he had made the assumption forgetting the new secretary, Suzanne, who, despite her advantage in having attended one of the right schools, sometimes emitted disturbing signs of not having benefitted from the fact.

"Not ill are you, Mr. Aitchison?" she enquired brightly as Peter passed through the office at three minutes to four. "I do hope not," she faltered uncertainly as she heard Miss Muir's stiffly ironed torso rustle reproachfully in her direction.

"I'm sure I'll be fine. Thanks for asking." Peter tried a re-assuring smile. "Good-night, Miss Muir," he said. "I doubt I'll be back before we close. Miss Murray Brown knows what to say if Mr. Black should phone."

"Thank-you. Good-night, Mr. Aitchison," she called as he opened the front door of the office sending a shaft of bright sunlight shooting as briefly as a lightning flash across the shadowless neon limbo of the reception and typing area.

He had allowed himself half an hour to walk the couple of miles to the *Potters' Haugh Medical Centre* where he and his father were registered. As the offices gave way to shops and the shops to tenement blocks and the tenement blocks to individually owned houses, his city persona threatened to mutate into the sulky, adolescent fifteen-year old raging inside, flexing his insecurities to show the world that he didn't care if he did become biologically fatherless. It might have been more sensible to have taken the bus and concentrated en route on his newspaper.

    "I thought perhaps Loch Katrine and perhaps a couple of smaller lochs nearby," Harry ventured. "Just a suggestion – based on the fact that it's large enough to accommodate everyone and equipped for all ability levels – but it's entirely up to you of course."

    He had poured over the map of the loch the evening before until he could almost feel the chill of the air rising from the unnaturally uniform cobalt-blueness of the paper loch. He had spent the half-hour in which he had waited in the doctor's surgery examining the tracks around the loch and those which connected it to one or two smaller lochs – scout sized perhaps. During both sessions he had hoped that he was giving Peter the impression that he was fully occupied with something far more important than the outcome of the blood-test. Peter, he had noticed, seated beside him in the waiting-room was making a complete cock-up of the crossword, even filling the answers to the clues into the wrong squares. So much for *his* sang-froid. After she had taken their blood, the young doctor had not seen them to the door. She had remained seated and spoken with her head bent over the forms she was filling out.

    "The results will take a few days," she had remarked casually, her voice slightly muffled because her head was lowered. "If you contact me in round about a week, I should have something for you."

"Fine," he and Peter had replied in unison, adjusting their ties in unison, clearing their throats in unison, before turning to each other to enquire hypothetically, "You O.K.?"

Now, at the Maitland's Harry found himself recovering from a sort of mental hypothermia, thawing slowly, becoming gradually more physically conscious of his surroundings, of the coldness of the nose that Jelly thrust into his hand, of the varying scent from a glass bowl of roses – now strong, now faint, of the glinting of the bangles that slid up Jenny's arm as she raised her fork to her mouth, of the lingering tang of marjoram and the grey smudges under Peter's eyes.

"Loch Katrine?" John swilled his wine round his glass slowly as he spoke. "Ah, yes. It's got an old steamer on it hasn't it."

"A bit touristy," Jane frowned. "Is it the sort of image of loch-netting that we want to give? I'm not meaning to knock your idea, Harry," she added slightly guiltily.

Unnoticed, Jelly had sidled in and lain down in the shadow of the table at Ham's feet and he took advantage of the fact that the others seemed to be absorbed in deciding whether Loch Katrine was too touristy at the height of the summer season to be viable to slip a thickly sauced chunk of meat under the table. She sniffed it, decided that the sauce had rendered the meat unpalatable and left his offering to exude its coating deep into the pile of the carpet. Ham wriggled on his seat in an effort to nudge the evidence away from his chair with his toe and, having done his best to incriminate Jenny, decided to contribute to the discussion.

"I'd really like to go on the steamer!" he said defiantly.

"Thing is," Peter put in, "there are other quieter lochs in the immediate surroundings and maybe the contrast would be good. Not all the Reynolds people are going to be keen on yomping or cycling around muddy tracks however much the rest of us might like it. So perhaps the steamer for those who prefer to taste loch-netting sitting down?"

He shrugged, and smiled around the table.

"I agree with Peter," purred Jenny sweetly. "Perhaps some of us could ride round. Any horses in the area?"

"Doubt whether horses are on, Jenny," Harry shook his head. "Loch Katrine's Glasgow's water supply and I don't think they'd allow horses around it. As far as I can remember there was at one time a bit of a stooshie about there being sheep on the loch-side."

"Bit of manure in the water'd do them good," pouted Jenny. "Make them grow. Well, Glasgow people are supposed to be small, aren't they?" Another happy thought diverted her from the stature of Glaswegians. "Is Helga coming, Peter?"

"I don't know," said Peter bleakly.

"Just wondered," she prattled on, "because ..."

"Jenny and Ham, help me clear away the dishes please," interrupted Jane.

By the end of the evening it was settled – in outline. It would be suggested that the factory party would concentrate on Loch Katrine, taking the steamer from the Trossachs pier to Stronachlachar and either walking back, cycling back or remaining on the boat for the return trip. The scouts could ramble up the west side of Loch Chon along a track which should carry little or no traffic. Then a minor road would take them to Stronachlachar from where they could get the steamer back to the Trossachs pier. For the rest of them – the "Foundation Lochnetters" - there were additional possibilities: they could cycle/walk round Loch Ard where the track followed the lochside closely and there was the possibility of exploring the site of a crannog; they could also follow the track to where little Loch Dubh nestled between Ben Dubh, Ben Bhan and Ben Lomond.

"Magnificent scenery around Loch Dubh." Harry's excitement was mounting. "And if your camera guru is looking for wild, woolly Highland shots, he could do no better. When did you say you were meeting him?"

"Monday and you can be sure it's going to mean more than one planning meeting!" John grimaced wryly. "There'll be meetings and sub-meetings. I feel it in my bones!"He shuddered theatrically.

"In the first instance," Caroline's voice sounded nasal over April's mobile and there was a vague crackling in the background which suggested that she was either stoking a bonfire or picking at a packet of crisps, "you need to offer your staff freedom of choice contained within a rigid framework."

"Uh-huh," April felt lost already.

There was the faintest sigh as Caroline registered that she and April were yet again not on the same wavelength.

"You need to fix the date, the time, the place and the mode of transport and offer choice vis a vis the activity each member wishes to pursue, their preferred refreshment opportunities ..." Her voice tailed off as she ran out of free choices. "Anyway we can fill in the details on Tuesday evening. I take it you will have invited a couple of representatives from your factory staff along?"

"Yes," lied April, blushing as she spoke.

It had been June's idea that the meeting with Caroline be held at Damhope Road rather than at the factory and, even though Caroline's evening fee was double, April had agreed readily enough, not only because it complied with her general rule of not interfering with the working day but because Caroline's presence in the factory unnerved her. She felt that her working relationship with the staff was constantly under Caroline's scrutiny and Caroline was given to those quick little sniffs followed by a straightening of her lips which seemed to suggest that she had criticisms to make but was holding them in check for the meantime – with difficulty. Caroline and her sniffs and her lips would be better in Damhope Road where her potential to stir revolt should be limited.

On the Monday evening before the meeting April took herself off to hoe feverishly, desperately, in between the cabbages and try to blot out the painful scenes of the last few days in which she seemed to have managed to fall foul of all three sisters.

After Caroline's phone call she had tried to confide in June – June, her right-hand 'man', whose support she had never before felt the need to question. They had been sitting in the car in the factory car park and April held felt a sudden urge to unburden herself and leave her misgivings behind her at work before she escaped home. She had relayed the gist of her conversation with Caroline, including Caroline's presumption that the shop floor be represented at the planning meeting.

"Things will never be the same after this," she finished running sweaty hands around the rim of the steering wheel. "The whole discipline of the factory relies on preserving the distance of management levels in order to retain the respect of the workers."

"You mean if they knew us better they'd cease to respect us." June laughed harshly. "You're probably right there. Same goes for us. I've a fair idea sisterly respect would dwindle if we knew each other too well."

"Don't be so silly!" April had snapped. "You know perfectly well that it was one of Father's unwritten rules that we should never fraternise." June leaned forward and switched on Radio 3 as though she'd heard enough, thereby goading April into adding, "Prue fraternised and look what it brought her!"

"Brought her William," June had countered evenly, "and I think he's rather nice."

"He's sweet, really sweet," put in May from the back

seat, feeling that the conversation had at last reached a level at which she felt qualified to contribute.

"Oh, shut up," muttered April under her breath as she turned the key in the ignition.

But the next day she had invited Archie, the foreman, asking him to bring two other members of the staff along with him and had been gratified by the fact that his embarrassment had been evident.

"Are you sure, Miss April? At your *house*, Miss April? Well, of course, Miss April! But are you sure, Miss April?"

She had taken great delight in reporting his discomfort to June who had neither responded nor raised her eyes from her paperwork.

She straightened her back and loosened her grip on the hoe. Her palm throbbed and she examined it to find that a splinter from the hoe had lodged in it. Deciding against returning to the house to extract it, she sucked it and made her way down to where Prue's dahlias blazed hotly despite the fact that Prue never weeded between the plants. "I like a good ground cover of weeds," she maintained, "and these dahlias are tough."

Prue could be tough too – tough and hot-tempered! On the previous Friday April had arranged for her old bedroom furniture to be collected and taken to a second-hand furniture shop in the morning and her new walnut suite to be delivered in the afternoon. She had arranged to take the day off work and had hoped that neither Prue nor May would be at home because for some reason that even she could not understand she had deliberately avoided mentioning to the others that she was changing her bedroom furniture. It had been her private decision – more than that really, more a private responsibility: the old bedroom furniture was an intimate part of the relationship between her mother and her father – to be respected at all costs. If *she* had decided to break taboo then surely *she* should be the one to bear the brunt of the decision, the guilt and any consequences that might follow alone and not make her sisters her accomplices. It was very complicated logic, something that she herself could not fully understand, but there it was. Last Friday morning the men had carried the furniture out onto the lawn at the front of the house where they had jettisoned the pieces in meaningless disarray while they enjoyed a statutory tea break before loading. May, returning from sketching the golf clubhouse as April had suggested she might, had seen the dark huddle of mahogany, dropped her sketch-book and run to trace the outline of the cherubs with a shaking forefinger, as she had often done as a child, before bursting into tears of inconsolable grief.

"Have you no feeling?" Prue had flared up at April. "Don't you think you could have told her, prepared her?"

She should have, yes, but she couldn't have. None of them had understood this and the gulf between her and her sisters had stretched still wider so that none of them had crossed the threshold of her bedroom to admire or even inspect her new purchases. And the following evening at the planning meeting she was going to need all their support.

"M-m-m-m-m-m," purred Mark, the producer, Jock's cousin's friend, yet again, at the end of John's carefully prepared presentation of loch-netting. John hoped that this was an appreciative noise but he could not be sure: the *m-m-m-m-ms* had been emitted on an upward glissando which had a vaguely questioning quality. He had outlined the aims of loch-netting and the progress of his band of lochnetters to date and Mark and Jock had listened without comment or interruption apart from the bland "m-m-m-m-ms" which Mark breathed intermittently through closed lips as he leaned back on a rickety chair in the scout hut, his eyes partly closed as though he was having to make an effort to visualise what John was describing. As he waited for a reaction John wished that the man's physical appearance offered more clues to his personality. The black cycling leathers covered up any hints as to his personal tastes and the thick jutting beard gave him the appearance of a jutting determined chin which might or might not exist. In the silence John began to wish that he had never agreed to this: his lochnetting project was too new, too especially his to be exposed to this man's calculating criticism or to this possibility of subsequent public ridicule.

"Well ...," drawled Mark folding his hands behind his head and continuing to gaze out the window with his tightly screwed up eyes.

"I'll make some coffee." So Jock was also finding the silence unnerving. "Sugar and milk, everyone?"

"No sugar for me, thanks," said John.

Mark ignored the question, gave no clue as to his taste in coffee.

Jock produced three mugs of coffee.

"Sorry mugs are a bit chipped," he grinned. "You just have to put your mouth where there isn't a chip."

"I think ... we're onto something ... that could be ... really interesting *if* and only *if* it's handled the right way," pronounced Mark sniffing the steam of his coffee and gazing through it into space. "Instant?"

"'Fraid so!" agreed Jock happily.

"Can't drink instant. Won't sleep all night. As I was saying, I think we're onto something here. Now what's the timescale for the next trip?"

"We are planning for the September holiday week-end," replied John. "That is the week-end of the 12th. The factory staff will go up to Loch Katrine on the Friday with the Reynolds sisters and Harry who thinks he can get leave of absence ...."

"Yes, yes!" The beard quivered impatiently. "No personal details now, please!"

"On Saturday, the scouts, Jock and Peter and others will walk up the side of Loch Chon, from there either walk or be transported to Stronachlachar where they will meet the paddle steamer and take it down Loch Katrine to the Trossachs Pier. On the Sunday, our original group will walk/cycle round Loch Ard where there is a crannog we wish to investigate and on the Monday we will make our way up to Loch Dubh, a small hill loch. By the way the incidence of crannogs is much more widespread than ..."

"Save it!" snapped Mark, holding out his hand. "Save all that sort of stuff for the interview which we can plan later. We've got to give this thing really wide appeal, think what grabs the public at the moment. Firstly there's the fitness aspect. Think of all the television-addicted couch potatoes who could happily visualise themselves shambling round lochs rather than walking up hills, believing that it would do them some good. We want that sort of anti-obesity, 'you too can be healthy' slant even if most of them probably couldn't be healthy if they tried. You'll need to have at least a couple of the very obviously obese in your clientele. And, talking of obesity, it would pay us to include disability."

John opened his mouth, struggled to make the connections between obesity, the disabled and the fitness level required for loch-netting and closed it again.

"Come on!" Mark was even more impatient and slapped his leather thighs resoundingly as he added emphasis to, "The *sport for all slant*!" He paused to stir his undrinkable coffee and expanded more calmly, "Seems to me that lochnetting would be ideal for combining able-bodied and disabled; team spirit between the two groups and all that. Well, you want to sell this thing you know and you need to engender sympathy between the viewing public and the participants and there's nothing like disability for engendering sympathy, take it from me!"

John wondered if he did actually want to sell lochnetting. It was a bit like a house you put up for sale. By the time you adapted it to suit the viewing public you hardly recognised it as being yours.

Mark was busy scribbling in a black leather diary. He looked up. "You submit to me a plan of your next venture. I'd like it by the end of the week. He looked at his watch. Well, it's Monday now so that should give you plenty of time. You need to try to get hold of a couple of obese and at least one token disabled – medically certificated of course - and let me know what the specific disability is. After which, I will draw up a shooting schedule, find you a suitable interviewer and we'll have lift-off. Easy as that! O.K?" The hair overhanging his upper lip parted barely discernibly which seemed to indicate that he was perhaps smiling.

John did not feel O.K. but he knew that any reply he made would fall on deaf ears. He took a gulp of coffee and looked across at Jock who winked at him.

Mark was on his feet, suddenly enormously tall.

"Now must fly. Got to be in Glasgow in less than an hour. Uneasy lies the head ... Great to meet you, John. See you, Jock!" And he added something else which they didn't catch because he was already halfway out the door.

"That," said Jock when Mark's machine had faded down the road, "was definitely one of his better days!"

The next day, over coffee taken anti-socially - and definitely not in accordance with the Head's cross-curricular, inter-mingling policy - in the library instead of the staffroom, Harry listened with sympathy and a twinge of guilt to John's account of the meeting the evening before.

"I ended up feeling as though the whole thing had slipped out of my hands," John said. "I don't want some snotty producer putting across a distorted view of lochnetting."

"Thing is though," Harry commented evenly, "that everybody who does it, who lochnets that is, is going to shape it to their own needs. You did. I did. The Reynolds sisters did. So if he does, he's not going to do much harm. You will get the chance to put your own philosophy of loch-netting across in your interview."

"Not sure what that is any more." John grinned rather sheepishly.

"Fine!" pronounced Harry. "Remember! The ethos of loch-netting is fluid! Anyway, I'm really sorry I couldn't be with you last night. I felt as though I'd let you down but I had stuff I really had to do. In fact I'm scarpering away early this afternoon to finish off."

He pulled a wry face.

"Nothing wrong?" enquired John.

"Nothing serious," lied Harry. "Just accumulation of stuff."

Harry had in fact spent the previous evening re-writing his will. It had struck him that in his existing will he had throughout referred to Peter as "my son, Peter". If the results of the paternity test were to prove that Peter was not his son, this could, he reckoned, potentially invalidate Peter's claim to his estate. The re-writing had proved taxing. Peter would of course still be his beneficiary. It was a question of how to define their possible new relationship legally. Peter was not his foster son, nor his adopted son. "God help me," he had muttered. "He *is* my boy, my son. What else can I call him?"

Finally, he had blown his nose, trumpeting violently, and completed the reconstruction to legal requirements if not to his personal satisfaction and placed the document in his desk drawer, ready for witnessing should the results of the test prove it necessary. He had turned out his study light and was about to rejoin Peter in the sitting-room when the phone rang and he heard Peter answer it.

"Helga!" The delight in his voice had been light years away from where Harry was.

He had retreated into his study and closed the door, leaving Peter to his Helga and his potential future with her and with all the little Peters and Helgas who would possibly have a choice as to whether or not they referred to him as their grandfather. In an attempt to blot out their little unrelated Nordic/Latin features, he had taken out an Ordnance Survey map and concentrated on the route to Loch Dubh. He was on the last leg of the return when Peter stuck his head round the study door.

"Coffee?" he enquired. "Really, Dad, you shouldn't be working so hard. That school's not worth it."

Harry had spent a sleepless night which, for Peter's benefit, he attributed over breakfast to nothing more than having had coffee later than usual. Not that Peter had appeared to be particularly interested, too busy sorting out the contents of his briefcase, obviously quite oblivious to the consequences of the information which the day might bring. He could not rely on himself to preserve his own outward nonchalance on hearing the result and had therefore decided to leave school early so that he could get the result and thereafter give himself plenty of time to assume equanimity before his cold-blooded possible-son arrived home from work. Having the last period free on a Tuesday afternoon, he was able to do just that. On the way home he found himself counting his footsteps because there was something reassuring about the predictable sequence of the numbers

"The gate needs oiling," he observed objectively to himself when he reached it. He swung it back and forward on its hinges "Could do with a lick of paint too."

"The grass needs another cut after all that confounded rain."

He was doing well, filling up all possible empty spaces in the next few days.

"Need to prune that cherry tree soon."

With his mind agreeably crowded with impending jobs there should have been no need for his key to tremble in the lock but it seemed to shiver of its own volition. It wouldn't turn because the door was already opening from the inside.

"Dad!" Peter, with tears on his cheeks, was hugging him tightly. "It's O.K."

"Why," muttered Harry through teeth clenched against the sob that was rising in his throat, "do I feel as though I've just given birth?"

June was sitting on a chair holding Caroline's long blonde hair clear of her face as Caroline knelt by the lavatory in the cloakroom of the Reynolds' house and vomited copiously.

"Moral is," she commented briskly but not unsympathetically when there was a cessation of retching, "never wear your hair down if you think that a meeting is likely to make you ill."

Caroline crumpled back on her bare heels - she had lost her shoes en route as she fled from the Reynolds' sitting-room – and just managed a wan smile in reply. Her face, pale and sweaty and mascara-smudged was, as far as June was concerned a great improvement on what it had been before.

As the factory lochnetting meeting had gathered pace, fuelled by its own momentum as June had known it would be, she had watched Caroline lose her grip on controlling its shape, had watched her floundering with more than a little satisfaction, had even deliberately needled her, provoking some of her discomfort. She had always suspected that the polish on Caroline's presentations was a brittle veneer which could be cracked to reveal a vulnerability which she, personally, would find much more attractive. Unobserved, from her bedroom window, she had watched Caroline stage her arrival at No 11 Damhope Road with considerable amusement. There was, she had decided, a very calculated simulation of professional competence even in the sharpness of the sound effects; in the decisive rasp of the handbrake, the firm slam of the car door, the loud click of the car-locks and the brisk, strictly rhythmical tapping of high heels on the crazy paving of the front path. Caroline had dressed carefully, June judged, to maximise her impact on and input into the meeting – heels high enough to convey leadership, jumper scarlet enough to stimulate discussion, jeans sufficiently distressed to demonstrate a bid for egalitarianism and hair loose around her shoulders to prove to them all that she, though their leader, was prepared to be totally relaxed and informal.

"Well done, Caroline!" she had enthused sarcastically from behind her curtain. "Just a pity about the body-language. You should be swinging your brief-case freely, you know, rather than hugging it to your chest as though you've had a mastectomy. Given the opportunity, I'll give you a wee tip about that." She smirked and went downstairs to where April had opened the door to a Caroline who was obviously thrown by the sudden appearance of a pyjamaed William who took his thumb out of his mouth long enough to point at her and enquire, "Who dat, Aunty Ape?" and then run for cover without waiting for a reply.

'Not good at coping with the unexpected!' registered June. Out aloud she said airily, "Don't let William worry you, Caroline. He doesn't bite, we've got him quite well house-trained and he's off to bed soon. Prue just thought that the factory people might like to see him."

Archie, his wife, Pat, and daughter, Tabitha, had apparently appointed themselves to represent the workers and it was not only June, but Archie too, who caught Caroline's frown indicating that she had doubts as to whether this was a fair representation of the shop floor and he consequently directed his excuse at her, rather than at April, clearly anticipating that she would be the source of any objection.

"I did ask round," he apologised, rubbing his hands together nervously, "but everyone else had something on to-night. Quite incredible!"

Caroline responded with a disapproving silence.

"Don't worry, Archie!" June was concentrating on pouring his lager carefully so as not to produce a head but she made sure her voice was loud enough for Caroline to hear. "After all, you and Pat are both on the staff and Tabitha has worked with us for four summer holidays. I'm sure that satisfies even Caroline's requirements."

"It's up to you," snapped Caroline. "I'm just the facilitator, you know."

"A facilitator," explained June very clearly and deliberately to May, "is some-one who makes things easier for other people."

Caroline's flush deepened, but she took a deep breath, curled her lips into a smile and assumed gaiety.

"I propose that we start with an ice-breaker. Now I want us all to get to know each other." She hunched her shoulders to indicate suppressed excitement at the prospect. "*Really* get to know each other. Get *under* each other's skin, *into* each other's shoes and ..."

"*Up* each other's noses," whispered June to April but April shook her head reprovingly at her and, anyway, her interruption was drowned by an ecstatic cry from Pat.

"Oh, Miss Prue!" She had caught sight of Prue entering with William on her hip and the floppy pink silk bow under her chin shivered with emotion as she rose and held out her arms, "Oh, Miss Prue, he's just gorgeous!"

"We'll just be a minute," apologised Prue but the minute stretched to twenty during which William monopolised attention effortlessly; baby adoration degenerated naturally into childbirth revelations and the meeting became so intimate with Archie's and Pat's second daughter's third delivery that everyone could picture the pathetic state of the ravaged placenta as vividly as if it lay on an occasional table before them along with the crisps and vol-au-vents. June watched Caroline: saw her pale at the account and gulp at her wine for fortification; saw her slip her ice-breaker sheets back into her brief-case as the need for deeper inter-personal intimacy became positively undesirable and, as William repeatedly peeped around the door to wave good-night, she intermittently wiped clammy hands down her denim thighs, moving her lips soundlessly in a desperate attempt to find her place after the omission of the ice-breaker. Eventually, April came to the rescue by saying firmly, "Good *night* now, William!" and shutting the door.

Caroline smiled round. "Ready now?" she enquired.

"Anybody want a refill?" asked June hospitably but no-one did.

"Well then," Caroline started and continued to speak slowly and deliberately, "on outings like this it's very important not to have a hierarchy; that is not to allow some people to be more important than others." She smiled round to make sure everyone could follow her. "Do you understand, Tabitha?"

"Yes, thank-you," replied Tabitha politely.

"There is a reason for this," she went on patiently, gathering momentum, getting into her speech-rhythm. "We want people to feel that they can mingle freely, say what they like and, most importantly, act in accordance with their own volition and the promptings of their initiative. O.K?"

Obviously concerned in case she had strayed into the white collar level, she glanced questioningly at Tabitha.

"Oh, you're O.K. with Tabitha," re-assured June sweetly. "She's bilingual, speaks English as well as medical jargon even if she is a third-year medical student when she's not at the factory. Has no problem reading jam labels, even long words like strawberry."

"June!" hissed April reprovingly.

Caroline straightened her back and tossed her head.

"Now, it has not escaped my attention," she addressed Archie, Pat and Tabitha directly, swivelling her head from one to the other and wagging a playfully accusing finger at each in turn, "that at work you call your employers '*Miss* April', '*Miss* June', etc. but on our trip this simply will not do. They are simply 'April' and 'June' etc. and ..."

"May, actually," interrupted June, keeping her eyes on the wine she was swilling around her glass. "Just so that everyone understands that by 'etcetera' you probably mean 'May'".

She took a swig and smiled at Caroline.

"Sorry!" With careful precision Archie placed his glass dead-centrally on his coaster, stood up and picked it up again, holding it out in front of him as though about to propose a toast. "Sorry, Miss Caroline, but speaking on behalf of myself, my family and the entire shop floor, I have to tell you that that we no can do and ..."

"You don't need to stand up, Archie," smiled Caroline evenly. "You are in a circle of equals, remember?"

"Maybe that's the way you see it." Archie's voice grew louder. "But when I'm speaking for others as well as myself, I prefer to stand. Same way as I don't expect young Eddie from *Labelling* to call me anything other than 'Mr. Macdonald' on a trip or anywhere else, '*Miss* April' can only *be* '*Miss* April' and that goes for the others ..."

"For the etceteras," smirked June.

April came to Caroline's rescue again with, "I think that's something we could perhaps discuss later. The important thing is that everybody has a good time and we can be grateful to Caroline because the trip was her idea. Now, just let me show you the variety of options for exploring Loch Katrine. Leaflets, May? There you are! Look! You can do Loch Katrine by foot, steamer, cycle, golf buggy, scooter or you can mix and match. Then there's a choice between bringing picnics or eating at the lochside restaurant and I think there could be a snack-bar on the steamer. Do you think people will enjoy that, Archie?"

While they were pouring over the leaflets, Caroline found it necessary to busy herself by folding her preparation sheets and stowing them back in her brief-case. Bending over to fasten it, the nausea returned and threatened to overwhelm her. She looked up and caught June's eyes on her.

"Could you direct me to the bathroom, please?" she gasped. "Quickly!" she added.

Now, looking down at the crumpled heap at her feet, June felt the justification for her behaviour. Caroline was indeed just the vulnerable, insecure creature that she had dreamed her to be, lurking behind a facade of professional slickness and immaculate self-presentation. She dampened a handful of tissues and wiped the sweaty face tenderly.

"There you are," she soothed.

"I'll be all right in ten minutes." Caroline made a ghost of a bid to regain control of the situation.

"Oh no you won't," June contradicted her. "We'll tuck you into bed here for the night and let you go in the morning if you're feeling better. Now, when you're ready I'll help you upstairs."

By the time June had completely secured Caroline's comfort, the shop floor representatives had left and April, Prue and May were in the kitchen loading glasses and plates into the dishwasher.

"I've put Caroline in my room," she said, putting her head only just round the door. "Careful you don't wake her when you go upstairs."

And she withdrew without making an offer of help.

"That's nice of June," said May happily.

"Yes, isn't it," agreed Prue.

'You weren't there, Prue, and you wouldn't notice, May,' thought April, 'and as for me, I just have to keep my thoughts all to myself.' She sighed, feeling so overwhelmed by a sudden feeling of isolation that she almost wished her old furniture, with all its ability to recall the past and a time when she was not in charge, back in the bedroom into which she would have to take her anxious, sleep-disturbing thoughts.

"You are tired, April." Prue put an arm around her. "You just go on up to bed and May and I will finish off."

"Good night, June." April paused in the doorway of the sitting-room, but June was plugged into her music, her eyes shut and a dreamy smile on her lips, so April left her to make her way up the stairs, treading very quietly so as not to disturb the sleeping Caroline.

On his return from his meeting with Mark, the producer, John had found it difficult to deal with Jane's bright, "Well, how did it go then?" There had been a shift of his scene: his vision had been re-arranged for him by a crass outsider. The picture of himself, lean and fit, leading a group of lean and fit lochnetters, among whom his own family would of course be prominent, around the lochs of Scotland would, it appeared, fail to attract the necessary interest of television viewers. If

Mark was to be believed, it would take a sordid display of superfluous flesh and/or a missing limb or two to coax the couch potatoes to the screen and loch-netting was now to become a purely therapeutic exercise. Who was he, the ex-leader? Head therapist? Or did he not even have a role? He felt rejected and after a sleepless night his disillusionment about the future of loch-netting had dropped to an all-time low.

Harry's philosophical re-action had helped, but Harry, though sympathetic, had appeared slightly distracted as though he had weightier things on his mind than loch-netting and he had left John with the distinct impression that the problem was really all his. At last, in the evening, when Jenny was upstairs doing "the sort of homework I *can* give my full attention to in front of the television" and Ham was outside practising goal-kicks, Jane looked up from the book she was reading, saw him staring bleakly at the blank wall opposite and said, "Well, do you want to talk about it now?" And he found he did. Even so he still phrased the problem carefully, omitting his own privately projected role as the lean, tough leader, but he did manage to express the fact that this "showcase for lochnetting" was not lochnetting as he had envisaged it.

"You wanted something more informal?" Jane suggested. "More of a recreation for family and friends?"

"Something like that," he agreed doubtfully, "but I did want definite aims – principally to cover all the lochs in Scotland, excluding lochans and sea-lochs. But then again Prue does want us to do sea-lochs."

"That's it," said Jane. "Everybody wants something different. I think with this TV programme, John, you'll just have to let the producer have what *he* wants. You can always make your own aims clear in the interview and in your book."

John frowned momentarily because he couldn't remember letting Jane in on his plans for a book. Uncanny! He sighed.

"That's almost exactly what Harry said. I suppose I'll have to rake around for the appropriate additions. But where to start?"

"We'll all help you," comforted Jane. "I'm sure we'll come up with some obesity reps at least. Just think! Three months ago you'd have fitted the bill perfectly yourself!"

"I may have been a little overweight," John admitted frigidly, "but somehow I doubt I would have met Mark's criteria."

He picked up his Sudoku puzzle to indicate that he did not wish to continue with the conversation.

Over the next forty-eight hours Jane put her mind to procuring the necessary token obese and by the following Thursday was able to inform John that he had at his disposal one morbidly obese male, two clinically obese females and a choice selection of overweights, all of whom were prepared to share their excess flesh with the entire British population.

"And," she added slyly, "you've got Moira to thank."

"She's not coming this time!"

"What? And loch-netting's a sport for all?" teased Jane. "No, don't worry! Her help was indirect."

Moira had put a scheme into Jane's head when she had arrived on the doorstep the morning after John had shared his problem, breathless with indecision and clutching a sheaf of leaflets.

"Help me, Jane!" she gasped as she body-swerved past her and led the way to the drawing-room where she perched on the arm of the sofa. "I don't know which one to go for."

"Slimming clubs?" Jane peered over her shoulder at the leaflets she held dramatically fanned out at arm's length. "What on earth do you want to go to a slimming-club for?"

"I've put on two kilograms," confessed Moira, sounding very much as though she was confessing to leprosy, "and I must take it off before Patrick leaves me. But which one?"

"That one," said Jane decisively because she had planned to put in an hour or two in the garden. "Definitely that one." She pulled out a leaflet and waved it knowledgeably in front of Moira. "I've heard it's excellent!"

Moira put the others down and, taking it from Jane, studied it minutely.

"I don't know," she mused.

"I do," lied Jane. "It's really good. Has the right sort of clientele too, if you know what I mean. Look how expensive it is! Now go and phone them now before you change your mind. You know what they say. The longer fat stays on, the harder it is to shift. Quick! Hurry! Go and phone them now!"

She propelled Moira to the door, through the door, shut the door and leaned against it.

"Well done!" she congratulated herself.

Over her lunch she herself looked at the leaflets which Moira had left behind, an idea forming in her mind. At length she selected the leaflet from *Melt Down* which advertised a fool-proof, medically approved, pain-free slimming course which combined regimes of exercise and diet with the most amazing results.

"You'd never believe that I was twenty-two stone," blew a bikini-clad waif into a bubble on the front cover.

"Probably air-brushed away," commented Jane cynically, "but you'll do and what is more you meet to-night."

The rather gloomy looking church-hall where *Melt Down* preached its good news and plied its trade was on the other side of Edinburgh, but Jane reached the door half an hour early and just managed to exchange her willingness to help the frosty-faced and initially suspicious fitness guru, Glynis, put out the chairs and carry her astoundingly heavy equipment in from the car in turn for Glynis to cock an attentive ear in Jane's direction. But, after the magic word, 'television', Glynis melted down. Yes, it sounded perfect: a very good advertisement for *Melt Down* – which would of course be mentioned? Perhaps accidentally in passing? Perhaps just an oblique reference? Jane was not to move any more chairs: she had done more than enough. What could she, Glynis, be thinking of to have let her do all that work. Yes, she would most certainly mention it, more than that she would *recommend* it, to her members and could almost guarantee three of her prime overweights. She would phone Jane the following morning with names and contact phone numbers. To-night they were giving away slabs of sugar-free, low-fat chocolate. Jane must take some. And some for the children too ...

In contrast, the acquisition of the token disabled required no preparation or planning: it was accomplished over the next week-end purely accidentally by Jenny – with some input by Katie. In response to John's casual invitation to "drop in one evening when you're out our way and meet the family" Katie dropped in on the Thursday evening, ringing the bell while he was making his introductory phone-calls to the trio from *Melt Down*. As she brushed past him in the hall, he failed to recognise her: dressed in black jeans and a black sweater with her hair now dark and very short, he dismissed her at a glance as yet another new friend of Jenny's. By the time he had welcomed the nervous-sounding *Melt Downers* into what he termed, reassuringly he thought, the brotherhood of lochnetters, and invited them to the planning meeting on September 4th, Jane and Jenny between them had supplied Katie with all the information she needed, and more: as he entered he was quite shocked to hear Jenny urging Katie to accompany her on horseback on a round trip of the seven lochs on the Grampian Range, which she had apparently seen advertised in the hotel on Loch Ness and never even thought to mention to him, her father and the leader.

"First I've heard of it," he commented, trying to sound jovial instead of miffed.

"No-one to ride with me before," shrugged Jenny off-handedly and she pulled a face. "You wouldn't expect me to ride with *Helga*, would you? Be real!" Then, as a concession to his parental right to information, she waved a hand in the direction of the door, "The leaflet's in my room if you're interested."

As Jenny's bedroom was a no-go area to the rest of the family and she didn't offer to fetch the leaflet herself, John's only choice was to remain in the dark.

"And when do you propose to do this?" he asked, interrupting the arrangements she was making to go for a hack with Katie at the week-end.

"October break," she replied briskly without turning her head in his direction and went on talking to Katie, "If I meet you at the stables at about two o'clock, Saturday, ..."

"I could easily pick you up." Katie sounded eager and excited. "Save your parents!"

John doubted whether saving her parents was high on Jenny's list of priorities, but knew that she would agree to anything that promised independence from them and this arrangement did at least mean that he and Jane would be able to watch Ham's last cricket match of the season. He sometimes felt that Ham was growing up in his sister's shadow.

Lolling in a chair where the boundary of the field was marked by faded red, white and blue bunting strung between low pegs, John felt his worries ebb away. The green of the field was tinged with yellow and there was a late summer smell of dried mown grass.

"What I like about cricket," he remarked to Jane through half-closed eyes, "is that they don't find it necessary to draw hard white lines all over the field. Very relaxing!"

"Perhaps some of them are a bit too relaxed," smiled Jane, nodding to where a small boundary fielder lay prone in the sun, arm over his eyes, with no hope of catching a ball other than in his mouth.

Whether his parents' presence contributed to his success or not, Ham's bowling certainly scaled unprecedented heights and he had just taken his fifth wicket when John detected the sound of his mobile through the applause. With his eyes on the retreating figure of the rather chubby young batsman, head hanging in mortification at being out for a duck, he picked it up, read Jenny's name and held it a good few inches from his ear in anticipation of the inevitable shrieks of glee, distress or whatever, but it was Katie's voice and she sounded nervous.

"John," she said, semi-whispering as though she didn't want to be overheard. "Jenny's had a fall. They don't think it's too bad, but she could have broken her leg. They've phoned for an ambulance. I said to wait for you but they're really bossy here. Wouldn't listen."

"The ambulance *is* probably best," said John. The next batsman appeared to be having trouble with his pads. Ham was engaged in throwing the ball nonchalantly high up into the air and catching it, but he sneaked a look in the direction of his parents and John gave him a thumbs-up. "Probably best if we meet you at the hospital. Let us know which one when the ambulance comes." Jane beside him was looking apprehensive. "It's all right," he mouthed to her and continued speaking to Katie. "And if you could go with her, please, one of us will run you back to your car. Give her our love."

They left almost immediately. Ham was concentrating on his bowling and Jane left a message for him with his pal

Ian's mother before joining John in the car. The traffic on the bypass was reduced to a single lane moving slowly past a row of police cones and by the time they reached A&E, Jenny had been given painkillers and taken through to X-ray.

"I suppose you felt you had to wait till the end of darling Ham's match," she murmured pathetically when they caught up with her and closed her eyes to shut them out from her world of pain which they couldn't possibly comprehend.

An orthopaedic surgeon in green pyjamas explained the nature of the break to them patiently, in minute detail, but although they tried hard to latch onto the odd English word interspersed amidst the medical jargon, they remained largely ignorant as to the exact nature of the injury. They did manage to grasp that Jenny's life was not in danger, that she would require an operation, followed by a couple of days in hospital, after which she should make a full recovery, and that since she was a minor he would require them to sign a consent form for the operation.

By visiting time the following evening, with the operation behind her, Jenny had begun to realise that there were pros as well as cons to her predicament. The cons had more or less dwindled to a throbbing sensation just below her knee, a rather unwieldy plaster cast that suggested that her leg was much fatter than it was and room-mates with whom she had little in common, namely two octogenarian hip replacements and a car accident victim too heavily bandaged to offer any clues about age or appearance. The pros were dotingly sympathetic parents who could be tapped for almost anything, a brother overawed into complete silence by the hospital surroundings, multiple supplies of cards, chocolates and teenage magazines and the fact that one or two of the medical students were definitely fanciable. On the third day after her operation, she was taken down to X-ray in a wheelchair, returning just as her parents and brother arrived for the after school visit. She did realise that over the next few weeks she could expect the level of attention she was receiving to wane, but she had expected them to keep up at least some pretence of compassion until she was discharged. She was accordingly shocked when her father, entering the ward and seeing her in the wheel-chair, instead of being overcome by pity, beamed with delight and spoke so loudly that the semi-slumbering, unidentifiable accident victim - whom she had learned was called Penny – gave a little start and waved a bandaged hand in the air.

"Jenny!" he bawled excitedly. "You'll be perfect."

She knew him well enough to frown suspiciously. "What do you mean?"

"For the disabled person on the next loch-netting trip. For the filming. We can put you in a wheel-chair and wheel you round Loch Katrine."

"Bad luck," she retorted sourly. "I'll be on crutches by then and, by the way, thank-you for not asking, I *am* feeling very slightly better today."

"So glad, darling," soothed her mother in a more appropriate tone. "Apparently, if the X-rays are all right and you can manage stairs on your crutches, you'll be home tomorrow or the next day. It'll be so good to have you back home. We've all been missing you."

"Well, Jelly's been missing you anyway," modified Ham suddenly, breaking his silence and plumping himself down on the end of her bed.

"Don't sit on my bed. You might have MRSA!" snapped Jenny.

"Kevin phoned," said her mother, taking a bottle of orangina out of her basket and placing it carefully in amongst the cards on Jenny's bedside table. "He had heard about your leg and he was very sorry. He wants to come and see you when you get home. Will that be all right?"

"Nice that some-one cares," said Jenny and managed "Thanks for the orangina."

"It's not that *I* don't care," said her father, taking her hand in both his. "Of course I care. I hate to see you in pain, but I am in a predicament over this disabled person thing and we may as well turn a bad thing into a good thing. Eh Jenny?"

She maintained silence, waiting for him to provide an incentive and wondering if, in a wheel-chair, she might in fact get a fairer share of the camera lens than if she was merely a junior member of the family. Then Ham made up her mind for her.

"Jenny, if you go in a wheel-chair, I'll let you have your party in my cellar."

That clinched it. She agreed. With some irritation she watched her father put his arm round Ham's shoulder and hug *him* in a display of misdirected gratitude but she couldn't help smiling at the thought of the glamour, the sophistication of a cellar party. She would have no lighting other than tea-lights strategically placed to leave secret nooks for those needing them and for music ...

"Can I have a live band, then?"

Eventually the parents left, her father glowing inappropriately. When she was out of their unsympathetic sight, she picked up her crutches and did a couple of agile and pain-free rounds of the ward. As she passed Penny's bed, Penny jerked up a thumb in her direction in a congratulatory gesture, winced at the effort and said something that sounded very much like, "Glad you're giving something back at last."

Realising she must have misheard, she smiled at Penny benevolently and returned the thumbs up gesture. With all those bandages round her head, Penny could hardly be expected to speak distinctly.

Back at No 10 Damhope Road, the ideas cuckoo chick

realised straight away from John's expression as he got out of the car that everything was now in place for the public launching of loch-netting; realised it with some relief because the summer days were definitely shortening.

"Foolproof now," he squawked to himself. "Even they can't go wrong."

And he put his head under his wing for an early night before his flight south and dreamed of the vast summer brownness of a land far across the sea that he had ever only visited in dreams.

After a dreamless sleep John woke suddenly in panic just after midnight and escaped through the kitchen out onto the lawn, pacing the damp, cool grass between the apple trees. The misgivings which he had been suppressing over the last few days had surfaced when there were no daylight distractions to dilute his sharp anxiety. This darling project of his was no longer under his control. As a source of escape, a scapegoat, a means of promoting business relationships, a spectacle to be distorted by the viewing fancies of the nation it was becoming all things to all people and it would be *their* purposes for it that would carry it forward and away from him.

"All I wanted," he moaned out loud. "All I ever wanted was simply to walk around all the lochs in Scotland – with my family – and perhaps a few friends –and ..." he had flopped down on the old rickety bench, landing on one of Jelly's squeaky toys which let out a piercing, agonised squeal, interrupting his soliloquy sharply and accusingly, "... and perhaps a moderate amount of publicity," he modified, removing the toy and staring at it. It was a grotesque misconception of an unidentifiable animal, perhaps a dog, perhaps a bear, but somehow appealing in its own distorted way.

He shrugged, smiled and went back to bed.

Chapter Twenty-three
Third Expedition
Planning and Planning Sabotaged

Mark, the producer, managed to disrupt the week-end plans of most of the lochnetters by giving John three days' notice via a message on the Maitland answer-phone to the effect that he would be unable to make the Saturday evening planning meeting and would therefore appreciate its being brought forward to the Friday.

"Same time absolutely fine."

As he left no contact phone number, no e-mail address and Jock, the scoutmaster, was on an orienteering course, John had no option but to re-arrange it.

"Bit high-handed," frowned Peter, looking up from the chess-board when Harry returned to their game with the news. "I had plans for Friday."

"Be able to change them?" enquired his father, fingering a rook. "If not, I can always give your apologies."

"Thanks, but I'd better go since I've not met the scoutmaster chap I'm supposed to be helping," sighed Peter. "I'll see if Suzanne can make Saturday instead."

Over the last couple of weeks Suzanne's name had been mentioned with increasing frequency, leaving Harry totally mystified about the Peter/Helga relationship. Since after all his paternity had been confirmed he could, perhaps, put out a feeler or two. With his eyes on the board, he tried to keep his voice as normal as possible as though he were seeking advice about the weather.

"Would Suzanne not like to go loch-netting?"

"Probably," replied Peter evenly, "but she's got her cousin's wedding next week-end. Your move."

Moira, though teetering on the very periphery of the lochnetting group, was even more put out about the change of date than anyone else. Prompted by a stern sense of duty, reinforced by the fact that she knew herself to be indebted to Moira for the inclusion of the token obesity element, Jane had informed her of the forthcoming trip, without actually inviting her or making any mention of television involvement.

"We might come along," Moira had looked as though desperately searching for a socially acceptable excuse, "but Patrick's hip's been playing him up, affecting his golf swing so that this year he didn't win the Hope Cup." She gathered momentum and became more certain, "And I'm not really one for crowds, prefer reading, the intellectual side of life." Then she finally triumphed with, "And I'm pretty sure that's the week-end I promised to feed the Simpson's cat. He got his OBE in the birthday honours. Of course we all knew it was coming – well, those of us in the know anyway."

"That's fine," purred Jane.

However, when on meeting Moira at the letter-box on the evening after Mark's phone-call, she mentioned casually that the date of the planning meeting had changed, Moira was aghast.

"You can't," she gasped, clutching her letter so tightly to her chest that the reinforced peak of her right breast threatened to pierce the envelope, "That's the night of our golf party. You know, the really big one."

"Don't worry," soothed Jane. "You don't have to come to the meeting, especially as you're probably not ..."

"No!" bayed Moira. "Can't you see? We're going to need all available parking close to the house!"

"Surely your guests can walk a few yards ..."

"Not in togas!" Moira glowered at her. "It's a *Classical* Party. Oh, Jane you're going to ruin everything. Muddy togas after I've worked so hard for perfection. Got *Flower Fairies* to

make laurel wreaths for everyone and for the statues too –
except for little Paddy, bless him who's having a flower chain
thing round his tummy for modesty's sake. Patrick's idea! I've
had the invitations made into scrolls and Patrick ..."

"Hold it," said Jane holding both hands above her head.
"I'll ask people to park at least two doors down."

"That might be all right," sniffed Moira.

"You'll not be having a barbecue then?"

"Of course we are. Everybody loves our barbecues!"

"Well tell Patrick to keep the toga out of the flames,
won't you," said Jane sweetly as they reached the gate of No
10.

As Mark had been the only person Jane had not
managed to contact about the parking, he parked a silver
Volkswagen Beetle immediately outside the gates of the
Maitland's drive half-an-hour early when Moira's toga-clad
guests were starting to struggle self-consciously out of their
cars and John was still running off the information sheets for
the meeting.

"Came early," he observed, dispensing with the
convention of a greeting when John opened the door to him.
"Wanted to have a word with you about the interview: date,
time, where,when,etc."

"I'll finish running off the sheets," Jane murmured
pointedly and disappeared.

"Orgy next door," Mark commented flatly as they
walked through the hall. "Bacchic rite or fertility ritual. You
into that?"

"No," said John.

Mark gave no indication of his own involvement in
such matters and had no more time for small talk. After a
cursory glance around the drawing room, he opted for one of

the large winged armchairs from John's mother's old house and sat down removing a cushion from behind his back and dropping it to the side of the chair. He then dug his heels into the carpet to adjust his seating position as though in the driving seat of a car His facial features, still partly obscured by an unkempt hairiness and topped now by horn-rimmed glasses, gave no clue as to his thoughts but, dressed in jeans and a faded maroon sweatshirt bearing a long since illegible legend instead of the sinister black leathers and with the capacious apron of the chair reducing his skinny limbs to an unhealthy spindliness, he seemed far less formidable.

"If we do the interview after the excursion," he said, "it allows more scope for potential questions to surface, helps the interviewer. Her name is Claire, by the way, and she'll be coming along on the Friday and the Monday, though she can't make the Saturday or the Sunday."

"Accommodation?" queried John. "We're booked into a local hotel. Do any of you need to stay overnight at all?"

"Uh-uh," he brushed the question aside, emphasising its irrelevance with a wave of his hand. "We'll travel up together on a daily basis. Get travel expenses."

After a few more questions, mainly about timing and exact locations, Mark signalled that the briefing was over by picking up a pen and incising a precise black line across a page in his notebook before leaning back in his chair and closing his eyes, an indication, John rather felt, that he had become incommunicado. However, he roused himself when the lochnetters started to arrive and turned over to another page on which he proceeded to make notes, presumably about the viewer appeal of each lochnetter entering.

When April had tried to insist that Prue and June

represent the family at the planning meeting, leaving May and herself to babysit William, Prue had frowned.

"Not fair," she had stated. "William is *my* responsibility."

"That's not the point," April had countered. "The point is that you have never been to a planning meeting and in fairness to the rest of the group, you should have some input."

"We'll leave it open," said Prue but both she and April had known that agreeing to "leave it open" meant that Prue was three-quarters of the way to acquiescing and on the Friday evening she set out with June without further discussion or protest.

In her own mind, April knew that she had not been honest with Prue: in fact she sometimes wondered whether she was entirely honest with any of them these days because her motives seemed rarely to be what she would have them think. In this instance her underlying motive had been her reluctance to witness what she presumed to be June's developing relationship with Caroline: to see June, steady, dependable June ricocheting uncontrollably between provocation and tenderness in her approach to Caroline, presumably so that she could shock her out of her professional formality into something warm, vulnerable and, above all, malleable. It was not the depth or the nature of June's affection for Caroline that concerned her, but rather the intensity of June's desire to manipulate and control. Was that always a salient feature of relationships, of the relationship between her mother and father, for instance? A situation in which one strove to dominate and the other submitted and surrendered?

"April!" May's voice held its distress quaver. She came into the kitchen where April had suddenly resumed putting away the plates she had been clutching for the past five minutes. "April, William is still awake!"

"Well," April started to assemble a course of action,

abandoned it and turned to May with a smile just beginning to form, "what do you think we ought to do?"

At the Maitland gate, June and Prue met Caroline conversing with the heavyweight trio from *Melt Down* under the mistaken impression that they were *bona fide* factory workers selected by Archie who had at last seen the error of his hierarchical ways.

"*So* glad you could come," she was saying, graciously extending a hand. "*Lovely* to see you. *Such* a pity you couldn't make it the other night."

"Make what the other night?" chirped Joyce, the leanest and therefore the most confident.

"Thought it was like that!" Caroline said knowingly, flashing a triumphant smile at June and Prue. "Thought Archie couldn't have told you!"

"Who's Archie?"

"Don't worry about Caroline," June advised them soberly. "She does get a little confused sometimes. It's her age. Right, Caro, old thing?"And she accompanied the 'Caro, old thing,' with a playful but none the less stingingly loud slap on Caroline's tightly skirted bottom.

"We better get inside." Prue felt the need to hurry things along. "We must be the last to arrive."

They were indeed the last. On their arrival, Katie and Peter vacated the sofa, Katie joining Ham on a cushion on the floor and Peter perching on the arm of Harry's chair. June, Prue and Caroline settled onto the window-seat and the three *Melt Downers* made for the sofa, all wedging themselves simultaneously, all sinking as far back as possible.

John smiled round nervously.

"Welcome again, everybody," he said."I'd better begin by handing out the information sheets because I intend to talk to them. After that, Mark will brief you on what he wants from you and then everybody can chip in. And, of course, we can carry on discussing things informally over supper. Oh, by the way, Jenny sends her apologies. Not quite up to making it downstairs but she is looking forward to seeing you all next week-end."

Jane leapt up to hand out the information sheets and hide her smile. Jenny had in fact been incarcerated in her bedroom by her father who was afraid that Mark might decide that she didn't qualify for the disabled provision if he saw her leaping about agilely on crutches. He had started off, over-optimistically Jane felt, by trying to manage Jenny's absence on the cheap, sending her to her room as a punishment for 'excessive cheek' and insisting that she stay there throughout the evening. Jenny, momentarily dumbstruck by this injustice, recovered her power of speech to declare eloquently and truthfully that she had been no cheekier than usual and Ham, fearing for his father's sanity, had backed her up. In the face of this joint protest and nagged by his own conscience, John had been forced to come clean and confess his motives whereupon Jenny had graciously agreed to stay out of sight in exchange for the definite promise of a live band for her cellar party.

John's sheet was sufficiently explicit for his expansion to be both largely unnecessary and boring. Mark, semi-screened in his wing-chair, closed his eyes and John could only hope that this was an aid to concentration. The three *Melt Downers* held their papers in front of their faces as though in a bid to conceal their identities and sought clarification from each other in whispers. Prue, seated between June and Caroline, felt inexplicably uneasy as though she was beside people she hardly knew. Through the open window behind her came the sounds of Moira's party, ebbing and flowing, now quieter, now louder, as though borne on a variable wind. It was funny, she thought, how humans in a crowd at a distance sounded like animals, like a herd of bleating sheep or the throaty cackle of geese. Behind the people noise was a thin metallic wail – obviously Moira's idea of the music of the ancients...

"Finished?" Mark's voice broke though the somnolence. His eyes were suddenly wide open and he gripped the arms of the chair as he stiffened and sat upright. "Good!"

John hadn't finished. He was merely pausing between *Day 3* and *Day 4* to allow the points he had made to sink in. If Mark had been paying attention, he thought, he would have realised that.

"Almost," he replied, stressing the first syllable reproachfully, "but feel free to come in now if you want to."

Mark felt free.

"Right!" he said and added, "Don't believe in hand-outs."

It was neither an excuse nor an apology. John took it as a criticism but it was actually just a bald statement of what Mark considered acceptable to which his habit of omitting personal pronouns at the start of his sentences lent his opinions a universality, an impression that his were surely the shared opinions of any rational beings. His voice, though neither raised nor didactic in tone, had a resonance that commanded attention and there was a general straightening of posture: even the two *Melt Downers* at the outer sofa seats struggled to sit forward, leaning away from the hollows they had gouged into the cushions and flowing plumply over either sofa arm.

"Don't believe in hand-outs," he repeated and aimed a ballistic index finger at his temple "You've got to keep what I say up here. First thing to remember is that even if a camera is pointing towards you, nine times out of ten it's not recording you so you forget it. Forget it anyway. Smiling at the camera and any 'Hello Mum' attempts will not be tolerated. Got to act as though you are unaware of the camera if the whole thing is to have any authenticity. We'll take far more footage than we need and any playing to the camera will be cut out. Out! Completely! Pretty sure all of you will feature so don't go forcing yourselves into the limelight."

"As if we would," huffed John quietly.

"Tell Jenny that," muttered Ham at the same time.

"You said something?" Mark wheeled round to face Ham who promptly shook his head. "Well, don't interrupt. Now Claire, our interviewer, won't be with us on Friday for the factory trip but she'll definitely want to record factory impressions of their trip re this becoming a regular exercise or not. That O.K?"

No-one answered.

"O.K. or not? Come on. Don't waste time."

"O.K.," obliged June. "Who is she likely to want to speak to? Employers or employees?"

"Both for heaven's sake. Balance is essential."

Caroline smirked audibly and said, in a syrupy tone, "That's exactly what I've been saying and now *at* last I hope that's what we are working to at *Reynolds Fine Preserves*."

Mark grunted uncertainly. "Who are you again?" he asked.

" Caroline Parry from the *Caroline Parry Pleasure and Productivity Programmes,* running courses on the roles of *self*-knowledge and *self* accountability and the need for *team*work in ...."

"*Do* tell me later. I'd be *so* interested!" The mimicry of her inflected speech was too accurate to be anything other than unkind and June glowered at him, but Caroline, missing the sarcasm, puffed out her chest and smiled.

"Delighted," she said and as he turned away from her she leaned forward to stick the tip of her tongue between her lips at June to express coquettish triumph.

Mark had now turned his attention to the *Melt Downers*, gazing from one to the other speculatively.

"Need an interview from at least one of you three," he mused and weighed up their relative demerits. "Not necessarily from the fattest. Claire will decide which of you has the most interesting history, who is the most articulate. Can't do that now. Previous eating disorders would be good. For instance if one of you were to be an ex-anorexic it would be great ..."

They attempted to flatten themselves against the sofa cushions, but his interest had switched from them.

"Jenny," he said. "Where's Jenny?"

"As I have already explained," replied John testily, "not up to coming down."

"Well tell her she'll probably have to speak too. She's quite young, isn't she?"

"Nearly fifteen, Mark," replied Jane before John could work it out.

"You might need to do a bit of coaching. Determination in overcoming the pain barrier goes down well we find. Try and gen her up on that. I take it she does have plenty of pain?"

"She *is* a ..." Ham started before he met his mother's eye.

Mark fingered his chin for a moment almost as though the unthinkable had happened and he had forgotten what to say next.

"Oh, we may have to do some re-takes at a later stage, but that's unlikely," he mused uncertainly crossing his legs at the ankle and rocking from side to side on the sides of his feet, before suddenly regaining his balance and continuing firmly "Oh, I know what I was going to say. Romance. Always goes down well with the viewing public. No chance of any of you lot pairing up? Or having recently paired up?"

Ham turned to look at Peter.

"Ham," intervened Jane crisply, "please come and give me a hand with the supper. It must be nearly that time."

"Actually," came a muffled voice from the sofa, "Jim

and I have just ... well..."

"Become an item, I think you mean, Joyce, but then we're already starring as ..."

"Starring's not a word I want to hear. Never use that word to me!" Mark hunched his shoulders and clapped both hands over his ears. "Never ever! People do not *star* in documentaries!"

"Fine," said Jim evenly when he eventually removed his hands from his ears. "Please yourself!"

"Well, where did you two meet then?" Mark sounded weary as though interest was an effort, but it was his duty to follow up.

"We both used to go to a healthy eating clinic," supplied Joyce timidly, " and it was no good. Hopeless! We both put on over a stone, although I'm sure we followed the rules ..."

"And we got kicked out – well sort of kicked out," smiled Jim, "and Joyce was very upset ..."

"It was so em*barr*assing," said Joyce, rolling her eyes round the room before taking a consoling sip from her glass of wine.

"So I took her out for a slap up meal to comfort her and after the meal ..."

"Don't tell them t*hat*!" Joyce giggled, a bubbly, gurgling sound. "Let's just say one thing led to another. Remember?" and she whispered something in his ear.

"The wedding's just as soon as Joyce's divorce comes through ..."

Mark held up his hand, "O.K., O.K.! Message received and understood. And you joined *Melt Down* because?"

"To look good in the wedding photos of course," Joyce shook her head at the needlessness of the question.

"Of course," said Mark drily. "Well we might use your story and we might not. Depends on Claire. Now, are there any questions?"He scanned the room with a frosty scowl that nipped any potential queries in the bud. "Well, that's it. Meeting over!"

"Unless," John said coldly, "somebody else would like to speak."

"I would," chirped Ham from the doorway. "Mum says supper's ready and know what? One of those people in sheets next door has fallen into Moira's fish-pond. We heard the splash from the kitchen and I ran up and looked out of the bathroom window and it was so funny and ..."

"This way," interrupted John firmly, although most of them knew the way.

As Peter walked through, Jock immediately in front of him turned and grinned.

"Don't mind Mark," he said. "He can be an utter prat over his job, but he's good at it. Very good! Perhaps you and I could have a word about Saturday over supper?"

Utter prat or not, Mark tucked into Jane's supper with an enthusiasm which warmed her to him and every mouthful seemed to bring an unexpected disclosure about a humanity which he shared with the rest of them . He bonded with Jane over culinary matters, shared hill-walking with June, supported the same football team as Ham and Jim, had visited most of the same old abbeys as Harry and even revealed to Prue, albeit with a shy self-consciousness which further proved him a man of flesh and blood, that he had a small son, a little older than William.

"Can't think how he managed that," John remarked sardonically to Jane later in their bedroom, adding for necessary clarification. "The son, I mean. I'm talking about that nerd, Mark. Yes, I can. He would have had him asexually cloned so that he could set up his special Mark Pitcher Admiration Society."

"You really don't like him, do you?" Jane slipped out

of bed and pushed up the sash window so that she could smell the secret dark scents of her garden. "Perhaps a personality clash?"

John shrugged his bare feet into his slippers and joined her.

"I don't want to see loch-netting distorted into something it isn't just to make it more viewable," he said. "I said that to Harry and he thought that it was O.K. because it would always mean different things to different people and I agree up to a point." He paused searching for words. "But I feel as though making a film of it defines it too specifically into something more concrete. People watching it will feel that they have to do it exactly the way Mark Pitcher chooses to show it. And *he* didn't start it. Do I sound petty?"

No," she slipped her arm around him, "but I'm sure you'll interview well and put your points about its fluid nature across then."

"That's what Harry said." He hesitated. "I suppose my point of view can also be a bit narrow at times?"

The question in his voice begged her to contradict him but she just smiled, hugged him more closely and changed the subject.

"Tell me why, when you're wearing nothing else, did you bother to put on your slippers?" He looked down at his feet puzzled. "You ought to go and stand at the bottom of Moira's garden along with the statues. That's where she celebrates the beauty of the human body."

He laughed and followed her gaze to where the classically incomplete white figures, their heads still crowned with laurel, seemed to tremble in the reflected light of the one solitary wicker torch left burning. On the grass at the feet of Aphrodite, a hump of sheets twisted, sagged and undulated.

"Moira and Patrick?" whispered Jane.

"Perish the thought!" he grinned. "Believe me they only

do it in full evening dress over the kitchen sink. Begging your pardon, I mean over their state of the art dishwasher."

"Bed!" said Jane severely.

Chapter Twenty-four

The Third Expedition

Loch Katrine – The Factory Day Out

"Reminds me of a school-trip," June had laughed, scanning the information sheet on Loch Katrine which April had spent all evening drawing up and intended to issue to all their employees on the eve of the factory loch-netting outing. "All it needs is a sentence at the bottom in small print to the effect that any infringement of rules will result in the miscreant being excluded from all further outings."

April had stared dismally at the sheet in front of her until the black lettering blurred on the stark whiteness of the paper. Prue peered over her shoulder.

"Don't see anything wrong with it myself. You could always get May to do a few illustrations round the borders to liven it up a bit. Otherwise it's fine."

Unbelievably May had shown a talent for cartoon figures and the finished result had met with an approving silence from June and appreciative comments both from her sisters and from the factory staff when it had been handed out to them. Quite a few had passed very positive comments and they were all clutching their sheets when they assembled in front of the factory steps on the morning of the trip.

In contrast to the other creaking, rectangular corrugated iron structures in the Industrial Estate, all of which spoke of a quick buck grabbed at before the ephemeral boom slumped, *Reynolds Fine Preserves and Marmalades* was a very solid, red-brick building that pre-dated all the flimsy prefabs and would surely outlast them all. It was Mr. Reynold's vision of eternal life rationally modified and logically truncated. The access to the high-walled forecourt was through a gateway so narrow that the gate posts from which hung the heavy wrought-iron gates embellished with a florid *R*, were dented at wing-mirror level of delivery vehicles. April stood on the top step with her back to the familiarity of the main door and knew panic as she faced the unknown alone. Without their overalls – white overalls with *Reynolds* emblazoned in blue on their breast pockets – and hatless in the morning sun this group looked shockingly like the ordinary, unfamiliar people that she might encounter walking down Princes Street or waiting on a platform at Waverley Station. Amongst the employees themselves some feudal sense seemed to have prevailed so that Archie and the senior staff formed a straight line in front and the cleaners a huddle at the back, smiling self-consciously because Caroline, aggressively stimulating in a blood-red top, had cunningly winkled herself into their knot. June, shunning classification, was lolling against the side wall, smoking a cigarette which she had acquired from Ted in *Labelling*, tilting her head back against the wall every now and again to exhale. But June had never smoked. Their father abhorred women who smoked. April remembered June of her university days coming home smelling of cigarettes because, she said, she had been sitting on top of a bus. After their father had wrinkled his aquiline nose in disgust, June had humbly agreed to stop travelling on top of buses – at least in Edinburgh – although, she had maintained that in Glasgow it was more difficult to get a seat inside. Behind the workers April could see the coach drawing up at the kerbside and feel the vibration from its running engine which meant she could delay no longer. Her mouth was so dry that her tongue stuck to her palate, parting from it with a click when she started to speak.

"Good morning, everyone!" She forced herself to smile. "We have a lovely day and the weather forecast is good so I hope you will all have a simply splendid time." The enclosing walls threw her clipped vowels back at her in unkind mimicry and the paper in her hand shook. Then she saw Harry in the gateway, raising his hand and smiling at her and she seized the chance to abandon her formal script. "Mr. Harry Aitcheson, the gentleman I mentioned on your sheet, has just joined us. He will be travelling on the coach with us all so that you will have the chance to get to know him on the way up. Any other notices can wait till later. Right now, it's all aboard!"

"You join the others," encouraged Prue after she had parked the car on Loch Katrine's Trossachs pier and May had said "Isn't it *love*ly, Prue," for the eleventh time since they left Aberfoyle – or it could have been the twelfth, or even the thirteenth. "I have to wait for William to wake up before I can move."

May clutched to her breast the rucksack in which she had carefully packed her sketching equipment and then checked and rechecked it, and looked dubious. Screwing up her eyes she could make out the figures of April and Harry. They must have emerged first, must have been sitting at the front of the bus because they were standing beyond the group who were still pouring out of the coach, laughing as they rejoined their friends on the tarmac.

"You could leave your sketching things in the car just now," Prue advised. "I'll bring them in William's buggy. You really ought to go and find out what's happening or you and I will both be lost."

She leaned across May and opened her door leaving her no option but to slide off her seat. May, still clutching the rucksack , closed the door behind her gently so as not to disturb the sleeping William, too gently so that the snib didn't catch. She turned and mouthed an exaggerated 'Sorry' at Prue before following an indirect route towards Harry and April, skirting the group of factory workers who had expanded from a tight circle into a loosely formed gathering.

"What wouldn't I give for a one-night stand," sighed Prue rebelliously, picking up and addressing the goggle-eyed Torty who had somehow landed on the car floor at May's feet while William, overtired by the car journey, had been throwing a particularly aggressive pre-nap tantrum, "but don't tell William there's a good chap."

Over the past few weeks No. 11 Damhope Road had provided her with a safe haven that was becoming almost stiflingly safe and she *was* grateful for it she told herself, grateful too for the companionship and support of William's aunts. That's what they were: aunts rather than sisters, prepared to devote themselves to Williams's needs and hers where they overlapped with his. She had, she supposed, the advantage of the comparative outsider's capacity to take an objective view of their relationships with each other, to understand how their very natures had become moulded by their interaction, but she had the disadvantage of not really belonging, of having both to express gratitude and to receive it for services which they could take for granted from each other.

"Thank-you so much for being prepared to drive the car up, Prue," April had said sincerely but formally, "and thank-you for agreeing to bring May too."

Even June, closer to her than the other sisters, had become recently estranged: her moods were unpredictable and she had become even less communicative. Prue picked up the map of Loch Katrine and ran her finger despondently around its perimeter.

"Land-locked," she sighed. "Know how it feels! Wish we could do some sea-lochs. I could do with a limitless horizon of sea, beaches littered with straggling seaweeds that crackle if you bed down on them, the tang of salt tasting like sweat. And I wish ..."

Happily, Torty was spared any further disclosures because William woke up at that point and Prue's sensual fantasies were channelled into the overwhelming maternalism that gushed through her veins obliterating her personal needs whenever he cried.

"Sh, sh, William," she soothed, lifting him out of his car seat onto her hip. "Look! There are the funny men with their cameras."

William looked round mistrustingly at the strange environment and, seeing nothing to lighten his mood, recommenced his wailing.

"We'll go see Aunty Ape and Aunty Jewjew and Aunty May," she promised enticingly. "Look they're talking to the funny men. Shall we take Torty to see them?"

"No!" bawled William, repulsed by the idea and buried his head into her shoulder.

"All right. Shall I put you back in the car then?"

"No!" screamed William even more loudly and offered no protest other than a few desultory sniffs as she carried him across to join the group.

On the arrival of the filming crew, the factory staff had once more closed ranks into a tight little bunch and were waiting silently for their orders from Mark who was deep in conversation with April and Harry. Caroline had planted herself beside them in readiness to offer advice but June, having yet again apparently abdicated all responsibility, was standing apart studying the loch through a pair of field-glasses and making a point, Prue felt, of not focusing on what was transpiring. She hitched William further up on her hip and went to stand behind April.

"... so if we give them time to decide how each of them is going to tackle the loch, we can meet back here in about twenty minutes. No, actually, we should meet by the bicycle park perhaps. Standing in a car park is not recommended under health and safety I believe. I'm going for a coffee. Hello, there!" And, ignoring Prue, Mark chucked William under the chin whereupon William smiled beatifically and threw, "Funny man! Funny man!" at his retreating back.

"Shall I tell them or will you," April with her employer status temporarily suspended sounded lost and lonely as she turned to Harry.

"I'll do it!" volunteered Prue loudly as Caroline stepped forward. "Listen up a moment everybody – that is if you guys haven't already heard what Mark said. You've got twenty minutes to choose how you want to tackle the loch. For those who've already decided I personally recommend coffee. We meet back at the bicycle parking area in twenty minutes. If anybody needs any help, just ask April or Harry. Good luck!"

"Miss Prue," Pat, Archie's wife, was at her elbow, "why don't you let me and Susie here," she indicated a thin sallow-faced woman with wispy hair which she kept smoothing nervously back, "take wee William off your hands? To begin with anyway? We could push him in his buggy beside the loch or take him for a wee walk? We'd love to."

Prue hesitated.

"Come on! Please!" Pat sounded really eager. "You know I'm good with the wee ones."

Prue smiled. "O.K. then. Thank-you. Actually I'd really like to go for a ride."

By the end of the twenty minute time limit, the factory had re-assembled at the bike park and after a further five minutes Mark and his crew joined them and took control immediately.

"To make it easier for us – and for Claire here who's going to interview some of you later" –he indicated a smaller figure in blue jeans and a blue sweater who Prue suddenly realised was female – "divide yourselves into groups according to the activities you have picked. Cyclists go and stand next to the sound recordist – that's the guy with the fluffy mike – walkers next to Claire – not difficult as she's the only woman. Those who are remaining on the steamer for the whole trip to your undying shame, go hang your heads and sit on the wall. Any who don't fit into those categories put your hands up now."

The four cooks obediently raised their hands.

"O.K., one at a time."

Mima, pushed forward by the others began with a self-deprecating "Why me?" before shrugging and obliging with "We're going to share a golf buggy in the morning and go on the steamer in the afternoon."

"O.K., Claire? You've got all your cooks together."

Not just the cooks, together. All the activity groups mimicked the factory job groupings. All the cleaners together with the security guards had opted to cycle to Stronachlachar from where they would be taking the steamer back. *Quality Control*, otherwise known as the 'belters' and which included Pat and Susie, would stroll along the lochside, picnic at a convenient stopping place and stroll back. *Labelling* would take the steamer to Stronachlachar and walk back to the Trossachs pier and *Office Staff* – two secretaries and two part-time receptionists – planned to take motorised scooters. Archie and the two senior floor staff would remain on the steamer throughout.

"Only because we want to leave time for historical research," remarked Archie pointedly not so much as an excuse than as if Mark had failed to take account of the obvious. "This area you *may* know or may have forgotten is renowned for its association with Rob Roy MacGregor who ..."

"Fine," interrupted Mark. "Glad to see you're wearing the kilt, Archie. Dressed for the role of Scottish historian."

Somewhat mollified, Archie sat down again on his wall, shifting his haunches and flicking an invisible speck of dust from his oversized sporran."

"Tha's no' frae a real badger is it, Mr.MacDonald?" asked Ken. "'Cos killing badgers ..."

"No talking, please," snapped Mark. "We need to get on."

He had half-turned to Claire when Caroline stepped forward and held out her hand imperiously as though she was stopping a bus.

"Just a moment!" She was flushed and bright-eyed with missionary zeal. "This may satisfy you, Mark, but it does not satisfy me."

He lowered his horn-rimmed glasses and gazed at her over them with a bemused expression as though struggling to identify her.

"You are?"

"Caroline Parry," she snapped, "whose job it is to facilitate team-work. How can this possibly be an integrating exercise when you propose to allow the different departments to preserve their separateness, segregating themselves in their activities?"

"How indeed?" mused Mark. "And how, Caroline, would you propose to alter this?"

"Easy!" pronounced Caroline triumphantly. "Everybody picks an activity out of a hat – or cycling helmet or whatever – and sticks to what they have picked."

There was a repressed murmur of disapproval.

"But, Caroline, dear," June was smiling indulgently, "you might pick cycling and you can't ride a bike!"

"And, Caroline, dear," added Mark, "dare I suggest that you are being a tad hierarchical. After all who are you to dictate what others should do? They all seem perfectly happy with their own decisions."

"From the interviewer's point of view," put in Claire slowly, "it makes it more interesting the way it is. It shows the way people like to stick with their mates when faced with something new and challenging."

"I think," April spoke with sudden assurance, "that we will leave it as it is this time and try drawing activities out of a hat when we get more used to these trips."

"Hear! hear!" said Harry.

"What will you be doing?"

Although Claire was smiling at her, April knew a moment of panic.

"I thought ..." she started and stopped because she hadn't thought.

"I mean is there a designated management activity?"

"Oh no!" April was relieved to be definite about something. "Absolutely not!"

"I'm cycling with the cleaners and security guards," put in Prue helpfully before she remembered that April might well have some qualms about her fraternising with security guards and added with a toss of her head that somehow reminded April of the adolescent Prue, "I planned to cycle, anyway."

"I think, April, that you and I could perhaps take the steamer up with the labellers and walk back," suggested Harry quietly. "Feel up to it?"

"Yes," replied April gratefully. "Coming with us, May?"

"No thanks." May responded with uncharacteristically brisk firmness. "I'm going up to Stronachlachar with the labellers but I'm going to stay up there and do some sketching. I'll come back on the afternoon steamer with the cyclists."

"That all sounds fine." Claire spoke while jotting in her notebook, smiled and ran across to where Mark amongst his crew was waving his arms about, gesturing expansively towards the loch."

June flicked the ash off her second cigarette of the morning and strolled across to where Caroline was standing on her own, swinging her capacious Gucci bag between her legs like a first former with a schoolbag.

"If I can get a tandem," she drawled, "would you care to come on the back?"

"What you said was really unkind, June," said Caroline, twisting her vermillion lips into a crooked little pout. "I told you in confidence that I couldn't ride a bike. I didn't expect you to humiliate me by broadcasting it."

"I've hurt your feelings then." It was a statement rather than a question. "To make up, I'll join you in any activity of your choice." She blew out a cloud of smoke. "And I do mean any."

Caroline blushed and hesitated before confiding, "I'd really like to try one of those motorised scooters that take two people. We could take turns driving. And, June," her voice grew shrill and triumphant with reproach, "you said you'd stop smoking."

"Nag, nag, nag," said June companionably as together they made their way to where the office staff were already examining the buggies.

Prue unclasped William's arms which he had automatically clamped around her neck when confronted by Pat and Susie and settled him into his buggy, tucking Torty snugly underneath his safety strap.

"Now he'll be absolutely fine," assured Pat, placing both pink, matronly hands firmly on the handle of the buggy and nudging Prue gently aside, "so you just go get your bike and forget you're a mum."

"He's not used to being separated from me," Prue was doubtful.

"Time he was," pontificated Pat crisply, exchanging a knowing glance with Susie at her elbow.

Prue knew a sudden urge to snatch William back, half-hoped he would bawl at the separation, prove her right. However, William did not give her a backward glance as Pat steered the buggy in the direction of the starting point with quick purposeful steps and she felt the absence of his warm little body on her hip as she slowly wheeled her bike in the direction of the group of cyclists, passing the Fourtrak from which one of the cameramen was unloading gear.

"Nice day for it," he remarked.

"Nice smile, nice eyes, nice, muscly, hairy legs and really nice bum so why not?" the part of her that was still not quite William's mother flirted with replying but she amended demurely to, "Yes, isn't it?" and reproved herself with the sudden thought, 'Perhaps sex for me is nothing more than the way I like to express rebellion. Perhaps it never has been love. Love is what I feel for William: it's warm and soft and good.'

To start with sex had been her escape from the sanctimonious claustrophobia of Aunt Margaret's knitting pattern life which dropped no stitches and left nothing to instinct. It had crept in accidentally when her aunt's embarrassment over her first innocent queries about reproduction had aroused such a frisson of excited power that she had quickly graduated to less innocent, to downright provocative demands. "Have you ever had sex, Aunt Margaret?" she had enquired on one ground-breaking day and had known triumph when the question had been answered by five sharp slaps of the ruler, smirking victoriously as her palm reddened, earning her an additional sentencing of a cloistering in her bedroom during which she had enacted a torrid love scene: Aunt Margaret – played by the petal-cheeked and appropriately stiff-limbed china doll her aunt had given her - was seduced and roughly deflowered by the hairy teddy bear she had rescued from the church jumble sale and which Aunt Margaret had regarded as 'dirty' and 'germ-ridden' even after it had endured two cycles in the washing machine. She alone had known that it had been her persistent raising of the topic of sex more than all her other naughtinesses that had secured her early release back to No 11 Damhope Road. She smiled to herself at the memory as she wheeled her bike across and then frowned, remembering that she had indulged her delight in shocking people much less excusably: when she was old enough to have known better, she had returned home, the prodigal, and learned to resent the way she was expected to become enmeshed in her sisters' arid factory obsession. True, with retrospect, she had felt shame at the unkindness of the shock she had given poor May when that easily wounded sister had discovered her in flagrante delicto on the chaise-longue with Hans, but at the time she had know unadulterated delight at the sight of May's horror, of her crimson face rising like an early morning sun over the crest of Hans' heaving buttocks. And now? Now she had William. William was a restriction against which she could not rebel and, she told herself, she must realise that the sisterly expectations that presumed to dictate her moves were kindly meant.

The cleaner-cum-security guard posse were leaning on their bikes in a close-knit group and she could tell from the way that they avoided eye-contact with her and turned their heads sideways to each other as she neared that they were passing comments about her. As she annexed herself to them, Mark drew up alongside them in his Fourtrak and leaned out of the driver's window, shouting to make himself heard above the impatient throbbing of its diesel engine.

"Listen up, guys!"he yelled peremptorily. "Listen up, guys, because I don't like repeating myself."

"Like you just have," laughed Prue.

He looked at her, blinked, shaking his head to show his utter non-comprehension, and continued.

"You lot are going second – once we've got the amblers and their buggies and what have you shifted. We'll take them setting out, then we'll take you setting out. Then we'll overtake you both and may or may not film you as we do. We'll proceed to a stopping-place about half a mile along and film you passing. We'll wait there for the amblers, film them having their picnic and then proceed with you. Don't get the idea that you are the main focus of attention. You're competing with waterfalls, historic islands and sites and views to die for. Believe me you come a very insignificant second. If there are no questions we'll get on to the amblers."

This was delivered at incomprehensible pace and he revved up his engine as he finished the last sentence so that any question would have been quite lost to him. They watched in silence as he cut a neat diagonal to where the amblers had lined up across the track like contestants in an egg and spoon race.

"You the conveyor-belt people?" they heard him bawl.

"Oh, they'll no' like that!" Linda, whose bright pink cycling shorts transformed her legs into soft, plump cylinders, shook her head and pursed her lips prudishly. "They're *Quality Control*."

Even at a distance the backs of *Quality Control* appeared to stiffen, either from annoyance or apprehension on Mark's approach. The crew who had disembarked with him were laughing amongst themselves as they extricated their gear and Prue looked idly but in vain among them for the cameraman who had spoken to her earlier. *Quality Control* remained rigidly in position as Mark backed a few steps from them to assess their photographic potential and then busied himself grouping and re-grouping them. When he turned his head in the cyclists' direction, they could hear odd phrases.

"...more relaxed...a picnic, not a funeral...meant to be enjoying yourselves...chat to your friends...let me hear you...exhausted all conversation on the bus?...the weather, damnit, your hobby, favourite soap. No! I want men and women mixed ...buggy on this side... just one of you ...doesn't take two to push a buggy." He appeared to be heaving his nervously rigid viewees around like dummies in a shop window. "Any minute he'll start yanking their clothes off and redressing them," muttered Prue to herself. The film crew took up positions and Mark's final instructions were so loud that they carried easily even though he had his back to the cyclists. "O.K., start chatting for half a minute and then move off slowly and try to keep your eyes on the loch. It *is* the reason you're here!"

While keeping his dark-glassed stare firmly on the walkers who were slowly approaching the bend in the road past the picnic spot, all heads dutifully turned in the direction of the loch, Mark motioned the cyclists forward with an imperious backward sweep of his arm. The party looked at each other and then at Prue, expecting her to lead them forward and, feeling this unsought role of leadership almost as a rejection of her efforts to identify with them, she deliberately slowed her pace as she moved forward, so that they had no option but to wheel their bikes alongside her. Without turning round, sensing no doubt with a producer's sixth sense that she was within earshot, Mark addressed Prue sharply.

"Prue, that your child and buggy?"

"Yes," she smiled proudly.

"Did common sense not suggest to you that you could have oiled its wheels?" He swivelled his torso towards her as he spoke, running an exasperated hand through his hair, the reflection in his outsized black lenses distorting her into a non-human caricature, a bulbous onion of a bosom topped by an ant's head.

She didn't reply. The shock of his fury caused hot tears to burn under her lashes and she turned away from him to blink them back. Across the car park next to the scooters the blurred figures that were June and Caroline merged together and separated as her vision cleared.

"... in pairs," Mark was saying, "except when out of consideration for other road-users you will go in single file. The two men will go at the back because they will probably be the fastest and it's important that you keep together as a group, show team-spirit." The film crew who had been tailing the walkers, rejoined them at that point. "Just a mo.," he said, holding up his hand although it was only his own speech-flow he was interrupting, and proceeded to hold a whispered conversation with one of the cameramen.

"I want you all starting off over there at the cycle park," he said, turning back suddenly and gesturing towards the cycle park with an open hand as though swatting midges. "You, Prue, and you," he pointed with his index finger at Ellen, "will lead because I imagine you're young enough not to wobble. At least I hope you are. The men'll be at the back and the others in pairs in between. You will follow the road, filtering naturally between the cars where necessary and continue past the cameras here. You will not look at the cameras as you pass." He took off his glasses the better to give them the benefit of a hard stare. "Is that quite clear? You will not look at the cameras at any time. If anything happens, for instance like one of you falling off your bike or falling into the loch, you will react to the situation as you normally would without looking at the camera. These little accidents provide humour, realism. We like them. O.K.? So you then proceed past the cameras here on towards your lunch-time destination. By all means stop and admire views, stop for a chat, stop for a rest. Ignore us when we appear. Right?"

Prue ignored the eyes looking at her, expecting her to acquiesce on their behalf and remained silent.

"Right?" he repeated, leaning in towards them and staring from one face to another.

"Right," came a lame, ragged chorus.

"Well, then, what are you waiting for? Rain? Off you

go and start out from the cycle park as soon as you've titivated and got into your pairs."

With Mark having established himself as supreme dictator, tyrant and despot, Prue lost her status as outsider. They whispered unselfconsciously including her in their huddle, readying themselves.

"If I was to behave naturally like that daft bugger wants," muttered Marion through lips folded back against her teeth as she replenished her lipstick, "I'd jus' have a fag right now and then catch yous all up."

"Except tha' you'd no' catch us up," taunted Ben. "No' wi' yer lungs full of nicotine and tar an' the like. You'd no' see us fur dust as you came wheezin' along behind ...

"Wizzin' no' wheezin'!" retorted Marion. "An' you ..."

"O.K.,"Peggy interrupted, running hands agitatedly along her handlebars while keeping a nervous eye on Mark. "Are we ready for the off, folks?"

"I'm no' sure I won' t go an' wobble," Ellen confided to Prue as they set off side by side.

"Won't matter if we do." Prue grinned at her. "As long as we don't look at the cameras as we wobble, I reckon we're free to wobble like jellies."

Ellen giggled. Overhead one seagull screeched and another screamed back as two by two they pedalled a trouble free passage past the cameras. The fresh scent of water off the loch rose up into Prue's face and the sun was ripe and invigorating on her back. She pressed down hard against the resistance of the pedals and felt herself swooping along the undulations of the rough road, rising and falling like a bird on thermal currents.

"This is Rob Roy's country," she shouted back to Ellen and Ellen shouted something back but she could not hear what.

'Another rebel,' she thought to herself. 'He was another rebel just like me.' And she found herself wondering whether the great folk hero had challenged authority from a sense of clansmanship or from a delight in challenging restriction and shocking the conformists. 'It was in his blood,' she told herself. ' He was a MacGregor, a member of a clan so notorious that upright citizens had legal permission to shoot them on sight. But if it's all down to blood why am I a rebel and my sisters so obedient to Dad's wishes? Beats me.'

They ate their lunch at the ruins of Rob Roy's birthplace, Glengyle, a cottage cradled between two small foothills, sheltered by Meall Mor and Stob an Duibhe behind and with the challenge of Stob a Choinn looming in the distance. She closed her eyes and tried to picture the scene in the cottage, the tiny red-haired rebel, a baby, like William; his red-haired mother, Mary Campbell, with lines of care already etched into her young face, screwing up her eyes in the gloom of the cottage as she worked at her spinning-wheel while her shawl-wrapped baby suckled at her breast. Dared she love him when infant mortality was so high that his chances of survival were less than fifty percent? Did she just concentrate on her spinning and try not to think about how vulnerable he was. The sheep around the cottage wandered through the door she had left open to give her light for her work. There were cattle too, grazing around the house, still fat from the summer but brought down from the hills in preparation for the winter. Some of them would have been the MacGregor's by right, others certainly ill-gotten. But at a time when the divisions between rich and poor meant the difference between greed and starvation who could afford morals and ...

"What was that?" she said to Ellen who was looking at her questioningly.

"Better be on our bikes," repeated Ellen nodding at where the rest of their group were fastening their hats and pushing their bikes forward.

April shivered as she settled onto a wooden bench on the deck of the *Sir Walter Scott*. The breeze off the water was only refreshingly cool and her shiver was part nervousness, part excitement, rather than the result of any drop in the temperature. Then, as Archie sat on the seat beside her, but a good half-metre away, not presuming to fraternise, keeping his eyes firmly on the receding Trossachs pier as though unaware of her presence, she drew her cardigan more firmly around her shoulders, wrapping her arms inside it. The throbbing engine drowned the sound of Harry's footsteps. He suddenly materialised before her with two cups of coffee, one of which he held out towards her.

"I even know how you like your coffee," he smiled. "Black, two sugars. What intimate information we have learned about each other."

"Ellen's Isle!"

Archie's observation addressed to Harry was startingly loud, loud enough for April to spill her coffee. As he spoke he gestured towards the little island with its clump of trees."

"Indeed," said Harry in a tone which offered no clue as to whether or not this was knowledge he had previously possessed.

"Walter Scott!" jerked out Archie at the same decibel level.

"Lady of the Lake!" came next and then, encouraged by their attentive silence, he launched into his version of the epic, of Ellen who was hidden on the island for her safekeeping by her outlawed father who later gained restoration to favour for himself and his henchmen because of the hospitality which Ellen showed to King James when his majesty was left stranded on the shore after the death of his noble hunter. His account took some effort as he had to shout to drown out the official, on-board commentary in response to which a chattering group had emerged from the saloon to watch the island drifting past. The cameraman, also alerted both by Archie and by the information system, took up position to film the cluster of factory workers as they watched.

"If I remember clearly," mused Harry, stirring his coffee, "King James wasn't just repaying hospitality: he really took a shine to Ellen, a very honourable, strictly above the waist, Sir Walter Scott type of shine, but a shine none the less."

Archie did not reply. Harry looked at him, wondering if he had implied too much knowledge about the poem, but Archie was staring, head stretched forward on a long purple, turkey neck, at the stern of the boat where his daughter, Tabitha, was standing close to Ted from *Labelling*.

"Bloody cheek!"

April's presence had become insignificant.

"The bloody idiot's actually got himself joined onto her."

Harry and April dared to look. It was a technical, a-sexual kind of contact in that Ted, had lent Tabitha one of the ear-phones from his MP3 player so that she could share his music. However, his generous action had indeed necessitated their standing closer to each other than they would otherwise have done and both were smiling.

"Can't wait to get his mucky paws all over her!"

The little group of *Labellers* around the stern had dispersed, settling on benches and allowing the cameraman an uninterrupted and photogenic angle on the young couple leaning towards each other against the stern railings with the island behind them. He smiled with satisfaction as he zoomed onto them.

"Hell's teeth!" Archie had had enough. With a grunt he heaved himself off the seat and staggered, swaying with the motion of the boat, to take up position beside his daughter where he stood erect, both hands on the rail. The breeze, more skittish over the open water, swirled around his legs, flicking up the pleats of his kilt.

"Mr. Mac*Don*ald!" screamed Alison, also from *Labelling*, "Mr. Mac*Don*ald! Ye're no' a true Scot! Get yer knickers aff, man!"

"Want tae help him, Alison?" followed the raucous laughter.

Without lowering himself to respond in any way, he took one hand off the rail and smoothed it down the side of his treacherous kilt hoping that Miss April and Mr Aitchison had not witnessed his humiliation, that the camera had not recorded it. Either uncaring or ignorant of his plight, Tabitha beside him was happily thumping the railings in time to the music.

"Just behave yourself!" he hissed sternly in her uninfected ear.

She smiled vaguely, uncomprehendingly as he turned to retrace his steps past his mockers to Harry and April to mutter, "Going down for a coffee," and to disappear below.

"Fathers and daughters!" sighed Harry to April. "When undesirables threatened to pay too much attention to Ellen, *her* father apparently had every skiff and boat removed from the shore and tied to the island so that the only access was by swimming this very deep and immensely cold loch." He took a meditative sip from his coffee. "Was your father fiercely protective?"

"Oh no!" said April bitterly. "He didn't have to be. He just planned my life so that I didn't have any options."

She shocked herself with the disloyalty of this bleak statement far more than she shocked Harry. She tried to think of some way to modify it, to relieve its brutality.

"He was a free thinker ..." she managed eventually.

" ... who allowed only himself to think freely?" he finished

She didn't reply. The hand free of a coffee cup

trembled in her lap. Harry laid one of his hands briefly over it. His hand was warm.

"Let's go downstairs," he suggested, "and see if we can cheer Archie up with a whisky."

June focused her binoculars on Royal Cottage, allegedly built for Queen Victoria to stay in for one night during her visit to open the loch as Glasgow's water supply, focused with difficulty because her hands were shaking. She steadied her view by propping her elbows on one of the buggies and swept the glasses from the cottage to the peak of Ben Lomond and then swung them giddily to the right, to find the Arrochar Alps. But though she concentrated hard, she could not blot out Caroline's brittle laughter as she ingratiated herself with the cooks with whom she had insisted they share their lunch break.

"We have to, June," she had argued when June had raised two objections: firstly that she was sure that the two of them would be happier on their own without the cooks; secondly that she was sure that the cooks would be happier on their own without them. Caroline was not to be persuaded and the reproach in her eyes had been both irritating and challenging.

"June!" she had expostulated, blowing out the June through tightly pursed red lips, "it is *my* job to integrate *your* factory staff more closely," just as though the relationship between the two of them was primarily on a business footing and she had then gone on to expand with exasperating grandiloquence with, "my job to gather up the loose threads of humanity and weave them into a team that ..."

"Oh, spare me the verbal garbage," June had snapped and strode away from their chosen picnic spot leaving Caroline, armed with her gingham-covered wicker picnic basket, her fraternising instincts and her too-ready smile, to winkle herself into the company of the cooks. Behind her now she could hear the tinkle of glasses, the popping of a cork and the silly giggle that inevitably follows when people cannot uncork fizzy wine properly. She could hear Caroline laughing with them, just being polite. She couldn't possibly be enjoying herself. For Caroline's own sake she would have to have it out with her, make her see that her behaviour was not only silly but also hurtfully disloyal. She could easily do that. When she was much younger, much less experienced, she had got Mattie to understand the same principle. When they first moved into the flat together, Mattie's old friends had persisted in dropping in of an evening, interrupting whatever it was she and Mattie had planned to do. Mattie, just to be polite as she had afterwards explained to June, had welcomed them, given them, as June had had to point out, the impression that this was their home too. The actual scene in which she had alerted Mattie to this had indeed been distressing initially, with Mattie throwing a rather adolescent tantrum and threatening to leave, but eventually she had broken down and cried and when June had taken her into her arms and consoled her, Mattie had sobbed her apology and promised that in future there would be no more interruptions, had agreed that when her friends called June should tell them she was out. It had worked very well. It would work with Caroline too, given time and ...

"Ju-une!" sang out Caroline on two notes. "We've saved you a glass of bubbly!"

June replaced her field-glasses slowly in their case and went to stand in front of them, looking down on them. Caroline was kneeling on a rug, holding out a glass which she did not take immediately.

"Drinking and driving!" Her tone was mockingly censorious.

"We're all naughty girls," agreed Caroline, placing herself and the cooks firmly in the same boat – with June still stranded ashore. "What were you looking at, June? Do tell us."

"Royal Cottage!" June took the glass from her and downed it in a single swig. "I think Queen Victoria stayed there."

"O-o-o-oh!" Caroline was protractedly ecstatic. She turned to Mima, laying a hand on her knee, "Can't you just imagine all her children playing in the water in those funny long-legged swimming costumes and ..."

"No," butted in June, "but I can imagine Victoria and Albert being sensible enough to farm their children out on some poor, royal relation and enjoying having their retreat all to themselves."

As she spoke she helped herself to a banana from Caroline's basket and unzipped it savagely with her teeth. Then, munching as she went, she returned to the golf buggy and climbed into the driver's seat to indicate that the lunch break should end and it was time for the workers to resume their driving duties.

Mark and the camera crew were stationed at the jetty at Stronachlachar to await the arrival of the cycling party. Prue, still in front with Ellen, saw them first and had time to shout back a wary, "Hey guys, remember not to look at the camera!" before they came into earshot.

"Who'd want to look at thae lot," came from Marion who had been toiling for over the last mile.

"Watch it!" warned Ben – or it could have been Bill – "Him with the zoom-lens can probably lip-read!"

"Terrible!" bawled Mark as the cameras lowered and they regarded themselves as off the hook. "Bloody awful! You'll just have to redo the last mile!" Then, "Joke! Joke!" he added hastily as their eyes, the only parts of their bodies which appeared still mobile, swivelled accusingly towards him. He then threw back his head and roared with laughter, a hard deep belly laughter, upsetting a pair of gulls who took off squawking their protest.

Linda, leaning on her handle-bars to rest her aching back, looked up shaking her head and eyeing him malevolently.

"That man!" she hissed.

"Ice-cream's on the house!" Prue said in an attempt to quell the incipient uprising. "Ellen could you help me carry the cones?"

"Fine as long as he's no' getting one."

May, glowing from a day in the sun and from pride in what she had achieved, joined them just before the steamer hove into view. "The one I like best," she said to Prue, "is Royal Cottage. Look!"

Opening her rucksack, she removed her sketchbook from its polythene bag and paged through slowly to find the right place.

"Some of those are bloody good!"

May had been unaware that Mark had been at her shoulder and was shocked by his sudden exclamation into dropping her sketch-book, retrieving it in confusion, only to drop her polythene bag which blew away into the loch.

"There!" he remarked unrepentantly. "Now you've gone and polluted Glasgow's water supply. The Weegies'll be dropping like flies!"

With that he turned away leaving Prue to calm May down and help her re-pack her sketch-book safely.

The small figure held up to the railings was William and as the steamer docked Prue could hear his ecstatic "Mummy! Mummy!" above the panting engines and the rush of water trapped between the jetty and the approaching hull.

"Have you been a good boy?" she asked hugging him and kissing the soft neck underneath his curls, thinking to herself that she really didn't care whether he had been good or not as long as he was safe and happy.

Knowing this instinctively, he didn't bother to answer but "Good as gold!" assured Pat triumphantly. "But we thought we'd like to bring him on the boat to meet his mummy."

Prue leaned back in her seat, exhausted, sipping hot chocolate, watching through the window as the shore-line slipped further away with William at her feet, safely playing with the laces on her trainers. From the deck above she could hear Mark bullying his camera crew and picking on some-one else with "Stand there! Don't look at the camera! How many times do I have to say that?"

"How on earth do you work with him?" she said to Claire, the interviewer, who had sat down beside her and was smiling at William.

Claire laughed.

"He's a pussy-cat underneath!" she said.

Chapter Twenty-five

The Third Expedition

The Loch of Dogs

Early on the Saturday morning on which he was to accompany the Scout expedition to Loch Chon, Peter awoke before his alarm sounded and was initially surprised to find himself alone in bed. He frowned. Then he remembered. Things had not gone quite according to plan.

As his relationship with Suzanne had developed he had analysed it carefully enough. Suzanne was not Helga. He knew that and had consciously made careful adaptations. The main difference, he had early realised, was that with Suzanne he was firmly in the driving seat controlling not only the direction in which they were heading but the pace at which they proceeded. He had, as every good driver, taken careful cognisance of the signs along the way – the 'slow down', the 'stay in lane' and, at last, with the Friday night absence of Harry, the unmistakable indication of a lay-by ahead. In anticipation, he had invited Suzanne to supper, visited Marks and Spencer's food department and changed his sheets.

Yesterday, he had picked the last roses out of the garden, damp as they were with the early evening dew of September. They were scented roses. It was an idiosyncrasy of Harry's that he would only grow scented roses. When he had lit the fire and all the candles the warmth had spread the scent pleasingly through the house. Assessing the result before her arrival, he had been quite happy with it, felt it gave off the right signals but not too blatantly. Suzanne had arrived smelling of roses too, soapy roses, a vague sign, he had decided, that their intentions were compatible. She was hungry, did not pick at her food like Helga, but downed it with relish, scoffed it even. A good appetite, he promised himself too, was probably also a favourable indication.

So far so good – until the *Cluedo*. Her eyes lit on it while she was congratulating him on the pear and chocolate dessert courtesy of Marks and Spencer. In fact she switched so quickly from the pudding to the *Cluedo* that he did not have to confess that it was not home-made. It was there, the *Cluedo* not the pudding, among the boxes of games now neatly stacked on top of the dresser, one of the many games that Harry had bought years ago to bridge the long silences between himself and his fifteen year old Italian son. He and Harry had started with Monopoly; had touched down tentatively together on the astringent lemon yellow of Piccadily, the purple plumminess of Mayfair and the plainly functional Marylebone St. Station; opened first moments of laughter when one or other of them landed in jail or won a beauty competition. Then had come *Cluedo* with the game extending their lives and their every day vocabulary with "Peter in the study with the pencil-sharpener" or "Dad, in the garden with the aphid spray." No, first it had been "Harry in the garden with the aphid spray." "Dad" had crept in later: he could not remember when.

"I *love Cluedo*," she had said and so they had passed on coffee, cleared the dishes just sufficiently to allow for the eager opening of the board and set to with passion.

"Great foreplay!" he said to himself now sarcastically, sitting on the edge of the bed and running his hand ruefully through his tousled hair. "Just great!"

It would have been hard – no impossible – to switch from the Rev. Green toying away in the conservatory with the rope or the candlestick or whatever took his fancy to his own attempts at seduction, especially as they had snuffed out the candles and turned on the lights in order to see their cards more easily. If only it could have been Miss Scarlet in the boudoir with a ...No, even Miss Scarlet wouldn't carry condoms, not in *Cluedo.* You couldn't suffocate some-one with a condom, could you? But it had ended on the Rev. Green doing his stuff in the conservatory, after which Suzanne had yawned a genuinely sleepy yawn, with all her teeth on display, not one of those lolling pink-tongued yawns with which Helga could bring him to wherever she wanted him.

"You're tired," he had heard the Peter his father knew say to her, "and you've a long day tomorrow with your cousin's wedding. I've been drinking so I'll call you a taxi."

But *she* had initiated the kiss just as the taxi drew up. And the kiss could have ... if the exasperated taxi driver had not interrupted them by ringing the bell ... Peter, still sitting on the edge of his bed smiled to himself and wondered vaguely if he was in the driver's seat after all. Perhaps they were co-drivers, he and Suzanne?

Better take a shower.

As befitted the leader of lochnetting, especially as one who felt his leadership under threat from a brash newcomer, John had decided that he would forgo the Loch Chon Walk for the time being and support the *Melt Downers* and the token disabled around Loch Katrine.

"It wouldn't be right," he had commented to Jane, "to leave them to the tender mercies of Mark. After all he knows little or nothing about lochnetting and his inter-personal skills, as our beloved head teacher would term them, are grossly, *grossly* underdeveloped."

She had smiled gently, recognising in the bitterness and pomposity of the statement exactly how insecure he felt about his role as leader and quickly agreed to accompany him. But by the time they reached Loch Katrine she had had to listen to so many similar observations that her sympathy began to wear thin.

"This public face of lochnetting," observed John drily in his car safely out of earshot of Mark who was prowling restlessly along the edge of the Trossachs Pier, "wears too much make-up for my liking."

Jenny, sitting beside him on the front passenger seat, carried on with the brisk, rhythmic filing of her nails as though she hadn't heard him. Jane, behind him, had definitely heard him; he could tell that by the little rustle as she shifted her seat position, a slight irritable movement, and refolded her legs. As she did not reply with ready sympathy, he found it necessary to enlarge.

"I had always intended that lochnetting should be a rather private experience," he continued.

"Well, how did you intend to advertise your private experience to the general public?" she snapped. "Were you thinking along the lines of 'come and hug a tree with me?'"

"Come and hug a loch," giggled Jenny who must have been listening after all.

"Come on, John," Jane's tone softened. He knew that was only because she wouldn't want him to think that she was 'ganging up' on him with Jenny. When would she realise that he did not need that sort of mollycoddling? "You know you wanted other people to be able to share in your lochnetting idea. Mark is helping you do that."

He looked away from them both, out the window, to where Mark was involved in conversation or, more correctly perhaps, in 'verbal exchange' with the *Melt Downers* who had struggled out of a silver merc., shaking themselves gingerly like blousy, damp butterflies emerging crinkled from compression within a chrysalis, and were now stamping up and down on the spot and swinging their arms to rid themselves of the stiff in-car cramp as they listened to him.

"We'd better go and support them," said Jane. "You

know what he's like."

"Don't move!" he cautioned Jenny as he unclasped his seat-belt and opened his door. "You're immobile! Think party! Think live band!"

"O.K., O.K.," drawled Jenny . "Keep your hair on – what's left of it. I'll just sit here and rot while ..."

The rest was lost as they walked over towards the *Melt Downers*, quickening their pace as the hostile tone of the conversation reached their ears. The problem seemed to be that the *Melt Downers* had arrived wearing *Melt Down* T-shirts – black with *MELT DOWN* unmissably in luminous pink across front and back.

"You'll just have to get them off!" Mark's voice was raised. "This is not a commercial. I will not have advertising. That is my last word!"

"O.K., if that's what you want!" blazed Joyce, her face red and her eyes welling with tears. She pulled her T-shirt over her head. "Is that better?"

She thrust her chest out towards him so that the mounds of her breasts encased in a metallic black satin bra focused their war-heads challengingly at him.

"Come on, you others," she cried, all but whirling her T-shirt around her head. "He wants us to strip off, the wee perv., so let's give it to him!"

Mark remained obdurately silent, his face unreadable behind his beard, his dark glasses and the peak of his cap.

"Now, I'm sure there's a compromise." John tried to put authority in his voice despite his discomfort at Joyce's quivering pink torso and Mark's inscrutability. "Joyce, we really need you three and we really want to have you with us. I'm sure Jane and Jenny between them can find a shirt or two in their cases for you and I can lend ..."

"Will you listen to him!" spat Joyce. "Only a man could think that me and Laura here could possibly fit into her (she indicated Jane) T-shirt. And as for the wee lassie ...She made a hissing sound through her teeth. But she pulled the T-shirt back over her head.

"If you had jackets with you," said Jane, "that would solve the problem. You'd get too hot walking in jackets all the time but if you had them in your backpacks, you could put them round your shoulders just when you're being filmed."

"S'pose," she shrugged.

"Well that's settled." Mark spoke while running his finger down his clip-board, stopping to jab at it with his finger. "And Jenny's here?"

"Resting in the car," said John.

"O.K., then," said Mark and took himself off to speak to his camera crew who had just arrived leaving John and Jane with no clear idea of how to appease the *Melt Downers*.

Half an hour later when the round scoops of greyish white cloud that had been squatting contentedly on the horizon like vaguely interested spectators had piled up on each other's shoulders and were threatening to obliterate completely the wedge of blue sky between the hills over Loch Katrine, Mark was still wearing both his sun-glasses and his peaked hat and still managing to indicate that things were not progressing to his satisfaction.

"Are you not," suggested John hopefully, "going to concentrate mainly on the scout party at Loch Chon today?"

Mark took off his glasses to focus more clearly on the person who had interrupted with such an irrelevance.

"Later," he said shortly and added in the low, reluctant tone of one called upon to give completely unnecessary information. "I've told my team there to delay their start. Now, as regards Jenny. You!" He pointed a ball-point pen in Jenny's direction with his eyes still on his clip-board.

"Me?" said Jenny from her wheel-chair, sitting up from

her miserably hunched position so quickly that she nearly dislodged the crutches laid across her lap.

"Yes, you! For all that you've been in a wheel-chair – or so I'm led to believe – for some weeks you give every impression of some-one who hasn't a clue how to operate one. Why are you letting your mother push you?"

"I'd be quite happy for it to be some-one else," co-operated Jenny, her interest having been drawn by the same cameraman who had inspired Prue with lecherous thoughts the day before. "This chair really is a bit heavy for my mum. She's no spring chicken you know."

"Shut up and listen up, will you? You should be working your own chair. How do you expect us to pull off the 'brave girl defies pain to join loch-netting group' slant when you act like a sulky adolescent who's been forced into this by her parents? Now, come on! Pull yourself together. And what is more, Miss Jennifer, I'll have a brave smile from you so wipe the pout off your face."

John looked at him with new respect.

"Good organising ability," he conceded to Jane.

Mark frowned him into silence.

"Now," he said, "the plan is this. For health and safety's sake neither the fat people - *Melt* whatever you call yourselves – nor Jenny will go beyond the point at which they can be picked up and returned in golf buggies if necessary."

"Hey, ..." Jim started to object.

"Hey nothing. We can't have you throwing heart attacks en route. It'll spoil the message we're trying to put across."

"Fine about the message," said Jim, "but you'll please refer to us as 'overweight' rather than 'fat'.

"I believe 'obese' is the correct terminology," mused Mark speculatively, "but it's O.K. by me if you want to be 'overweight.' That aside," he waved the argument away, "remember that you will walk together but not in groups. That is I don't want all the fa-overweight people together. Spread yourselves! Trust *that* doesn't cause offence? One of you can walk beside Jenny, chatting to her encouragingly and she will, I hope, if she can that is, respond politely – at least when she's on camera."

"One point!" Jenny raised her hand as though she was in the classroom and Jane recognised with apprehension the glint of challenge in her eyes. "This is not lochnetting. It's just doing a cheap publicity stunt parading about on the edge of a loch and I think it's a cheat."

"Jenny!" breathed her father reprovingly.

"Well, in the car just now you said ..." She caught sight of her mother thrumming an imaginary guitar and thought 'live band' just in time. "Nothing," she finished sulkily.

"You're not stupid, are you?" Mark grinned at her, a sudden unnerving flash of predatory strong white teeth. "I'm not denying it's a publicity stunt but, believe me, if you want lochnetting to catch on this is the way to do it. Sometimes, one just has to prostitute oneself!"

Jenny, discomforted by some-one agreeing with her when she was doing provocation, was silenced.

"All ready?" said Mark. "Remember! Don't look at the cameras! Look at the loch! Look at each other if you can bear to! And if it starts raining, as seems highly likely, remember how much you *love* walking in the rain!

"He's not really all that bossy," opined Simon to Ham re Peter in the car park at Loch Chon.

Ham sniffed his disagreement.

"Well, put it this way," modified Simon, "he's not as

bossy as Jock."

"M-m-m," Ham reserved judgment. "Wait till you do something wrong – like row a boat across a river which he thinks is too dangerous for you because he just hasn't bothered to find out how good at rowing you really are."

"You did that?"

"Uh-huh," Ham agreed casually and bit into his lunch-time chocolate. "Often!"

Not even the fact that it was fairly chucking it could spoil Ham's upbeat mood. By now the news would have filtered through that his dad was the leader of the loch-netters; he himself, as veteran loch-netter, had the edge over everyone-else – well excluding Peter perhaps; Harry, April and Prue were there too but everyone could see that Harry was old and sort of past it, April was old and past it *and* a woman and Prue was in a complete dither as to whether or not it was too wet for her to walk with William. Jock, he had to admit, was the boss - sort of – and Jock had done loads of hill-walking and such-like but not loch-netting! That left just Peter and himself to offer any real expertise and, as long as the others knew to disregard Peter's bossy ways, he was free to take the reins.

And then too he had Jelly which was an added bonus, further marking him out and raising his profile. Despite unfortunately audible protests from Jenny who had rolled down the car window to voice her objections all the more clearly and woundingly, his dad had handed over Jelly with an appropriately nonchalant "Take care of her and yourself, son." Apparently this had been pre-arranged with Jock but no-one had told him – arranged with Jock no doubt on what his dad would call a 'need to know' basis – an infuriating phrase of his which, if it meant anything at all, meant that he, Ham, was not to know about it. Actually, it probably meant that if Jenny had found out that this was the plan all hell would have broken loose. As it was she had been bad enough. Most of what she said had been drowned by Jelly's excited barking but there had been the odd clear snatches – "scarcely out of nappies" and "can't even mend his own punctures" being the two he personally found most offensive.

"Ignore her!" he'd said loudly to the circle of rustling waterproof surrounding Jelly. "She's always jealous about Jelly liking me best."

With the others now fully aware of his loch-netting prowess, Peter hopefully demoted and Jelly, definitely *his* dog, frisking around, the Labrador half of her dominant as she scrounged crisps and unwanted sandwiches, his cup, his virtually unbreakable, orange (to make it conspicuous) with *Ham* marked on it with freezer pen (in case he left it lying around) mug was running over.

It was still fairly full two hours later when Mark arrived to release them from a stuffy wait in the minibus, Jock having insisted, seconded by Peter and further reinforced by April and Harry that they all return to the minibus in order to keep as dry as possible. Despite the fact that Ham had been eager to point him out to the rest of his group, he failed to recognise this Mark who had divested himself of his dark glasses and peaked cap and was sporting a brilliant red PVC jacket and rusty looking waterproof trousers of a more subdued shade of red.

"He looks like he's wearing a Santa outfit," sniggered Simon as Mark, having squelched gingerly across the sodden ground, eased the top half of his body through the door of the minibus. Jelly, appalled by this disembodied, vermillion torso, uttered a whine of horror, followed by a steady crescendo of yelps.

Mark held up his hand to silence her, a signal Jelly mistook for aggression. The hackles around her neck stiffened into a Jacobean ruff and she prolonged her barking, still steadily increasing its volume, while performing a complicated haka in the aisle.

"I'll hold her outside," volunteered Peter.

Ham passed over the lead reluctantly.

"Told you he was bossy," he murmured to Simon. "Poor old Jelly won't like being with him at all."

But when he rubbed a hole in the misted up window he could see that Jelly was sniffing happily into the undergrowth as Peter strolled her around the periphery of the parking bay.

"Listen up good!" bellowed Mark climbing up the steps so that the whole of him was now visible and shutting the door firmly on any further interruptions from Jelly. "You too!" He jabbed an index finger in the direction of Ham who had just noticed that Peter had allowed Jelly to pick up a stick which was certain to get jammed down her throat and was anxious to bring this folly to Simon's attention. "We'll start filming as you emerge from the minibus. The cameras are over there. Look at them now! Look long and hard and don't dare look at them again! Jock will come out first. You will follow in the order in which you are sitting. There will be no push and shove to get out first and absolutely no lingering in front of the camera once you are out. It's too wet for repeat performances. Anyone who spoils the shot will not go on the steamer this afternoon. We'll go with you for some of the way and then double back and meet you from the other end. If at any stage you don't know what to do, look at the loch, skip stones across it – NOT PLEASE NOT if there are any birds floating nearby because that won't look good and do exactly what Jock tells you. Got that? Remember, we are going to be doing English scouts as well and I expect they will film better. Prove me wrong!"

"Scotland! Scotland!" came a single patriot.

"Scotland! SCOTLAND!" came the howl of the masses.

He covered his ears in mock horror before holding up his hand.

"I'll signal Jock in a few minutes so be ready!" he said.

With the scouts having spent a good part of their incarcerated two hours quaffing cans of fizzy drink, the expedition was off to a slow start with plenty of communal peeing, most of which was off camera. Jelly was less discreet and she cast her eyes around as she squatted as much as to say, "Anything you can do I can do better." At least that is how Ham interpreted it for Simon's benefit.

The rain was fractionally less heavy, allowing them to walk with their hoods down and, if the view of the loch was hazy with the rain, in the damp air they could better smell the sweetness of it and taste it on the wind. The loch, a silver grey sliver of water between deeply wooded hills held three small wooded islands, the largest of which, Harry explained gave the loch its name. According to folk lore it was on this island that a rabid dog was abandoned centuries ago and the surrounding hills echoed night and day to the sound of his howls until he died. The loch was reputed to have been haunted by the ghost of a dog but whether it was the ghost of the rabid dog or that of some other poor beast, Harry was not sure. It was also reputed to have been the haunt of fairies he explained; not your dainty type Tinkerbells with pretty dresses and wands but powerful subterranean creatures who lived beneath the conical mounds at the far end of Loch Chon and as late as the nineteenth century, people who lived in the area would not walk past the mounds at night for fear of disturbing the "good people" and annoying them.

Ham felt that Harry was monopolising too much attention. He and Simon placed themselves right at the front with Jock so that Ham would be able to give them both the benefit of his advice and regale as many highly coloured accounts of previous loch-netting trips as possible. Interruptions to his narrative were, unfortunately, quite frequent as Jock repeatedly paused to look back on the progress of the flock behind him and to receive a reassuring thumbs-up from Peter that all was well with the rearguard he was shepherding. Ham obligingly stopped his account at these pauses so that he didn't reach the story of the body in the water of Loch Ness until they were about halfway. Jelly, scampering on ahead was out of earshot and with no other witness present, Ham was free to give his own version of events and was relishing every sordid detail of how he had heaved the sodden body aboard single-handedly when he was interrupted by a shock of brakes, an agonised yelp that made his stomach contract and an expletive never used in the playground, not even under exceptional circumstances.

Then he was kneeling into the sodden earth beside the inert, mud-bespattered body of Jelly. Some of the mud was still wet; some of it had formed a hard crust. He was crying. He heard his own voice far away screaming, "Jelly! Jelly!" but she didn't even lick his hand, just lay there with her eyes shut and her lovely, long, soft eyelashes. Over his head there were blobs and blurs of speech like the distorted sounds you hear from above when you are under water and your ears are thrumming.

"Jelly!" He tried to put his arms around her but Peter was kneeling beside him stopping him and he could not push Peter away.

"She's not dead, Ham." Peter's voice was suddenly very clear as though his ears had suddenly popped. "Look! She's breathing!"

Peter put Ham's hand on Jelly's chest and through the thick fur he could feel the thin, bony rib-cage moving in and out and in and out. She was warm too and his hand was cold.

He turned his head towards Peter.

"It was my fault," he said. "I was telling lies. That's why she's hurt."

"Absolute rubbish!" said Peter with re-assuring sharpness. "It's not your fault. She's hurt because this bloody fool here came round the bend thinking he was Chris Hoy."

There was a murmur of protest somewhere above which died under a loud chorus of recrimination.

"I'm no vet," Peter went on, "but I think she's concussed. There's no external bleeding but she could be bleeding internally, Ham. She'll need a vet pronto."

Ham went on stroking Jelly's fur with the tears alternately blurring his vision of her and then clearing to course their way over his cheeks. His nose was streaming too. He didn't care if the others saw. There were no others. Only Jelly.

"So what's best?" Jock had hunkered down beside them and it seemed that he was patting Ham's back soothingly. Well, some-one was patting his back.

"Ham and I'll take her to the vet," Peter said. "We'll go back the same way because we know the way and my car's there." He took off his coat as he spoke and slid it gently under Jelly and wrapped it around her. "You," he said to the cyclist, "can use your racing speed to good effect and get a vet to meet us at the car park." The cyclist looked at him helplessly. "Try your mobile, man! Be there waiting for him! Fucking heck! Have you no initiative? Don't you think you should be trying to do something to put things right?"

"I would if I were you," said a familiarly sarcastic voice stemming out of an aggressively red PVC hood. "We were behind you, *if* you remember, and, despite the fact that you splashed us *and* our equipment, we've caught the whole thing on camera, *television* camera. That means you might well be seeing yourself blazoned across the screen on *Crimewatch*."

Peter lifted Jelly very gently but Ham heard a little yelp, low and soft, more like a sheep than a dog, a sheep bleating far away in the distance.

"Careful!" he cried.

"I'll be very careful," promised Peter.

Ham had to trot to keep up with Peter's strides. About

halfway along Jelly opened her eyes.

"She's awake," said Peter. "Would you like to speak to her?"

He held Jelly down towards Ham. Ham could only just whisper her name but he stroked her head and she licked his hand and his feelings for her surged up out of control and he found himself sobbing against Peter's arm.

"Come on," Peter said gently. "For her sake we've got to keep going."

He could see the car park as he mounted the rise towards the main road, see the minibus, Peter's car, April's car and, a little apart, a sort of van thing against which a man was leaning while talking to the cyclist.

"That man might well be the vet," encouraged Peter.

Ham didn't argue because he should never have called Peter 'bossy', but secretly he disagreed. He knew that the vet at home in the surgery that smelled of disinfectant and fishy dog biscuits, always wore a white coat, a very clean white coat with no blood or urine or anything else you might expect on it. This man had on one of those greyish green waxed jackets, a flat cap so that you couldn't see the colour of his hair or even if he had any hair, jeans and large dirty black wellingtons. When he saw them, he started to meet them, running briskly towards them even with his wellingtons and not as if he was running through mud.

"Hi," he said briefly to Peter, although he hardly looked at Peter and didn't look at Ham at all. He was just looking at Jelly. "She's awake. Now that is good!"

When the vet said, "That *is* good!" as if it *were* good, Ham wanted to cry again but he managed to swallow back the crying.

"Bring her over to the van and I'll take a proper look at her."

The proper look took forever and everything was very

quiet apart from the occasional yelp from Jelly. Ham could only hold Peter's hand and watch while the vet moved his stethoscope around so that its silver mouthpiece thing gleamed through her black fur. Ham felt anxious. The vet didn't appear to know where Jelly's heart was. Stethoscopes were for your heart, weren't they? When the vet left his stethoscope to dangle and started moving Jelly's legs very gently, she yelped again, this time lifting her head in protest.

"She go up in the air?" the vet asked the cyclist.

The man shrugged guiltily. Then, "Yes, I think so," he said. "It was all so quick!"

"Telling me it was quick!"Ham put in bitterly.

"Sh now!" commanded Peter soothingly and squeezed his shoulder.

At length the vet turned to face them, or rather to face Peter.

"It's early days," he said. Was that good? His tone gave nothing away. "She's definitely broken her left front leg and dislocated her right hip. The leg's quite badly broken. You can see that looking at it." Peter leaned forward but Ham couldn't look. "No wonder she's feeling rotten. I need an X-ray to be certain but I suspect her back and her neck are fine. I can't tell for certain that there's no internal injury. I'll need to take her back with me, X-ray her, check her bladder and bowel functions. Give me a number and I'll phone you if there's any serious decline. Otherwise you could phone me at eight o'clock to-night for a progress report."

"She could still die?" Ham gasped.

The vet looked at him. "Your dog?" he asked.

"A quarter of her is mine." Ham was determined to be very strictly truthful now. It was in Jelly's best interests.

"I really hope she'll be all right." The man had very blue eyes in a very brown face with deep lines on it. "I promise you I'll do my very best for her."

"Can't I come with her?"

The vet shook his head. "She really needs to rest and she'll find you much too exciting! I'll sedate her, make her feel sleepy and she won't worry about a thing. You'll be more unhappy than she will. I'll give her a wee shot just now and it would be nice if you could stroke her while I'm doing it."

"I'll give you a ring; find out how she's doing," said the cyclist flapping his hands about awkwardly when the van rounded the bend out of sight.

"Fine!" said Peter and wrote his mobile number on the back of an *Alderson McTavish* card. "And I'll get your name, address and number too if you don't mind." As he spoke he furnished the cyclist with another *Alderson McTavish* card and a pen.

The cyclist read the card carefully.

"Think she could have buckled my front wheel," he countered nervously.

"Good!" said Peter unprofessionally. "Come on, Ham. I've got a thermos in my car. You need a hot drink and some chocolate while we wait for Jock to come for the minibus."

Ham gulped down hot tea and tried not to think of Jelly lying in that cage thing in the back of the van.

"Will it hurt her a lot to be lifted out?"

"No," said Peter very definitely. "Remember she's had an injection and will be having a beautiful long sleep, dreaming away happily, not sitting in a car worrying her heart out." Ham felt Peter turning to look at him before he added gently, "Whatever happens, Ham, the vet won't let Jelly feel any pain."

Ham nodded and looked out the passenger window because the tears were threatening yet again.

After the departure of Peter, Ham and Jelly, Mark made

a stab at lightening the mood with a cheerful, "Dramatic shot that! Cyclist kills dog!"

"Jelly's NOT dead!" Simon was nearly in tears.

"Well, either way we don't lose ...." Mark was interrupted by his accompanying cameraman calling out, "Mark, I could get a good shot of the loch from here, don't you think? That angle ..." and his voice faded as he drew Mark aside for a closer inspection.

"Let's have lunch now." Jock removed his own backpack as he spoke. "It'll save stopping further on. Remember what happens to those who drop litter?"

"They have to clean out the minibus when we get back. We-e-e kno-o-ow."

With appetites suppressed by shock and the more appealing snacks having already been consumed anyway, lunch was a token meal during which the boys picked unenthusiastically at sandwiches while Mark leaped amongst them shouting, "You're starving! You're ravenous! Tear at your food! Chomp that apple! Now if you were English boys ..."

Even that failed to elicit more than a muttered, "Shut up."

Prue eyed him with disfavour.

"What about a boys-are-naturally-upset-by-friend's-tragedy slant," she suggested brightly.

Jock re-organised the walking party to compensate for the loss of Peter, placing Harry in Peter's place at the rear and asking April to walk beside him "to keep things going in case I have to dodge back for anyone."

She could hear the honking of an invisible goose sounded across the water, a sad, lonely, questioning honk as though it was searching for the whereabouts of its mates, needing to be rescued from its loneliness. A small lichen-covered bridge crossed the stream running beside the path, leading blindly aimlessly into the green light of the forest. The loch's three islands, all covered with trees were clearly visible now. April remembered Harry's story of the dog of the loch, a story true or untrue of the dog, abandoned on the island after it developed rabies, whose howls could be heard day and night until it died. Not a story for boys grieving over another dog's mischance. A fading rainbow spanned the mist lifting off the surface of the loch and through it she could see that the trees on the far bank were already partly copper. The liquid sunlight catching the hillside above them, showed it already toasted with the gold-brown of the autumn bracken, and she could smell the sweetness of bogmyrtle drifting up from the banks of the loch or down from the hillside or perhaps both. Despite all this beauty, her conscious awareness centred on her bladder which was uncomfortably full, and having exhausted polite preliminaries re the view and the weather, she could think of no possible topic of conversation with Jock to distract her from her discomfort. 'Now, if I were interviewing Jock for a job,' she thought to herself, 'what would I say to put him at his ease? Possibly, 'Did you have much difficulty finding us?' Even that is out of date now that everybody has sat.nav. and it certainly won't do here.' She wished she could be walking with Harry. Since the start of her loch-netting her social comfort zone had expanded to include Harry and Jane and, possibly, John although she still felt slightly uneasy in his presence. She would, she decided, have to face the fact that she was boring because her world was limited and her vision restricted to a sort of tunnel vision which focused on the factory and left her with a distorted peripheral perception of the outside world. Even Prue, usually kind, had hinted as much in the car that morning when she had remarked that she felt that June had rather let the side down by not rejoining them this morning as had been expected.

"Saying she's tired after going back on the bus with the

factory workers is a bit feeble," she had commented. "After all she had Caroline with her to help."

"It's probably Caroline who's tired her out," laughed Prue.

"Ridiculous!" April had snorted.

'Ridiculous' had been one of her father's terminating words, used when he wanted everyone within earshot to understand that he wished the present topic of conversation immediately snuffed out. Prue would know that and the moment the word escaped her lips, April regretted it: regretted that she had snapped at Prue; regretted that it might have given Prue insight into just how unsettled she felt about the relationship between June and Caroline and more than anything regretted what had prompted her outburst - the bleak ban on the discussion of sexual matters which had been instilled into their childhood and remained with them like a small, hard, sour green apple picked too early and never allowed to mature naturally into its full sweetness.

"April!" Prue had ejaculated, hard and stern. "You really must get a life beyond the factory. I hoped that loch-netting might have helped."

Although she didn't need to conclude with, "but it hasn't," April felt the full, cold draught of the criticism. At the moment loch-netting seemed only to expose all her weaknesses, and especially her complete lack of confidence in her non-factory self.

"Bloody midges!" Jock remarked, swatting at his face with savage cheerfulness.

"They don't bother me," she latched on eagerly to a familiar topic. "I've never been bothered by midges. I don't know why but they just don't like me."

"I'm sure it's not personal," he grinned. "It's probably just your smell that puts them off."

She was not sure that this was entirely complimentary

but she smiled and anyway Jock had turned the conversation and was blurting out unskilfully, "What does Prue's husband do?"

She hesitated, suddenly unsure about whether Prue had ever actually married Hans. She rather thought not.

"He's not around any more," and hearing the curtness in her tone, mellowed with further information "and he doesn't have anything to do with William."

"Oh, shame!"

Jock didn't look sorry. If anything he looked more cheerful than ever and the thought crept into her mind that he might just have taken a fancy to Prue. She glanced over her shoulder to where Prue was walking with the cameraman. Both burdened, she top-heavy with William on her back and he laden with photographic equipment, they had quite naturally fallen a little behind, but seemed happy in each other's company. She didn't seem to be showing any interest in Jock. Still, one day Jock or some-one else would come along and the house would become very, very quiet again; no toddlerish screams of laughter or tantrums of frustration; no midnights with William's teeth and Prue's soothing crooning. June would eventually be lost to Caroline. May would be pouring exclusively over her painting with her easel set at just such an angle and her paintbrushes washed and laid out in the correct order. And she herself?

"Oh please God," she breathed.

Jock looked down at her.

"Not much further," he said.

Loch Katrine

As the electric whine of the golf buggies bearing Jenny and the *Melt Downers* receded into the distance, following submissively in the wake of the Fourtrak carrying the last of the cameramen and the sound recordists and their poles and their wires, the silence that ensued made John very conscious of the loudness of his own breathing, of his own thoughts even. In fact it seemed as though there was altogether too much of himself. The rain was falling steadily now, pockmarking the surface of the water and nullifying the hills, the peak of Ben Lomond, the Arrochar Alps, enclosing him in a world in which he was the predominant feature, giving him nowhere to lift his eyes away from himself except to Jane and having Jane with him couldn't make him less aware of himself because she was so unnervingly tuned in to him that she could invade even the privacy of his thought world and reflect it uncompromisingly, unflatteringly. In her he could see himself projected onto an infinitely wide screen with every pixcel of his being distended, every pitiful flaw in his make-up faithfully but unmercifully represented.

"Nice to be alone," he said to her because that was surely what he was expected to say.

"Oh yes," she replied, too obviously trying to breathe into the flatness of her voice a shared relish of the prospect.

A part from the odd break-through, like the one that had taken them both by surprise at Loch Quoich, theirs seemed to be a stagnating relationship he now decided: a relationship between himself and himself-as-reflected in Jane. It was restricting the enjoyment he should be finding in loch-netting which was after all *his* idea, *his* dormant passion. When he was a boy accompanying his father on fishing trips around the lochs his father's enthusiasm had infected him. Their relationship extended him as he took in new experiences, rejoiced in the opportunity to leave behind the restrictions of the daily routine imposed by his overbearing mother and share instead in a world in which they responded together to the rhythms of the sun, the moon and their own physical needs. They had gasped together at the coldness of the water when they bathed, discovered together how the numbness of their emerging feet softened the sharp stones on the shore at the water's edge wept, laughing at their tears provoked by the acrid smoke of the damp wood fires. And when the mist descended, as it did today, and wrapped him into a cosy world peopled only by his father and himself, he had been aware not of himself but of his father with his tales and his silences, of a music in the sweet, clear whistle of his father's line when it spun invisible from the rod and music in the rhythmic tapping of his pipe on a stone. Now, with Jane, most likely because of Jane, there was much too much of just himself.

"Like to stop for a rest, dear?"

They had reached a small settlement with large trees and she had stationed herself in their shelter in anticipation of his reply, having of course assessed his comparative lack of fitness with tedious accuracy.

He bit back the "No thanks, I'm not tired," because it was useless to pretend to her.

"I think it's lost its magic," he said with cruel, meaningful ambiguity.

She was silent for a moment, taking in his words, weighing them up in the context of himself and at the same time unpacking her knapsack and concentrating on its contents. 'Bloody irritating multitasking' he thought to himself. She was just like his schoolmates had been in the park, displaying their cycling skills and taunting him with their wordless 'See, *we* can do wheelies!'

"Magic changes," she pronounced wisely. "If it didn't it wouldn't be magic! Would you like a cheese roll? You always get grumpy when you're hungry."

As far as she was concerned he was just all stomach. What about his feelings, his heart? Next Valentine's Day he would draw her a card with an arrow piercing a stomach. He might suggest it now. Come to think of it, when had he last given her a Valentine's card? Better keep his mouth shut.

"That magic enough?"

She was holding out a crisp brown roll with golden cheese and a hint of pickle smiling up at him out of its slit.

He couldn't suppress his own smile as he took it.

It was dry under the tree with heavy drips forming an intermittent curtain around them, screening them from the other world. The cheese was delicious and he could feel the warmth of Jane's arm pressing against his in the confined space. It came into his mind in a sudden flash of inspiration that if he were more aware of Jane's individuality, the part of her there must be which didn't reflect himself, he could possibly be less sick of himself. He toyed with the idea as he munched. It should be easy. After all he did love her. Of course he did. That went without saying. Perhaps he should get to know her a bit better. Her tastes, her likes, her ambitions, if she still had any, could well have changed during the eighteen years they had been married. He should perhaps rediscover her.

He made an inspired start with, "What is your favourite roll?"

"Prawn," she replied. "Why?"

"Well, why do you always do cheese?"

"Because nobody else likes prawn, of course," she laughed.

"I do," he lied magnanimously with his mouth full. "Next time we'll have prawn."

"It was absolute hell!" hissed Jenny proudly when she embraced Katie after disembarking from her golf-buggy. The hiss was unfortunately loud enough for Laura, hovering nearby, to hear and to re-act to by shrugging her flesh-padded shoulders self-consciously and edging away from her.

"Come for a coffee," said Katie comfortingly, smiling at Laura who did not return the smile and ushering Jenny firmly out of general earshot, "and tell me all about it."

Having settled themselves at a table with mugs of hot chocolate and sandwiches next to a window from which they could watch the general activity on the pier and in a corner where Jenny could lay her crutches where they were unlikely to trip up any tray-bearers, Jenny knew a selfless moment.

"Did you have a good run up then?"

"Not really!" Katie pulled a face. "There was a long tailback with road-works near the safari park and then an accident just outside Callander."

"Oh no!"

"But tell me about your filming."

"Least said," replied Jenny before taking a deep breath. "Mark – the queer film producer guy – I mean queer as in odd. I don't think he's gay – or straight for that matter. He's just got absolutely no sex appeal. None at all, believe me. Anyway, talk about bossy! You'd think my dad was a saint compared to him. He made me push my own chair and look! I broke a nail trying to turn that wheel because he made me look longingly at the loch at the same time. That was the easy part, looking longingly at the loch. I could have thrown myself into it no bother. Then he wanted Laura to walk beside me and talk to me. What did he think Laura and I could possibly have in common? Anyway, fortunately she was puffing and panting so much she couldn't talk, just wheeze out a few comments. He told the cameraman, not the one that's fwah, the one with B.O., to get alongside us and get some close-ups and that would have been O.K. if he hadn't made Laura walk on the camera side to emphasise her fatness. So, what do you think anyone would see of me? And, all the time, he was telling us to look natural as if we were relaxed and enjoying ourselves. Eventually, he made all the others walk ahead of me and then I had to hobble slowly after them on my crutches looking limp and pathetic when I could have overtaken them no bother. *And* they filmed me hobbling along from behind and you know how your bottom sticks out when you're walking with crutches. Best part was when he left to go and do the Scouts. Do you want another sandwich?"

Katie shook her head.

"Don't you feel just a wee bit sorry for Laura?" She was looking out the window to where Laura was standing a little apart from Jim and Joyce. "You can see she finds her size embarrassing. The other two are so wrapped up in each other that their common problem is almost a bond between them."

Jenny registered the mild rebuke sufficiently to turn from Laura to Jim and Joyce with a giggle that blew bubbles into her hot chocolate.

"Oh them!" she expostulated putting down her mug in order to flutter her fingers dramatically. "Well, I was listening behind the door at the planning meeting and I distinctly heard Mark say that a love interest would be good." Katie frowned in an effort to recollect. "Well, he said something like that I know he did. But in the meantime he must have decided that having Jim and Joyce at it wouldn't be photogenic. You must admit he's got a point. Anyway, he split them up, said it looked better to have fat and thin interspersed. First time anyone's called my dad thin! He looked well chuffed but Jim and Joyce were raging. Soon as the golf buggies came to get us they tried to dive into a back seat together but they wouldn't fit and Jim had to sit in front beside the guy who drove to meet us. Expect they'll make up for it later but can you just imagine how difficult it must be for them to have sex?"

She lowered her voice for the last part so that the couple two tables along who had been homing in to her account swayed in their direction in an effort to catch the last few words.

Katie looked out the window to where Jim was helping Joyce into a white plastic raincoat and Laura, standing slightly to one side, was holding Joyce's backpack for her while watching the operation attentively.

"You could be like that one day." She stifled a yawn as she spoke for all the world as though Jenny's account had been boring.

"Me?" Jenny was scandalised. "Never!"

"People overeat for all sorts of reasons – loneliness, boredom, pain, unhappiness ..."

"Do you think I'm unkind?" Jenny's lip trembled at the possibility. "Do you think I'm horrible?"

"No," Katie smiled. "Well - perhaps a bit unkind but I would have been the same at your age. You've just got some growing up to do."

Jenny was silent, stirring the remains of her chocolate, the bits that she would have fished out with a teaspoon and eaten when she was a child. She had thought of Katie as a mate, had thought of inviting her to her cellar party. Perhaps she still would. Katie would no doubt be impressed by the sophistication of it, would realise that she, Jenny, was mature after all and be sorry that ...

"Jenny, you look really tired." Katie sounded like her mother but *she* would not be rude enough to retaliate by pointing that out. "No wonder after all that exertion. Why don't we go ahead to the hotel instead of getting on the steamer to meet the others. You'd feel much better after a hot shower and a rest."

Admittedly, the idea was inviting – even more inviting as she limped through the puddles with her arms aching from using her crutches while Katie asked Laura to explain the change of plan to Jane and John and packed the wheelchair into the boot of her car. The steamer would have been nice but not with all those scouts and Ham and after what Katie had just said she wouldn't feel free to make witty observations on any of her fellow passengers.

Ham sat opposite Peter in the little cafe on the pier at Stronachlachar and looked from the thick triangle of chocolate cake which Peter had set before him out the window over the waters of Loch Katrine to where diluted sunlight shifted patterns of cloud on hill slopes now hygienically free of the sheep whose droppings might pollute Glasgow's drinking-water.

"I'll be the only member of our family not to have done Loch Katrine," he said mournfully. "Going on the steamer doesn't count, does it?"

"Not really," agreed Peter with his mouth full. "We'll have to have a cycle round it one day."

Ham thought.

"We can't take Jelly if we cycle though," he pointed out, "and that wouldn't be fair because she hasn't done it either, not even on the boat. Perhaps she never ..."

"Ham," said Peter firmly, gesturing out of the window, "do you see that small island over there, the one with the wall round it and lots of rhododendron bushes?"

Ham followed Peter's finger out of politeness.

"While you were in the loo, I was reading a notice which said that Rob Roy marooned the Duke of Montrose's factor on that island as revenge for the cruel treatment of his wife and family and demanded a heavy ransom for him from the Duke."

Ham considered the island, taking a large mouthful of chocolate cake as he did so. The cake was delicious – comforting and chocolatey.

"I don't think I'd mind being on that island," he said

dreamily. "Did he have a tent?"

"Shouldn't think so and you'd get very hungry."

"I'd catch fish."

"And eat it raw?"

"I'd have to if I was really hungry and anyway I'd build a fire to send smoke signals to people to rescue me."

"Do you know how to start a fire by rubbing sticks together?"

"Oh yes," said Ham and then it struck him that if Jelly was to live he had to be truthful. "No, I don't really but I am good at fires. I used to make them in the cellar – great roaring ones- before they found out."

"At least when they found out they didn't stick you on an island."

"No, but they can be terribly cruel! No, they've never really been cruel at all. Do you find telling the truth hard?"

"Impossible, sometimes," laughed Peter.

He heard his mother's voice outside, "Well, Peter's here." The door half-opened on the sound of the brushing of muddy boots and her voice grew louder. "Look there's his car."

Ham knew panic. "You tell them, Peter, please," he whimpered. "Please will you tell them. Please tell them I didn't mean it."

"Ham, listen to me!" Peter leaned across the table towards him. "Ham! Jelly's accident was not your fault!"

"I'm going to the loo," said Ham and, as John limped towards their table behind a smiling Jane, he fled past them but instead of going to the lavatories he walked out onto the smooth pier, damp and shiny from the afternoon's rain, felt the cool breeze against his face, tried to concentrate on the little round island on which the factor had been imprisoned and tried not to so see Jelly with her head lolling limply over Peter's arm. Just as he was about to wipe his sleeve across the dampness in his eyes, he felt arms around him, hugging him close, so he burrowed his streaming eyes and nose into his father's chest and breathed the rancid smell of stale sweat.

"Poor Ham," murmured Dad stroking his hair and he knew he must own up.

He looked up leaving a snail trail of snot against his father's dark green sweatshirt. "It was 'cos I told lies," he said. "It was my fault. I was telling lies and not watching her properly. I told lies about Peter being bossy and lies about me and how clever I was."

"What a lot of claptrap," said his father severely, placing both his hands on Ham's shoulders. "It was not your fault at all. Put that sort of silly rubbish out of your head now. Jelly's in good hands. The vet will do his best for her and he won't let her suffer and you can just be sensible and come inside. The chocolate cake looks superb."

"I know," said Ham. "I've eaten loads. Well, one slice," he modified because telling the strict truth had become a sort of habit.

Jane leaned against the rail of the steamer, feeling the vibrations of the throb and thrust as the boat, manoeuvring out from the pier, heaved itself against the resistance of the water and she watched the turmoil of the swirling water being sucked back around the prow and the stern. Stronachlachar with the figures of Harry, Peter and April preparing to drive two cars and a minibus back to the Trossachs pier receded smoothly and she envied those three their opportunity, brief though it would probably be, to be alone in their respective vehicles. The wind was sharper now and the dark loch was flecked with sporadic whiteness flinching in and out of the water. Overhead the clearing sky was a mess with the detritus of fraying clouds metamorphosising uncannily into different shapes as they traversed the wide expanse of sky from hill to hill. The day, she decided, had been a huge disappointment.

"It's just because of Jelly," she told herself. "You're upset about Jelly."

With determination she pushed Jelly firmly to the back of her mind, forced Jelly with her toffee-brown eyes and her plumy tail to skulk behind a coldly analytical assessment of the day, an impersonal, logical assessment

"It fragments us, all this filming," she concluded. "It has broken up our day into too many presumably photogenic facets, involved us in superficial relationships with people we're not happy with and who would never dream of going loch-netting if it weren't for the chance to appear on television. We were, after all a very compatible group until that Mark came along."

But that did not really help her because she knew that she was scapegoating Mark unfairly and that there was a deeper, more personal reason underlying her disquiet which she could not verbalise into sanity. At worst he, Mark, was only highlighting differences which had already occurred. At the root of her unhappiness was her own insecurity when seeing people she thought she knew weirdly altered in different lights, the fickle way they changed under different circumstances, changed like the clouds above, still constitutionally the same and yet unrecognisably different. Like her own John, now unrecognisably confident, with absolutely no need of her support, not once glancing in her direction as he told the boys stories about Rob Roy MacGregor and they listened spellbound, respectful. Subconsciously of course she had known that he had a natural gift for dealing with and holding the attention of youngsters, but at home he showed little expertise in handling his own son and daughter, leaving most of the difficult stuff to her. Jenny, at least was uniformly difficult - no fear or hope of change there - but Ham, her own son, irrepressible, resilient Ham, had surprised her with his unsuspected sensitivities. It was natural that he should be upset over Jelly but then there had been his anguish over the drowning in Loch Ness.

A clawing dragon of cloud overhead disintegrated completely, its bits adhering to a nebulous sister to loom into a misshapen cotton boll.

It was not only her own family who were different: Prue, devoted mother of William, had five minutes ago snuggled sensuously into the jacket held for her by Jock, with a conscious wriggling of her shoulders, calculated to draw attention to the pertness of her breasts with the result that Jock, devoted scoutmaster and every mother's son if there ever was one, had immediately responded by ushering her downstairs for a coffee, abandoning his charges without a qualm to John who now was heavily into the finer techniques of cattle rustling.

People were better at staying the same when they were only acquaintances, like distant mountains, like the Arrochar Alps over there, having emerged from cloud cover with a reassuringly constant outline. When they were far off and indistinct, when you didn't think you knew their individual quirks, when your knowledge of them was only skin-deep, people could be counted upon to remain the same. So she could, perhaps, take herself across to chat casually to the mountainous forms of Jim, Joyce and Laura, without bothering to get to know them too well, postpone her good weep over Jelly to later and even later than that, admit to John that he had been right in his opinion that this filming thing was suspect and that she too hoped it would never be repeated.

But, even as she turned, she was joined by Mark at the railings and, in no mood for his caustic humour, she braced herself to retaliate if necessary.

"See Royal Cottage over there? I hear its coming up for sale. Fancy sleeping where Queen Victoria laid her head?"

"The point is she didn't lay her head there." He might

sound uncannily and uncharacterisitically human but she was still wary and now glad of the opportunity to set him right. "They built it especially for her to sleep in when she came to launch Loch Katrine as Glasgow's water supply; all that expense to house her for just one night. But when they fired the twenty-one gun salute, the windows shattered and she had to sleep elsewhere to avoid a draught on the royal neck. It was all just another anti-climax."

He looked at her shrewdly, "Another?"

Jane didn't feel like enlarging. She remained silent drumming her fingers on the rail

"I could get to like this," he mused softly and dreamily, staring out over the water as he spoke. "Loch-netting is a really good idea, something I might like to get into myself."

Unprepared, it took her a few moments to think up a suitable reply and at last came up with, "It's still at its experimental stage, but I've enjoyed it up till now."

"And what's wrong with now? Well, of course, I'm sorry about your dog but I take it that's not all?" She could just see his eyebrows rising over the rim of his glasses.

"Too many cameras. Too much bossing about." But this time she smiled as she spoke and his beard undulated in response.

"But being in a film," he said, "gives people the chance to see themselves as others see them but don't worry. I'll leave the gear behind next time I come on an expedition."

He straightened and jerked his head towards John.

"I'll just get a bit of footage of the kids listening to Rob Roy and then hopefully, I'll get the *Melt Aways* to ..."

"*Melt Downers*."

"*Melt Downers* to sink their teeth into some cream buns or whatever and we'll be able to pack up our gear for today. Hurry up guys!"

And he was safely back to nagging the camera crew.

Even after they docked at the Trossachs pier, Jane felt jangled, anxious to be on her own with just her own family behaving predictably. Eventually, the scouts left with loud good-byes and multi-coloured scarves hanging limply out of the windows of the minibus. Mark and his crew took their leave with just a curt valedictory threat of "See you tomorrow!" and the *Melt Downers* melted away for a stirrup-cup with more alacrity than they had displayed before. "A stirrup-cup *plus*," Joyce was heard to qualify. "After all we'll have burnt off plenty of calories."

"I'll drive," Jane held out her hand for the car-keys as she spoke. She wanted to keep active. They still had to face Jenny with the news of Jelly. On the way to the hotel she tried to concentrate on the view and ignore Ham who was snivelling on the back seat because he had unearthed a squeaky toy of Jelly's from below the front seat.

Their hotel, *The Sleeping Swan*, situated on the northern shore of Loch Ard, was a long, narrow building with the upstairs windows so deeply embedded in the combed slate of the roof that they gave the building a sleepy, dormant appearance. They found Jenny and Katie waiting for them in the hotel lounge. Jenny, looking unusually pale and fragile, had changed into a black top which emphasised her pallor and Jane took a deep breath and tried to think of a more gentle way of breaking the news than the speech she had prepared on the way, but she was forestalled by Jenny enquiring, "Is Jelly in the car?" at which Ham promptly had yet another bout of weeping.

Incredulously, that same Jenny on whom she could rely upon to be unpleasant at all times both to and about her brother, on hearing the news, hugged him fiercely, glaring over the top of his head and whispering determinedly, "It's not your fault. It would have happened if she had been with any of us," thereby shocking Ham into responding more positively than he had done to the reassurances of either his parents or Peter.

"Too right!" he agreed, adding triumphantly, "That cyclist was a bloody bastard, a bloody, fucking bastard!"

Whereupon, John lapsed back into his familiar role of giving Ham a row, going over the top about foul language in spite of Ham's vulnerable state, and showing none of the empathy with the younger generation that had characterised his story telling to the Scouts on *The Sir Walter Scott*. Life, superficially at least, seemed to be returning to a quasi-normal state

Later, long after the phone-call to the vet had brought the good news that Jelly was progressing satisfactorily and that he was cautiously optimistic that there were no internal injuries to worry about; after Prue had returned to being the model of maternity, completely monopolised by William, and after Jenny, despite the benign influence of Katie, had embarrassed her mother three times during dinner which was about average and had referred to her brother (after the phone-call) as "that unnecessary evil", a phrase she had launched so proudly that they could expect it to be repeated, Jane pressed her cheek against her pillow and reassured herself that she had been right in her earlier supposition that people were only behaving out of character because of the filming and closed her eyes on the day.

"You asleep?"

John was standing in the bathroom doorway towelling his wet hair vigorously. Of course! As per normal he would be wanting a post-mortem on the day's events so that he could write up his record. She sat up dutifully and forced herself to smile encouragingly at him. But, when he, warm and smelling of soap and shampoo, sat down on the bed beside her, he kissed her so that although it was late and they had had a tiring day and would have to make an early start in the morning and Ham was in the next room and the hotel bedroom walls were made of parchment, she got her priorities completely wrong. With hindsight.

"We're being silly," she protested feebly as she traced a line down his spine.

He looked up from kissing her left nipple.

"It's like Ben Lomond, now," he said, husky with job satisfaction.

Lying close beside him when they were both happily exhausted she considered the subject of change more favourably.

"Change can be good," she decided aloud. "What are those lines? Something about nothing fading ... you know in *The Tempest* ... something ..

....will suffer a sea-change
Into something rich and strange.

"Uh-huh," he grunted.

"Should be suffer a loch-change."

"Uh."

"The change is fine when it has been completed," she continued. "It's the process of change that's so ...so.... discombobulating and ..."

She drifted into a sleep in which she and the other loch-netters were standing on the edge of a loch, looking into the water and the water was moving so that all their reflections swayed and snaked into different unrecognisable shapes, just blending, blurring colours. When she woke, because the pressure of John's head on her arm was giving her pins and needles in her hand, she knew that it had been a dream and not a nightmare and she tried to lose herself in sleep again to that living, swirling chaos waiting resolution.

Chapter Twenty-Six
The Third Expedition
Loch Ard

The hotel, it seemed, followed a policy of anti-social breakfasting on the Sabbath. The tables that had been adjoined to accommodate a communal dinner for the loch-netters the evening before had been firmly separated, permitting a maximum of four to each table. The woman in charge of breakfast had brittle blonde hair, a metallic nameplate inscribed *Heather Harrison*, a steely glint and a snakeskin belt that would have looked good on a dominatrix. She could obviously only be approached with extreme caution. John, insufficiently awake to take in any warning signs – the inevitable clicking of the ball-point pen with which she ticked off the straggling breakfasters and the terseness of the "You are ready to order," without the slightest inflection of a question – started to ask her if they might draw up an additional chair for Katie when she came down, only to lapse into a despondent "Doesn't matter" half-way through.

June, who had left Edinburgh at sunrise, coupled with the unexpected addition of Caroline, arrived at the Reynolds' table to bring Heather striding across the dining-room to remonstrate. While May tried to screen herself behind a flimsy paper table napkin, April pointed out belligerently that William's high-chair hardly constituted at-table-seating but before the argument could become too heated, June agreed that she and Caroline would sit at a separate table and was even gracious enough to smile at the prospect. During the altercation however Katie slipped in unnoticed and joined Harry and Peter at their table, an arrangement which was allowed to remain although Heather had other ways of communicating that Katie's late arrival was not to be tolerated.

"Eggs is off," she informed her triumphantly. "Bacon's

off."

Katie opted for "Continental" only to find that continental people no longer enjoyed croissants and that they were not fussy about whether or not their rolls were fresh or their coffee hot.

The loch-netters escaped from the discipline of the dining-room in a body without exchanging a word until they had shut themselves into the 'conservatory', a flimsy glass and PVC attachment which, presumably, had only been passed by the planning regulators because it could be felled if necessary with one blow of a sledge-hammer. The narrowness of this extension meant that the wicker-chairs were drawn into a row along the front, an arrangement not unlike that frequently seen in a residential home for the elderly, where the incapacitated elderly are obliged to be entertained either by the view or by their own reflections. This view, however, relied on the viewer having more than a passing interest in parked cars and was intermittently obstructed by stiff, prickly cacti which seemed to thrive in a mixture of soil and stubbed out cigarette ends.

"When are Mark & Co. due?" asked Peter.

"They're meeting us in the car-park at the west end of Loch Ard at ten o'clock," John replied. "We've got a few minutes before we can expect to be marshalled around."

"To-day we shouldn't be marshalled around at all," declared Jane. "We're not carrying any extra bodies for publicity's sake: no scouts, no *Melt Downers*. It's his chance to film us as we really are."

"Frightening prospect!" Unable to see her properly past Ham, Jenny and Katie who filled in the row between them, Peter smiled at her reflection, slightly distorted by imperfections in the glass, giving her a lopsided jawline. "But of course you're right. We should just be doing our thing."

"What about me?" Jenny's voice was calculatedly small

and pathetic. "Do I have to stay here with (she stopped herself in time from saying "with May") ... with Heather and ... and knit?"

"Tell you what?" Peter leaned forward to face her. "The cyclists are going to be much quicker than the walkers. When we've finished our cycle, I'll come back and take Jenny and any other cyclist out for the afternoon. O.K., Jen?"

Jenny purred. It sounded almost like a date.

Jane stood up and pushed back her wicker chair decisively.

"I'm just going to phone for an update on Jelly and then I'll be ready for off."

"By the way," John remarked, suddenly twisting round to face her, "I've remembered that quotation you were on about last night. It was

Nothing of us that does fade
But does suffer a sea-change
Into something rich and strange.

"Very good!" Jane replied tersely, blushing as she did so. Would the man never realise that there were things to be felt and done and said at night which should never be carried on into the harsh light of day?

The cyclists set off first. Harry, chewing ruminatively at the end of his pipe in the car-park noted with satisfaction that Peter's preliminary cycle check was more relaxed than before, but this could just be because he was confident of receiving little opposition: Ham, though in ebullient mood after this morning's bulletin on Jelly, describing her as definitely on the mend, was still sufficiently aware of the support Peter had given him after the accident to obey his every word and Katie was sure to prove cheerfully compliant. Harry had arranged to travel with Jane and John, leaving his car for Peter to use in the afternoon and he stumped out his pipe on one of the rockery stones as he saw them emerge from the hotel, turning to wave at Jenny who was still in the conservatory, her mobile clamped to her ear.

Harry was glad to sit in the back of the car with the humming of the engine drowning any need for him to attempt to participate in conversation. He would like to have been altogether alone in this early autumn. He could feel its movement, its stirring as it busied itself to shift the somnolent stagnating remains of summer, copiously sprouting fungi, new life springing from decay, angels' wings hovering over dead stumps, the defiant blood red of the fly agaric and the smaller insignificant mushrooms in their edible and lethal conglomeration all rising up through the withering grasses. This year there had been an upsurge in interest in magic mushrooms in school among some of his less committed students. He knew that because having to teach the moral welfare type subjects meant that you got to know what went on in the school's underworld. Why did school always intrude into his thoughts – even here where the leaves blazed wonderfully before falling?

Do not go gentle into that goodnight ...

Dylan Thomas had written that for his father, forbidding him to slip unresisting towards death, wanting him to go out in a rebellious blaze. He smiled to himself, wondering vaguely if Peter would have similar thoughts about him when the time came. Never! Peter would want him to be the model of convention, preferably clinically hospitalised and sedated against any upsurge of protest. But it was not up to Peter.

Now that he and Peter had been proved to belong to each other so definitely that the slightest sliver of doubt was unable to insinuate itself between them, it became more possible, desirable almost for them to flaunt their differences, almost a celebration of the fact that the bond between them could never be severed. There was love of course. Went without saying. He loved Peter and he was now certain that Peter loved him and that set him free to do his own thing and leave Peter to the tender care of Helga or Suzanne or whoever. After he retired next summer there would be a lifting of restrictions on his time and place.

"Today Loch Ard; tomorrow the Med.!"

"What was that, Harry?"

Jane had turned round and was smiling at him. He had forgotten that his voice would carry forward more easily than theirs would carry back and had assumed a privacy he did not have, but before he could attempt a reply, he was saved by Jane's reaction to the appearance of Mark and his team in the car park.

"Oh no! They're here already. Good-bye, peace."

Mark, barely recognisable, dressed like a normal hiker in the faded greens and earthy browns of the naturalist, was standing at the notice-board in the car-park with two of his crew, tracing a line down one of the maps with his finger. As they turned off the car engine they could hear him laughing at some joke. John didn't think he had heard him laugh before.

"At least there are only three of them," he said comfortingly. "He did say that he was bringing a skeleton staff today, whatever a skeleton staff means."

"It means," said Jane drily, "that he's going to work them to skeletons. Them *not* us! We are calling the shots today, remember!" She leaned out of the window and smiled sweetly. "*You're* early, Mark! I'm afraid that means you'll have to wait while John fetches April from the other car park where she's to leave her car."

"Whatever you say, ma'am." He touched his forelock in mock acknowledgment of her authority, a gesture she chose to ignore. "It's fine by us. We were hoping for a fly cup of coffee before the off anyway."

Jane frowned without knowing why and turned her

attention to Prue, William and May who were emerging from the Reynolds' car. April seemed to be in a hurry to take off to the Milton end car park and May was fretting about what she should take and what she should leave behind.

"There's no hurry," she called out. "I've told Mark he'll have to wait for us."

"Funny men!" shouted William, running delightedly towards the group round the notice-board in a desire to fraternise. Prue left him to it but Jane followed after William in an attempt to inhibit his over-enthusiastic welcome. By the time she caught up with him he had already launched himself at the cameraman who had accompanied him and his mother the day before with a "Hello, Dames!"

"Hello, William! How's Torty today?"

Torty had been left in the departing car and a grisly scene might have ensued if the three cyclists had not arrived, distracting the bereft William and prompting Mark to action.

"That was great! You looked superb coming round the bend," he commented enthusiastically, "but unfortunately we missed your entry on the scene because James here was going ga-ga over William. If you wouldn't mind, please, just doing your entry again, I'll not bother you for the whole of the rest of the day."

"Fine," agreed Peter before Jane could think of a valid reason to obstruct this. "We'll just wait for June to clear the road, I think."

As he spoke June came down the little lane leading to the car-park like a boy-racer and with a squeal of brakes, swerved into a reverse parking position which caused Caroline on the front seat, firmly knotted into a head-scarf to rock forward stiffly like a dummy in a test-car. They caught the tail-end of her shrill remonstration as she swung her white corduroy legs out the door into the mud and dead leaves mix on the path.

"... too fast. You really do!"

June, her car-keys dangling from one finger, pushed the driver's door shut with her foot and smiled her satisfaction.

"You've churned up our road!" protested Ham.

"Never mind," said Mark who was obviously in a mood to object to nothing. "All the more atmospheric!"

"You mustn't look at the camera," Ham primed Katie as they retraced their entry route. "He goes absolutely bonkers if you do." He remembered his resolution to be strictly truthful and amended self-consciously to a tamer version, "Well, not 'bonkers', but he doesn't like it."

"What Ham means," grinned Peter, "is that Mark is bonkers most of the time so it's hard to tell if he is going extra bonkers. Right, Ham?"

"Right!" agreed Ham. "He bonks most of the time."

Peter and Katie were still grinning as they cycled down the lane into the car-park to greet their fellow loch-netters but Ham, already lagging behind, suddenly caught sight of the dog-poo bin on the corner of the car-park, a bin which poor Jelly was in no position to utilise, and he could only manage a subdued salutation, half-raising his hand from the handlebars with a wan smile. Mark, however, was perfectly satisfied with their performance and waved all three of them off with his blessing.

"Careful round the corners!" Jane called after Ham, responding to a sudden urge to assert maternal authority. "You don't want to knock anyone down."

Fortunately Ham, habituated to ignoring his mother's good advice, paid no attention but Mark drew alongside her, raised his eyebrows and whispered in tones of mock horror, "Hardly tactful, considering yesterday."

"When you are a parent," Jane rejoined coldly selecting her words for maximum impact, "you will discover that in the interests of safety it is occasionally necessary to sacrifice tact."

"But I am a parent," countered Mark. "I have a son, conceived, you will be glad to hear, in the marriage bed."

"It is of absolutely no interest to me where you beget your offspring!" she snapped back, only to realise that the asperity of her reply assured Mark that he had won the round.

She didn't need to walk away from him. Mark's attention had slid round to June and Caroline while he was still speaking to her and he approached them with his hand held out confidently in a gesture of friendliness.

"Who have we here?" His gaze swept down from the knotted silk headscarf to the sheepskin boots via the white trousers. "Ah yes! I remember! Our Friend of the People and her Staunch Ally."

Caroline, remembering only too well that she had been the butt of his sarcasm only two days earlier, eyed him with suspicion. June watched them both.

"I am a professional you know," parried Caroline archly with a provocative toss of the silk headscarf, "not just a social worker."

"My wife's a social worker," he mused. "She thinks she's a professional but I'll have to tell her she's wrong, won't I?" He smiled down at Caroline's discomfiture. "Never mind, my dear, it takes all sorts to make a world – professionals, unprofessionals, the lot. What say you?"

Caroline, hopelessly lost in Mark's verbage, said nothing but June, putting her arm around her protectively took up the challenge.

"Professionals, unprofessionals and television producers, the latter of course being in a category all of their own, their main function being to annoy everyone else."

Mark threw back his head and brayed. Caroline joined in uncertainly with a polite titter. June remained sober, keeping her arm very tightly around Caroline. They were still standing like that when John drew up with April in the car.

"What do you expect me to do about it?"

The sharp retort was to May but April's eyes remained fixed on June and Caroline.

"It's just that it's my favourite pencil," May whimpered. "All my best sketches are done with it. I know it was in my rucksack. I put three pencils in my bag this morning and it was the second one I put in and ...."

"Well, May, if it's not on the ground here it's fallen out in the car where it will be perfectly safe." She added more kindly, "Remember you did agree to leave your drawing behind to-day and be one of the group."

"Yes," said May awkwardly because she did remember agreeing and yet she had a nagging doubt that she could ever qualify as a member of any group. "What do we do now?"

"We just follow *John*," said Jane who had just come up beside them and with arms outstretched she attempted to round up the small flock and shepherd them towards a holding place in the middle of the car-park. She spoke loudly enough for Mark to hear her and for John to raise his eyebrows quizzically at her uncharacteristic assertion of his authority. "We just *all* follow *John,*" she cried.

"Raise your standard, John, man," exulted Mark.

They filed slowly forward. John, alone at the front, kept turning round, waiting for some-one to come alongside him but June and Caroline who were immediately behind him remained as a solid pair and were monosyllabic in their replies when he turned to address the odd remark to them. Behind them Jane walked with April and May, followed by Harry, Mark and Jim, the sound recordist. Prue with William and James with his camera brought up the rear.

They left behind the white houses of the little village of Kinlochard with their doors and windows shut against early morning disturbance on a Sunday, with their children's swings hanging idle and their dahlia's heads still heavy with dew and started up the hill above the loch.

"What are you focusing on today?" asked Harry of Mark. "There are one or two interesting features: the remains of a crannog can still be seen and then there's Helen's rock where Helen, the wife of Rob Roy, wrought some unspeakable revenge on some-one."

"Actually," Mark lowered his tone confidentially, "I'm more interested in the group dynamics today."

"Group dynamics?"

"Aye! How the members of the group fit in with and affect each other. It'll help Claire with her interviewing, help the programme come alive. We'll film from time to time but the main focus will be the members of the group and what makes them tick. I'll be keeping a low profile."

Harry smiled at him. "Is that possible?" he asked.

May was walking with April and Jane with her mind firmly set on being a member of the group but with undefined doubts of her eligibility clouding the brightness of her determination. April and Jane were talking gardens, discussing the relevant efficacy of slug pellets versus beer-traps. She could see no way into their discussion. If May found a slug in amongst the vegetables when April was present she kept very quiet about it. If April was nowhere in sight she would dispose of it humanely by lobbing it over the nearest fence where it could take its chance in a neighbour's garden. She knew that April would not be pleased if she were to reveal this and Jane, frequently the recipient of her slugs, might well be even less pleased. This she felt instinctively was not the conversation she should be joining and she fell back slightly so that they would not need to converse over her head.

"You'll be May, the elusive May."

Mark had caught up with her.

She nodded, not quite completing the nod in that her head went down and stayed down, her eyes on the road before her feet. She made pretence of picking her way carefully over the smooth tarmac.

"I believe you're an artist, May?"

"I wouldn't call myself an artist," she muttered, blushing a purplish-pink. "I like to draw. Just draw."

They walked on in silence and she hoped that if he insisted on prolonging the conversation he would move to a subject other than herself.

"Draw people?" he persisted.

"What? I beg your pardon?"

"I just wondered if you drew people."

"Oh no! Oh, I couldn't! Just houses and trees and hills and ... and things."

"Why don't you draw people?"

She thought about it, raising her head and focusing on the next bend in the road. She had never dared to draw people. Faces had expressions which changed as you looked at them, never the same. It would be like drawing a sun-dial and she had tried that once and been thrown by the steady if almost imperceptible movement of the pointing shadow. And if faces were difficult, bodies were impossible. You couldn't just draw the clothes, you had to see through them to the nakedness beneath.

"I might try animals," she compromised, hoping that would satisfy him.

"You should try drawing people," he persisted. "It helps to get to know them. Talking to them, drawing them, filming them is all communication."

"Very interesting," she managed and was rescued by Jane who was pointing to where a red squirrel was leaping from a birch to an oak so that Mark turned back to alert his cameraman.

Her mind raced on with its attempt to interpret what he had said.

'That's why I can't draw people,' she worked out. 'It's because I don't know them. I don't know how to talk to them. I can't be a member of a group and I don't want to be. I want to be an artist all by myself and draw whatever is not a person.'

She quickened her step determinedly, to catch up with April again.

The road was broad, wide enough for the passage of Forestry Commission vehicles and John felt the ludicrousness of his position out in front, a bit like a punitive exclusion, like being made to stand in the corner or being plonked down on the naughty step. If he didn't know Jane better, if they hadn't been so close the night before, he might even suspect that she was trying to teach him a lesson. But what lesson? Earlier she had seemed to be encouraging him not to monopolise the leadership; now apparently he was to take his position as leader to what he felt to be ridiculous lengths.

They were climbing steadily. At times the loch below them was invisible behind the foliage; at others he had clear glimpses of it. He was walking through mixed woodland with the fickle light and shade of the birch glancing through the static gnarled fretwork of oak, the fresh green of young ash slow to respond to the onset of autumn and the rowans bristling with hairy grey lichens. Unbidden, he slowed down so that June and Caroline overtook him, June in stoical silence, Caroline with a fleeting, almost illicit smile, and he fell back to walk beside Jane, April and May. He did not look at Jane's face to gauge her reaction, just took her hand, interlocking her fingers with his and felt rejected by its impassivity. They had reached a bend where the road spread into grass under the shade of an oak. To make up, to satisfy her inexplicable whim of the day, he made an executive announcement.

"We'll wait here," he said in a commanding tone. "Give Prue and William a chance to catch up."

"Good idea," said Jane pressing his fingers.

Prue and William had indeed fallen behind and so had James, the cameraman, mainly because William had insisted on walking and, as well as having very small strides, he tended to tack and veer in his explorations so that by the time they had caught up with the others he had probably covered twice the distance they had.

"Get some good shots, James?" Mark enquired as his cameraman drew up beside him. "Or was your focus elsewhere?"

"Got a good shot of the red squirrel," James was examining his camera minutely as he replied as though it could offer evidence if required, "and a lovely one of William trying to eat an acorn."

"Acorn dirty!" William pulled a disgusted face. "Acorn not nice!"

"Acorns are squirrels' breakfast," agreed Prue, "not William's. Look," she addressed herself principally to John, "if you guys don't mind, William and I'll drop out."

"We could all help carry him," offered Jane, "don't you think, John."

Prue shook her head before John could agree. "Carrying William when William doesn't want to be carried is a nightmare. He and I'll stroll back down, have a break at that nice fattening tea-room at the telephone box and then wander on to the hotel. We'll be fine."

"Well, we're sorry to lose you of course," said John, "but you must do as you think best."

"That's a good woman," Mark remarked sagely as she turned at the bend of the road and waved. "Puts her child before pleasure." He turned to James, putting a hand on his shoulder, "Come on, *Pleasure*! We've got work to do!"

James continued to fiddle with his camera before following.

June and Caroline were waiting for them at the rustic crossroad sign which offered a divergence of routes. Caroline was seated on the verge, her legs splayed out in front of her, her hands massaging her knees. June, surveying the distant hills through glasses, ignored their arrival.

"We weren't sure which way to go," smiled Caroline as they drew up, "so we thought we'd better just wait for you."

"You mean *you* weren't sure," muttered June, still raking the distant landscape.

"I mean *I* wasn't sure," responded Caroline obediently.

"I smell the remains of a lovers' tiff," observed Mark sotto voce to no-one in particular.

"They're not ...," April began heatedly and stopped because in this clear open space where she stood between sky and land and where the sun was shafting so sharply between the rows of pines on the slope above her, she realised that she was exposing her own prejudice as clearly as June and Caroline were exposing their relationship – if it was a relationship. There was surely still doubt.

"Come on, Caro!" June was holding out a hand to Caroline to coax her from the ground with no eyes for the rest of them. "I'll take your water in my bag; it's probably the heaviest thing you've got. And, look, it's downhill now!"

Downhill all the way for *them* now; now that Mark had translated it into words, had brought it out into the open, whatever you called 'it', thought April. And she had a sudden deep sense of loss, not just the possible loss of a sister but the loss of a way of life dependent on not probing too deeply, not knowing too much. 'Like Eve in the Garden of Eden,' she thought, 'needing not to taste of the fruit of the tree of knowledge of good and of evil.' She and June had sat together in Sunday School when her mother was alive and they had listened together to the story of Eve and how she couldn't resist a bite of that apple and their teacher, a woman with wispy hair, round spectacles and a lap for the children, like May, who were not good mixers, had told them not to worry too much about Adam and Eve being driven out by the angel because there was a happy sequel. Only she had never heard the sequel, been left in limbo, because the death of her mother had meant an end to Sunday School. From then on her father had grafted his own values onto the tree of knowledge: there was from then on good – white, evil - black, the things you don't talk about - grey and the things you don't even want to know about – no colour at all because they didn't even exist. Her father would have put June's relationship into the latter category: to label it would have been irrelevant to all their needs and superfluous to his masterplan.

She fell back on the pretext of a call of nature to allow June and Caroline to disappear out of sight.

They skirted the finger of water projecting inland or was it a finger of land projecting into the loch before their path turned away from the water into evenly spaced, cultivated pine woods among which a small clearing presented itself with fallen tree trunks offering seating.

"Lunch?" suggested John. "I'm starving. I don't know about the rest of you."

This was greeted by a general agreement expressed non-verbally by everyone starting to unshoulder their backpacks. Jane, seating herself on one of the trunks, saw that a thick protruding branch carried a thick coating of small caramel coloured mushrooms and leaned forward curiously to examine them. Looking round to alert John's attention, she found Mark standing right behind her.

"Mushrooms," she said, when what she wanted to say

was "Go away I find you annoying."

"Coprinus flocculosus, I think" he replied biting into a sandwich from which she noticed the crusts had been carefully excised.

"You know your mushrooms." She knew her statement sounded like a concession.

He shrugged. "Only the common ones. I didn't specialise in fungi." Her curiosity was aroused and he proceeded to answer the question she did not want to ask in case it prolonged their conversation. "Yes, I did botany. Studied at Reading. Came away with a degree in botany and a wife." He chuckled drily. "Fortunately my marriage has lasted even if my botany career was short-lived. Still love my garden though."

She looked at him suspiciously, wondering if this confidence was prompted by his having eavesdropped on her conversation with April. Seemingly, he could also have acquired a degree in mind-reading.

"I did hear you and April on about your gardens," he said. "Seems we've an interest in common." He selected another sandwich and held it in front of him as though it was relevant to his thought process. "Rather be a gardener than a botanist any day," he remarked, took a small experimental bite, evidently decided the sandwich was to his taste and quickly took another. "Gardeners just have to love their plants; botanists analyse them."

"So what on earth made you switch to this sort of thing?" He would probably be able to read her thoughts and tell her anyway but, on balance, she preferred to verbalise her own questions. "I can't see any connection between this and either botany or gardening, analysis or loving."

"Don't you?" he sounded surprised. "Mind you it is sometimes very difficult to love people after you have analysed them."

"Tell me you're not analysing us!"

"On the contrary that's just what today's all about for me!" Her intake of breath demanded that he justify himself which he did with passion. "How on earth do you suppose I can present you to viewers without analysing you; without knowing what makes you tick, why you are doing this, in short what sort of people you are?"

"And what sort of person, may I ask, am I?"

"A control freak."

"A what?"

"You can't help it," he said forgivingly. "You're used to having your family-life revolving around you; used to supporting them; used to controlling them. You feel that they're not safe if you're not at the helm. You have to control."

"I think that's ..." she could not find the words "just impertinence" would be prissy, "totally incorrect" would be a lie; both would show how wounded she felt.

"That's why you're pushing John to be leader to-day," he went on remorselessly, "leader with a capital 'L'. You were determined that I was not going to dictate the pace. You wanted it to be John because you knew that was a socially acceptable, if manipulative, way of gaining control yourself. You know that he listens to you whenever you want him to. Excuse me, I've left my yoghurt in my backpack."

A detached part of her felt as though she had been listening to some wildlife programme expounding the characteristic behaviour of some non-human species; the sort of thing that should be delivered in a David Attenborough-type stage whisper; something like *the queen-bee is always the centre of life within the hive* or *the dominant sow in the badger sett can be relied upon to protect her cubs with her life*. That's how he had analysed her; the dominant matriarch, confident of her supreme position, aggressive to the point of despicable manipulative techniques when she felt threat to the status quo.

He was back at her side delving unconcernedly into his yoghurt pot.

"You've forgotten one thing in your scientific analysis of us all," she remarked very impersonally, very calmly, as though not ruffled at all.

"And what is that?" He paused, spoon in hand, eyebrows raised.

"You're not exactly an objective viewer."

Unpredictably he laughed, shaking his head as though at his own stupidity.

"You're dead right," he gasped. "Absolutely one hundred percent right!"

She would have preferred him to have appeared at least slightly humiliated.

"Everybody ready to move on?" and John looked towards Jane for some indication that his timing was right but she appeared to be concentrating on re-packing her backpack. Everybody did appear to be ready except for May who was concentrating on shading in a group of mushrooms nestling into a hollow in a large grey boulder.

"May!" April's voice was sharp. "May! We're going now!"

May looked up, frowned and continued with her work.

"I'll wait with May," offered Jim. "Seems unlikely that I'm going to be needed. Could have had my golf after all."

"We all have to make sacrifices for the sake of art," pronounced Mark loftily, waving his hand in a mock effete gesture. "Even you, Jim. Actually, it might be an idea, James, to do a bit of footage on May sketching so you can stay too. O.K.?"

April half wondered if she should remain behind with May as a sort of chaperon, but May appeared not in the least discomforted by, in fact oblivious of, the company of two attendant males. She had not looked up from her work throughout the discussion.

"All right then, May?" she said.

"Nearly finished," replied May without looking up.

"It's repacking her bag that's going to take the time," April confided very quietly to Harry and Jane as they moved off together. "The pencils have to go in in a certain order and she'll have to check three times that all is in. I hope they're not unkind in their filming."

"Probably determined to show us all in a bad light," replied Jane ominously. "I'm dreading the film. It'll be like those sneaky holiday snaps taken on the beach from behind – the ones that give you a supersized bottom."

Harry chuckled. "So far I've escaped interrogation. Probably because I've been typecast as the archetypal sixty year-old – all bowling green and faded memories- but from what I've observed there's been some pretty intense scrutiny and it rather looks as though John's in for it now."

Jane nodded soberly. She had noticed that Mark had joined John but it was not an attempt to share leadership that worried her now, it was whether John's sensitivity could withstand Mark's invasive questioning and brutal analysis. But after Mark's assessment of her as a control freak, how could she possibly prove him right by interfering?

"Harry," she said suddenly, "could you please join them on some pretext or other? Join Mark and John, I mean?"

He looked at her, puzzled, and then catching her meaning, he nodded and moved forward.

"I was just being manipulative," she said to April and laughed. There was no point in trying to explain to April: she couldn't possibly understand.

Disappointingly, their path took them further away from the loch than they had imagined from studying the map, becoming a picturesque walk through the woods, very lovely but hardly a lochside ramble. They caught up with June and Caroline by a small waterfall. Caroline was sitting by the edge of a stream dangling her feet in the water with June standing over her, leaning forward slightly in the attitude of a school matron delivering a dose of unpalatable medicine.

"Keep them under the water," she commanded.

"I can't," wailed Caroline. "I can't feel my toes. Look, my feet have gone purple!"

"If they're numb they won't hurt you," retorted June logically. "You'll benefit in the end, you'll see."

"It's called being cruel to be kind," opined Mark sagely. "Which do you enjoy more, June, being cruel or being kind? Or perhaps you like the way one leads to the other?"

June probably did not even hear him. She was kneeling before Caroline now, drying her feet on her own spare sweater and massaging them gently before replacing her socks and her boots for her. April, who felt that Mark's words were meant more for her than for her sister, averted her eyes and was glad when, with the sudden arrival of May and her escort, he became involved in a technical debate with his team.

"Not got an awful lot on Loch Ard," he reported back after consultation. "Views of the loch I mean with you guys in it. Too many trees along this path. Fortunately James here is prepared to be a martyr and stay behind and hopefully, persuade one or two of the cyclists to do their thing along the road on the other side of the loch where we can get a better view of it. I'll have to persuade your hotel to squash him in to-night somehow. Is that O.K.?"

April was aware that the question was directed at her, that somehow he had judged her to be her sisters' moral guardian and was careful not to allow her expression to change as she said, "No doubt something can be arranged."

"Or perhaps some doubling up?" said Mark.

"Perhaps," she said evenly.

Jenny was quite unaware that she was shedding friends. When she phoned the mobiles of those she wished to impress and most were switched to voicemail she latched on to what she chose to regard as the most obvious reason.

"It'll be their mothers," she muttered to herself, "into brain damage or being a sociable family member or something."

It never occurred to her that any of her loyalish band of friends could possibly have reached saturation point with accounts of her leg agonies, not to mention the party to end all parties or the fact that she was to become a television star – no not quite a celebrity- she had joked, but in all seriousness, who knew? She might yet reach the heights, might even make Big Brother. So it just had to be Phoebe for her latest and surely most breathtaking bulletin and Phoebe kept saying that she had to go and practise her clarinet. Good thing that she, Jenny, had rehearsed this intimate confidence, a confidence to be passed on discreetly to most of Senior 3, so that she would be able to aim the most important bullet points through Phoebe's increasingly pressing excuses.

She had had a date with Peter. Actually, Katie and Ham had come too which was a bit of a drag, but they were in the back seat in more ways than one.

After tea at Stronachlachar – chocolate cake too – Peter had sent Katie and Ham ahead to Royal Cottage so that he could walk beside Jenny. "Yes, O.K. Phoebe, I may be slow on my crutches but that was not the reason, I'm sure! Come *on,* Phoebe!"

On the way – "now listen will you" – Peter had told her that he wasn't going out with Helga any more. What? Well, Helga had been his girl-friend, bit of a slut if you asked Jenny, but she had thought it polite to ask how she was and whether she wanted to come on any more loch-netting trips and why she hadn't come on this one and whether Peter was sorry she hadn't been able to come and Peter had stood stock still on the path and raised his eyes to the sky – "and you should have seen his eyelashes, Phoebe" - and said "wait for it, Phoebe", he had said, 'Jenny, just give it a rest! Helga is in the past! Finito!' "That means it's over, Phoebe and ... Phoebe... Phoebe ..."

Phoebe's phone must have run out of charge and she had forgotten to ask her how her granny was, the one Phoebe had been crying about on Thursday. That was a bit mean, perhaps. Not like her. She would make a point of sitting next to her at lunch on Tuesday even though Phoebe was not, well not ...you know.

Now what to wear for dinner!

Prue leaned her forehead against the cool glass of her bedroom window to cool her brain, slow down her thought impulses, slow down all her impulses. Behind her she could hear the rhythmic sucking of William's thumb, indicating that he was at last falling asleep but she dared not move towards the door just yet. She had tried twice and each time he had sat up alarmed, holding out his arms towards her with an imploring, "Mummy, Mummy!" and she had sat on the bed beside him and patted him and sung to him.

In the car park below she could see Harry, the whiteness of his hair luminous in the twilight. He was standing feet apart, rocking slightly as he sucked on his pipe. There was a slow crunch of gravel as Peter joined him. She could catch the odd word of their conversation: they appeared to be commenting on the position of the stars that were pin-pricks of light in the semi-dark, semi-light of the sky. The nights would be closing in soon, something that always filled her with a desperate sense of urgency, perhaps a primitive need to provide for lean times ahead, perhaps a need to accomplish, to finish before darkness fell. And there was so much in her life that was unfinished, so many threads left dangling, some to be discarded, some to be caught up and woven into her future.

The urgent sucking noise had subsided. She gently removed the thumb from his mouth, leaving his lips slightly parted, placed Tory on the pillow beside him and went out, gently closing the door behind her.

She half knew that James would be in the hall; knew too that he would hear as soon as her bedroom door opened. 'Like William,' she thought to herself with a smile. 'Males don't change. They're born with super detection gear.' April was there too, apparently studying the maps of the Western Highlands. Apparently!

"I was just thinking of going for a short walk," he said casually. "Like to come?"

"I can't leave William," she said regretfully. "I've had a real job getting him off to sleep and I'm not sure ..."

"Prue, I'll listen for him." April took over. "If he cries, I'm sure I can look after him. You're not going to be long?"

Somewhere deep inside her a tiny flame of rebellion flared up fanned by the suspicion that April was trying to limit their activity by curtailing the time she gave them.

"Go on!" urged April. "You look as though you could do with some fresh air."

Good healthy exercise could well be all April had in mind. Prue brushed a kiss against her cheek.

"Thank-you, April. We won't be long."

They walked past Harry and Peter still deep in conversation, both looking down at the gravel although the stars were clearer and brighter now, shifting pebbles with the toes of their shoes. Harry raised a hand in vague acknowledgment as they passed. Peter who was talking, paused in his conversation until they were out of earshot.

"Which way, m'lady?"

"We could walk towards Loch Chon," she said. "I'd like to look at it at night."

Once Kinlochard had petered out he took her hand.

"You're cold," he said. "You should have brought a cardigan or something."

"I'll soon warm up – walking."

Conversation was light and easy between them as they walked briskly along the road that skirted Loch Dhu.

"Such a small loch," she said. "I wonder why it's a loch and not a lochan."

"Some-one will be writing a thesis on the distinction between a loch and a lochan," he said soberly, "and it'll mean that some lochs will be downgraded to lochans and some lochans will be upgraded to lochs and John will find that he has done some lochs which don't count because they are lochans and will rush round trying to cover the lochans- to- lochs he's left out and you ..."

"Stop!" she laughed. "You're ..."

He had turned and was smiling down at her.

"I'm what?"

The undipped headlights of a car passing from the opposite direction reduced the moment to nothingness and they moved on.

"Want to go down to the water?" he asked when they reached the mirror of stars that was Loch Chon?

Did she? Did she want to go down through the darkness or did she want to stay on the road in the safety of interrupting headlights. On the hill behind them a stag started belling, a sound wrenched from his loins, and in the windless night his echo from the hills beyond, amplified into a roar over the dark plane of the loch, mocked his challenge giving him false hopes, false fears.

"Let's go down a little way," she whispered so as not to

provoke an echo, "not all the way. Just so that we can see the water more clearly."

Harry and Peter had retired to the conservatory by the time Prue and James returned walking easily, their arms around each other's waists, matching stride to stride, ghostly shapes through the reflecting glass which confused the inside and the outside worlds. Only the cacti bristled sharply against their own sharp mirror images. Harry raised his whisky glass in salutation to Prue and James and took advantage of the fact that their appearance had interrupted the impasse, the uneasy silence between him and Peter, a silence broken only by the odd, sharp knock of a glass being replaced on the glass surface of the table.

"Looks as though they've enjoyed their walk."

"Yes."

Peter's reflection was staring determinedly into the reflection of his whisky glass, deliberately avoiding eye contact, real or illusory.

"Look, Pete my boy, I'm really sorry if I've put things clumsily, hurt your feelings. Of course I'd miss you if you moved out but I feel – well to be honest I felt particularly when Helga was around – that you need your space. I think you'd enjoy having your own place and, of course, goes without saying, you can come and go from home as much as you like. My home will always be your home whenever you want it."

"You're not getting any younger," Peter spoke slowly. "Do you think I want to leave you just when you're going to want to need me around?" In the silence that followed Peter felt the need to qualify a rather brutal assessment "It's not that I'm suggesting that you're going to collapse into senility or anything but ..."

"Peter, you can't insure against the future. None of us knows what is going to happen to us. Just have to concentrate on our present needs."

Peter revolved his glass slowly, studying the liquid closely, "Looks like honey," he said and turned to smile right at Harry, not at his reflection. "It's just so sudden."

"Uh-uh," Harry shook his head as he drained his glass. "I've been thinking about it for years but it's easier to suggest now that we're, well ..."

"Definitely blood -related?" grinned Peter.

"Something like that. More closely related anyway."

"Let me sleep on it," said Peter.

"Good idea! Tomorrow should be good: Loch Dubh, the dark loch, one of my favourites."

Chapter Twenty-seven

The Third Expedition

Interlude - A Means to an End

It was exactly three o'clock in the morning after the moon had gone down and before the sun had risen - and perhaps the sun would never rise it was so dark. A deadline. April awoke as suddenly as though her alarm had been set, awoke to two ringing realisations:

that the purpose for which she had been conceived, which had
    been adapted to suit her unfortunate gender, was no longer
    relevant to her life

that, for her, a life without purpose was unlivable.

Numbed by the realisation that her useful life had ended, she felt no bitterness. May, the artist, no longer needed her and, looking across the hotel bedroom with a certain amount of distaste at the lump of bedclothes curled in on itself and on its talent, she felt a sense of relief at the thought of freedom from May's clinging sensitivities and invasive vulnerabilities. June had Caroline and the two of them would take over the running of the factory without her sticking her spanner in their works. With the income from the factory being divisible by three instead of four, Prue would be financially secure and, it would seem , had every prospect of rearing William within a family setting rather than amongst increasingly elderly and therefore needy aunts. The fact was that she would be living any future life among the family as an observer, watching it play itself out on a life-size plasma screen, knowing that she could play no meaningful part in any unfolding scene. She could either watch it or switch it off and she had never been one for spectator sport.

Unwilling to disturb May, she dressed in the dark and packed in the dark, feeling carefully around drawers to make sure that she had cleared her desk – so to speak. She pulled up the bedclothes and straightened the sheets, erasing every crease where her body had rested. Then she felt in the drawer of the small desk for a pen and a sheet of hotel writing-paper.

Have gone back to fix something. Love, April.

"Typical April," they would shrug. "Always puts the factory first."

It was true too about going back; going very far back; going back further than Prue went back. With a sense of purpose she inserted the key in the ignition and set out for far back, joining, just North of Callander, the same road they had taken so long ago – and taken countless times since no doubt, but those more recent times had ceased to be relevant.

She could hear her mother singing in the car as she drove, singing about the Braes of Balquhidder as they twisted around the bends of Loch Lubnaig where the road moved with the loch. She was sitting in the front seat beside her mother and she could hear her voice clearly although June and May were girning and squabbling in the back and her mother sang on as the road straightened through Strathyre and climbed up into the hills beyond. The first sign of light came as Buchaille Etive Mhor rose up above the mighty desolation of Rannoch Moor.

"The Big Shepherd of Etive," her mother told them.

"Well, if it's a shepherd, where are its sheep and how much longer?" grumped June.

"Its sheep," said her mother, "are the clouds. "Sometimes they are so close together that the shepherd has a problem counting them."

Today for her, April alone, superfluous to requirements, the sky around the shepherd was clear with no sheep grazing on it – the faintest grey-green sky with the shepherd's shoulders squared against it – and the road was dipping down now out of the half-light into the darkness of Glencoe and the sound of rushing water had drowned her mother's singing.

The road led stark and purposeful between the hills "towards the sweet grazing grass" her mother had said, but just as she reached what was surely the sweet grazing grass the road lost its sense of direction and dithered towards what was nothing but a small overgrown track and she pulled to the side so that she could carry on in her mind down the track to a busy car park behind which the Saltire and the National Trust flags fluttered bravely in the teeth of the January wind over a small raised building. Her mother picked up May and carried her - although May was too old to be carried but she was such a baby - and then out of the cold and to the sound of bagpipes they drank hot chocolate and bought packets of crisps and funny pencils. "Piped bagpipes," her mother had said. That was funny. What else would they be? Outside again and surely that was snow against her face and "Run on down across the bridge," said her mother and they all ran. Behind her, her mother's running steps were echoed by the light, breathless sprinkling of May's footfall and June was charging ahead to take on, as her mother said, "the Campbells and all comers" and she herself gulped in the cold air and converted it into warm mist as she screamed in delight over the bridge into a dark wood where dark meant mystery and the probability of revelation, not pausing until she reached the top of the hill.

She smiled as she took up her seat again beside her mother or was she herself in the driver's seat where there was no busy car-park and no bright flags, where there was only silence and the dark hills, tear-stained with rock-fall, lifting their heads into the lightening sky from what they did not want to contemplate. She had to go.

"Are we half-way yet?" queried June peevishly from the back but she and her mother ignored June. There were three worlds in the car, three planets spinning around their own private axes in the universe of the car. May and June, girning discontent, was one planet, she spun contentedly on her own and her mother beside her spun joyously, more of a star than a planet, a star radiating hope and excitement.

They smelled the salt air that hung above Loch Linnhe, although being January, it was cold salt, disappointing like vichy-something, that soup that was meant to be cold when everybody knew that soup should be hot, and they bypassed Fort William, half asleep both because it was semi-hibernating in January and because it was still before seven in the morning in September, and turned off along the road to Mallaig.

The sun rose at Glenfinnan "where the bonnie Prince raised his standard to bring hope to Scotland" said her mother and then on towards Loch nan Uamh where he had landed and April paused to watch again as the boats, many, many boats, triple oared like triremes churned the waters of the loch into a single straight furrow. First to land was the prince himself, splashing bravely through the water to kneel and kiss the soil of his kingdom while around him, brooding on the future, stood the followers of Lochiel and Lochiel himself, she saw, was the first to declare his allegiance as the prince rose from the ground.

The sands of Morar were so white that she thought it was snow lying fine on the beach and the sea was so flat that Rhum and Eigg and Muck floated on it motionless at anchor. She stopped by the beach to walk again on the sand but she didn't stop long because this was not her final destination and she had left the car engine running with the keys in the ignition which was not a good thing to have done.

The cottage still stood, the one they had stayed in, so warm and cosy around a fire, that they welcomed the nights falling early and dark and cold and she waved at her small self, looking possessively out of the window of the coomb-ceilinged bedroom as she drove past. Even when she reached Loch Morar she didn't stop but followed the road to the right place. When she climbed out of the car she shivered, not because it was cold because, remember, it was no longer January but because her present purpose was catching up with her past recollection and threatening to overtake it. She had come here because Loch Morar was deep, so deep that its waters ran far underground connecting and interconnecting with great caves of water that had remained pure, spurning entry into the sea. No-one had plumbed these caves and, surely, if no-one had plumbed them, no-one could and it would be possible to sink without trace or inconvenience to anyone, to dissolve into oblivion, leaving as heritage the one good thing she had done, followed her paternally prescribed destiny and preserved the preserve factory.

She turned her thoughts backwards. Her mother was sitting beside her on the bank, stroking her hair, her one glory, and whispering, "It's deeper than you would ever guess, April, but then life and love run deeper than you would ever guess."

A queer thing to say but then it was altogether a queer day because she had been sleepy and confused from the night before when she had woken suddenly to the sound of wind beneath the door and then realised that it was not the whistle of the wind but the passage of air through June's lungs that whined so bizarrely. She switched on the light to June's white face and heaving stomach and rushed in panic through to her mother's bedroom.

"Mummy! June's asthma! She ..." and she had paused, half in relief, half in disappointment because her father was lying in bed beside her mother with his arm over her and it was not a dream although the watch was fastened onto her father's wrist with a thick leather strap instead of the usual gold one and her father's arm was now brown and covered with a smooth coating of silky, black hair. Her mother chivvied her back to bed, excessively worried that she would catch cold if she lingered and, although it was night, the doctor had come out from Mallaig and been very kind and eased June's breathing.

They had all slept late and by the time they were up, her father had gone.

"Did he just come for one night?" she had been puzzled.

"Silly child!" her mother laughed harshly, brushing her hair cruelly hard. "Your father was never here. Do you honestly think he'd leave the factory? You were dreaming. Now I'll hear no more of this nonsense or I'll get very, very cross."

She had sounded cross but later on when Mrs Maxwell who cleaned the cottage for them agreed to stay with the coughing June and whiney May, she had taken April for a long walk along the lochside, holding her hand and speaking gently to her and they had sat down right here, although it was January and her mother had admired how far she could throw stones, past the ice, into the black bit of the loch where there was no ice which meant she could hear them splash.

She could see even now where the black bit had been. It was surely where the loch was at its deepest. Her mother was still smiling at her. She should perhaps write a quick explanatory note to the others but, pen in hand, she had nothing to say. Perhaps, *Archie has spare keys to all departments* would be useful. She wrote that and then, feeling that that was a bit impersonal, added *All my love, April* and penned four kisses – for June, for May, for Prue and for William. She pinned the note down with a smooth, grey stone and then carefully took off her watch, as she always did before a bath and laid it beside the stone.

The water was cold around her knees and she sensed that the bottom of the loch was about to shelve steeply.

"No man can plumb the depths," her mother re-assured

and she turned now so that she could face her mother squarely.

"But you don't always tell the truth, Mummy," she said with child-like matter-of-factness. "I did see Daddy last night."

"No, you didn't," said her mother triumphantly and her words carried the ring of truth this time.

She had nothing more to lose.

"Well, anyway, it was a ..." She had fallen forward and her feet were automatically treading water. "It was Prue's father," she gasped as she surfaced, but her mother had disappeared from the shore, leaving her alone because she April had moved on irreversibly, moved past that January holiday into adult realisation and her present purpose.

"Prue was born the following October," she gasped, and although she could no longer see her mother she could hear her voice, weak but with a mocking laugh in it, rising up from the hospital bed, " ...call her Prudence because, John dear, that is the one thing I was not."

She tried to swim out further towards the black place but she was so cold that her limbs were lead and then the coldness changed into numbness and the numbness into a sort of warmth which overcame her with a surge of contentment.

Choosing death is nothing more than choosing a new way of life she decided. Far below, the waters of the loch would be pumping deep arteries of life through the earth to feed underground wells, homes of strange unearthly creatures, feeding them a dim recollection of the world above. "It's a good thing," she bubbled into the water ...

"A good thing!" her ears were blocked but the voice, strangely not hers throbbed through her head, rhythmic as a heartbeat. "A good thing! A good thing!" The phrase developed a life of its own and evolved into a sentence. "A good thing I saw her! Just caught sight of the top of her head. It was her hair caught my eye."

"My mother's hair!" she explained but her lips were so

numb that her voice didn't get past her throat and she heard another voice this time.

"A long way to go yet, "said that other voice. "We can't be sure ..."

'No,' she thought, 'you're wrong because the road ends at Loch Morar ...I think ...'

Chapter Twenty-eight

The Third Expedition

The Dark Loch

On seeing April's bed empty, May felt only relief. She had woken with a sense of purpose from which she did not wish to be distracted by the vagaries of "Did you sleep well?" or "Do you want first shower?" or any other preliminaries to the day ahead. The bud of an idea which she had taken to bed with her had swelled to open during the night, unfolding wide its petals so that there was simply no room in her head to question April's whereabouts. It was Prue, calling in on her way down to breakfast with William on her hip, who drew her attention to April's envelope and, in the face of May's lack of curiosity, opened it herself.

"That's really odd," she commented holding the note at arm's length out of reach of William's grabbing hand. "She never said anything last night about going back though I can't remember having any real conversation with her last night ... We do take her rather for granted."

"Yes," agreed May happily, "we do." And she hoped that that was the end of the conversation and that she could get back to the idea that was obscuring all else with its loveliness.

In retrospect she rather thought it was James who took April's place at the breakfast table: it was certainly some-one who absorbed Prue's and William's attention, leaving her undisturbed. She left the table early, excusing herself to whoever was there on the grounds that she needed to sort out her things. The right pencils were very important today: she would put in a few extra just to be on the safe side and each of them would need to be inserted at the correct angle into the sharpener and the sharpener twisted three times clockwise for each of them.

June's mathematical inclinations meant that she viewed April's absence first and foremost as a disturbing lack of symmetry of the seating arrangement at breakfast – eventually corrected by James' late arrival at the table which meant a restoration of the four, three, three, two table groupings. June still tended to take refuge in numerical balance and symmetry- which for her was closely aligned to harmony – when her life was proving difficult and Caroline, this morning had been proving so much less malleable that she could almost be called obstructive.

She had planned that she and Caroline would set out together for Loch Dubh, walking until Caroline reached her limit and would depend on June for support. They would then sit down on a convenient pile of logs. There were, she had assured Caroline, a plethora of piles of comfortable moss-padded logs on all Forestry Commission land. Seated comfortably together on their pile of logs they would enjoy a spectacular view and listen to the bird-song – there was always the odd robin even in September – when they could hear it above the resonances of the waterfalls – and there had been plenty of recent wet weather – and they would munch the delicious packed lunch provided by the hotel in perfect harmony with man – or at least with each other – and nature. This she had considered to be a most inviting prospect, had delivered the plan with all the charm at her disposal and when Caroline had turned it down flatly had felt a personal sense of rejection.

"You're quite free to do your own thing," Caroline had said and the way she had said it had sounded very much as though she herself was relishing the prospect of personal freedom. "I've asked Jenny if she'd like to chum me along to the little tea-room at Kinlochard and, poor girl, she seems really keen. So we're going to hobble along together – she with her broken leg and me with my blisters! What a sight we'll be!"

It wasn't a sight June cared to imagine and she scowled instead of smiling the sympathetic smile that Caroline, glancing up at her from pouring too much milk on her cereal, seemed to be anticipating.

"You might have consulted me before you spoke to Jenny," she had muttered.

Caroline chose not to hear her and since then there had been the minimum of communication between them. She had managed an indirect snub when Prue had come across to their table to tell her that April had gone back to work by remarking, "I wish I had gone with her!" and saying it loudly enough to cause Caroline to blush and toss her head, a mannerism which under other circumstances she would have found very attractive.

The rest of the party greeted the news of April's defection with little surprise and varying degrees of concern.

"I just don't like it," Harry remarked to Peter when they assembled in the car-park at Loch Chon.

Peter was frowning at his mobile.

"No network coverage here," he muttered. "What don't you like, Dad?"

"April's having taken off like that."

"You know what a workaholic she is."

"A very unhappy workaholic!" Harry shook his head and swept some of the fallen leaves into a neat pile with the toe of his boot. "Why didn't she tell anyone? I can't believe something cropped up at the office since last night." He looked accusingly at the mobile in Peter's hand. "And talking of workaholics, you're just as bad! You don't need to phone the office on a holiday."

"And who said I was phoning the office?" asked Peter, raising mocking eyebrows. "Actually, dear father, I was phoning Suzanne. Now she and I may be work-connected but, believe me, it was an off-duty call."

"Another good reason for you to have a place of your own," said his father, grinning sagely.

"I completely fail to see the connection," huffed Peter because he could see it only too well and forestalled any attempts by his father to elucidate with, "Here comes Mark. Wonder what guise he'll assume today. Bully? Artist? Friend of all? Can't wait to find out!"

Despite the fact that this was his fourth day of lochnetting, Mark exuded drive and enthusiasm for the project from the time he swung out of the front passenger seat before the car had stopped.

"Claire," he jerked a thumb in her direction, completely oblivious of the fact that he was interrupting three separate conversations, "has been doing research into these parts over the week-end. It seems that round here is a favourite haunt of the fairies, known locally as the Men of Peace."

"I rather think that could be a placatory name," added Claire, coming round from the other side of the car, "because it seems that they generated quite a bit of fear locally."

"Anyway, we're latish because we drove up to the other end of Loch Chon to see if we could see any of the conical mounds there that they were reputed to inhabit. Seems they're a subterranean lot."

"Any luck?" smiled John benignly, leaning against a tree-trunk with his arms folded, an attitude calculated to mislead himself and everyone else into believing that he had no qualms about the steepness of the hillside ahead.

"We found some promising mounds," nodded Mark. "Have to get James up there afterwards with his camera. However, we didn't see any fairy folk, just some hairy folk i.e. Highland cattle."

"There are so many subterranean workings through these hills," mused Harry, "carrying water from Loch Katrine to Glasgow. Their construction must have caused considerable headaches to any resident fairies."

Conversation flagged as they had to walk in single file back along the narrow road to the start of the Forestry Commission track they were to follow. The track itself was rough; newly laid stones causing William's jaw to judder as his buggy jerked along and he clutched Torty to himself apprehensively, but Harry was very confident that this was just a temporary phase and so it proved to be. They crossed the bridge over the Water of Chon as they skirted the south side of little Loch Dhu, so screened against the brisk breeze by the tall trees sheltering it that its waters scarcely moved, just puckered into dimples from time to time. At the far end a floating white boulder became a swan and flew away, dragging bright sprays of water as it lifted with difficulty, straining its neck forward.

"We thought we'd concentrate on you lot today," Mark interrupted their enjoyment of the scene, walking backwards in front of them so that all could hear him. "Get some shots of you *au naturelle.*"

"*I* thought *au naturelle* meant naked," confided Jane to Claire who had fallen into step beside her.

"You never know with Mark," she replied with a grin. "He might have it in mind to send you all skinny-dipping."

Lip reading was obviously among Mark's many skills.

"For the benefit of those who need to extend their vocabulary," he said testily, "I mean that we want to record you just lochnetting the way you always lochnet so ..."

"So don't look at the camera!" chanted Ham triumphantly

Mark looked at him approvingly.

"Quite right," he said, "and for heaven's sake enjoy yourselves. I take it you're not all doing this as a penance for some outrageous sin?"

"Wouldn't you like to know?" giggled Prue.

Following behind June so as not to irritate her, May pressed on up the hill in search of the right time, the right place. It was all too vast. The expanse of hill and loch that gradually flattened out below them was too wide, indivisible into cameo portions although James' camera swept hungrily from north-west to south east stroking the velvety pile of smoky green pines on lower slopes, skimming bare, brown hill-tops softly moulded by cloud pressure and flanked with deep, dark, water-spliced folds. Beside their track the trees soared too high, shirred by the wind which set them mewing like buzzards as their rough barked branches chafed and winced against each other. Over the crest of the hill the lochnetters followed the track towards the sky, parting into the sparse, spindly grass of the verge on either side as a jeep rattled towards them with the slumped body of a stag jerking spasmodically as the trailer bumped over the pitted surface. On the hillside opposite felled trees, bleached ashen to the colour of bone, lay where they had fallen and around them a fringe of young spruce, green to blue-green, fidgeted stiffly with the wind.

"Desirable residence," somebody said, somebody right beside her and a long way off.

"Yes," she agreed politely without smiling because her eyes were probing the roofless ruins as a possibility, but they were not quite right.

Nothing was quite right until she came to the place

where the road divided.

"I'll wait for you here," she said.

They all stopped. They all looked at her

"Are you all right, May?" John asked kindly.

"Yes thank-you," she said taking out the folding stool that April had given her, shaking it three times, watching the striped canvas billow in the wind before setting it squarely before her.

"I'll stay with you," offered Jane.

"No," said May and she didn't add thank-you. "That would spoil it."

Before her a broad, brown valley unfolded like an opened book, parchment leaved and with a darker brown river marking the fold between the pages. Beside the river the track ran companionably, narrowing on and on until both river and track disappeared into a misty, immaterial distance. The simplicity of it reminded May of a background illustration in a children's story-book, the sort of background into which a Pied Piper might lead his joyful band of children, or against which a black sheep might proffer its wool. In all events it was the perfect background for her purposes. It didn't take her long to sketch in the valley, the river and the road and then, pencil pointing upwards, she paused not to look at the departing figures but to delve into her inner self for the knowledge she now knew must be there. They would have their backs to her because she wasn't ready for the intimacy of faces or the inconstancy of their fleeting expressions. Prue and William would probably be nearest to her because they would be at the tail-end of the walkers and her pencil traced gently around the slenderness of Prue, her hair blowing around her head, her hand reaching towards William, the sturdy diminutive figure beside her, trotting along with his hands firmly clasped behind his back in a bid to show his independence, his refusal to take her hand, but his head twisting up towards her, his most important reference point. Jane and April took their places naturally just ahead of her, such very different figures, such different people with the tenuous link of their gardens spanning the gulf between them: Jane with her shoulders relaxed, head up, swinging so easily into a walking rhythm and she would be smiling, even though of course May could not draw the smile, and she would have her head turned towards April, ready to listen. By contrast, April was a slightly hunched figure, her head poking awkwardly forward as though ready to anticipate or forestall something and May frowned as she sketched her because she could not quite work out what it was that April was so worried about. June might know but then she would be choosing to walk by herself again, squarely independent, braced against any intrusive conversation, digging her heels firmly into the surface of the road with such a loneliness around her that May drew her shadow long and dark. The pencil moved hard and sharp around her contours and then skimmed on to Peter's shoulders , running down the straightness of the spine, the smoothness of the broad back which tapered to narrow hips, rounded, muscular buttocks, long legs. It was a pity that she had to dress him. She glanced round nervously to see if anyone had read her thoughts, so wicked, so suddenly exciting. Then she put on his jacket and jeans and made his head tilt back because he was at his water-bottle again, ever health-conscious, keeping himself hydrated. Harry, a comical figure beside Peter, stocky and compact with walking poles bristling out of his backpack and peculiar bulges on his legs because his trousers were, as always, tucked into his socks against midges, even in September. He was slightly bandy too. Odd that she had known that for so long without noticing it. On the other hand, Jenny, just in front of them, slim to waif-like in her tight jeans and cropped jacket, was slightly pigeon-toed, so that her small hips swayed as she walked and the long blonde hair that hung free down her back swung from side to side. There was a brightness about her, and an alertness and May kept her pencil strokes light and soft, almost feathery. She held her head high just like her mother but there was a pertness in her carriage and a tension too which Jane had lost. John's shoulders were as broad as Peter's but there was little tapering from there down, perhaps more of a thickening around the midpart which she was quite happy to cover up with his outdoor gear and his head was bent forward with the pain of his feet and the dogged effort of his walking. Ahead of him the irrepressible Ham, a towsled mop of hair like the wispiness of old man's beard on a thin stem of a body, leaped and bounded. She captured him in mid-leap twisting his head back to converse with his father. Between him and John she drew the shaggy body of Jelly with difficulty because the dog would not keep still, dodging from one side of the track to the other in an ecstasy of verge-sniffing.

Looking at the finished work she felt a deep satisfaction. She had left out the new ones because they were not inside her head yet and she had left out herself because she didn't know herself at all. That was fair enough. For now. She started to put her pencils away in the right order, in their right places.

The breeze had dropped and the surface of Loch Dubh was still: it was a black depth. It was like looking into the blackness of the pupil of an eye, June thought, like peering into that soft most vulnerable part of an eye. She had a sudden urge to pierce it, to throw a stone into the middle of it, right into its softest and most vulnerable part. She liked vulnerability, liked the feelings of power and control that it gave her. It was what had appealed to her so in Mattie, what she was looking for in Caroline. Her hand closed round a flint so sharp that it hurt her hand as she squeezed it.

"Do you think May will be all right?"

That was Jane spoiling the moment for her.

"She'll be fine," she said firmly without turning her head to look at Jane. "She wanted to be alone." 'And so do I,' she all but added.

There was a thing. May was definitely vulnerable, but she didn't find that attractive at all. Maybe that was her childhood conditioning, the restriction on being 'masterful' with May. Doing things, saying things even, to May had been a punishable crime from very early on.

"Very ugly!" she had once pronounced joyfully on one of May's interminable flower arrangements, causing May to cry which had temporarily made her quite endearing, but only very temporarily because the cause of her tears had been rumbled and June had been sent to bed without supper. It had been May who had sneaked her up a piece of bread and jam, with the jam spread on both sides making it a pulpy, sticky mess, and she had thrown it straight out of the window just to show May that it was not her place to dole out pity.

May hadn't even had the guts to complain when June had taken the pinking shears to 'tidy up your hair' remaining mute in front of the mirror while the extent of the mutilation became screamingly obvious. And she would have taken the blame for it herself too, if April had not told on June.

April had been the one to interfere too when June had carefully worked on May to persuade her to try sleeping with a plastic bag over her head so that they could see what happened. The anticipation of the danger to which she was exposing May had caused her a frisson of excitement, a delightful burning sensation deep in her loins. For this she had actually been beaten; the only time her father had ever raised his hand to one of them. When she came out of his study with her face flaming with humiliation and her behind stinging, May had been waiting at the door crying like a baby and June had kicked her hard on the shin.

'I could have killed May with that bag,' she thought and

then comforted herself with, 'but I was only a child. I don't get pleasure out of people's suffering now.'

Staring down at the loch with her stone still in her hand she knew that the last part wasn't quite right and that there could still be times when she needed to rely on April's intervention. Odd that – needing April. Then the surface rippled. Peter, Ham and Mark were having a competition skipping flat stones. Peter was winning but Ham was considerably more skilful than Mark.

"You're not holding the stone right," he advised Mark critically. "Look, you do it this way."

Mark's subsequent effort was no better. Ham looked round with a gesture of despair, saw June watching and grinned.

"Come and have a go, June," he invited.

She dropped the sharp stone and, picking up a suitable flat one, flung her arm back and watched it gently skimming the surface.

On a dryish patch on the hillside above the stone skippers, Prue, Claire, Katie, Jim and James were stretched out sunning themselves, talking and laughing, with William clambering over their recumbent forms, the occasional exclamation of pain indicating that he had successfully found a foothold on a sensitive spot. Attracted by the cheers and jeers of the stone skippers below, he grabbed Torty and wandered down towards them in search of a more interesting pursuit than inflicting pain on adults.

"Frowing," he remarked, "frowing into the water."

"That's right," replied June without looking down at him, but pronouncing the 'th' of 'throwing' very distinctly, "we're throwing into the water."

"Me," he decided. "Me frow." And he went on muttering 'me frow' to remind himself of his objective while seeking out stones small enough to fit into his hand. The pebbles he managed to unearth, the few that did actually reach the water, made a very unsatisfactory splash which he found greatly disappointing.

"Me frow Torty," he announced.

"That's right," agreed June absent-mindedly her eyes on Mark's latest attempt. "You throw ... No! William, no!"

Torty had already hit the water with a very satisfactory plopping sound indeed and could be seen bobbing on the surface.

Suddenly made aware by June's reaction that Torty was no longer accessible, William let out a piercing scream, bringing everybody to his side. Torty, gradually becoming more water-logged, was definitely sinking. It was James who, stopping only to kick off his shoes, waded in to the rescue, successfully grabbing Torty just before he became completely submerged.

"Did it have to be you?" Mark, exasperated, asked him when wet to his thighs but clutching a soaking Torty triumphantly to his chest, he struggled out. "It would have made a marvellous shot if you had only been on the bank to take it. Could you not have thought?"

"Fuck off," muttered James, shivering as he pulled down his sodden trousers to reveal boxers with pink elephants on a blue background.

"Just couldn't wait to show off his legs," remarked Jim.

"That was very, very silly!" scolded Prue sharply, ostensibly to William, but allowing her glare to linger on Mark and Jim. "Very silly indeed! Say a big, big thank-you to James, William."

William, howling not at his mother's reproof but because he was being denied the sodden and sorry-looking Torty, glanced dispassionately at James and continued to howl.

"Those were the days!" Jane remarked to Harry. "I remember Ham being inconsolable every time his cuddly blanket had to go into the washing machine. You must remember similar?"

"No actually," said Harry so bleakly that Jane immediately realised her blunder and changed the subject.

"I hope today hasn't spoiled your special liking for this loch ... I mean with Mark and all his gang tagging along ..."

"Not at all," he smiled reassuringly at her. "I love it in all its moods. I love the way it opens to the sky. The last time I was here was just this last Easter. I must have been quite mad but I decided to come up here on my own in the evening. Probably was mad because it was the time of the full moon: they say it affects you – affects women more than men, I believe."

"That," said Jane, "depends on what you did when you were up here and whether you grew whiskers and started howling."

"As far as I can remember I just sat where I am now and watched the moon rise through cloud bank at the mouth of the valley and from here it looked as though the moon was at eye-level and that Ben Dubh and Ben Bhan were towering above it. It was unreal and there was something about the way the colours faded into brightness – no more greens and blues and browns and blacks, just silver. And the loch, believe it or not, was a luminous pearl, hard and as bright as though there was a light buried deep within it, not reflected light, a sort of intrinsic luminosity. And the sky was so low that the stars seemed to swing on threads between the hills. And from all this you have probably concluded quite rightly that men are as vulnerable to the full moon as women and even more likely to start baying like wolves."

"And looking at it now?" smiled Jane. "Now in the rational light of day?"

"Now it belongs to us: it's not part of another world." He packed the remains of his lunch into his backpack.

"I can't think why they gave us all prawn rolls today, ghastly things prawns."

May still sitting upright with her sketch on her lap even though her pencils were safely packed away watched the approach of her loch-netting companions with growing agitation. Coming towards her they looked very different, she thought, from the way she had drawn them. April and Jenny were absent, it seemed. Peter had William on his shoulders, lengthening and distorting the beauty of his proportions. John and Jane were holding hands and June, of the long lonely shadow, appeared to be chatting to Ham. James, wearing Peter's waterproof overtrousers walked awkwardly with his legs wide apart under the monstrous hump of his camera, making him not only unrecognisable but even subhuman. Even William's buggy looked peculiar, as though it had wet trousers strung across the handle and a lump of sodden substance on its roof. She referred back to her sketch and panicked but they were on her before she could hide it. And they were so enthusiastic that her misgivings vanished and her heart beat so fast with pride that she felt as though she was having palpitations.

"It's the first time ..." she started and then felt self-conscious about finishing,

Jane thought she had John just right. "You see," said Harry to Peter, "you *are* an Adonis!" "Jelly's cool!" said Ham. "I love William!" said Prue. But best of all, June, her harshest critic, said nothing at all.

Downhill on the way home and it was not only May who was in an ebullient mood. Although James still stopped for the odd shot, the odd buzzard being mobbed by the odd crows, the filming ordeal was over. The forthcoming interviews with Claire posed no threat: Claire was not a Mark. Even Mark seemed happy with what he had done. By the time they reached Loch Dhu they had all burst into song to the private embarrassment of Ham who later reported to Jenny that June had a really loud really quavery voice and that he had nearly died when a posse of birdwatchers emerged from cover and shouted at them. "We *all* thought they'd just gone in there for a pee. We didn't see their telescope things until they came out."

At Prue's suggestion the filming group tailed them back to the hotel for a stirrup cup and a pair of more comfortable if equally ill-fitting trousers for James. They were met at the door by Heather with her face set in the rigid lines of Sunday breakfast frostiness.

"The police are here for the Reynolds sisters. It is very rare for us to have police at this hotel." She put out an arm to prevent Prue from entering the hotel lounge where she anticipated the police would be. "They are certainly not in the lounge. I have taken them to wait in the laundry room where you will conduct your business with them and, if they require you to accompany them, please exit through the kitchen."

Chapter Twenty-nine

The End of the Beginning

Into Something Rich and Strange

.

April sat in Jane's kitchen, stroking the top of Jelly's head.

"She's been terribly spoiled since the accident," said Jane.

"Her and me both," smiled April. "June actually tried to bring me breakfast in bed!"

"I'd make the most of it if I were you." Jane placed two mugs of coffee on the table and pushed a plate of biscuits towards April. "That sort of thing doesn't last. I hope you're not going back to work too soon."

"I'm not going back at all," said April airily, dunking a ginger nut and shaking the drips into her mug. "I may not have succeeded in ending myself but I've certainly ended my old lifestyle." She stirred sugar into her coffee. "My father always used to say that no hot drink should be sweetened." She added another spoonful, happily watching the grains trickle in and returned to the subject of her new improved lifestyle. "I've known for a few months now that things have to change. Where I went wrong was in thinking that I had to escape from my life whereas it was my factory life that had to go. That dip in Loch Morar really cleared my head. I'm leaving the factory – apart from helping out on the odd occasion when June is really stuck, although I'm pretty sure she'll be getting help from another source, and I'm going to start a market garden."

Jane sat motionless her mug halfway to her mouth.

"I've put in an offer for a piece of land. Fairly confident

I'll get it. Not too big, just two acres. I have to be sensible and make sure it's not too big at first. I want to divide it between vegetables and flowers. I like my cabbages – comfortable and motherly looking – but I am really looking forward to the flowers – to having a riot of colour and I'm going to have a special place for wild flowers – poppies and cornflowers, ragged robin and campion... Prue says she'll help me but Prue has William and, I'm glad to say, he's not the only man in her life."

"James?" suggested Jane innocently, deciding against disclosing that they already knew that Prue's relationship was burgeoning from the number of times James' red Corsa could be spotted outside no. 11.

"M-m-m," April nodded. "Hope it works out. Prue is very sensible, taking it slowly."

"The market garden's a really exciting idea."

"Yes," agreed April. "It came to me when I was in hospital. At first I was so disappointed that the drowning attempt hadn't worked out because I couldn't bear to go back to being *April, the Factory.* Then I realised I didn't have to. There were better ways of escaping." She took a sip of her coffee and chuckled. "They suggested I should have psychiatric help you know and the odd thing is I've never been so sane."

They sat smiling at Jelly who was rubbing herself alternately against Jane and April in the hope of cadging a bit of ginger nut.

"If it hadn't been for you and your loch-netting, I don't think I would ever have thought of a life beyond the factory. I've actually come to say thank-you and to see if you'd like to come across and see my seed catalogues."

"Love to," said Jane.

At about the same time Peter was sitting in the office of James Brown, senior partner at *Alderson McTavish*, mildly aware of the fact that he was being given a dressing down; a watered down dressing down - because there was a glass of single malt in his hand - but none the less a dressing down. He could tell this because James – for the last ten years it had been first names only – was calling him 'my boy' instead of 'Peter' rather, Peter felt, to emphasise the generation gap between them than from any attempt at indicating affection, thereby giving James the chance to assume experience in the matter under discussion.

"I do realise, my boy," said James slowly and deliberately, "that you are at an age when the blood is hot. Get my meaning?"

Peter looked as blank as he could.

"Shall we say at an age when one's heart rules one's head. Now, take me. I am a man of the world and, believe me, in my time I sowed my wild oats."

'Sweet-pea seeds more likely,' thought Peter, fortifying himself against James' sexual revelations with a burning gulp of the malt, 'sweet-pea seeds accurately spaced out into very deep trenches with absolutely no organic manure.'

"... and must cut your teeth somewhere on some-one," James was saying. "Must, absolutely *have* to, test one's virility. Now to get to the point: Miss Muir is frankly very concerned that you may just be forming an attachment to one of the girls in the office. Susan I think her name is? Pretty young thing. I've noticed her myself I don't mind telling you." He coughed a fairish attempt at a dirty laugh. "Nice bits ..."

'Not *bits* but they do rhyme with *bits*,' thought Peter "... and so on but relations with the secretarial staff can lead to complications. Nothing against secretaries as a breed. My own wife was a secretary. Still is my personal secretary at home. After thirty years would you believe? I know, it surprises me too. But the difference is she *never ever* worked in this office."

He tapped his desk as though the secretaries might be lodged in one of his drawers.

Peter swilled his whisky around his glass and tried to think of something to say, failed and put his glass down. James swung off his chair, laid a paternal hand on his shoulder and stared down into his face breathing whiskily.

"All I want to say is, my boy, all I want to say is ... don't take it too far. Get what I mean?"

"No," said Peter mischievously. "Could you explain, please?"

"Well then if you insist," said James a trifle tetchily, "don't get her, to be crude, in the family way. In fact it would be better not to .... not to... to keep sex out of the relationship. "

'Better not to keep sex out of our relationship? I could certainly consider that,' thought Peter swilling his glass. Out aloud he said humbly, "Thank-you so much for your advice, sir. I appreciate your concern."

"You know we hope for great things from you, Peter my boy."

Peter left the office of his superior full of self-respect, having just received a testimonial to his virility. Miss Muir looked up from her computer as he passed and he flattered himself that he read apprehension together with well-trained respect in her glance. When she had lowered her eyes demurely back to her keyboard he grinned at Suzanne and mouthed, "See you at six."

While Peter and Suzanne were walking along Middle Meadow Walk with their arms around each other's waists and respect for neither James Brown's paternal warnings nor the advice of Miss Muir who had taken it upon herself to counsel Suzanne along the lines of secretaries being "easy prey, something which I have had to guard against all my working life", Harry was rooting in his attic for a couple of ancient and out of date travel guides to Italy and Greece. He found them eventually, dusted them by wiping them down the front of his sweater and clambered back down the creaking Ramsey loft ladder to pour over his findings.

He had assumed after Peter's arrival in Scotland that the boy would want to pay frequent visits to his native land, visits on which Harry would have enjoyed accompanying him and he had consequently stocked up on travel guides to both Italy and Greece and showed them to Peter with the suggestion that while he was enjoying time on his own with his Italian relatives, Harry would skip across to Greece. Surprisingly, Peter who had acquiesced to all Harry's other suggestions readily if not enthusiastically, had simply shaken his head with a bleak "No thank-you". Harry, sensitive to the boy's embarrassment, had not pressed the matter further but a few weeks later he had found the travel guides hidden under fruit tree prunings at the bottom of his garden bonfire. He would not have found them at all if he had not decided to poke around for the odd stray hibernating hedgehog. He had been initially furious but, before he had been able to confront Peter, his anger had given way to pity and he had simply hidden the offending books in the attic out of Peter's sight.

Recently images of Italy and Greece had floated in and out of his daytime plans and his night-time dreams because with Peter having finally agreed that it might be a good idea for him to have his own place just for a trial period and with retirement from teaching brightening his horizon, these long postponed visits were definite possibilities. He was, he mused at the dawn of a new personal classical golden age. Of course it would be euros now not drachmas he mused while leafing through the yellowing pages and there would be a wider choice of flights and packages and so forth but these were minor details. The important parts were still there as they had been eleven years ago or, in fact, two thousand years ago and sitting by his fire he contemplated threading through the ruins of Pompeii, still lying under the threat of an erupting Vesuvius; staring through the fissure in the rock at the oracle at Delphi while a pair of eagles circled over the Omphelos; climbing the Areopagos where the diminutive figure of St. Paul told the Athenians the identity of their Unknown God; walking beneath the archway of the lion gate at Mycenae, the palace of Agamemnon, through which the proud king had returned triumphantly from Troy and where his fickle but lovely Clytemnestra had hung the walls of the palace with purple cloth in his honour and a few hours later murdered him in his bath. He hummed contentedly to himself as he paged through the book until he fell asleep with the books still on his knee, dreaming of Venice in the early autumn when the sun was mellow and golden on the Doges Palace and was woken by Peter entering the room.

"Hi, Dad."

The books slipped from his knee to the floor as he started out of his sleep and Peter bent and scooped them up, looking at them incredulously.

"These were the books I ..."

"You put in the bonfire?"

Peter turned them over in his hand, studying them.

"It was a really sneaky thing to do but I just couldn't bear the thought of going back. I think I was terrified in case you left me there." He laughed. "I must have been half-witted!"

"You really mean you think you're sane now?" asked Harry.

A few hours before Peter was called upon to defend his sanity, Jenny stared into the looking-glass in her bedroom in an attempt to face a few home truths about herself. The sordid truth had to be faced. She would have liked to have had someone there to contradict her assessment which she had made up her mind would be frank to the point of brutality, but on the other hand there was something commendable, she felt about the humility she was flaunting. The fact was that most of her friends, the ones that mattered, had declined the irresistible invitation to her cellar party. Worse still, some of her friends hadn't had the courage to refuse: it had simply leaked out that they would not be coming. They all had different excuses. Her ex-best friend, Hannah, had three separate excuses.

"What is wrong with me?" she had asked Phoebe despairingly at lunch-time because for the last week or so she had been reduced to lunching with Phoebe. Phoebe, being relatively unpopular, could be relied upon to offer some palatable, sycophantic assurance to save Jenny's face.

"They think you're too full of yourself," Phoebe had blurted out without looking at Jenny. "Sorry, Jenny, but that is the truth and you ought to know it."

At the time Jenny had been too shocked to be hurt and when the shock had worn off and the hurt was really hurting she had been too proud to let it show. But the thing needed facing so here she was, staring at her reflection with her hair scrunched back and no make-up on, ready to face the worst about herself.

"I am unkind," she said slowly. "I know that because Katie thought I was unkind about the *Melt Downers*. And then I'm selfish and take too much for granted because that's what the bandaged girl in the hospital was trying to say." She frowned with the effort of remembering more of her bad points. "I'm cheeky to my parents but that doesn't really count because it's natural at my age. O.K. then, and I do show off and that's why nobody likes me."

She began to feel that she had been a bit hard on herself.

"I've got a few pluses," she informed the looking-glass, "and I ought to mention them to balance things out. I am very pretty, even now that I've a plook coming on my nose and I've got a figure to die for – everybody says so."

She paused again.

"It's really only my character that could do with improvement and that's easily fixed. In future I shall be really nice to everybody."

Having assessed the bleakness of his sister's mood earlier, Ham's knock on her door was the gentlest of taps.

"Supper, Jenny," he called. "We're having it early, remember, 'cos of the interviewing. Claire's coming."

"Get lost!" she shrieked. "I'll come when I'm ready." Then she added for the benefit of her reflection, "I meant really nice to everyone who deserves it."

It struck her though that her reflection looked a tad guilty.

"I'll offer to do the dishes for him," she promised it.

With the interviews completed, Mark and James brought a DVD round to No.10 for a private viewing.

"This is just the rough edition," Mark said to the assembled company which comprised the same group he had met at the planning meeting but with the addition of Suzanne. "We'll have to edit it further but thought if you saw it at this point you could make any objections you wanted to.

"Do you do air-brushing?" squeaked Joyce.

"No," he replied good-humouredly, "just total elimination."

"You won't need air-brushing, Joyce," said Jenny sweetly, hoping that Katie heard her and earning a suspicious glare from her mother. "You'll look lovely."

The film opened with an interview in which John

outlined his reasons for launching loch-netting very lucidly – not quite the way Jane remembered them - and explained how he hoped it would develop. It then switched to a still of a close-up of John, standing on the west side of Loch Chon, staring out over the water with his hand shading his eyes. The still lasted just long enough to cause him acute embarrassment before switching to the expedition to Loch Dubh.

"That's the wrong order," Ham frowned.

Mark paused the DVD. "You' re right but we thought that we ought to show loch-netting by the original loch-netters first and then see it spreading."

"But Jenny won't be there ..." Ham started.

"I don't mind," put in the ostentatiously self-effacing Jenny.

"And April's not there because that's when she was trying to kill herself."

"Ham! Go to ..."

"No, he's absolutely correct," pronounced April calmly. "It's just what I was doing and it's quite all right, Ham."

"You could put them in as insets like in the school team photographs when people are missing?" suggested Ham.

"To move on swiftly," said Mark switching to play.

Jelly's accident was shown in all its horror "as a salutary lesson to aggressive cyclists," said Mark but the face of the cyclist had been distorted to make him unrecognisable.

"No! Name him and shame him!" cried Peter.

"And you a lawyer!" retaliated Mark.

The *Melt Downers* thought that their girth had been amplified by the camera angle and Caroline and June thoroughly enjoyed a heated discussion on whether the factory interviewees had been democratically selected, but eventually everyone pronounced themselves satisfied.

"What next?" asked Mark with his mouth full of Jane's quiche.

"Well, Harry and I need to spend some time systematically dividing Scotland into loch areas," replied John. "Jenny wanted to go riding up North with Katie round some lochs just South of Loch Ness. Unfortunately her leg won't be up to that just yet but we've agreed on Loch Leven during the October break. Apparently it's a wonderful time of year for migrant geese."

"Can I come?" asked Mark. "Please?"

"If you behave," John smiled, "and leave your camera behind."

"And so?" said Jane later, sitting up in bed with her arms around her knees.

"It's the end of a chapter," said John.

"Just the first chapter."

"Yes, of course."

He continued to stare out of the bedroom window, elbows propped on the window sill although with the darkness of the night and the cloud of his breath on the window-pane she knew that he could see nothing. She waited for him to frame his thoughts into words.

"The film was fine," he said.

"But?"

"Well, it showed loch-netting as something that could be enjoyed by people of all ages; showed the beauty of the lochs and I was really touched by what some of the people said – the factory people in particular. Said it had opened their eyes to something they'd never thought of. Said they liked the way you didn't have to be clever or sporty, just reasonably fit. *The Melt Downers* too. They said it was a great way to get fit even though, actually, I can't see any of them persevering."

"But?"

"The scouts too. They were so enthusiastic and the wee chap who said the rain just made it more fun ..."

John drew a dog with his forefinger on the condensation on the window-pane.

"But?"

He turned to face her. "Remember what you said that night? That night when you quoted those lines:

Nothing of us that does fade
But does suffer a sea-change
Into something rich and strange

Only you said it had to be *loch-change?*"

She nodded

"Well, that is what happened but the film didn't show it."

Jane thought for a good few minutes before speaking very slowly, "I don't think that matters. We all know ourselves what we have experienced and some things are too private for public viewing."

"You're quite right as annoyingly usual," he smiled, "far too private for public viewing."

Chapter Thirty

The End of the Beginning

In October when it is not quite light yet, the waters of a loch are brighter than the sky. Around the edges of the brightness which was Loch Leven were the hummocks of geese, plumply irregular feathery mounds, not quite motionless, with the occasional fuss of feathers rippling through the gathering. As the dawn greyed they anticipated the day with the odd premature call, the odd shuffling of position, small waves of feathery mounting and falling, restless with that breeze which is the change of air as night blows out into sunrise. And the periods of restlessness grew louder and more frequent as the light left the water and spread into the sky but it was not until the rim of the sun behind the hills became too bright for human eyes that they rose. In layer upon chaotically overlapping layer, layer upon layer of quavering call and quivering feathers they rose up in their thousands so that the wind from their wings flattened the surface of the water. Airborne and easy, the chaos splintered into arrowheads, into precision of purpose, as they alternated leadership to allow each other choice, to spare each other, to shield each other from wind-resistance, in perfect group formation.

And John, Jane, Ham, Jenny, Katie and Jelly; and Mark, Harry, Peter and Suzanne; and April, May, June, Caroline, Prue, William and James rose up from their cramped positions, huddled behind the gravestones in the graveyard in Kinross and watched them until the last call faded into silence.